NOW THE WIND SCATTERS

NOW THE WIND SCATTERS

J. DONAI

Asteria Press

I

those who come ungarlanded

Thick roots carved painful indents into her knees, but Iphigenia did not cease her prayers. No, the words, foreign in shape and ancient in origin, flowed ceaselessly from her lips with a fervor that would rival that of the most pious priest. Trying her best to replicate the phrases she'd been taught, she focused on the little bundle of herbs at her feet. With each syllable, power flooded through her fingertips, traveling up her arms and down into her chest. Apparently, she was doing something right. Elation bloomed in her heart. *This is the goal,* Iphigenia thought. As she continued, she couldn't help but smile. *This is what will save me.*

The world plunged into darkness. Gone was the forest where sunbeams pierced the thick canopies of its trees like arrows, and gone was the ever-present cicada song of summer. Even the sky, that bright visage of heaven, had withered away into nothingness. As she climbed unsteadily to her feet, Iphigenia faced only unyielding blackness. Terror crashed over her like a wave. Still, this was the only way. She took a step forward.

A soundless scream exploded from her lips as she was slammed onto cold marble. Pain bloomed from every part of her body, the very worst of it radiating from the center of her ribcage. When she went to clutch at her chest as she desperately tried to regulate her breathing, Iphigenia found that she couldn't move either of her arms. The same was true for her feet; attempting to kick them resulted in only the slightest of twitches. Her body was entirely immobilized, save for her head. This small freedom allowed her to look around enough to see that she now rested upon some sort of altar, and the blackness had solidified to form a floor to support it. The heat of a torch somewhere above her head gave her just enough light to stave off a full-blown panic attack.

Just as Iphigenia had gathered her bearings enough to realize that the altar rested in the center of a forked path, an apparition blinked into existence above her. Somehow formless in the darkness and yet impossibly dense, it leered ominously. Its face was hidden beneath a hood as inky black as the void surrounding them. A woman, maybe— but she couldn't be sure. The darkness only allowed her to see the barest trace of a figure.

"Choose," the apparition whispered, and terror rippled through Iphigenia anew. Why was this blackness, this being, so familiar? Then she looked closer. It was as if a mirror hid beneath the hood; the face peering out at her was her own.

Clasped tight in one hand was a dagger, dripping with crimson. With it, the woman who looked like her shadow made flesh gestured at her chest. Iphigenia followed the blade's point to see a gaping wound bleeding there, staining the pale marble beneath her. She couldn't bear to look at it as the pain throbbed anew, and so she redirected her attention to the weapon's wielder.

In the crook of her shadow's opposite arm rested a bundle of cloth. Unsure of what it could be, Iphigenia squinted in the darkness to get a better look. A wail cut through the air, and the cloth fell away like ash to reveal a nude infant, angry and red. It was pathetic, scrawny; like its mother had denied it the opportunity to suckle and left it to starve. Instead of pain, Iphigenia only felt pity.

"What are you asking me?"

"You know why you came. This is your choice alone," a woman's voice, *her voice*, soft as morning dew, whispered. "Everything is up to you."

"Up to me," Iphigenia repeated, turning the words around in her mouth. It wasn't often that she got to choose anything. Iphigenia looked between the sharp bronze and the squealing child — a beat, and her mind is made up. Suddenly able to move again, she extended her arm, ready to grasp...

* * *

Iphigenia awoke with a gasp — not on a cold altar but amongst leaves and pine needles. There was no woman wearing her face here, she realized as she wheeled around, no woman, no dagger, and certainly no child.

"Just a dream," she whispered, disappointment roiling through her as she brought slim fingertips to her chest. They come away not with blood, but with the tell-tale dampness of saliva. She must have fallen asleep during her prayers. She glanced at the sky; the sun had already crested its zenith. She'd have to return tomorrow to try again.

"Iphigenia," a voice called, grating and raw.

"Who's there?" she replied, suddenly on her guard. First that awful nightmare, and now someone was sneaking up on her? She whirled around, scanning the fig trees and the slope behind her. It was only when her eyes fell on the gorge, to the edge of that deep gash in the earth that she'd spent the morning praying—no, *begging*—at, that she saw it. Her.

Iphigenia's back slammed against a gnarled fig tree as she skidded away. The herbs at her feet had been knocked aside, their heady scents rising from the dry cracked ground. Lavender and sage coated every shuddering inhalation. She shivered even as the oppressive heat of the afternoon bore down on her skin. Any other day and she'd say what was glaring at her with open malice was a trick of the air, a case of far too potent plant fumes blended with a touch of heat stroke, but this was no ordinary day, and what was staring at her was far from simple illusion.

The being she'd seen in her dream, the other her, had materialized, and Iphigenia knew now it had been the furthest thing from a dream. It was across the gorge, covered from head to toe in heavy black garb. Its presence was hardly substantial; far different from the vastness she'd communed with as she lay on the altar, the being was hardly more corporal than smoke. Despite this, a rush of triumph cut through Iphigenia's fear: she had succeeded. The tree she leaned against teetered at the edge of the cliff side; the entity stood on the opposite rim, motionless. Then Iphigenia blinked, and it was right in front of her, a slender hand reaching out almost as if to caress her face.

All around her, the forest seemed to stretch into infinity. It was a soundless vacuum; absent was the near ubiquitous birdsong of these woods, and gone as well was the sound of small creatures scampering underfoot. It was as if they had dropped right back into that dark place. The apparition's eyes were piercing a hole straight into the depths of her soul, and despite the desire to cry out, locked her own gaze with the being. There could be no backing down now. She braced herself for the worst, for nails like talons to rend themselves down her cheeks, for her chest to be pierced by a well honed blade. A single bead of sweat slithered down her neck and splashed onto the thirsty earth.

"Princess!"

And the spell was broken. The spirit blinked out of existence as if it had never been there at all. Iphigenia whipped her head around.

Behind her, at the bottom of a rocky slope, stood a soldier so scrawny and thin that his breastplate looked as if it were going to slide off one shoulder. His overly large helmet hung low over his eyes. Good. He'd seen nothing.

"What?" She hissed, decidedly very unprincesslike. She found herself unable to give a damn.

"Your mother sent me." The soldier pointed at the sun. "You were supposed to be weaving an hour ago."

"Ugh," she groaned, clamoring to her feet and stepping out from the shade of the fig trees at the top of the hill. With a final forlorn glance at the ravine, Iphigenia gathered the basket into her arms before picking her way down to where the soldier stood. She saw the way he eyed her admittedly light basket, and struggled to resist the urge to kick him. She'd come out here under the pretense of gathering some figs as a treat for her siblings; there was no way in hell she was letting him have any of the few she'd bothered to haphazardly throw in the basket.

"Thank you," she said, false sweetness flavoring her voice like rancid honey. "I'd let the day get away from me."

Iphigenia shoved her free hand into a pocket of her chiton as her bag of hastily packed away tools and herbs bounced against her side. They were on the way home now, a steep pine needle strewn trail adapted from old goat herding paths. She could feel her lip jutting in an irritated pout, no matter how fiercely she was trying to keep up the facade of an oblivious princess called back for lessons. Weaving was the absolute *last* thing she wanted to do right now. All those long hours of research, of exhausting practice, of following false leads from the occasional roadside crone, and she'd succeeded! It had almost touched her, even! She'd finally conjured something more substantial than the last wisps of a long dead shade…only to be interrupted by some pimply faced boy whose only purpose in life was to escort her to something as banal as weaving lessons, of all gods affronted things. She'd collapse to the ground in laughter if she weren't so angry.

"So uh," the soldier began, voice cracking. He gave his chest a thump and coughed before continuing in the sorriest attempt at a baritone Iphigenia had ever heard. "I hear you're still yet to be promised to anyone, Princess." False bravado dripped from every one of his oversized pores.

Iphigenia can't help the venom in her glare, her mask once again threatening to slip. "This again, Lysander? Really?"

Lysander raised his hands, palms outstretched. "I'm just making small talk."

"Well, make it smaller. Say less." Iphigenia pinched her brow. Lysander darted out in front of her, throwing his thin arms wide. Stuttering, he said, "You...you should really be nicer to me, Princess. I'm not that little kid you used to shove around anymore—" he took a step forward.

Iphigenia crinkled her nose. Interesting choice of fish he must have had for lunch; by interesting, she meant absolutely disgusting. The boy reeked. She watched as his thin nostrils flared. "We're all alone out here. I could do something horrible. Then you'd *have* to marry me."

"Really now?" Iphigenia asked, raising an eyebrow and crossing her arms.

Lysander nodded furiously. Iphigenia shrugged before delivering a sharp kick to Lysander's unprotected groin.

The boy crumpled to his knees. He gagged as if he were going to splash sick all across the forest floor. "Why did you do that?" he wailed at an octave so high that a flock of birds responded back, hands cupping his injury.

"Because you're disgusting, and more than that, fucking annoying!" The coarse language was comforting. "I should have your head on my mantle!"

Letting loose on Lysander almost made up for his interruption, and she was about to hurl a few more kicks at his prone form when the blast of a trumpet seized her attention. She sprinted to the low wall overlooking the valley below and scrambled up the stone, perching at the top just as the horns blare again.

Mycenae spread out before her in all its stone glory. Encased by walls so large only a team of cyclopes could have erected them, the grounds of the palace proper and the town surrounding it bustled with life. The Perseia Spring gurgled down the mountain opposite the one she stood upon, disappearing into the walls. Boys, sons and grandsons of minor nobles, practiced spear play in the dust of the royal courtyard. Serving women ran to and fro with heavy wicker baskets. Merchants peddled their wares through the city's narrow streets, donkeys pulling their carts laden with items as rare as rubies and as delicious as apples, just as red. Within the walls, sloping streets separated the many homes and artisan workshops from one another. Clay, wood, and stone interlocked to form two and even three story buildings. The many shades of brown were broken up by splashes of scarlet from the city's banners, and the ever present greenery hanging from every wall. While incomparable to the lush forest that Iphigenia had just emerged from, the carefully cultivated cypress trees and giant ferns were charming in their own right.

Iphigenia was normally content with gazing at the vista of her father's city. It was a beautiful, endlessly evolving place, and she loved to watch its little machinations. But today, an undercurrent of anxiety roiled beneath her nostalgia. Mycenae was the city that made her, and it would also be the city that shall unmake her, if she failed.

She shook her head, trying to clear her thoughts. This was not the time to focus on *that* issue. Instead, she diverted her attention to the source of the trumpets, the reason she was even looking down at the city at all.

The main road of Mycenae exited at a narrow gap in the massive walls, flanked on either side by more walls that extended outward, atop of which sat the trumpeters still furiously blowing. *I would've collapsed a lung by now*, Iphigenia thought as she watched.

Below the heralds, two chariots passed through a heavily fortified gate. Of all its ornate decorations, the most impressive of them were the two roaring lions carved into the rock at the gate's apex. Iphigenia's father had said the lions were to intimidate any visitors to his city; to Iphigenia, it appeared that the drivers of the chariots were totally unbothered as they spurred forward the largest horses she had ever seen. The chariots were unaccompanied; instead of the usual assortment of carts and wagons, the drivers and their steeds were the only members of their miniature entourage. Strange—the Lion Gate was reserved for grand shows of power, not fickle ventures or quick visits.

"That's a lot of drama for only two chariots," Lysander said, gingerly taking a seat several arms lengths away from Iphigenia. She threw a blistering glare at him, and he tenderly clasped his still sensitive groin.

"I'll behave this time!" His voice still held the pitch of a young child. Hopefully it was stuck like that.

"You better," Iphigenia said, scooting further away from him, "or I'll push you so hard you won't stop until you ram right into their ankles." She pointed at the men disembarking the chariots so far below. They were dressed brilliantly in full bronze armor, plumes and all, a far cry from Lysander's rusty, oversized chest piece. The men were being met with vigorous claps on the back from elders tripping over their long robes in their haste to greet them.

"Bunch of grifters," Iphigenia muttered.

"They're not invaders, then," Lysander said. A hint of disappointment weighed down his voice.

"That was obvious from the trumpets. Invasions are what the bells are for. For your sake and mine, I'm glad they're not. You're a piss poor excuse for a warrior." Still, worry crept in at the corners of her mind. These men, with their magnificent steeds and shining armor, had to be of the highest importance—kings, most likely. She furrowed her brow. All the kings of Greece would have set sail for Troy a month ago. There was no way they'd landed that quickly, let alone won the war and returned. Something was up.

She'd seen enough. Iphigenia swung back over the wall, dropping to the pine needle strewn grass below. She dusted herself off and resumed the narrow path that she and Lysander had detoured from. She needed to get closer, find out why these strange kings had just arrived in their finest battle attire. Peering down at them like a curious vulture wouldn't accomplish that.

She was already a good hundred or so feet away from the wall when Lysander let loose a shout in surprise. For someone so skinny, his footfalls were aggravatingly heavy as he sprinted to catch up.

"Why do you have to be so damn difficult?" he grumbled. "I wanted to keep watching them. Electra would've watched them with me."

"Then maybe you should be up Electra's ass instead of mine," Iphigenia spat, not even bothering to face him as she marched down the hillside. "It would save us both a headache."

The mention of her sister served as a grim reminder of what she had to look forward to once back inside the palace walls. She shuddered. At least she had much to think about while she blanked out during the ordeal weaving was destined to be.

Eventually, the two of them finally exited the forest. As they continued walking, they brushed up against one of the great walls, almost four times Iphigenia's height. Lysander immediately started walking to the left, toward the imposing main gate where the strange visitors had entered, while Iphigenia made a swift break for the right.

"Where are you going now?" Lysander whined. "The warriors are this way!"

"Not anymore, idiot!" She thought it was obvious—no one dallied at the gate. The visitors would have been graciously welcomed into the city proper by now. Iphigenia sprinted for the southern entrance, the one most used by slaves and traveling merchants. The Lion's Gate was for shows of power, with all its snarling statues and heavily armored guards, but the Southern Gate put purpose over pomp and circumstance. It was the fastest way to the palace courtyard, where the men were bound to be heading before they entered the royal receiving chamber, the *megaron*. Iphigenia, if she had her way, was going to meet them there.

She looked over her shoulder as she ran. Lysander was wheezing and coughing as he struggled to keep up, his thin red hair plastered to his scalp with sweat. Good, she thought, pumping her legs faster as she threw a wave to the archers perched on the walls above. They waved back, grinning as they held their bows.

She smiled, turned a corner, and slammed head-on into a woman whose arms were full with several layers of fabric.

They crashed to the ground, and it was as if a switch had flipped inside of Iphigenia. Her bravado had fled; she was already on her knees furiously apologizing as she flung broadcloth after broadcloth off the woman buried beneath her. It was only when the pile of linens began to shake that Iphigenia paused. Had she caused the woman to crack her head against the hard flagstones of the path? She was about to shout for someone to fetch a palace healer when she heard not sobs of pain or the moans of one caught in a seizure, but a suspiciously familiar snicker. Eyes narrowed, she reached out for another piece of fabric when the woman sprang up, tossing one of the discarded cloths over Iphigenia's head.

"Hey!" Iphigenia yelled, struggling to disentangle herself. Finally free, she found herself face to face with a plump, olive skinned girl, whose toothy smile stretched from ear to ear.

"You should really watch where you're going," the girl laughed, brushing the dirt from her dingy dress as she climbed to her feet. Her Greek was accented with the thick tones favored by the Egyptians living in Mycenae. She offered Iphigenia a hand. It was accepted with a shake of the head and a smile.

"Very funny, Euthalia. Just as funny as the last dozen times you've tricked me."

"I know, right?" the girl replied with a toss of her sable curls. "Maybe those nursery hags will promote me from laundry mule to a job with a little bit of dignity. I'm thinking royal diaper changer?"

Iphigenia laughed before pulling her friend into an embrace. Euthalia's hair smelled like the wildflowers that grew on nearby Mt. Zara's hillside, and she indulged herself with a brief inhale.

"Why the hug? Somebody dead?" Euthalia gave Iphigenia a light squeeze.

"Listen," Iphigenia quickly whispered. It wouldn't be good for too many to have too many people overhearing. She desperately wanted to tell Euthalia about what she'd seen up on the ridge, how she'd finally pulled it off, but there were more immediate concerns. Deciphering the apparition would take a far more involved discussion than they currently had time for. "We don't have much time before Half-off Heracles catches up with me, and there's some interesting strangers who've just arrived in the courtyard, if you get what I'm saying?"

"I'd heard the horns, but figured it was normal. I'll take your word for it." Euthalia clapped Iphigenia's shoulder as the two girls separated. "Research mission it is."

Iphigenia felt Euthalia's hand slip into hers as the girl tugged her towards the entrance to the citadel. Anxiety welled up inside her as soon as their fingers interlocked. Was it because she hadn't told Euthalia what she'd seen up on the ridge? There would be time for that soon enough; she wasn't hiding anything. So why did she feel like every step she took with the girl's hand in hers was a betrayal? She tried to tamp it down, willing her palm not to clam up with sweat, but before she could even begin to unpack the growing maelstrom of feelings rushing through her, a sharp "ahem!" broke the moment.

Iphigenia turned to come face to face with a tall hawk of a woman, her severe bun held together by pins just as sharp as the glare she was giving the girls. *Shit.* Sitamun, her weaving instructor and the strictest member of the palace staff, was the absolute last person she wanted to see.

"Where do you think you're going, and why are you leaving this mess?" the woman asked, a finger pointed at Euthalia. The sternness in her voice, coupled with the thick Egyptian accent, was sharp.

"Nowhere, mother," Euthalia said dejectedly, already lowering herself to retrieve the scattered linens. All sense of mirth had fled from the girl, and Iphigenia was sad to see the sudden dejection in her friend's eyes. Still, she had a mission to accomplish. She began to slip away.

"No ma'am, not this time, young lady," and Euthalia's mother's hand had encircled Iphigenia's bicep in a vice grip. Her nails dug into her skin like talons as she spoke. "Your mother will have my head if her darling daughter misses another weaving lesson." The sarcasm in her voice was plain. "Come on."

She jerked Iphigenia forward before calling over her shoulder. "And you—Timycha is due to have her child any hour now! Get to her, and be snappy about it."

Euthalia nodded, but as soon as her mother had turned her attention forwards, she slipped Iphigenia a sly wink. Iphigenia winked right back.

An ugly laugh erupted from over by the wall. Lysander stood there, hands on his narrow hips as he gave another guffaw. There wasn't much Iphigenia could do as she was being dragged away, but she certainly could make a rude hand gesture at the boy. The next time she saw him (she hoped that was in a few hours of never), she'd make sure he knew just how much she wanted to force his head into the cool waters of the Perseia until the bubbles stopped.

II

do not aspire to touch the sky

Firm hands pressed Iphigenia into her seat in front of the loom. Her sister was seated next to her, already working. Electra's nimble fingers flew, deftly transforming the bright threads from individual fabric to a unified image of a fantastic naval battle. Iphigenia's expression soured when she saw the little men drowning in swathes of blue and gray. Some clutched at the waves while others were tossed into the gaping maws of beasts larger than the ships they had fallen from. It was a terrible scene, but she had to admit, it was expertly done.

"It's for Father," Electra said, thin mouth curling in a smirk when she saw that her work had caught Iphigenia's eye. "When he returns from Troy."

Iphigenia frowned as she plucked at the frayed and messy threads on her own loom, leftover from the day before. No real image had emerged. Still, it was better than anything the man who called his self her father deserved.

"You try too hard."

"And you don't try hard enough."

"Shut up, Electra," Iphigenia grumbled.

13

There was a sharp tut. From across the room, Sitamun glared. The tall, bony woman's small eyes needled into Iphigenia in such a way that she just knew yet another chastisement was imminent, and it wouldn't be kind. A phantom ache ghosted across her knuckles, and she began to halfheartedly run the woolen fibers back and forth in an attempt to prevent the inevitable.

"I still don't see why Mother bothers with you with lessons," Electra continued, hands flying across her tapestry. "You can't weave, you can't dance, gods forbid you ever open that horseish mouth of yours to sing—"

"Electra, I swear—"

"There's no way you could nab a husband, and even if you could, you clearly wouldn't know what to do with him."

"Don't want one," Iphigenia said succinctly before shifting so that her body was angled away from her sister as she scoffed. All Electra wanted was to get a rise out of her; there was never any point in arguing.

Instead, she allowed her thoughts to wander back to the entourage she'd seen roll through Mycenae's massive gates. It had been a small coalition, with only a couple of chariots. Clearly built for speed rather than a display of grandeur or power then. Perhaps her father had fallen gravely ill before setting sail? She didn't dare let herself hope.

Then there was the question of the woman on the ridge. Why today, out of all the days she'd tried to summon something? Was she an omen, or a premonition of a blessing? The idea that her appearance was a simple coincidence with the visit of these strange men was laughable. Fate was a trickier mistress than that. Iphigenia needed to talk with Euthalia, sooner rather than later.

A measuring stick cracked against her knuckles; she shrieked, snatching them back from the loom to cradle them against her chest.

"Focus!" Euthalia's mother snapped, jerking her head up with the stick. Sitamun may have been a slave, and a foreign one at that, but that didn't mean that as a teacher, she didn't hold all the power in this chamber. "An idle mind makes for idle hands, and idle hands make for sloppy work like that mess in front of you."

"Sorry, miss," Iphigenia murmured, face on fire. Next to her, Electra stifled a snicker. Never so badly had she wanted to sock her sister right in her smug little mouth.

The next hour passed in dull silence. The summer heat had followed them indoors and showed no sign of relenting. Iphigenia found herself often tugging her chiton away from her neck. As she fidgeted, she tried to imagine she was still in the woods, the cool shade of the trees providing some relief. If it were up to her, she'd be walking to the bubbling source of the Perseia, ready to submerge herself completely beneath its cold mountain waters. These dreams did nothing to alleviate the crushing stuffiness of the weaving chamber.

Sitamun had long ago collapsed into a chair in the darkest corner of the room, fanning herself intermittently. Iphigenia longed to stand at the window under the guise of catching a bit of fresh air, to get even just a glimpse of the courtyard below to see what was happening. It was wishful thinking to believe an excuse for air would work, even if she'd genuinely love to feel the breeze against her sweaty skin; the wind hadn't blown in weeks. Even Electra, normally the perfect picture of a proper princess, had cast off her veil and sandals and dug her feet beneath the straw covering the floor to the cool stone beneath. As the god of sleep worked hard in bringing drowsiness to the chamber, an idea came to Iphigenia.

She fiddled with a small bag in her pocket. It was a tiny thing, made of goat bladder and hardly bigger than a mouse; and it was full of enough powdered poison to kill even a warrior on par with Heracles. She only desired the barest pinch — her targets were already half asleep. It would be so easy; one slip of the hand, a breath, and both Sitamun and Electra would slump to the floor, unconscious. The effects wouldn't be permanent, of course; a little vomiting upon waking never hurt anyone other than the very young or very elderly. They'd be incapacitated, and she, who would somehow have the miraculous foresight to use the restroom at the very same moment of their collapse, would be free to investigate the mysterious visitors. She could see the look on Euthalia's face now — hopefully words of praise would be falling from her lips at Iphigenia's utilization of the nightshade they'd spent all spring and half the summer nurturing in the mountain gardens behind Mycenae's great citadel.

Dreaming of future praise and secretive laughter, Iphigenia closed her eyes, falling victim to the drowsy warmth of the room. Just a few minutes of rest, and then she'd get up and enact her plan.

The door to the chamber slammed open with a bang that was quickly followed by another as Iphigenia's head crashed into the heavy wooden loom.

As she groaned in pain, a neurotic looking young boy dashed into the center of the chamber, his hands waving. Iphigenia grimaced. Of course it had to be Lycus, little twerp. A visit from Lycus, half as old as his brother Lysander and somehow twice as annoying, was never pleasant.

"The Queen requests the presence of her daughters for an audience!" His struggled to get his words out as if he'd just run the length of the palace twice over.

He approached Sitamun and, standing on his toes to reach her ear, deposited some swiftly whispered words behind his hand. Euthalia's mother nodded solemnly and the messenger dashed out of the room. Next to Iphigenia, Electra sprang to her feet.

"Maybe one of those handsome men is here to beg for my hand," Electra sang as she hopped on one foot, struggling to get her sandal on.

So, Electra also knew of the strange men who'd arrived. Iphigenia pressed a hand to her head and winced. Her fingers were sticky with blood, and worse yet, she had a sneaking suspicion that her and Electra's sudden summons was going to be more complicated than a simple chat with their mother. Any of her and Euthalia's usual espionage missions were out of the question now. A sneaking suspicion crept into her mind that someone had seen her dabbling in a foreign religion, one of a rival nation at that. The room wobbled as a sudden wave of dizziness hit her — they'd have her head on a pike for that, princess or not.

"You're insufferable," Sitamun says, pressing a scrap of scratchy wool into her hands. Iphigenia recognized it as a portion of one of her failed tapestries, the broken bodies of poorly woven horses almost taunting her.

"What am I supposed to do with this?"

Sitamun sucked her teeth. "Stop the bleeding, obviously. There's no point in calling a healer. You've got an audience to get to."

Iphigenia gingerly tied the beige cloth around her head, wincing not from the pain of the harsh fabric brushing against the gash, but from the thought of how she would look, dusty and bloodstained, next to her perfectly composed younger sister. Mother wouldn't mind, she never did, but if word got back to her father...an image of the man, broad and angry, loomed in her mind. Iphigenia shuddered as she exited the chamber with Electra strutting proudly in front of her.

* * *

The winding walls of the palace twisted and turned as they made their way out of the women's quarters, across the dusty courtyard, and toward the fortress proper. Along the way, many of the staff stared, whispering to each other behind their hands. Iphigenia couldn't help but feel the sickening pull of anxiety deep in her gut. Why did everyone but her suddenly seem to know what was going on?

She couldn't help but take a second glance at the strangers' chariots, now parked in the courtyard. The horses had been reigned in and were eagerly drinking from one of the many troughs lining the walls. They were beautiful creatures, tall and strong, and their saddles were just as gorgeous, richly dyed with purple native to far off Tyre. Still, the chariots themselves were unladen with the normal assortment of gifts and treasures that the kings of the surrounding cities brought to her father's house. This was a visit planned in haste, if planned at all.

Inside, the audience chamber loomed with its doors flanked by bronze statues twice a man's height. Perseus stood on one side, and her father on the other, his heavy brow caught up in a frozen scowl. The founder of their city and the self proclaimed lord of all men, side by side.

Iphigenia pointedly looked away from them, focusing instead on the heavy wood of the door as she stopped. What awaited her on the other side?

Electra and Sitamun kept strolling past the *megaron*, however, sandals slapping against the stone as they rounded a corner.

"Where are you two going?" she called, hand on the door. "Didn't Mother—?"

"We're going to the inner *megaron*. It's gotta be something extra special," Electra replied over her shoulder, and the arrogant glee in her tone dripped like venom.

Iphigenia raced to catch up before Euthalia's mother could start yelling. The apprehension in her chest bubbled, threatening to boil over.

She'd only been in the inner *megaron* once before, when Orestes had been born. She and Electra had never seen their father so happy; he had held the newborn aloft in his arms and laughed, his deep voice bouncing around the brightly painted room. It was as if something wild had gotten into the man as he paraded the infant around, pointing out the scenes of long ago battles and ancestors coursing with gods lovingly depicted on the walls. It had been funny at the time; there was no way the hours old Orestes could understand a word of it, but their father had insisted on telling the ancient tales, and none had the courage to interrupt. Her mother had quickly let her and Electra know that their father had a much more subdued reaction at their births. It was not the happiness of a new father, but of a king who finally had an heir that they had witnessed that day. They'd feasted for weeks afterward, all the way up until Orestes was three moons old. Iphigenia was positive they'd be feasting even now if it weren't for the tragedy at Sparta grinding their whole world to a halt. That had been almost two years ago.

The trio made their way up a set of rough hewn stairs until they stood before a single bronze door, much smaller than the one a floor below. "Try to behave," Sitamun murmured.

Electra feverishly raked her fingers through the mass of blonde on her head and Iphigenia swiped away an errant stream of blood off her cheek as Sitamun rapped her knuckles against the door frame.

There was a pause, and then the door swung open onto a room swathed in light. Iphigenia squinted as their little group trooped inside, the change from the darkness of the palace corridors a stark contrast to the sunlight streaming through the massive glass skylight above them. She was pleased to see that the room was still awash in colorful paintings and tapestries. Frescoes of leaping dolphins intermingled with warriors clashing spears, the dry battlefields they fought on thirsting for fresh blood. The room was twice as long as it was wide, and at the end stood a pair of thrones, raised high upon a dais. The thrones were flanked by two men, cloaked in shadow just beyond the skylight's reach. Between the two, in the smaller throne, sat the unmistakable figure of her mother.

It was funny; when they were together, it was easy to see just how much Electra resembled their mother. They had the same long blonde hair wound up in intricate coils, high cheekbones, and strong, straight noses. Coupled with the several inches Electra had over Iphigenia in height, a gift from Clytemnestra's own impressive stature, she wouldn't blame anyone who thought Electra was the elder daughter rather than her.

Iphigenia had heard her mother described by traveling merchants and foreign dignitaries as many things: devastatingly beautiful, second only to her sister, was one of her most common epitaphs. Others referred to her as an absolute eagle of a woman. The smartest of them even dared to call her shrewd, rivaling even her husband Agamemnon in her cunning. But today, Iphigenia saw something far different in the woman before her in the throne.

For the first time in Iphigenia's life, Clytemnestra looked nervous.

She could see it in the way her mother's chin, held high as always, warbled slightly, and how her long fingers tapped against the armrest in quick little spurts. Iphigenia wished she had paid more attention during temple rites; even if her gods had turned a deaf ear to her, perhaps they'd protect her mother from whatever had her so on edge.

Sitamun gave a quick curtsy and swiftly exited the room. Next to her, Electra sank to her knees in an elaborate bow, and Iphigenia immediately followed, thankful for the soft carpet that greeted her. Where Electra lowered her gaze, ostensibly in an effort to play coy, Iphigenia kept hers high, searching the darkness for any hint of the men's features. It was risky move, almost defiant, but when had that stopped her before?

"Girls," Clytemnestra said in greeting, rising from her seat. Her voice was strong and proud, full of her normal resolution, but the furrow of her brow and the way she worried at her lip betrayed the queen's true emotions. "Our guests have journeyed a great distance to deliver a message from your father." Clytemnestra gestured towards the men, and they stepped forward from the shadows.

They were polar opposites of each other; where one was tall and broad, the other was wiry and barely came up to Clytemnestra's chin. The large one was pale, whereas the smaller man was dark of skin and even darker of beard. Neither were as old as her father; wrinkles had yet to decorate their visages, but Iphigenia took careful note of several scars that only sharp blades could leave. They were both dressed in light clothes, plain and comfortable on a day as sweltering as this one. Still, armor rested against one of the walls, gleaming bronze and inlaid gold sparkling in the sun. These were the same men she'd watched ride in, no doubt about it. The wide one's face was empty, betraying none of his inner thoughts. He was no simple brute — as she searched his face, Iphigenia recognized him as one of the kings that oft came to her fathers banquet table. The skinny one, with eyes as black as the unlit coals lining the hearth, stepped forward, and as he prepared to speak, Iphigenia could already smell the heavy stink of lies upon him. He spoke first, his small eyes locked on her and her sister.

"Your great and noble father King Agamemnon," the man began, his voice gravelly, "has sent I, Odysseus, King of Ithaca, and my companion Diomedes, King of Argos—" he waved an arm at the other man, who nodded solemnly "—to announce the marriage proposal of Prince Achilles of Phthia. Agamemnon has accepted, and wishes for Achilles' bride to join him at the port of Aulis at haste for the wedding."

While Electra looked hardly able to restrain herself from an excited shout, all the tension in Iphigenia's shoulders slipped away. While she was of a more marriageable age than Electra, pushing her seventeenth naming day, for as long as she could remember, her father had said that Electra would make the better bride. Judging by the rumors of Achilles that made their way to Mycenae, Agamemnon would want the finest bride he had to offer for his young colleague if they were to cement a formidable alliance.

Iphigenia gave Electra a small smile, taking her sister's hand in hers. Electra returned her grin, and for the first time since they'd both been small children, Iphigenia felt that she and her sister truly were happy for each other. Finally, Electra would get to play the bride she'd so desperately wanted to have been since she was five years old, and Iphigenia would get near unlimited privacy to practice her craft with no nosy little sister looming over her shoulder. This was how things should be, how they'd always been meant to be. Despite being two years her junior, Electra had surpassed her in weaving, cooking, cleaning, and praising the household gods. She was far better with Orestes, often cooing to him and demanding to be the one to change the baby's linens. In all things domestic, Electra had always been the superior sibling. Iphigenia didn't mind; she'd much rather be down by the market shooting dice with the lowborn children, or roaming the hills and forests surrounding their small city.

A warm feeling spread through her as she pictured the future. Electra, far away and happy with a handsome husband, baby Orestes learning statecraft to be the ruler Mycenae would one day need, and her, free to test the limits of her ability. She may have been the firstborn, but she was more than happy to bequeath all the trappings of an heir onto her two younger siblings. Yes, this would be the best way.

Still, she wondered: why now? At this point, the wide Trojan plain should long have been in the mens' sights. A wedding was the last thing she expected her father to be organizing.

As Odysseus rattled off the amount of goblets, gilded bracelets, and shields that would serve as the bride's dowry, Iphigenia's eyes wandered to the large tapestry directly above her mother's head. This one was her favorite, the rich red thread connecting panel to panel. It was oft repeated throughout the castle, but they were all pale imitations of this one, the largest and most richly dyed by far. Up in the left corner stood a man, a boy, and a roiling pot, followed by a savage feast — goddess Demeter of the waving grain munching away at the flesh of the boy. Then the boy, raised anew with bright white thread for a shoulder, and the man far below, emaciated and reaching heavenward, the boy just out of reach. The boy's life followed, the tapestry chronicling both his own deceptions and those of his descendants. Iphigenia's eyes traced the journey through the ages, murder and treachery continuing in a cycle until she reached the end, where two men stood shrouded in gold threads, arms clasped around each other in triumph. Agamemnon and his younger brother Menelaus, with their kingdoms sprawled out beneath their feet. She turned her eyes away. If only this part could be cut away — she was positive not even Aunt Helen, scion of the loom, could weave something more elegant, save for that.

As soon as Odysseus finally finished, Electra scrambled to her feet. "I accept noble Achilles' proposal," she said, her chest puffed out with pride. "When do we leave?" When there was no response, Iphigenia looked up, roused from her daydream. Her mother was frowning fiercely, looking almost as if she could jump out of her throne and throttle Electra, while Diomedes was barely hiding a snicker. Odysseus shook his head.

"You have me mistaken, young Electra," Odysseus said, his voice sweet with sympathy. Despite his tone, his smile did not reach his eyes. "This proposal is not for you." And Iphigenia watched with horror as Ithaca's king diverted his attention to her. "It is for Agamemnon's eldest, Iphigenia."

III

ever shall I be a maid

Iphigenia stumbled down the hall. After they'd told her everything they'd deemed necessary, Odysseus and Diomedes had asked if they could speak with her mother alone to iron out some of the more nuanced details. With limbs like jelly, Iphigenia had nodded and excused herself. She'd felt like she was burning alive the entire time she'd been forced to hear the details of what she could only describe as a transaction. She'd yet to have even shed her first blood and here these strangers were, discussing just how soon she'd be able to produce an heir for Achilles. She'd been reduced to the status of a broodmare, just like that.

"It's not fair." The tight voice cut through the fog in her mind. Iphigenia looked to her right, and there was Electra, a deep pout marring her pretty features. "You don't even want it."

"I don't have time for this," Iphigenia mutters, speeding up her stride. She couldn't bear yet another of her sister's tantrums. Not here, not like this.

"You *never* have time!" Electra whined, and then she smashed a vase to the stone floor. Through the numbness, some portion of her was shocked. Perfect Electra, resorting to violence? "And now you're going to be married and you'll be gone and I'll be *alone!*"

24

Iphigenia, stunned, could only say one thing. "You'll have Orestes." Then she ran, desperate to get away as her sister devolved into full blown tears.

* * *

Three days. That's all they'd given her — three days to pack her things, to say goodbye to the only home she'd ever known, to prepare to be shipped out to a foreign land and a foreign man's bed. Odysseus had said the wedding needed to be an expedient one, before the ships left, as a good omen for the war and a morale builder for the soldiers. Iphigenia wondered if anyone gave a damn about the morale of the bride herself.

Iphigenia staggered across the palace grounds in a daze. She desperately longed to race up onto the mountain, to weep at the same springs and wells she'd had to comfort her from the time she could walk, but even that was denied to her. Ever since the announcement, she'd been expressly forbidden from venturing alone beyond the walls of the palace, let alone those of the city itself. The elders said it was a matter of "preserving her integrity". No longer could she be the wild princess who journeyed onto Mt. Zara each morning — that morning, she may have been a child, but by dinner, she was a woman, and a promised one at that. Mycenae couldn't risk any damaged goods being delivered to Aulis, so to speak, but Iphigenia felt like the eyes that followed her every move were checking if she was a flight risk, not if she were sneaking off with a boy at her side. The constant supervision was almost as suffocating as the whirlwind of attention that she was now subject to.

Everywhere she went, servants piled congratulations on her, but she found herself unable to even muster up a smile — half heartedly waving them away was the best she could do. The people of the city openly celebrated in the streets, throwing garlands at her feet when she was escorted through the same wide avenues that she'd once played in with their children. Once familiar faces became strangers in their adoration, as if something had intrinsically changed about her. There was Glaukos the chicken skewer salesman who had often chastised her for sneaking out before slipping her a piece of meat, weeping openly in the street. Philomela too, the woman who'd once tried to teach her to sing, heavens bless her. Cheering amongst the ferns were Apollonia and Dionysia, the twin girls she'd spent her earliest days making mud pies with in the castle courtyard — they too melted away into nothingness in the crowd of doting people. Iphigenia's face burned hot each time she spotted someone she knew, and it took all she had in her not to leap from the litter that she was now required to be carried upon and dash her skull against the stone pavers of the street.

The whole palace doted on her any time they weren't preoccupied with preparations for the journey. Rare perfumes from the far off empires of the east were often left at her door at night, and there was a constant influx of fine robes and tapestries delivered to her bedroom. Women would tell her that since Achilles was going off to fight in the war, it wouldn't be so bad, and she could essentially still live as a maiden while she waited for him to return. Iphigenia found herself snapping back that that was almost worse, living alone in a foreign palace with foreign people. She'd never even *heard* of Phthia, let alone been there— she wasn't even sure if it was connected to the mainland, or if she'd be shoved onto a boat and forced across the sea.

Clytemnestra sent her all sorts of presents, ranging from expensive ivory combs to sweet figs doused in honey. Iphigenia would have thrown them all out the window in exchange for a minute of her mother's time. Both she and Clytemnestra were surrounded by a maelstrom of attendants in constant motion, and there was seldom opportunity for a hello, let alone an actual conversation. She longed to confess to her mother just how much she did *not* want this. Her mother was the most powerful woman in all of Mycenae's history; if she could just get a few seconds with her, maybe things could end differently.

The palace staff tried their best to bring her a little cheer, often preparing her the hottest bathes and sweetest wines. She was sure they were confused at her constant sullenness; the whispers behind the smiles were far louder than their owners intended them to be. Normally a princess off to be wed was a joyous event, and even better that it be to a young hero. Iphigenia couldn't emphasize with their disappointment. If they wanted smiles, they would have been better off building her funeral pyre.

Even Lysander, scrawny lewd Lysander, was being nicer to her, but that may have had something to do with the fact that she would be out of his life for good very shortly. The only one who didn't seem ecstatic for her was Electra, who was now much more prone to slamming doors in her face. Iphigenia was tempted to knock her sister over the head several times, especially when Electra had outright called her a bitch, but she restrained herself, opting instead to focus on the more pressing matter at hand rather than her little sister's raging jealousy.

Marriage was the last thing she wanted, not when she'd been so close to preventing it from ever happening in the first place. Even though she'd grown up knowing it would be almost impossible to avoid, she couldn't help but feel like being violently sick every time she thought about it. Her stomach was near constantly twisted in knots. The idea of being uprooted from the only life she'd ever known to be married to a man, one she had never met, one who was purported to be the blood thirstiest warrior Achaea had ever seen? It had her wrenching at her hair in the night when she thought no one else could see.

* * *

Her fears grew more extreme the closer departure approached. The day before they were scheduled to load up the wagons, she stumbled out of the healing house, where she'd just been given a long lecture on just exactly what she was supposed to do on her wedding night, and promptly vomited into the street. The concept of doing *those* things, with a *man*, down in the dirt of a tent—?. Her skin crawled with the thought of it, and bile rose in her throat again as the very same women who had induced this feeling in her fretted about her health.

"There, there," one of them said, patting her on the shoulder as she dry heaved. "A little bit of fear is good — keeps your lad excited." As the sun beamed down on Iphigenia's back, she found her vision skating past the tutting old crones surrounding her and up the hill. There, the state temple, the largest in the valley, stood, its gleaming pillars almost calling out to her in the sunshine. She wouldn't have long; this was the first time she'd been allowed outside the palace in days, and her handlers would be at hand momentarily. She pushed the women aside and staggered towards it.

As she stood at the bottom of the marble steps, Iphigenia began to reconsider. She'd never been much for prayer, only performing the occasional state rite when asked to by the priests via her mother. What was she even supposed to say? And to who? She struggled to figure out who to appeal to as she entered the building, wiping furiously at her mouth. Her first thought was Athena, goddess of war and wisdom; wasn't she too a woman? And a virgin at that? She cautiously approached a burning altar, above which a small statuette looked down at her almost cruelly. A nagging suspicion tugged in the back of her mind that perhaps she'd approve of a marriage between the head general's daughter and the strongest soldier on the basis of strengthening bonds between the army. After that, she drew a blank. She could hardly discern most of the pantheon from each other, let alone remember their specific attributes. And why should she? It wasn't as if they'd ever heard her pleas — it was only when Iphigenia spoke Euthalia's strange Egyptian words that anything had ever happened.

When the priests began to approach her almost menacingly, she threw her hands up and went back outside. Of course they'd object to her presence; not only was the temple closed to the public at this hour, she was still an unaccompanied woman, princess or not. The Temple of Zeus would give her no aid.

Iphigenia found herself slapping the stone wall in frustration. Her good for nothing father had always said that those close to the gods were the closest to the seat of power and he was the most powerful king Achaea had ever seen, surpassing even Theseus if he was to be believed. Agamemnon, if his records were to be believed, had never lost a battle. "The gods are on my side", he'd proclaim, drunk on victory and tributed wine, at banquet tables overflowing with bounty.

To Iphigenia, if the gods were on his side, that meant that they were against hers, and that was the open and shut case of religion for her. She wanted nothing to do with anyone who allied themselves with that man, deity or not. Now she was deeply regretting her own agnosticism. She thought back to her childhood, which was filled with instructions on weaving and how to be a good wife rather than tales of heroes and gods. She knew their names, and she knew what to sacrifice at their annual state festivals, but further than that? It was all a mystery. Still, her rejection from the main temple had sprouted an idea, one that might just work— but she didn't have much time.

The next morning, she was posted at the city's smallest temple on the outskirts of the grounds, wringing her hands as she waited on the chilly marble steps. She'd been there since dawn, having snuck out of the palace proper. It hadn't been hard; the guards had been getting drunker and drunker each night as the engagement celebrations continued, and by morning they were all too sloshed to even pause in their snores as she tiptoed over their prone forms.

Now that the sun had fully risen, the dew had begun to dry. Iphigenia was contemplating moving to a seat in the grass instead of her current hard throne when the sound of a heavy door creaking open broke her out of her reverie. She swung around, watching as the gaggle of priestesses descended the steps in their swirling sage robes. They were all talking animatedly among one another, but quickly dissolved into silence when they saw her at the bottom of their path. Iphigenia rushed to approach them.

"I need help," she began, but before she could get any farther, the woman in the front, with the shining diadem, raised a hand. Whereas the other women were veiled, this one was not. Iphigenia recognized her as the head priestess, the one who had always sat conspicuously at her father's side during state addresses in the *megaron*.

"I already see where this is going, and no. I've heard the rumors. This marriage is a *good* thing," the head priestess stressed, and the attendants behind her nodded in unison. Iphigenia thought they rather looked like starstruck fools, the way they were clearly parroting the woman they were standing behind.

"What about if I want to be a priestess instead?" Iphigenia challenged. The role of priestess was sacred, something only for unmarried women. Princesses before had done it, even firstborns. No mortal king dared interfere with those the gods had picked as their servants, lack of piety be damned. She had long wondered what happened in that secluded cloister of women, but she was completely open to a trial by fire if it meant she could get out of this.

"It is not your fate—"

"Please," she pleaded, panic rising in her voice. "I'll cook, I'll clean, I'll cut the necks of the beasts myself—"

"Princess," the head priestess said, pinching the bridge of her nose. "Every girl looks forward to her marriage. Why do you fear what is natural?"

It's not natural for me, Iphigenia wanted to scream. All through her childhood, she'd known nothing but contentment in Mycenae, save for one little thing. It was that age old ailment that plagued her, an affliction really, an aversion so stomach churning that she'd sought out ancient magic rather than confront it head on, and now she was being thrown right into its gaping maw. Ever since she'd been old enough to form with her mouth the vowels and consonants of desire, she'd known hers to be abnormal. "You didn't look forward to yours," Iphigenia accused, avoiding the question as she stared the priestess down. "Why else would you be here?" She gestured towards the cotillion of women behind her.

The priestess scowled. "My personal affairs are of no concern, as I was not born a *princess*. Every one of us is to serve the kingdom to the best of their ability, and the best ability a princess possesses is a good marriage. You are the first daughter of the most powerful king in all Achaea. See for yourself." The priestess gestures towards the hearth just inside the temple's entrance, where the foul scent of burning flesh wafts up. "It is as the gods have ordained in the entrails, and it is beautiful. Accept it."

"If there is beauty to be found in gore," Iphigenia spat, "let it be that of my own corpse." Her mind was made up. No matter what, she would not be wed.

IV

hail, gentle evening

Iphigenia was back in her bedroom, head in her hands at her table. Just hours left, now. The stone walls shone with the flickering of several candles; coupled with the moonlight streaming in from the open window, the chamber was awash in light. Across the room, Electra snored in her own low bed. *What I wouldn't give to sleep like that,* Iphigenia thought, fingernails digging into her forearms. The sleeping draughts had stopped working; whether it was from developing a tolerance for chamomile or genuinely suffering from a malady even her own brews couldn't help, she did not know.

For hours now, ever since she'd excused herself from the dinner table after barely picking at her meal, she'd been pouring over hastily scrawled notes, searching for anything that would help her escape the fate that awaited her at dawn. It was pointless; Euthalia had vehemently opposed teaching her anything useful, beyond simple medicinal potions. She wanted to swear — naturally, she'd *had* to have been denied access to anything of real power. Despite her slowly growing resentment, Iphigenia still wanted to see Euthalia desperately. She hadn't seen her since before being summoned to the *megaron.* Apparently Timycha's labor had only grown more and more difficult by the day, and the midwives had needed all hands on deck around the clock. Her screams, loud enough to be heard halfway across the palace, had been the stuff of Iphigenia's worst nightmares — in less than a year, she had a very good chance of making the same agonizing wails.

She was seriously considering the logistics of stripping her bed of its blankets and using the paltry skills she'd gained from weaving lessons to fashion a noose when a knock rapped at the door. Iphigenia jumped to answer it, desperate for a distraction from the growing panic in her mind.

One of Orestes' nursemaids, a thin woman named Myia, stood at the door.

"Apologies for disturbing you, Princess. It's your mother. She wants to see you."

"Mother? At this hour?" Iphigenia was confused. Her mother had already kissed her and Electra goodnight before rushing off to her chambers before Iphigenia could get more than the slightest word in. It had hurt, but she supposed she understood. The queen was a busy woman, and she'd need plenty of rest for the journey tomorrow. "Is something wrong?"

"Nothing is wrong. She told me she wanted to chat with you before you depart in the morning."

Iphigenia shrugged before returning to her desk to retrieve a small candelabra. Mycenae's wide halls would be ablaze with oil fueled torches at this hour, but a little extra light against the often uneven flagstones was always welcome. She gave one final glance towards her sister's lolling head; Electra was still snoring away. That brat could sleep through a siege of giants. Iphigenia slipped out into the hall.

It wasn't a long trip. The royal wing of the palace couldn't be described as particularly small, but Clytemnestra had always called for her children's chambers to be close to hers, breaking with the tradition of separating regents from heirs. Iphigenia had asked her why once, and her mother had muttered something indistinct about Aunt Helen and a place called Athens before promptly shutting the conversation down. A few paces down the hall and around a corner, and Iphigenia was gliding through a sparsely furnished antechamber. A pair of guards stood watch, heavy spears in hand. They nodded at her, and she gave a halfhearted wave before moving between them to push through a beaded curtain to the royal bedchamber.

Clytemnestra was seated on a chaise beneath the open window. The Queen was as radiant as ever, her blonde hair hanging loose around her shoulders. At Iphigenia's entrance, a small smile graced her lips. She was dressed in a richly embroidered nightgown; it was sumptuously dyed as red as the hyacinths that dotted the plains, and a trick of the light almost made it appear that the golden threads winding up and down its sleeves glowed on their own. Iphigenia couldn't help but feel self conscious in her threadbare gown from childhood, but the evenings had been so warm that nothing else was anywhere near as comfortable.

"Come, sit with me," Clytemnestra said, patting the space next to her. "I want to spend my child's last night as a little girl with her."

Iphigenia felt her first smile since the arrival of Odysseus and Diomedes creep onto her face. She hadn't been allowed to sleep in the same chamber as her mother since before Electra had been born. No matter how much she'd pleaded, her father had been adamant about not allowing it. She almost ran to the chaise, plopping herself onto its cushioned surface. Her mother immediately wrapped an arm around her.

"You're so big now," Clytemnestra began, stroking her daughter's hair. "I remember when you were small enough that you fit right in the crook of my arm."

Iphigenia allowed a laugh to bubble up out of her throat. "That was a long time ago, Mother."

"Not really. It feels like just yesterday for me. It might as well be." Clytemnestra's brown eyes, one of the only features shared between the two, welled with unshed tears. "And now...another baby is being taken from me."

Iphigenia's eyes drifted towards Orestes' crib in the corner of the chamber. The baby cooed in his sleep. A twang of guilt pulsed through Iphigenia. She normally played with him every day, parading him amongst the goats and olive groves; she hadn't so much as held him since the night before the announcement. Clytemnestra followed her gaze. "Of course, he and Electra are my babies too, but not like you were. Not like you *are*."

Ah. So that was what this was about. The secret Clytemnestra had whispered to her from before she could even remember, the one shared betwixt only the two of them. Not even Electra knew — her mother had made her swear by the river Styx that she'd never tell her younger sister, lest it irreparably harm her.

Her mother began to hum the beginnings of a song. Its chords were as familiar to her as the back of her hand, but Iphigenia was unable to grasp its name, no matter how fiercely her mother's voice tugged at the edge of memory.

"I hear your betrothed is exceptionally beautiful," Clytemnestra said after a few more notes. "They say his eyelashes are darker and fuller than a woman's. The beauty of his hair apparently rivals yours," she chuckled. Iphigenia picked at the strings of her night gown, not making eye contact. She didn't want to talk about him right now.

"I know, its hard," Clytemnestra said, her voice soft. "I've seen how you've struggled. I just want it to be easier for you."

"It'll never be easy," Iphigenia murmured, turning away. "Mother, please. Can't you do anything to stop this?"

Clytemnestra grimaced, but just as quickly, her gaze smoothed into a far more tender neutrality. To Iphigenia, it almost looked like pity. "Iphigenia, would you humor me for a moment?"

Despite her discomfort at her mother's expression, Iphigenia nodded. "Anything you'd like."

"Do you remember the story of Persephone?" her mother asked, looking down at her wistfully.

"Not really," Iphigenia responded. She had paid even less attention to myths than she had the gods. They seemed far off, problems for other people, cautionary tales in a world that was harsher than that of the worst stories. Still, memories of a festival only a few months prior float to the surface. "Doesn't she have something to do with spring time?"

Her mother tutted as she gently brushed Iphigenia's hair out of her face. "Well, at least I know I won't be boring you." She then took a deep breath before beginning to speak.

"Long ago, there was a goddess named Demeter. She reigned over the fields and the grain, and she made sure everyone the world over was well fed." Iphigenia felt a tingle of embarrassment at how baby-ish the story was already shaping up to be. It sounded like something Orestes should be hearing, but her mother was already so earnest in her retelling that she didn't have the heart to do anything more than nod appreciatively. "She broke the hard soil of the earth alone, and tucked each seed into the ground with her well calloused hands. The work was backbreaking and the people she kept alive through her efforts took it for granted. They ate and grew fat, but their praises were lacking. Demeter found herself lonely. So lonely that she wished and prayed for a companion to be by her side forevermore. She had to pay dearly," Iphigenia looked up in alarm as her mother's grip grew stiff, "but eventually, her wish was granted by the king of the gods in the form of a gorgeous girl, her own daughter, grown from her flesh as the stalk of wheat grows from the ground. This was Persephone." At this, Clytemnestra's eyes softened.

"Persephone shared in her mother's work, and what was once a labor of obligation became one of love. Never had Demeter loved humans more than when her daughter was at her side. Demeter could face any injustice or humiliation, as long as she had her darling daughter to come home to." Clytemnestra's voice had grown morose, and despite her lack of background knowledge, Iphigenia would bet a golden calf that Demeter and Persephone's idyllic circumstance was about to come to an end.

"The problem arose when Persephone's father, Zeus, decided that it was high time for her to be married. Demeter's daughter was just a little girl, younger than you are now." Clytemnestra pulled Iphigenia closer. "Of course, he neglected to consult the girl's mother at all, for she would have declined *immediately*. Not that it would have mattered. No one stood up to the king of the gods — but for her daughter,

Demeter would have overthrown the man a thousand times over if she could've.

"Either way, while Demeter was out in the fields, Persephone was frolicking in a nearby meadow, as was her custom. There, the lord of the underworld broke through the earth and swept her up in his dark and terrible chariot. Zeus had promised his daughter to his own brother. By the time Demeter had returned from her daily labor, her daughter had been long gone. At first, she thought she was playing a game with her, hiding amongst the waving stalks of barley, but Demeter grew panicked as the night washed over the land. She begged the other gods to help her search for her child, whose cheeks still held the roundness of one not far from sipping her mother's milk, but all denied her, claiming to not want to offend the will of the girl's father."

Clytemnestra spat out the final word with such sudden venom that Iphigenia instinctively recoiled before relaxing back into the embrace.

"Demeter was inconsolable. She wouldn't eat or sleep. She wailed all hours of the day as she wandered, searching for her lost daughter. She was so grief stricken that she didn't even notice as she was fed the flesh of your ancestor. Above all, though, she was angry. Angry for her child, snatched away without a trace. Angry at the others, for being complicit in the plot. Angry at herself, for not being there, and for being too weak to do anything about it. Most of all, she was angry at Zeus, who'd not only taken her dignity, but the only good thing to come out of that vile union. So, she plotted revenge in the only way she knew how.

"The other gods underestimated her. Poor, weeping Demeter, they would say, as they shook their heads when they passed her in Olympus' wide halls. Gentle Demeter, who had never harmed a fly. 'One day, she'll move on,' they'd said. She had no arrows she could release, nor could she bring forth waves as tall as mountains, but they forgot that she held the key to life itself: sustenance.

"Demeter had been robbed of her only joy. Why should she provide for anyone else's? If they wouldn't tell her where her daughter was, she'd simply quit. And so, black soil became dry dust, the wheat ceased to grow, the bounty of the grape vines shriveled to raisins as hard as rocks, and the olive trees withered into ash. Worse yet, the animals, cows and goats alike, ceased to produce milk, then stopped giving birth, as if they feared their own young being seized. Soon, the humans began to starve and perish beneath the burning sun, and the gods, all the way at the top of that lofty food chain, began to feel the effects when their primary nourishment, worship, was denied to them."

Iphigenia felt her eyes growing heavy, her mother's gentle cadence enveloping her. It was more powerful than any sleeping draught she could brew.

"They all grew weak, and even Zeus found his strength lacking, his thunderbolts little more than crackles in the air. Finally, he relented, and told Demeter where she could find her daughter. Like a woman transformed, Demeter raced to the underworld, wrenching the earth apart with her bare hands. But she was too late." Clytemnestra's voice was soft.

"She found her daughter in Lord Hades' house, and she wept and embraced her, but when she tried to pull her away to bring her home, her daughter began to wail. She'd been tricked, she told Demeter, forcibly starved by her husband as punishment for Demeter denying the world and overfilling his court. The only food she was permitted to eat was the wicked fruit that grew without the sun, without her mother's loving touch."

"And so she couldn't leave," Iphigenia whispered. She didn't remember much of the story, but the idea of food being an avenue of punishment conjured visions of an emaciated Tantalus reaching for food he'd never taste. She found that she sympathized far more with Persephone than her ancestor.

Clytemnestra smiled down at her encouragingly. "Persephone was led to believe by her new husband that she couldn't leave, but she told her mother that she'd only eaten enough of the cursed food to sustain herself, never truly filling her belly. Demeter immediately wrapped her daughter up in her cloak to bring her back above the dry, cracked earth, and along with Persephone too came the rising of the green shoots of spring. For a time, it seemed as if they could put this dark episode behind them. Mother and daughter returned to their old patterns of planting and nurturing.

"The two were not truly free, however. When summer waned, and all the bounty was harvested, Persephone had to sink below the ground back to her cold husband, who would not be denied, and Demeter locked up her house and settled in for the long wait until her daughter returned to her side again. But her rage still simmered, and that's why nothing grows in the long winter months, for Demeter would rather the whole world perish than to be full and healthy while she is robbed of her little girl."

By the end of her tale, Clytemnestra was staring out the window. Iphigenia followed her mother's gaze, but there was nothing to see but the faint outlines of the surrounding mountain ranges.

"That was a wonderful story, mother," Iphigenia tentatively began, pulling at a loose strand of hair. There was nothing *wonderful* about any of it, but the sound of her mother's voice had lulled at least some of the horrible anxiety she'd been grappling with since the announcement. Still, she wasn't stupid. Her mother's meaning was clear as day. "Thank you for telling me. Did grandmother tell it to you when you married father?"

Clytemnestra still did not face her. "Iphigenia," she said, and there it was again, that strange hesitation, heavy in the voice of one who'd never hesitated before. "Promise you'll visit me, as Persephone visited Demeter? That you won't forget about me?"

Iphigenia gripped her mother's hand, committing the feeling of her soft skin to memory. "If it were up to me, I'd never leave. Why wouldn't I visit?"

"I'm nowhere near as brave as Demeter," Clytemnestra said. Before Iphigenia could argue, she did the one thing she'd never expected to see her mother do — tears, pearly in the moonlight, slid down Clytemnestra's cheeks. "I've failed you. You're well within your rights to never wish to see me again."

A pang of guilt struck Iphigenia. So her mother had known all along?

"If you can find it in your heart to forgive me, come back. These halls are too dark and cold without the promise of one so vibrant as you. Sometimes, I think that if I never had you, I would be just as dark and cold as they are." Before Iphigenia could further question her mother, she had risen from the chaise and moved to the bed, wearily pushing back the heavy throw. Her face was unreadable. It was as if she'd never cried at all. "It's getting late, and we have a long journey ahead of us."

As she crawled into her mother's warm embrace for the first time since childhood, Iphigenia knew the journey was going to be far longer than a three day ride to Aulis.

* * *

Something tickled her shoulder. Iphigenia swatted it away, curling back into the warmth of her mother's side. Then the sensation returned, gently shaking her. She jerked her shoulder away.

"Wake *up*," a voice hissed, and then Iphigenia opened her eyes to see Euthalia standing at her side, arms stained red.

"Did Timycha have the baby?" Iphigenia whispered, mindful of the gentle rise and fall of her mother's sleeping form next to her.

"Timycha is dead."

"And the child—"

"Never was. A white mass, with hair and teeth, but never a child."

"What does it mean?" Iphigenia breathed.

"It means it is time. I know what you saw. You'll get your wish, Iphigenia, and I will get mine."

V

in my ear all thy secrets tell

"Where are we going, and just how do you think we'll get around the guards?"

Despite the tightness in her voice, Iphigenia was close on Euthalia's heels as the two of them picked their way along the exterior wall of the palace. Slipping out in the first place hadn't been a problem, surprisingly enough; Clytemnestra hadn't stirred, not even when Iphigenia had accidentally nudged her while slipping out of bed. Even the guards who'd welcomed her into the royal bedchambers accommodated her exit, no doubt thinking she was only returning to her own bed.

Euthalia scoffed, not even deigning to turn around. "What guards? This city has nothing but children and old men left to defend it. Just look."

Iphigenia followed Euthalia's extended finger to the top of the wall. Beneath the flicker of torch light, she could see two boys leaned against a crate, heads slumped. Further down the catwalk, the sound of drunken laughter and clattering dice rose up from a gaggle of gray haired figures.

"So? This doesn't mean anything. The main entrance will still be heavily fortified."

"Luckily, we have no need for the main entrance. We won't even be leaving the palace grounds, technically." Iphigenia felt a flutter in her stomach as soft fingers encircled her wrist. What on earth was *that* about? "Now come. We won't get a chance like this again."

The two of them took a sharp left and then, embedded into the wall, stood a nondescript wooden door. In all her years of living in the palace, Iphigenia had never noticed it. She had no idea where it could lead; the only thing on the other side of the wall was the mountainside.

As if she could read her mind (and sometimes, Iphigenia wondered if she really could), Euthalia spoke lowly.

"You'll have to trust me."

Iphigenia nodded. Euthalia had yet to lead her astray. She watched with bated breath as Euthalia wrenched the door open, its rusted joints straining under the force that she applied. A set of descending stone stairs greeted them, roughly hewn and unlit. An impenetrable gloom seemed to extend beyond them forever.

"Are we—"

"Yes."

The hair on the back of Iphigenia's neck stood up as her flesh broke out into goosebumps despite the balmy weather. More darkness. *Fantastic.*

As Euthalia pulled the door shut behind them and even the light of the moon was denied to them, Iphigenia broke into a cold sweat, the tell tale tremors already beginning. Then a hand slipped into hers, just as a torch was struck into blazing life.

"I'm here," Euthalia murmured, stroking her knuckles with a thumb.

The relief was instant. Iphigenia told herself it was from being able to see ten feet in front of her again, rather than any reassurance gained from the soft hand lacing their fingers together.

Trying to suppress the shake in her voice, she asked, "Where are you taking me?"

"Far beneath the city, to a place long neglected by your people," Euthalia answered matter-of-factly. Her sandals clapped against the stone as they walked, echoing hollowly throughout the narrow corridor.

Iphigenia wished she'd thought to strap some on; she could feel moisture seeping into her own soft slippers. "We're going to the last place that can offer you any sort of reprieve."

"How?"

"If I told you the answer, and what we're going to do, you may not have the strength to continue."

Iphigenia wrinkled her nose, and it was not from the stale stench permeating the still air. "Euthalia, I would do *anything* to not be a part of that caravan leaving tomorrow."

"And yet, in all these years, you've never told me why."

"That's not true! I must continue my studies—"

"Which being in another's household won't prevent you from doing. Arguably, you'd have more leeway as mistress of the house."

"I'll miss my mother."

"All daughters miss their mothers. Tell me the truth, Iphigenia. Why did you choose this path?"

Iphigenia couldn't suppress the feeling that the answer lay in their interlocked hands, but rather than confront that startling revelation, she formed her mouth into a tight line. "You ask too many questions for a slave."

Euthalia dropped her hand, doubling her stride so that Iphigenia was left alone in the rapidly encroaching darkness.

"Wait!" she shouted, although it came out as more of a strangled sob. "Don't leave me!"

Iphigenia broke into a frantic run, trying to keep up with Euthalia as she descended deeper down the narrow staircase. So panicked was she that she didn't realize she'd made a wrong turn until she was alone in a chamber of empty cells, lit only by a single torch.

"Help," Iphigenia squeaked, sinking to her knees. Where had Euthalia gone?

"I can help you," a man's voice rasped, and Iphigenia could not contain the shriek that fell from her lips.

"Don't fear me, little Atreid," the man whispered, and as Iphigenia's eyes adjusted to the light, she could just make out the figure of a thin man behind the bars of one of the cells. "We *are* kin, after all."

"I don't...I'm not supposed to—"

"Of course you're not supposed to be down here. Your father would never allow it, wretched rat that he is. Let me out, and I'll take you back to where you're supposed to be, little one."

"I don't know who you are."

"Because your father wouldn't allow you to. Come closer."

Iphigenia, despite her better sense, approached the man. Now that she could see him better, she could make out ruggedly handsome features. He looked like he could be a brother of her father, save for his unkemptness. His beard was wild, and his hair was even wilder, but his eyes were entirely clear, unclouded by the madness that she'd seen in the gazes of prisoners of war as they were marched through Mycenae's streets.

"A fine young woman. What brings you to my little corner of the world, cousin?"

"My father, he..." How should she phrase it? Her father was about to sell her off as he would livestock? Why should this man even care?

"He's wronged you too, hasn't he? Agamemnon knows no honor."

Just as Iphigenia was about to reply, a tug at the neck of her chiton dragged her roughly away.

"Get away from him!" Euthalia hissed.

"But he's going to help me—"

"*I'm* going to help you, not this lunatic."

"Don't forget about me, little Atreid!" the man called. "I'll be waiting!"

As the room of cells began to recede back into the darkness, Iphigenia couldn't help but lament that she'd never even gotten the man's name. She hadn't even known of an underground prison; just how long had he been trapped in that cell?

"We're here," Euthalia said, her voice chilly as she pushed past a beaded curtain that reeked of rot and mildew. Dozens of shiny red beads clattered to the stone floor as she disturbed them, finally breaking the bonds of the threadbare fibers that had once held their weight. Iphigenia followed, doing her best not to slip against them as her friend held the torch high.

They'd exited into a circular chamber. Massive stores of gold and gemstones littered the floor, rivaling even the wealth store in the royal treasury. Faded murals occupied every inch of space on the walls. In the dim light, Iphigenia thought she could just make out the figure of a man, triumphantly holding a head aloft while its owner bled out at his feet. What really caught her eye, however, was the massive pair of stone boxes in the center of the room.

"This," Euthalia said, passing the torch to Iphigenia as she strode towards the pair, "is the burial chamber of Perseus, first king of Mycenae. Tonight, I'm going to show you why we Egyptians do what we do with our dead."

"Why Perseus?" Iphigenia breathed, letting her fingers run lightly across the ornately carved lid. The coffin was huge — the size of it brought to mind the massive statues that lined the streets of Mycenae. This was the grave of the man who slew the gorgon Medusa, rescued Andromeda from a fearsome sea monster, and founded a city to rule when his own was denied to him. If he was that powerful in life, how strong would he be in death?

"Not Perseus. It is his mother, Danae, that we're here for." Euthalia stepped towards the smaller, more nondescript coffin. She laid a hand on it, looking at Iphigenia expectantly. "Well? Are you going to help me, or is this just another task better left to *slaves?*"

Sheepishly, Iphigenia joined her side. She wasn't sure why Euthalia was so angry — *she* wasn't the one who purchased her off that boat from Egypt, after all. She made a mental note to remind Euthalia of that fact after all of this was over.

"Push. We need to get this open."

"What? Why?"

"Do you want to get out of this marriage or not? Because I've been up for three days delivering a —"

"I get it!" Iphigenia didn't have the patience for any more arguing.

Together, they began to push. By the time the lid had moved an inch, sweat had Iphigenia's thin nightgown clinging to her back.

"I don't think we're strong enough."

"Then you're not strong enough to change your fate," Euthalia replied succinctly. She barely had a hair out of place as she looked at Iphigenia with intense coal-dark eyes. "Are you giving up?"

"I'm not—"

"Then get back to pushing."

Iphigenia groaned in frustration, but resumed pushing all the same. At last, after what seemed like hours, the lid hit a critical point and began to slide in earnest. There was a proper gap now, large enough to reveal the upper half of whatever remains may lay within.

"Well?"

Euthalia picked up the torch and raised it high, illuminating the stone interior.

The contents were unsurprising.

"Nothing," Iphigenia yelled. The urge to kick the coffin was overwhelming, but she knew that'd only result in her limping all the way up the stairs again. Shouting was the only viable method of releasing her frustration. "We came all the way down here and did all this work, just for dried up old bones?"

"Will you shut *up*?" Euthalia hissed, and her tone mollified Iphigenia immediately. "Do you think so lowly of what I've taught you? This is not an obstacle."

"I've yet to see any magic."

Euthalia gave her a sharp look; Iphigenia couldn't help but take a step back. "That's because *you* need to do it."

"Me?"

"This is your quest — if any magic is to happen, it must be performed by the one seeking it. Anything else is slavery, and that's antithetical to true magic."

Iphigenia couldn't help but respond to Euthalia's glowering gaze with one of her own. Yes, they were definitely going to have to have a long talk after all of this was over.

Think, Iphigenia brooded. *What did I do on the mountain?*

That was where the true problem lay — she'd done nothing particularly different from all the other times. It was all the same; enter a deep solitude, say the words just as Euthalia had taught, pray, burn the right herbs and call upon the right gods. That day on the mountain had been no different. She'd gone seeking something ancient, and it had only come to her when it had deigned to.

That's when the thought stuck her, chilling her to her very bones, and she was certain it would be considered sacrilege in every civilized religion. If she wanted whatever spirit she'd summoned to aid her, she would have to meet it on its own playing field, in a sort of reversal of what had happened that day by the gorge.

"I'm going in," Iphigenia said, standing abruptly. "Inside the coffin, I mean."

Euthalia, leaning against Peresus' coffin, didn't look up from her nails. "Don't get lost."

Iphigenia scoffed, and then she closed her eyes, steeling herself for what she was about to do. One, two, — as she breathed out *"three"*, she gingerly began to pick her way inside.

The stone was unforgivingly cold, and the dust was so unbearable that she couldn't help but descend into a fit of sneezes as she settled in to lay on her side. As soon as she recovered from the assault on her nose, she blearily opened her eyes.

Solid white met hers.

Iphigenia's back collided against unyielding stone in her scramble to get away. It was futile; what had once been a pile of brittle bones was now a grinning skull, sallow skin pulled tight. A pair of eyes without irises had locked onto hers. Clammy arms clamped tight around Iphigenia's torso as she fought to put distance between them. Then the coffin lid shut, plunging the two of them into total darkness.

"Let me go," Iphigenia whimpered, still struggling to get away.

"But you're amongst friends," a voice purred in the darkness, both familiar and terrifying. "Remember? And don't friends call upon each other? I called you, and now you've called me — now, shall you choose? The babe, or the blade?"

Her theory had been correct, then. Iphigenia didn't know if she should feel triumph or terror. She forced that thought out of her mind, focusing on getting this over with as soon as possible.

"The blade!" Iphigenia gasped, and it was as if the coffin was plunged into the forge of Hephaestus himself, the way the temperature suddenly shifted from cold to sweltering heat.

"I had hoped as much." The corpse's horrible finger was trailing itself down Iphigenia's cheek. "You'll seal it in blood."

"Blood?" Iphigenia whimpered. The word sent a pang straight to her heart. Blood had defined this whole quest, from the first moment red had bloomed between her thighs and whispers of courtship and dowries began to float across the palace. It was a pact of blood that had been her solemn vow to Euthalia to go through with her studies, and she'd been promised blood on her wedding night if she'd failed.

"All blades thirst for blood — their very existence is predicated on quenching that thirst. The sort of blade you seek to hold must be sated in full before it can truly be wielded."

"What?" This was all descending into hallucinatory territory very fast. Had she accidentally inhaled some fumes off the mushrooms she'd seen growing on the staircase?

"The world is on the cusp of change, Iphigenia," the corpse whispered, excitement dripping from its every rasped syllable. "It is caught in a state of flux, trapped betwixt that space where the old order falls to ruin while a new one claws itself from the ashes. The gods themselves prepare to lay down their arms, to relinquish their crowns. Only one as liminal as the age itself can become the catalyst to bring about the new age, and for that one to *be*, great sacrifice is in order. Hence, Iphigenia, the blood for your blade."

"I don't understand," Iphigenia replied. Fingers like talons were digging painfully into her side, and she was unsuccessful in her attempt to pry them away.

"You do, and more," Danae's corpse said, hot breath mingling with hers. It reeked of decay. "You shall be the catalyst." Then, lips as dry as tinder met hers.

Iphigenia thrashed, useless beating against the sides of the stone coffin that had become her prison. She'd never been kissed, but she was positive it was supposed to go nothing like this. It was like she was choking, no, *drowning* — something was being forced down her throat. It was painful, like thousands of shards of glass were slicing the insides of her lungs to ribbons. She was forced to take and take until she could breathe no longer and spots began to form at the edges of her vision. All the while, Danae's corpse held her in a bruising grip.

As soon as it had begun, it was over. The fingers digging into the soft flesh of her arms had disintegrated into moldering bones once again. Iphigenia was left with only a piercing noise that threatened to make her ears provide the blood that the corpse so desired. Had the horrors yet to cease? It was only when Euthalia's concerned face, the rest of her body obscured by the coffin lid, appeared above her that she realized that the noise was coming from her own mouth — she'd been screaming.

Euthalia's arms wrapped tight around Iphigenia's torso and hauled her through the narrow opening, head and shoulders first.

"You've done it," she heard Euthalia murmur as she clung close to her, sobbing all the while. "You don't have to worry anymore. The power you sought is within you now."

She'd done something, certainly, but as Iphigenia tried and failed to stop shaking, she couldn't help but wonder — how much more blood would have to be shed to pay for what she'd just endured?

VI

we will give, says the father

A gentle shaking of her shoulder aroused Iphigenia from her sleep.

"Mother?" she asked, rubbing sleep's residue from her half opened eyes. Instead of her mother's tall figure, Euthalia stood over her, a smirk painted across her features.

"The wagons have stopped."

At this, Iphigenia sat up from where she'd been reclining, groaning as she stretched. They'd been traveling for what felt like weeks, and the rockiness of the roads had done a number on her spine. The breakneck speed at which they'd been journeying didn't help either; Odysseus had told them to make haste, and so the horses pulling the vehicles of the caravan had been working from before dawn 'til late after dusk each day. She hadn't been sure of just what "wagon sickness" was when the nursemaids had warned her before they left, but she was well aware now. With every turn of the wheel, her queasiness multiplied. The knowledge of what was waiting for her at the end of the road was already enough to make her retch; combined with this new sickness, it made for a journey as bad as any punishment in Tartarus. Any break from that hell was sent straight from the isles of the blessed.

She raised an eyebrow as she took in her surroundings. She and Euthalia sat in the center of a great mass of wagons, horses, carts, and a handful of chariots. The low braying of mules broke the hum of cicada song that buzzed through the air. Mycenae had spared no expense when it came to travel preparations; it looked like half the palace staff had embarked on this journey with her. Iphigenia was positive that even her grandstanding, luxury-loving father had departed for Aulis with a smaller caravan than this one.

A great grassy field was to the left of the road they had stopped on the side of, while just beyond it the landscape transformed from fertile plain into rocky, wooded hillside. At its apex was a long ridge nestled against a low mountain range. To the right, the earth sloped downward toward a river, judging by the sounds of gushing water. From this area wafted the scent of smoke and sounds of song and dance, filling the early evening air with a sense of mirth that Iphigenia only wished she could feel.

Her mother and their shared retinue of attendants were nowhere to be found; instead, the open air wagon was empty save for her and Euthalia, who eased herself next to her on the cushion lined bench. Above them, the late afternoon sun began its descent towards the amber horizon.

"They're all down by the river," Euthalia said, twirling a long strand of her dark hair. "Your mother said you were sleeping far too peacefully to wake up." She snorted and pinched Iphigenia's cheek. "A little nymph, she called you. In my opinion, you look more like a slack jawed harpy drooling over her next kill."

"Don't touch me." Iphigenia knocked Euthalia's hand away from her and rubbed furiously at her mouth. There was nothing there.

"You're too easy to mess with. Now get up." Euthalia pressed her traveling shawl into Iphigenia's hands and pulled her upright.

"No! You lied to me. I'm not going anywhere with you, witch," she said, throwing the shawl to the ground.

"What did you think would happen?" Euthalia spat, her jovial attitude disappearing entirely. "That you'd sprout wings and fly away? That you could just make everyone forget?"

"I thought enough would happen that I wouldn't be halfway to the marriage bed!"

"It took many moons to build the pyramids."

"Well, I don't have *any* moons left. Tell me — what did you make me do in that tomb?"

An awkward silence hung between them. Euthalia sheepishly picked up the discarded shawl, thumbing at the pale fabric.

"Just come with me. You won't regret it." Euthalia pressed a small kiss to Iphigenia's cheek as she wrapped the shawl around her shoulders. "I promise."

"Is that all you have to say to me?" Iphigenia said, unable to hide the rising anger from her voice. All of it, the studying, the magic — it had all been for *nothing*. Euthalia couldn't even tell her why.

She turned on her heel and ran.

Iphigenia did her best to block out Euthalia's shouts as she bobbed and weaved through the throng of carts. She needed to get away, gather her thoughts, figure out why her best friend had played such a cruel trick on her. She passed the last cart and beyond, running through the open field in earnest. The grass was coarse against her skin, and moving so swiftly only exacerbated the irritation. She swatted away a fly buzzing around her head only to miss the mosquito drinking greedily from her ankle.

It took mere minutes for her to reach the beginning of the slope, and without any hesitation, Iphigenia began to climb.

As soon as she reached the top, she turned back to see if she'd been followed. "Shit," she swore. The grass was heavily depressed all along where she had run. Hopefully no one noticed she was gone — she couldn't count on Euthalia to cover for her this time. She sat, arms wrapped around her knees, and watched the sun begin to arch its way behind the caravan.

Amongst the jumbled mixture of wagons, chariots, and horses, Iphigenia could see dancers weaving in and out of the narrow passages towards the campfires by the creek. They twirled and spun to drums and horns that she had to strain to hear. They looked like minnows as they waved their long silver scarves in their dance. Soldiers with heavy spears watched as they passed flasks back and forth, and a few tapped their feet to the sounds of the lyre. Even at this distance, she could hear their boisterous laughter.

"They're all so happy," Iphigenia murmured, clutching at her shawl. With the heat of the sun disappearing, the dampness of night was settling on her bare arms like morning dew.

Something plopped next to her, and she scrambled back in panic, frowning when she realized it was only Euthalia. "Of course they're happy! They're only helping to orchestrate the most magnificent wedding of the age. Plus, it doesn't hurt that their wages are doubled for the journey."

"I want to be alone." Iphigenia cursed her lack of physical strength. It wouldn't have taken Orestes very long to catch up with her, let alone a strong young woman like Euthalia.

"And I would give anything to be home, looking at the Nile instead of this empty field, but we can't all have what we want, can we?"

"Just leave me alone, Euthalia!" Iphigenia shouted, clamoring to her feet. "Nothing you've done has helped! I wasted so much *time*, all for nothing!"

"I just wanted to meditate with you, to calm you. By the gods you don't have to be such a bitch about it." Euthalia scowled at her as she too rose. "It's not as if I have any say in my situation either. At least we're equal in that respect."

"You have power though."

It was the wrong thing to have said. Euthalia's gaze was as hard as she'd ever seen it. She took Iphigenia's hand in hers, but instead of one of the affectionate caresses they often shared, her grip was tight to the point of bruising. She did not relent, even when Iphigenia tried to pull away with a wince. "Never mistake magic for power in front of me again. Swear it."

"You're hurting me!"

"I said swear it!"

"I promise!"

Euthalia released her hand, pushing her away. "You'd do well to keep your promise, lest you end up in something much worse than a political marriage. What I wouldn't give to see my countrymen, my brothers—"

Iphigenia's face burned for a different reason now. "I'm sorry, Thal," she began, voice meek, but Euthalia had already turned away.

"Let's just get back. It'll be faster if we go up and over; you zigzagged us so far that it'll be a miracle if we make it back before dark."

Iphigenia reached for Euthalia's shoulder in an attempt to further apologize, but Euthalia moved just out of reach. Confidence lost, she opted instead to walk in strained silence. She couldn't help the tears that began to slide down her cheeks. Regret and guilt seemed to coat every interaction she'd had with Euthalia these past few days, and yet it seemed she couldn't stop herself from spouting cruelties.

By the time they were at the apex of the hill, night had begun in earnest, the patches of sky visible through the trees a deep violet. Together, they crossed the crest.

"Is this what I think it is?" Euthalia murmured, sinking to one knee.

Before the two of them stood the ruins of what had once been a forest altar. It was a tiny thing, hardly up to Iphigenia's knees. Flowers, still vibrant with color, had been laid on top of the crumbling stone.

"This is what I wanted to show you...I could smell the magic from miles away. We might as well see what you can do. Sit, and cross your legs like this, lotus position."

Iphigenia followed Euthalia's instruction, seating herself at the altar. "Euthalia, please," she began, unable to hide the pleading in her voice. "How do you know...what happened in the coffin...how do you know it worked?"

"The same way you can tell when a woman is about to give birth," Euthalia said from her seat across the altar. "There isn't much difference between calling to those souls beyond the veil and bringing new ones into the world."

Iphigenia frowned. That really didn't answer her question; of course something had come and spoken to her, but whether or not that had any effect on her impending marriage had yet to be seen. She didn't argue, though. Despite her frustration, she was sick of fighting.

Euthalia closed her eyes and drew in a deep breath. "Focus."

"On what?"

"On whatever you desire."

Desire. What a complicated notion. Iphigenia desired a lot of things. She desired to be at home, wrapped up in her familiar blankets. She desired a hot bath to soothe the itching bites on her ankles. Frightening as it was, what she desired the most was the hand of the girl in front of her interlocked with hers. Somehow, even that felt like it wasn't enough.

Think. She inhaled slowly, letting her chest fill completely before expelling the air within. Still, nothing came to her.

Her frustration must have been palpable. Euthalia began speaking softly, her hand finding Iphigenia's across the altar. "I wasn't lying earlier; magic isn't power. Magic is a tool; a wonderful one, but a tool the same way a sword is just mindless metal until it's in the hands of one strong enough to wield it. Anyone can learn magic; it takes someone with real, true conviction, someone willing to risk everything, to utilize it to its fullest potential. The rest of us can only get a glimpse of the truth."

Iphigenia nodded, listening intently despite the little flip her stomach did when Euthalia's fingers interlocked with hers.

"Imagine you're a frog, sitting on the lotus leaf," Euthalia continued. "You have the energy coiled inside you, the magic; all you have to do is leap."

Iphigenia clenched her friend's hand tight, willing the same shivering sensation she'd felt inside the coffin to come forth again. Deep down in her navel, she felt a pull. Was this it?

"There," she gasped, climbing to her feet. She was pointing just beyond the trees, to where the ground began to slope downward. She staggered over, letting the feeling draw her in as she broke through the trees.

Before her stood something far more fearsome than any ghostly apparition could ever hope to be.

Standing directly in the path of the sun's final dying rays in his full regalia was her father. Agamemnon stood tall, his black beard reaching halfway down his armored chest and his lion's mane of hair racing down his back in tangled glory. His stillness was unsettling; Iphigenia had always known her father to be a man in constant motion, whether that was swinging his spear in the palace training grounds or hurling vases older than the palace at his wife. If not for his face being flushed with barely restrained ire, Iphigenia would've believed he was a perfect copy of his marble statue at Mycenae rather than flesh and blood.

At his side, a thin, white-haired man cowered, hands gripping the reigns of an alabaster stallion. She didn't know the man, but she'd know that steed anywhere: it was her father's finest horse, Leukos, said to be a descendant of those steeds raided from Troy long ago by Heracles. Iphigenia had spent many a long afternoon begging to just be allowed to brush its soft mane. She'd been refused every time; the horse had been far too valuable, the stable slaves had explained. She was positive that the horse's monetary value had nothing to do with it, and her suspicions had been confirmed when Orestes had been allowed to feed the horse, his chubby toddler fingers poking dangerously near to the creature's eyes every time.

Iphigenia slowly pulled Euthalia down flat to the ground. There was no indication that her father or the old man had heard them approach, but she still couldn't help the thunderous pounding of her heart. Why was *he* here? Aulis was still a full day's ride away. And if her father was here, why hadn't he met up with the bridal party not even a half hour's trek down the mountain? He had to be aware of their presence— the smoke from their campfires alone had to be visible for miles across this lonely valley.

The elderly man stepped close to her father, placing a wizened hand on his arm. Iphigenia thought he looked rather like a rat with the way his hands curled like paws. His voice was tense as he began to speak.

"My King, the day grows short. We should be departing—"

"She will come," Agamemnon snapped, throwing the priest's hand off his gauntleted wrist. His voice was low, anger barely restrained. Iphigenia knew his tone all too well. "Not even a goddess can resist the call of the King of Men, Calchas. She will come, and make a liar out of you yet."

Iphigenia felt Euthalia draw closer to her side. She couldn't help but grip her companion's arm and feel relieved when Euthalia didn't protest, despite the disagreement between them. Had her father finally gone mad? Invoking the gods was always a practice in futility; she knew that well by now. Her very presence on this hillside was proof enough.

For a few precious moments, all was quiet as the sun finally slipped beneath the horizon and the stars emerged in all their twinkling glory. At one point, Calchas and Agamemnon both lit torches, and it was by that firelight that Iphigenia saw Leukos sink his muzzle and front legs to the ground in an equine bow. Calchas, skin leathery with age, looked at the horse as if it'd suddenly sprouted a second head.

An arrow whizzed past his face, and he sank to his knees immediately, arms raised above his body in supplication. Agamemnon, to Iphigenia's surprise, did not draw the heavy sword at his side, but instead acted as if he'd noticed nothing, standing stock still with his arms crossed and legs spread.

"Goddess," he called, voice as crisp as a winter's breeze, "Reveal yourself."

The forest stood still. Iphigenia could hear nothing but her own breathing. Then the air changed — damp heat transmuted into a chill she had once thought exclusive to the darkest days of winter. The sensation was the same as that day at the gorge, when her ghostly doppelgänger had first appeared to her.

And then, from the trees opposite, the figure of a woman emerged. Her features were enshrined in a swath of light so silver and bright that Iphigenia felt it must be the very essence of the moon and stars themselves. She knew she must be drawing blood as she dug her nails further into Euthalia's arm, and she stifled a swear as she watched the woman—the *goddess*—strut towards her father.

Agamemnon stroked his beard slowly, his face set firmly in a scowl. Finally, movement. The light began to dim to a soft glow, fully allowing the features of the woman within to emerge.

She was short, much shorter than Iphigenia would have expected of a goddess. A round face was framed by tendrils of dark curly hair that had escaped the bounds of a haphazardly tied ribbon. Dark freckles from the sun were splashed across her nose. Dressed in a short belted chiton, the well defined muscles of her arms and legs rippled with practiced strength. Across her back, she carried a broad silver bow, and circling at her side were two enormous hounds, each easily twice her weight. Atop her head, a circlet gleamed, catching the light of the half moon above.

"Artemis," Iphigenia whispered, hardly able to breathe. The woman could be no other than the goddess of the moon; she carried all the symbols. She'd heard stories about her from spooked hunters, even sacrificed to her once or twice at city festivals, but here in the flesh? She'd tangled with magic, even summoned a spirit, but nothing had ever threatened to make Iphigenia weep in awe like the goddess' presence before her.

"Goddess," Agamemnon greeted, briefly dipping his chin. He never took his eyes away from the goddess. "I'm sure you must know why I'm here."

The goddess' face, which to Iphigenia looked awfully young, slipped from impassivity to tight-lipped annoyance. "At the scene of your crime? Yes, Agamemnon, I know exactly why you've deigned to further aggravate me, and my answer remains the same: no."

Agamemnon stepped forward; a reverberating growl rumbled forth from the dogs at the goddess' side, and he came no closer.

"Calchas has informed me of your...conditions, but your price is too high."

Artemis threw her head back and laughed, and the sound of it was simultaneously terrible and the most wonderful thing she'd ever heard. It sent a thrill racing through Iphigenia; she'd never seen a woman defy her father so openly, so gleefully. Clytemnestra had been his match, of course, but Agamemnon had his armies to stand by him. Here, against a goddess, he may as well be a beggar slave.

"You, willing to wage genocide for mere wealth, and *my* price is too high? You make me laugh, 'King of Men.'"

Agamemnon bristled. "I fight for the honor of my brother—"

"You cannot lie to a goddess, little man," she interrupted, leaping onto the altar with a preternatural swiftness. She stood above Agamemnon now, and Iphigenia watched with wide eyes as she leered at him. "You wronged me. You denied me what is owed to me, and therefore I must take it from you by force."

Agamemnon hurled his torch to the ground, splintering its fragile wood and causing the flame to sputter out and die. Iphigenia had to squint to see as the darkness grew. Calchas, still holding his own torch, dared not look up as his thin frame wracked itself with tremors. If it weren't for the soft glow of the goddess herself, the scene would be nigh impossible to observe.

"It is my right alone to decide the fate of my household, but you orchestrated this sickening stillness!" He waved his hand through the air.

"That I did," Artemis replied, her gaze cool. "And what about it?"

"You seek to punish me for doing what is in my natural right with an abomination double fold! You pause nature for petty quarrel and seek to rectify it with atrocity."

"Incorrect. I seek proper compensation for your trespasses against me, both past and present, and for the atrocities you've yet to commit."

Artemis leaned forward, and though she did not step off the pedestal, her motion had Agamemnon fumbling backwards. "You will not deprive me of my prize, Agamemnon," she said, her voice haughty with loathing. "An eye for an eye, and my reward for your conquest. My terms alone, or you do not sail. Now take your sorry excuse for a substitute," she jerked her head towards the horse, "and be gone from this place and never return."

Agamemnon raised a fist as if he intended to argue further, but another smoldering gaze from Artemis had him turn sharply on his heel.

"Fine," he said, straightening his breastplate. "Have it your way, goddess. You grease your palms with innocent blood. Calchas, rise. We will be taking our leave." He swung a long leg over the horse as the priest struggled to his feet, avoiding the intense gaze of the goddess and her hounds.

Silence blanketed itself back over the night, save for the trot of the horse as the men disappeared back into the forest from which they'd come. Iphigenia, despite the initial shock of seeing her father here, now had eyes only for one. Artemis stood watching the departure of the men until they'd moved completely out of sight. Then, she turned.

Despite distance and shadow, dark eyes met pale gray through the trees. Iphigenia's mouth was dry; the thundering of her heart was worse than Zeus' fiercest storm. Euthalia had long slipped from her grasp. She hardly registered the sound of her friend crashing through the undergrowth as she held the goddess' gaze.

It was a vivid reminder of the gorge: a ripple of power, coupled with the sensation that she was gazing on something truly eternal. Those eyes, shining bright with what could only be the divine, locked with hers and Iphigenia feared the worst — hounds set upon her, an arrow piercing her heart — but still, she didn't dare break the moment. Something deep inside her compelled her not to, no matter how much she longed to tear through the trees at Euthalia's heels.

Then, the unthinkable. The corners of the goddess' mouth perked up in a radiant smile.

"Princess!" A man's voice broke the reverie.

Iphigenia only turned her head for a moment, but that was all it took; Artemis had disappeared with her hounds, melding back into the night just as easily as she had emerged from it. It was as if she'd never stood upon the altar at all, a hazy dream brought on by the oppressive heat that had sunk back into the night air.

She slunk to the forest floor, head in her hands. Life swelled back into what was formerly the vacuum of the night. Birds sang, insects buzzed, and above all rang the din of a large search party to drag her back to reality. But to Iphigenia, the only reality that mattered was the truth she'd seen behind those shining silver eyes that had looked up at her with a fondness unlike any she'd ever seen before.

VII

golden pulse grew along the shores

Sweat rolled down Iphigenia's face in rivulets. The weather here was sweltering, far hotter than it had been in Mycenae, and despite the scent of salt on the air, the approaching sea provided no relief. The foliage had grown sparse as the caravan journeyed further east, and what few trees dotted the sandy brown landscape were more akin to overgrown shrubs than the olive groves Iphigenia had grown up amongst. The only shade to be had was beneath her thin veil, and even that sheer fabric was near unbearable.

Next to her on the bench, baby Orestes dozed, his sable curls plastered to his forehead. A tiny thumb was planted firmly in his mouth. It'd be an issue if her father saw that; he'd said time and time again that Orestes was far too old to still be suckling like an infant, in his mind a worse crime even than the child still not speaking.

As she gazed down at her brother, alone with her thoughts, Iphigenia let her memories wander back to what she'd seen on the ridge. At the time, it had terrified her, but now, the whole situation left her feeling exhilarated. A real living, breathing goddess had noticed her, and had *smiled*. That had to have been a good omen, no matter what business Artemis had with Agamemnon. Hopefully it was something particularly nasty.

She'd briefly considered confiding in her mother, informing her that her father had been consorting with and was even in debt to a goddess, but Clytemnestra was frazzled enough. Iphigenia felt bad; her mother had looked genuinely beside herself with fear when the guards had returned her, shell-shocked, from the mountain that night. It just wasn't in her heart to frighten her mother further — the explanation had been that she and Euthalia had gone off to do some immature exploring, nothing more. Euthalia had been punished immediately, forced to walk with the rest of the common slaves at the back of the caravan instead of riding in the wagon as part of the bridal party, while Iphigenia herself had been very sternly instructed not to leave her mother's sight for the rest of the journey. She was lucky that was the extent of it. She wasn't going to push the envelope further to get Euthalia out of trouble, even if it had been her idea in the first place to run off. So, to the back of the caravan she'd been sent, as a way to get her "influence" away from Iphigenia, as Clytemnestra had put it.

Orestes began to fuss in his sleep.

"You're lucky," Iphigenia whispered, pushing his bangs back. She traced the scar that ran up from his eyebrow into his hairline. The poor thing had run into the loom chasing toddling after Electra a few weeks prior. "I ought to be the one whining here. Boys have nothing to cry over."

A shout startled the child awake with a gasp. "Ay! Camp, just ahead!"

Iphigenia gathered her wailing brother into her arms and followed the herald's outstretched arm with her gaze. They had just crested a ridge; in the distance, mountains rose against the perfect blue sky. Before them, a thin channel of sea, so narrow that it may as well have been a river, glittered bright blue in the blazing sun. The strip of sea was clogged with hulking wooden things, bobbing in the waves. They competed fiercely for space, and many times it looked as if one of the vessels would capsize another, sending it and its garishly colored sails straight to the bottom of Poseidon's realm. Ships, hundreds of them, all decked out for a singular purpose: war. Iphigenia had never seen more than a fishing boat on the rare occasion she'd been allowed to journey to the shore. Even Orestes was curious, pausing in his sniffles to lift his little chin up at the boats.

As they moved closer, and the land before the sea emerged into view, a black mass seemed to shimmer in the noonday sun. It stretched for what looked like miles, bordering the sea in a long row. It was only when she squinted that Iphigenia realized the mass was full of thousands of pinpricks of movement, darting back and forth across the sand: men. When they weren't running, they marched in tight formations that had to number in the dozens, if not hundreds. The clamor of them was deafening. Orestes had clasped his hands over his ears and Iphigenia was sorely tempted to do the same. Tents and lean-tos dotted the landscape, and the occasional burnished bronze of a blade flashed in the sun as whole armies sparred.

Iphigenia covered her eyes. This was the camp of the Achaeans, and it was far larger than anything she'd ever seen before, surpassing even Mycenae's farthest reaching walls. Her nails dug into her palm. There would be no running from this.

"I know you're scared," and her mother was at her side, pressing a kiss to her scalp. "Don't be. It is a beautiful time in a girl's life."

Beautiful, Iphigenia thought. *Only as beautiful as a dove in a cage of gold.*

She spent the rest of the ride in silence, fidgeting as fiercely as her baby brother, especially when her mother made her put on her veil and then proceeded to fuss over its placement for the entire descent to the shore. The stifling fabric only increased her urge to rise, roll out of the wagon, and run back the way they'd come.

At last, the caravan rolled up to the walls of the camp, and Iphigenia understood why she'd seen no trees for the last several leagues. Between them and the sea stood a towering palisade built from whole trees rammed into the earth, so new and so hastily built that branches still hung with green leaves waving. She looked up in awe. What kind of men lay beyond the barrier to have been able to construct it?

A gaggle of boys greeted them at the gate, all clumsy limbed and oily faced. They were hardly older than Iphigenia, and they gawked at the processional before a few broke off into a sprint, yelling in such heavy accents that she almost thought they were speaking an entirely different language. Ugly, gangly, but the way they laughed and shoved at each other as they ran freely made a whole different sort of misery well up inside her. She averted her eyes, scowling down at Orestes.

As the wagon slowed to a stop, the ache in Iphigenia's legs returned in full force. Despite her fears, she was dying to stretch her legs after the long ride and made to climb down. But as she moved to stand, her mother's hand held her back. When she turned with a questioning glance, her mother only raised a finger in response.

Seconds passed. Then, a group of women flowed towards them through the wide gate, singing loudly with garlands of white and yellow flowers bunched up in their arms.

"There are women here?" Iphigenia asked out of the corner of her mouth as she raised her arm in greeting. Clytemnestra briefly glanced down at her, a rueful smile on her face.

"Where your father goes, there are always women."

Some of the women paused in their song to help Clytemnestra down from the wagon. She held her arms out, and Iphigenia gladly passed her wriggling brother to her mother. He was on the verge of tears again, the women having startled him, and Iphigenia could only take so much more. The women turned to Iphigenia then, smiling broadly at her. She couldn't help but blush when an especially pretty brunette, the one with the eyes like spring's first green shoots, took hold of her by the wrist and waist when she stumbled on her way down.

While her mother gave the women instructions for the wagon and their luggage, Iphigenia bent her head as the girl who had helped her down offered a garland of yellow and white. The girl crowned her with a wink before twirling away back into the throng of women she'd arrived with. To Iphigenia, it felt almost flirtatious. She'd have to find her later, get her name.

She caught herself. Get her name for what? Gods in Olympus, she was going to be married. What was *wrong* with her?

The camp bustled with activity. Mycenae's highest feast days couldn't even compare to the fast paced throng surrounding her. Despite the oppressive humidity, men labored in the dust as if their lives depended on it, bare backs gleaming with sweat. It was on these men that Iphigenia narrowed her focus. They were a rough contrast from the women who'd greeted her and her mother; they kicked at the dogs running between their ankles, spit on cowering slaves, and, judging by the stink of alcohol in the air, guzzled wine by the barrel. These were not the noble heroes of myth, but an army of slovenly drunks. Her focus narrowed on the two closest to them as they, beards matted with filth, hurled insults back and forth at one another.

"Your mother's a whore and a shit one at that," a broad shouldered man slurred as he roughly snatched a wineskin from an equally large compatriot. "My dick's never been so dry."

His companion, who'd been sharpening his sword on a whetstone, angled his head towards Iphigenia and her entourage. "Why don't you try her out for size? Might get more bang for your buck with that little doe."

The man took a deep draught from the wineskin before peering closely at Iphigenia, who'd shrunk back behind her mother's skirts. Clytemnestra was silent, but Iphigenia could see the way her mother's fist curled just a bit too tightly to be coincidental.

"Nah, I like mine a bit more used up, keeps 'em looser. The young ones cry too much. Hey!" and then the man was stumbling towards a woman dressed in garb just as gray as her hair. She looked up from her washing in alarm as she was harshly jerked up. "Why don't you and I get out of the sun?"

Iphigenia forced herself to look away as the old woman was dragged through the broad thoroughfare, no one even blinking an eye. Was Achilles going to be like that? She began to seriously contemplate wrenching one of the ornate pins from her hair and carving open her wrists.

The men gone, Clytemnestra clutched her hand. "Don't worry," she murmured, so low that only Iphigenia could hear her. "You have special protection as Agamemnon's daughter. None would dare to harm you, lest they have to go through him, or worse yet, me." Her mother passed Orestes, sleeping soundly again, to one of the women.

There was a sudden blaring of horns, and Iphigenia watched as Clytemnestra stiffened and rose to her full height, face set with cold impassivity. She had transformed from the warm mother of the bride into the stoic Queen of Mycenae.

"Your father approaches," she said. "Look sharp." There were no traces of congeniality in her tone now.

From the same gate the women had emerged came the throng of boys from before, this time accompanied by older men, all dressed in brightly dyed tunics and expensive bronze armor. Iphigenia recognized many of them; they'd often visited Mycenae before the great departure for Aulis. Half of them were her distant cousins, but more importantly, they included all of her father's staunchest battle allies.

Out of the center of this group emerged her father. Agamemnon looked no different than he had in the grove. His beard was long and extensively manicured, the perfect compliment to his hair, acorn dark and tangled with beaded braids. A sword swung at his waist, and his expression gave off an air of grim sternness, along with something Iphigenia couldn't quite place. Was it apprehension? She wondered if her father was just as nervous as she was.

"You're early," he said, deep voice terse.

Clytemnestra dropped to one knee, and Iphigenia clumsily followed. "Hail, Agamemnon," she said, not breaking eye contact for a second. "We heard your order. Odysseus said to be swift, as the ships were ready to launch at a moment's notice."

For a moment, all was silent as mother and father, husband and wife, stared each other down. Iphigenia felt discomfort twist at her gut. The animosity was thick, and it was already too much, just like home. "No matter. We will make adjustments. The ceremony will take place tomorrow at dawn."

He looked at Orestes, bundled in his mother's arms.

"Does the boy still not speak?"

"He does not, my lord."

A grimace darkened Agamemnon's features. He looked as if he were going to lash out, but then his shoulders deflated. "No matter. Even if his mouth remains dumb, his sword will speak for him. Where is Electra?"

"At home, with the elders."

Iphigenia remembered the morning they departed and how Electra had wailed, demanding to be allowed to accompany them. With a certain amount of smug glee, she'd watched Clytemnestra try and fail to explain that at least one member of the royal family needed to remain behind to keep any would be coup attempts at bay. In the end, they'd left Electra weeping by the gates.

"Good," her father's gravelly tones wrenched her out of the memory. "She'll make a fine proxy in the meantime."

Then Agamemnon turned to her.

He was not the proud father, happy to give his daughter away. Quite the contrary, in fact; Agamemnon was all grimaces as Iphigenia cautiously rose and stepped into his outstretched arms. The embrace was stiff, and she wondered just how dearly a price he'd had to pay the goddess for him to be this morose. How many prize heifers? A dozen tripods? She couldn't imagine what he had that would be worth more than his steed.

"Hail, father," she whispered, the fibers of his beard irritating the delicate skin of her forehead. "I'm happy to see you well, after so long." If her parents had taught her anything, it was how to lie.

Agamemnon gave her a rough pat to the head. "If you are happy, then I am as well," he said gruffly. "A joyful bride is the best omen a father could hope for."

Despite his words, Agamemnon looked far from happy. Red veins formed little tributaries across the whites of his eyes, and no amount of musky perfume could banish the stink of wine on his breath. Iphigenia thought of his exit from the grove, and just how fast he and Calchas would have had to push their horses to beat them to Aulis. The men had to have been run ragged.

"For one so happy," she cautiously began, "you look weary. Perhaps we could've taken more time in getting here, to give you time to prepare. It isn't as if the ships could launch today; there's no breeze."

Agamemnon pushed her an arm's length away, looking her up and down with both hands on her shoulders. It had been a risky statement, baiting him like that, but Iphigenia had to know. He grimaced, and for a moment Iphigenia feared he would strike her; it wouldn't be out of his character. Instead, he surprised Iphigenia by doing something he had yet to ever do: he stroked her cheek.

"One has much responsibility when one is both king and general, as well as father of the bride. Weariness is my duty."

That wasn't the answer Iphigenia wanted. Agamemnon had looked positively distressed at their arrival — what did it have to do with Artemis?

Before either could say anything more, there was another great cacophony as a figure clad in armor from plumed helm to gleaming bronze greaves strode into the dusty space.

The figure was tall, towering over his compatriots in armor that aided in filling out his figure. He had walked in front of their group with a javelin firm in his grasp, and Iphigenia didn't miss that its sharp point was already coated in dried blood. His helm hid all of his face, save for his eyes, two unreadable pinpricks. This, coupled with the gore on his weapon, made his fearsome appearance rival some of the darkest tapestries in the *megaron*.

"Agamemnon?" the figure asked, voice muffled behind the helm as he waved his spear arm at the wedding caravan. His accent was thick, and decidedly northern. "What is all of this?" Iphigenia shuddered. It was said that men from the north had a particular penchant for brutality in all that they did.

Agamemnon's lips stretched to reveal his teeth, as straight and blocky as the meticulously carved blocks that composed Mycenae's walls. The gruesome imitation of a smile stayed plastered on his face as he strode over to the warrior, even as the kings and generals he'd arrived with murmured among themselves.

"Ah, Achilles, my boy," he clapped the figure on the back, ignoring his flinch as he did so. "I was just speaking to my wife, Queen Clytemnestra, and my daughter, Iphigenia, as lovely as the blooming crocus."

So this was Achilles, the man who was to be her husband. Her anxiety had returned tenfold. She took a step back in trepidation as he snapped his gaze onto her.

Clytemnestra either felt no such apprehension, or was just incredibly adept at hiding it, because she was already taking Achilles' free hand into both of hers. Iphigenia had not even seen her mother approach him.

"Hail, son of the sea," she said, laying a kiss upon his knuckle. Achilles jerked his hand away as if he'd been burned, and the maids collectively gasped.

"Agamemnon! Control your woman!" His voice, still muffled, oozed not with ire despite the bite of his words, but distress. Before Agamemnon could speak, Clytemnestra was already laughing.

"Was that too forward? I understand nerves, by the gods I know my husband had them on our wedding day—" at this, she threw a dark glance to Agamemnon before returning her attention to Achilles, "—but if I am to become your mother-in-law, we should become well acquainted with one another, yes? We're family now."

Iphigenia stepped forward, kneeling before Achilles just as she'd been instructed. She looked up at him, attempting to be demure, but she was sure her expression was more akin to the one she'd make if she'd bitten into a bad piece of fish. Achilles' mouth popped open. For a moment, it was as if time itself had paused as he glared at her in alarmed silence.

Iphigenia thought of the frog coiled inside her. She leapt.

"This unhappy marriage embarrasses me. I pray that you die in Troy so that it shall never go beyond this beach."

Achilles' mouth popped open. For a moment, it was as if time itself had paused as he glared at her in alarmed silence. Then, he roared.

"Agamemnon!" he thundered, and suddenly he was hurtling towards her father. He lunged: there was a flash of bronze, the clang of metal on metal, and then all Iphigenia knew was shrieking women and swirling skirts as she was lifted bodily and spirited away by the handmaidens.

* * *

The women's tent was a flurry of activity, and Iphigenia wished that it would all come to a standstill, even if for just a moment. The high fabric walls had been piled up to the thin wooden rafters with trunks of treasure, as if the entire contents of the caravan had been dumped here, even though this was far from their permanent home in Phthia. Iphigenia couldn't help but swear each time she narrowly avoided tripping over the various crates and vases that littered the earthen floor as she sought somewhere quiet in the chaos. Women dashed through the chambers of the tent, carrying piles of linens, clothes, and more flowers than Iphigenia had ever seen. How they'd acquired them on this barren shore, she'd never know.

The feast celebrating her arrival was still raging outside; she should have known under no circumstances would she be able to attend. The roar of hundreds of men was palpable, even this far from the feasting grounds. This was the celebration of a marriage in a war camp; the purpose for the whole ceremony was to boost the spirits of Agamemnon's soldiers, not the bride. This exclusion didn't even take into account the hundreds of heavily intoxicated soldiers attending; her, her mother, and their entire retinue would remain in the royal women's tent for safe keeping. No one would challenge Agamemnon by approaching the tent of his family, but if any woman was caught carelessly wandering the camp, well...it wouldn't be the first case of drunken mistaken identity.

Iphigenia didn't mind. In fact, she vastly preferred taking her meals as far away from the spotlight as possible. She wasn't sure if she would be able to handle the thousands of eyes upon her at the wedding itself, let alone at any extraneous events. It was difficult enough playing the role of smiling bride-to-be whenever any of her father's guards checked in on her. So, she found a spot in a back corner of the tent to chew her roasted lamb quietly while the women around her arranged garlands and fussed over clothing. The meat, despite its delicious aroma, was like a block of salt in her mouth.

The sound of hundreds of animals rang cacophonously through the camp. Iphigenia had looked out of one of the many flaps to see a large flock of sheep being led through the dirt paths; the half-picked meat on her plate was evidence enough of where they had been going. Still, that didn't explain the cages full of fluttering doves that were being carried by the dozens past the tent. She had asked one of the nearby slave women what their purpose was, and was surprised to hear that the birds were going to be offered up as sacrifice.

"I thought one only needed to sacrifice a single heifer for a wedding?" she'd asked with incredulity, only to receive a shrug from the woman in response.

"The men here, they do strange things often." The woman had walked away, leaving Iphigenia to watch the white birds be led away in silence.

Something is going on, she thought from her perch on a crate. Doves were an expensive sacrifice, and for there to be so many? That didn't even take into account the appearance of Artemis, or, more recently, Achilles' violent reaction to the news of his impending marriage. Agamemnon had never been known for restraint, but her father was pushing envelopes he had no business going near.

She pushed her plate aside, hopping down. She needed Euthalia.

It was difficult pushing her way through all the attendants without being roped into having a sea-silk scarf pressed to her cheek to check if the color set off her eyes (it most decidedly did not), or to be asked if the temperature in the tent was to her liking (it was sweltering), or if she'd met Achilles yet (she never wanted to see him again). Still, she endured, and at last she made her exit.

The air outside the tent was much cooler, despite still bearing a heavy humidity. The stars above had just begun to emerge into the indigo sky; their brightness, coupled with a nearly full moon, gave her enough light to survey her surroundings. A couple of dejected looking guards sat outside the tent. The boisterous sound of drunken men laughing rang out in the distance. One rose at the sight of her.

"Princess, we're under express orders to keep you here tonight," the man said, giving her a slight bow. "We can't allow you to leave."

"I don't want to leave," Iphigenia lied. "I'd just like to go for a walk around the women's area, get some fresh air."

The guard looked as if he were about to object, but his companion laughed, standing. "It's fine, Titarus. Gods know we could stretch our own legs. Let the lass go."

"Her mother says she's a flight risk."

Ah, betrayed by her own mother. She knew the woman meant well, but was she to be under another's thumb for the entirety of her existence?

"She won't leave these grounds if she knows what's good for her," the guard said with a wink. "I'm sure if she comes up, ah, less than whole, that lion Agamemnon wouldn't hesitate to have her head, eh? He's got *two* daughters, after all."

Iphigenia nodded and smiled, despite the bile that had risen in her throat.

"Fine," the first guard, Titarus, said. "Keep it quick. I don't want to lose my noggin."

That was all it took for Iphigenia to turn on her heel, making long strides towards the royal slave quarters. Euthalia would be here no doubt, sleeping off the fatigue of her march. Why else would she not have met up with Iphigenia by now?

That was why she was so surprised when, as she rounded the corner to where she had seen slaves lining up to receive their rations for the evening, she saw Euthalia not keeled over from exhaustion, but standing in the arms of a lean man. She squinted through the darkness; that was her friend, no doubt, caught in the caress of a lightly armored soldier. Iphigenia felt a tight lump grow in her throat. She cleared it loudly, and the two whirled around in shock.

The man was young, red haired, and horrifically familiar. He gave Iphigenia a leering grin before stepping away and around the corner. There was a series of excited whoops; he must be kissing and telling to some of his fellow guards.

"What are you doing?" Iphigenia hissed, stalking over to her friend. Euthalia frowned at her as she dabbed at her mouth with a cloth.

"Trying to help you?"

"Doing that with *Lysander* isn't helping!" Iphigenia struggled to keep her voice low. The thought of him with Euthalia, kind, smart Euthalia...she wanted to throttle the boy currently laughing it up with his friends just around the corner.

"I'd argue the contrary. Lysander is a part of your father's inner retinue now. He's only here instead of at the feast because Agamemnon trusts him so. I was getting information from him."

"Oh." Shame rippled through Iphigenia. Here was Euthalia trying to help her again, and again she'd stuck her foot in her mouth. Why the Egyptian girl continued to support her was anyone's guess.

"I think something beyond just a wedding is happening here," Euthalia continued. "You saw the animals, right?"

Iphigenia nodded. "I've never seen so many doves."

"That's not normal. In my training, we were told to only lead that many animals to slaughter if the pharaoh committed some heinous wrong against a god. From what we saw on the mountain, that seems to be the case here."

Ah. So it hadn't been a hallucination after all. Euthalia remembered. "So what happens now?"

"I don't know. They've been slitting throats all afternoon, and even now, priests are still at it, but—" Euthalia gestured towards the black sea, its surface as still as glass. "She still won't return the wind."

Dread gripped Iphigenia's heart. "It was never going to be enough," she whispered. "I don't know what he has planned, but you've got to help me."

"What do you think I was just doing?" Euthalia asked, grimacing.

"Not like that," Iphigenia quickly said. "With magic."

"You're not strong enough. Besides, magic won't appease an angry goddess."

"Then what else will?" Iphigenia couldn't hide the fear rising in her voice. She didn't understand anything going on, and it was threatening to make her lose her mind.

"Lysander says the wedding will do it, and if all else fails, they row. What I do know is that it's your father's burden to bear, not yours."

"I don't understand — why would a wedding appease her? Fathers have their daughters married off every day, that's nothing."

"That's what I told Lysander, but he said that even the priests agreed it would be enough. Perhaps it's because you're so unwilling?"

Iphigenia felt a twitch behind her eye at the mention of the soldier's name again. "I don't want you seeing him anymore. Maybe Achilles could do something, I heard his mother is a goddess—"

"You're lucky Achilles didn't black your eye for what you said to him today. I've already heard all about it."

Iphigenia didn't want to admit it, but Euthalia was right. Cloying fear crept up the back of her neck.

"What if I ran away? I could go to Delphi, ask the oracle there for advice? I have cousins there."

"Iphigenia, you and I both know you're not that naive. Lysander said—"

"Shut up about Lysander!" Iphigenia snapped. "I don't care what he knows. Don't talk to him again."

Euthalia's eyes narrowed. "Is that an order, Iphigenia?"

"Yes." The moment the word had left her lips, Iphigenia wanted to snatch it back and swallow it up. Her friend's face smoothed into blank indifference.

"I don't even know why I bother," Euthalia said, and Iphigenia was horrified to see her friend turning away. "You're just like the rest. I'm just a slave to you, as much a thing as a pretty comb. You're a hypocrite."

"That's not true!" Iphigenia reached for Euthalia's arm, but the other girl smacked her away. Her mouth hung in shock. Euthalia had *never*, in all their years of knowing each other, struck her. Again, she reached for Euthalia, this time holding the other girl's forearm tight in her grip. Her mind raced, but she could think of no decent explanation for just why seeing her wrapped up so tightly in that man's arms had her so repulsed. So, she did the only thing she could think of. She tugged the other girl close and pressed her lips to Euthalia's.

The other girl's reaction was instantaneous.

"Get off of me," Euthalia spat, trying to twist away.

"Listen, I'm sorry, Euthalia—"

"*Iset.*"

"What?"

"My mother named me Iset, *not* Euthalia. *Now let go of me.*"

Iphigenia stared down at her friend with wide eyes. She'd never considered that she'd had any other name before she'd been brought to Mycenae.

"I'm sorry," she repeated in a whisper. Tears pricked at her eyes.

Iset shook her head at her, disgust evident across her pretty features. Iphigenia did the only thing she could at that moment; she fled.

VIII

release me from cruel cares, and let my heart accomplish all that it desires, and be thou my ally

She didn't know how long she ran, but by the time she stopped, drenched in sweat and lungs on fire, she was in an entirely different portion of the camp. Here, guards weren't posted every few tents, nor were there any torches gleaming bright in the darkness. There weren't even any chickens pecking underfoot. No, this area was all but deserted, and the only illumination came from the moon and stars above. The spears and shields littering the sides of the tents, coupled with the scent of sweat and musk, told a far different story than that of the women's camp. With a start, Iphigenia realized she must be in one of the army's warrior camps.

This was dangerous. She thought back to what the guards had threatened, and her insides swam. She had to get back, lest any stragglers too drunk to carry themselves to the feast found her. She stood on her toes, craning her neck.

There were no obvious paths. She was in the center of the mass of tents, and all around her dirt trails weaved their way in all directions. Any one of them could take her back to the women's camp, but all the others spelled certain danger.

Iphigenia forced herself to breathe. There was no use in panicking; if there was one thing she'd learned during her long hours practicing with Euthalia, panic always led to ruin.

"Why did I do that?" she whispered, wanting to kick herself for being so stupid. Was she no better than Orestes, a weeping child who fled when they couldn't get their way?

Her heart ached. Euthalia was just a selfish dream; Iset was the true girl, and Iphigenia had severed any hope of anything real with her. Still, as she continued scanning her surroundings, she considered the idea that it may never have been possible in the first place. No wonder she'd hit her; she was a slave, and Iphigenia her master, no matter how they'd dressed it up. Iphigenia kissing her had only served as a painful reminder. She was no different than her father, than the men populating this accursed camp.

The gentle gurgle of water on rocks gave her the direction she needed. It had to have been the sea. She could walk along the shore, and from there make her way back to the camp. She stalked towards the sound, cautious not to kick up any rocks. Silence was her only ally now.

Murmurs made her stop in her tracks just as she found the narrow path running parallel to the sea. Judging by the position of the stars, following the path south would take her back to the women's camp. She ducked behind a large barrel just as two figures picked their way down to a large boulder on the sand.

The murmurs grew louder and higher in pitch; Iphigenia realized that she wasn't witnessing a stroll between comrades in arms, but an argument. She braced for the worst. For the whole journey, her mother had warned her of the passions of men — at any singular moment, they were likely to erupt into violence if they felt their honor had been slighted. Men had killed even those considered their dearest friends over the pettiest quarrels.

She wasn't surprised therefore when one of the men pulled the other into his grasp; the stunning part was that instead of a violent grapple to the sand below, she was a witness to him tilting his comrade's chin heavenward. There was a glint of silver moonlight on hair like flames, long tendrils framing his face like a girl's. Accompanied by the long eyelashes of legend. Iphigenia realized that it was Achilles standing there on the beach being embraced by a man who, judging by the plain armor he wore, was far below Achilles' own station.

Iphigenia was of two minds. One was ecstatic; out of all the soldiers she could have encountered, Achilles was the only hope she had of being escorted back safely. On the other hand, his "friend" there might not want any witnesses to their moonlight tryst. It could be incredibly bad for the both of them if it were to get out that Achilles was caught in the arms of one of his lesser lieutenants — it'd be different if he was the one taking charge, rather than what looked suspiciously like a role not unlike that a woman would take. Despite it all, excitement buried her initial shock — she and Achilles were more alike than she had thought. No wonder he had been so utterly incensed with Agamemnon: their reasonings for not wanting any parts of this marriage must be eerily similar.

Her mind was made up. She stepped from behind the barrel with a light cough.

The two broke apart as if Aphrodite herself had severed their embrace. The tall one dropped into a battle stance while Achilles unsheathed the sword at his side.

"It's me, Achilles!" Iphigenia called out. She stepped down onto the sand, lifting her veil so her face could be clearly seen.

"Is this her?" the tall one asked. Iphigenia noticed that he did not break his stance, until Achilles placed a hand on his shoulder. Only then did he relax.

Achilles to his credit immediately put away his sword. "What are you doing over here?" She'd been expecting that harsh voice that had screamed at her father, but the tone of the youth before her was shockingly gentle.

"I got lost." She'd leave out the rest of the details for now. She wasn't sure if she was able to open that wound quite yet. "Can you help me get back?"

"That depends," the tall one said, and as he came closer, Iphigenia could see that he was young, probably around Achilles' age, but a dark beard studded his jaw. "What did you see?"

"Patroclus, I told you — it doesn't matter. They wouldn't dare stand against me."

"What did you see?" the man repeated, his gaze as steely as his voice was stern.

It would be easy to say "nothing," to pretend she hadn't witnessed what they all knew she had, but Iphigenia felt that she finally had some leverage. Her mouth had been running reckless all night, what was one more thing?

"I saw my future husband embracing another," she replied simply, not breaking her stare with the man called Patroclus.

His nostrils flared, but before he could say anything, Iphigenia turned towards Achilles. She could hear her heartbeat in her ears. It would be a leap of faith. She jumped.

"I guess we're more similar than I thought."

"What?" A flush had crept up Achilles' neck. This close, Iphigenia could see that what she had thought was a tan was truly an amalgamation of dense freckles. "What are you talking about?"

"Is your friend here going to be joining us in the marriage bed? Because if so, I'd like to bring a handmaiden of my own."

There was a pause, then laughter. All sternness had fled Patroclus as he doubled over, gripping his middle as he guffawed.

Iphigenia's heart fell. She'd never told anyone that before, and Patroclus was laughing at her as if he didn't just have his hands entangled in Achilles' long hair.

"Patroclus, stop," Achilles said softly.

"I'm sorry," Patroclus said, wiping a tear from his eye. "It's just— it sounds like something out of a play. I mean no harm, really. Take her back, Achilles, and then rejoin the feast. I'll be at the tent when it's all said and done."

Patroclus gave a little wave to Iphigenia before turning to stride up the rocks back towards the tents, whistling all the way.

"He's a strange man," Iphigenia murmured just as soon as he was out of earshot. Achilles nodded.

"Strange, but he's mine," Achilles said, gesturing Iphigenia closer. "That's why he's the only one here I trust."

"I guess we're all a little strange." Iphigenia fell in step with Achilles as naturally as if she walked with her own siblings. How surreal to be walking alongside the one that had been the stuff of her nightmares. "I won't tell anyone if you won't."

Achilles rolled his eyes. "Who would care? Don't worry about that." The two of them were walking along the surf now, the water lapping softly at their ankles.

"I can't help it." The memory of Iset shoving her away had not even had time to dull its sharp edges. The girl must think her vile and cruel.

"Iphigenia, do you have any idea what goes on in the camp every night?" Achilles had a strange look on his face, as if he were remembering something especially salacious. "Love between warriors is love in its truest form. It's not just Patroclus and I. It's normal." He leaned down, picked up a particularly round stone, and flung it into the sea. "You shouldn't worry either. It's not like anyone cares what women do, as long as they're in their husbands' beds when they seek them. It doesn't count."

"Oh," Iphigenia replied, looking at her feet before swinging her head back up. If love between soldiers was the best, where did love between women stand? She doubted it was anywhere near as sacred. Achilles was surprisingly sweet, but he was still a warrior. She gazed at him for a long moment, watching the way his eyebrows furrowed as he concentrated on choosing which rock to skip next. By the time he sent one arcing into the waves with a splash, she'd made up her mind.

"That's the problem," she said softly. "The husband thing." Achilles flinched, and Iphigenia inwardly cringed. What she was about to say would be a blow to his honor, no matter what.

"When I look at a man, I feel nothing. It's like looking at a tree, or a mountain. Just another part of the scenery." Iphigenia didn't understand why she was taking the risk of revealing the secret closest to her heart, more secret than the magic, even, one she hardly understood herself. Achilles may be treating her gently right now, and clearly he was similar to her in that he preferred Patroclus to sleep in his tent over any of the varied camp girls he could have, but at the end of the day, she was to be his wife, no matter the circumstances of their arrangement.

To his credit, Achilles wasn't angry. He rolled a stone between his palms, stance open and easy. "So you don't like men," he said, and it sounded as if he were talking about her lack of preference for a certain cheese. "I can understand why, believe me, but does that mean you feel differently towards women?"

Iphigenia thought of her mouth going dry at the sight of a girl raising toned arms to pile loose hair into a bun, her pulse quickening when a well meaning serving girl placed a hand on the small of her back to guide her to noon day lessons, her endless daydreams of inviting girls she'd never said more than two words to back to the palace gardens at night…and finally, the war between shame and ecstasy she had felt at the sensation of Iset's lips on hers.

"Different is one way to describe it," she said, leaving it at that.

Achilles gave her a warm smile. "Thank you for telling me. If we have to do this, then I promise that as long as you and I are wed, no man shall touch you."

* * *

"I never wanted to be here. I shouldn't be here, if I'm being honest with you."

"I hope you'll be honest with me."

"I think I can be."

Iphigenia and Achilles sat in the shadow of a beached ship, its tattered sail hanging over them as a shield from any prying eyes. Any useful wood had long been pillaged, leaving only the brittle skeleton. In the distance, ships bobbed in the water while men scurried up and around their scaffolding like ants. Moving out of the water and into the shade had been a welcome respite from the afternoon sun. Here, at least, they would be able to talk openly away from any prying ears. Achilles sat with his arms wrapped around his knees, while Iphigenia lay on her side, propped up by her elbow.

"Achilles, what I am going to say may sound fantastical, but I need your guidance."

"My guidance?" Achilles asked, his brow furrowed. "No one has ever asked for my guidance...my blade, yes, but—"

"The rumors about your mother, are they true?" Iphigenia interrupted, urgency creeping into her voice.

Achilles turned his head away, lips caught in a pout. "There are many rumors about her, none of them good. What does she have to do with Agamemnon's treachery?"

"He's found himself with a blood debt to a goddess."

Achilles moved so fast that Iphigenia shrank back from him. He had whipped his head around and held her bicep in a vice grip. "Which goddess?" he breathed, gaze even more intense than when he'd quarreled with Agamemnon at the gate.

"I believe it to be Artemis," Iphigenia said as she gently extricated her arm from Achilles' grip. "She said he committed some crime against her, a theft, and that he must pay if he wanted a breeze to Troy."

"He's doomed us all," Achilles groaned. "Of all the gods to anger...I knew the wind not blowing was no coincidence. She won't back down without her price. They never do."

Iphigenia looked out towards the sea. "He said it's too high a price to pay, but he'd pay it nonetheless."

"He doesn't have a choice. The army'll kill him if they don't sail soon. I don't know what he did, but there's no changing destiny now." Achilles' words were weighty with bitterness. "Not for him, not for me, not for anybody."

Something in the back of Iphigenia's mind was desperate to disagree, but she held her tongue. "So, we're here now. There's clearly more to this than a wedding for good fortune."

"Is there though? He tells me nothing, even though I'm supposedly the linchpin behind this whole operation. No offense to you, but this marriage is clearly a scheme to trap me further. I have no desire for any parts of his household, but it'd be a mar on my honor to renege on your hand, even if I never consented to it in the first place."

"I take no offense. I don't want it either. Still, there's more to it than just keeping you under his wing." Iphigenia looked Achilles up and down. Even though he was slight of frame, defined muscles stood out in sharp relief under his sun browned skin. The blood on the tip of his spear hadn't left her mind either. She couldn't see Achilles being beholden to anyone if he didn't want to be, even if that person was the most powerful king in an age. "They think this marriage shall appease Artemis?"

"I don't know. All I know is there's no escaping this. Not that I haven't tried. It's as if Agamemnon has forgotten I'm already married."

"To who, Patroclus? How?" Iphigenia was confused. Achilles was hardly older than her, and he had already been wed once and was hours from another?

"No, though I wish to the gods it were true. In exchange for her assistance, I eloped on Skyros with the isle's princess." He didn't elaborate.

"Skyros?" Iphigenia asked, frowning. This was growing more and more difficult to follow. "I thought you were from Phthia?"

"I am, but I've lived on Skyros the past two years. My mother, she...*we* came up with the idea for me to stay there, disguised. Away from this." Achilles fully turned to Iphigenia, tugging at his hair. "The king's daughter was the only one who knew my other identity, and she helped me hide it. Deidamia loved me enough to take me in, show me what to do, let me become who I always should have been, and I loved her for it."

"But why did you have to hide?"

"You know of prophecies, correct? They had to have taught you that at the very least."

She thought back to the grim-faced men and women that ran the temples of Mycenae, and how they'd waxed poetic about the prophecies that had driven the most vile actions of her ancestors. They had said it was fate, that it had all been preordained by the gods, but to her, it'd seemed like excuses made after the fact for nothing more than human greed.

"Yes, I know of them."

"One less thing to explain then," Achilles said, giving a terse smile. "I was unlucky enough to get two. The first one isn't so bad, for me at least. They say I'm supposed to surpass my father, and who wouldn't want that? But the other...apparently, I either die a "young, glorious hero," or I live a long happy life of being a nobody." He looked down at his gauntlets. "They say I chose honor and glory, but I chose Skyros. No one knew 'Achilles' there, and I was happy. I was *myself*." He pointed out towards the sea. The island across the strait loomed large. "Cross the mountains of Euboea, swim to the middle of the sea, and rocky Skyros rises from the waves."

Iphigenia followed the line of sight that Achilles' finger drew. "How far is it?"

"Not far at all. If I swam as swiftly as I run, I could be there in a day, maybe two. A ship would have to go the long way, and it'd be slow rowing," he said darkly. "It's not like the wind will speed them along."

Iphigenia stood. "So what's stopping you from leaving?"

Achilles smiled sadly and shook his head. "I don't have a choice in the matter. Even if the Skyrans take me back—which they won't, not after what Odysseus did to me—there are some things here that I can't lose." His dark eyes were wistful as he gazed back towards the camp. "I know what I must do."

What had Odysseus done that was so bad that Achilles couldn't return to the home of his wife? A sympathetic ache rocked through Iphigenia. The man from Ithaca had intruded on both their lives. "I never wanted to come here either. I thought I had more time..."

"Before marriage?" Achilles asked.

"Before a lot of things," Iphigenia responded, looking back across the strait. She'd barely had a chance to explore the heavy power that dwelled within her. "Now I'm here."

"Now *we're* here." Achilles took his helm into his hands, shaking sand out of his scarlet plume. "If it makes you feel better, you may still have time despite this. We'll be wed in name only. I'm not coming back from this war."

A pang of guilt struck Iphigenia as she recalled her words earlier that afternoon. "You know this?"

"I know it. I...wish that this was a world without the burden of destiny, one where I could be the real me, where I could be with Patroclus. It's not though, not for me. I can't change my path. I have to walk it, but *you* don't. Live the life you want to live for me, Iphigenia. You'll be protected under my name for as long as I fight."

Here was the warrior who just a few hours before had threatened to throttle the life out of her father, vowing to defend her on his own honor. They barely knew each other, and yet Iphigenia could see the sincerity behind Achilles' stormy eyes. There was power behind an oath like that; swearing it was proof enough of Achilles' conviction.

Iphigenia tentatively placed a hand on Achilles' bare shoulder, frowning as she watched him flinch at the contact. "But Achilles, who will protect you?"

Achilles stood abruptly, shrugging her hand off. "Let's go back; I can smell meat sizzling. They'll be expecting me at the feast." His face hardened as he put on his helm again, the mask of the warrior back up. Iphigenia smelled nothing on the stagnant air but salt. "But we'll talk again before the wedding, Iphigenia of Mycenae. I swear it on the River Styx."

IX

and delicately woven garlands round tender neck

As they made their way back into the walls of the women's camp proper, Iphigenia felt the lightest she had in years. To be able to actually voice her feelings, no matter in how small of a way? It may be a forced marriage for the both of them, but at the very least she knew even if she had agency nowhere else, she could find it with Achilles. Their talk had cheered her, and she even found herself drumming up the courage to seek out Iset and apologize the right way.

Her spirits were high when she and Achilles reached her mother's large tent. It was mostly quiet, save for the low murmur of what she recognized to be Clytemnestra's voice. She was probably telling Orestes a bedtime story. The thought of it made her feel a slight pang of envy. He'd have so many more years of stories, she was sure. She shook her head. There was no sense in being jealous of a baby, and this whole situation had turned in her favor seemingly overnight.

"Goodnight, Iphigenia," Achilles said, tilting his head. "I'm sure your mother has much to tell you before we share vows in the morning."

"And goodnight to you, Achilles." She hesitated for a second. The question of what dealings Artemis had with her father was still unanswered. "Your mother is a goddess, correct? Does she have any sway with the others?"

"Well—"

An enraged shout cut off Achilles, followed by the ear splitting wails of a child. Achilles sprang into action, drawing his weapon, but Iphigenia's hand on his arm stopped him.

"Hold on," she said, pressing an ear against the thick canvas. Just as she thought, two familiar voices were mingling in rage. "It's my parents," Iphigenia said, motioning for Achilles to come and listen as well. "They do this every time they're alone with each other." She wasn't bothered; why would a change of locale stop her parents from their ceaseless feuding?

And then, she heard her father mention her name above the din of Orestes' tears. Had he found out about her excursion out of the women's camp, and that's what he was laying into her mother about?

"You can't take another from me!" her mother screamed, and Iphigenia's blood turned to sleet. Iset must have ran straight to the elder maids and complained about what she had done to her. They would have nearly tripped over themselves to tell Clytemnestra — what had Iphigenia digging her nails into her palms with anxiety was the idea that her mother, the same woman who not a week ago had likened the two of them to Demeter and Persephone, would find her sickening. She could lose everyone else, but her mother?

"It must be done," Agamemnon yelled, and Iphigenia watched his shadow pacing back and forth as Clytemnestra stalked after him. "If the gods ordain it, then it is as natural as breath itself."

Panic washed over her and she turned to Achilles, who could only offer a shrug in response. What did she have to do with the gods? Artemis' words about her "prize" rushed to the forefront of her mind.

"I don't care what she told you," Clytemnestra shrieked, "but you'll kill *my* daughter over my dead body!"

Iphigenia took a trembling step back and looked at Achilles, who'd gone pale with shock. Had she heard that right? And then, the memory of the goddess in the woods came back to her, and she began to understand. It had all been a trick, an awful ruse.

Achilles gripped her arm. "Listen, I don't know what's going on, but no one is going to harm you." His words poured out of him in a rapid torrent of hushed whispers. "If I have to fight off the entire army myself, I shall, but I won't let you die. We'll head for the mountains—"

There was a great clamor, and then Clytemnestra's shadow was swinging a great double sided axe, the bride gift meant to be from mother to daughter. It came within mere inches of Agamemnon's back, who dodged with the speed of a practiced warrior despite his hulking size. Within seconds, he'd tackled Clytemnestra to the ground and began hammering his fists down onto her snarling form.

Achilles was struggling to pull Iphigenia away, but she broke free, rushing into the tent. She couldn't abandon her mother, he'd kill her. She was greeted by scared servant women lining the walls, her brother's wails, and the sight of her father's broad figure laying heavy punch after punch upon her mother. Clytemnestra was clawing at his face, scraping deep gouges into his skin with all the force of a lioness. Iphigenia couldn't bare to watch a moment longer. She leapt onto her father's back and pulled at his long hair, attempting to reign him in.

It was to be a short lived attack, as Agamemnon shrugged her off his back with minimal effort. She rolled right back to her feet and was about to lunge again when Achilles thundered into the dimly lit tent and wrapped his arms around her, holding her back.

"Get off of me!" she screamed, desperate to return to her mother's side.

Clytemnestra clambered to her feet, having used Iphigenia's distraction to get out from under her husband. "Get out! Run! Achilles, take her and go—" and then Agamemnon slammed his fist into her mouth and she crumpled.

"Shut up!" Agamemnon then turned. "Achilles, leave us. This is a family matter." The calmness of his voice was horrifically juxtaposed with his panting breath and the weeping red wounds carved into his cheeks.

"No," Achilles insisted, his grip around Iphigenia growing tighter. "We heard you—"

"You heard nothing. Leave my daughter and go."

"She is my fiancée—"

"She is no one to you!"

Clytemnestra, arisen once again, released a guttural scream and rained her fists down on Agamemnon's back as dark blood flew from her mouth. Iphigenia saw her father reach for the dagger at his belt and she yelled for Achilles to do something, anything. He was already flying towards him, sword raised, when the tent was flooded with the heavy footfalls of soldiers marching in. Within seconds, it was over. Iphigenia and her mother were being restrained by two soldiers that she realized with a start were Odysseus and Diomedes, and Achilles was struggling against an entire group of men. Hatred coursed through her as she fought against Odysseus' slimy hands.

Agamemnon, composed as if nothing more than a few choice words had been thrown, wiped at his face carefully with a handkerchief. The men in the room all looked to him, quietly awaiting instruction. Meanwhile, Clytemnestra raged, laying curses upon Agamemnon so violent they made even Achilles blush.

Iphigenia could not tear her eyes away as Agamemnon swaggered over to his wife. Her head held high, she glared at Agamemnon with a fury that could rival that of Nemesis herself.

Agamemnon cleared his throat before spreading his arms. "I do this for the good of all Greece—" he began, voice projected.

"Fuck Greece," Clytemnestra swore, and then she spat in his face. "And fuck you."

For a moment, Agamemnon regarded her coolly. He then smashed his closed fist against her face. He relished in the sick crack and gush of blood running from his wife's nose before spinning on his heel to face the soldiers.

"Don't let them out of your sight. I'd chain her if I were you," he said, pointing to Clytemnestra. "Don't touch the girl."

Achilles surged forward, body trembling with rage in the arms of his captors.

"You've used me for the last time. My name, my honor, for your treachery? I'll cut your throat myself."

Agamemnon looked Achilles up and down. "I'll pretend I didn't hear that. If I had, that handsome friend of yours just might find himself drowned in your beloved stinking sea tomorrow morning. Don't think I would hesitate, *daughter* of Peleus."

Achilles instantly deflated.

As Agamemnon exited the tent, barely sparing her a second glance, followed by most of the men, Iphigenia knew hope was lost. She and Achilles met eyes one last time as he walked away. He was free now, while she was still ensnared in the bruising grip of Odysseus. His eyes were mournful, but Iphigenia knew he had no regrets leaving her there. No matter how nice to her he'd been, no matter how sincere he'd looked as he'd uttered promises to her, Patroclus came before everything. She didn't have it in her heart to blame him.

As her mother's head fell limply against Diomedes' arm, and Orestes' wails reached a fever pitch, Iphigenia felt as if her brother cried for them all.

* * *

There was a ruckus at the tent's entrance; morning had come too soon. Iphigenia shrank against the canvas wall as a few of her handmaidens traipsed in. Gone were the radiant smiles and songs of celebration; the assortment of women was silent and their eyes were downcast as they set their baskets of perfumes and basins of hot water onto the floor. It was just as well, Iphigenia thought to herself. She couldn't bear this burden as it was; to have to sit and listen to the chattering of girls who thought they were preparing her for a wedding rather than the funeral it was always intended to be would have been impossible.

They'd shackled her to one of the heaviest chests. She had rubbed her wrists raw fighting against the chains all night, but she didn't mind the pain. It helped to distract her from the real torture. They'd dragged her mother out of the tent just after they'd restrained her. Sleep had been out of the question; she may have been able to bear it if Clytemnestra had been at her side, but her mother had been taken from her without her senses. She hadn't even been allowed to say goodbye.

Odysseus had left her with the guards who'd let her leave the camp earlier that night. Neither one dared look at her, no matter how desperately she'd pleaded for her life. Her throat was as wounded as her wrists. Now, she was silent. There was nothing left to say.

The tent shifted again, and two more women rushed in. With a start, Iphigenia realized who they were— her mother, more bruised and battered than Iphigenia had ever seen her in her life, and Iset, whose brown eyes were rimmed with red. They almost tripped over themselves in their haste to reach her, and the guard, Titarus if she remembered correctly, standing over her sneered at the women as they shoved him aside.

"Leave us," Clytemnestra barked at him, and Iphigenia felt a spark of relief. Her voice was stuffy, like she had a nasty cold, and her nose was bent at a sharp angle, but no matter what they'd done to her, her mother had not lost her ever-present pride.

Titarus stood steadfast, his companion watching the exchange with an air of boredom. "Can't do that. I'm on orders."

Clytemnestra drew herself up to her full height, towering over the man as venom dripped from her voice. "I don't care what your orders are or what rat bastard gave them. I came to prepare my daughter; she is owed at least the dignity of privacy. She and I will not suffer yet another humiliation here."

The two glared icily at each other. Then, the guard broke, grunting and pushing past the women gathered.

"Fine," he said over his shoulder. "I'll be outside, just until she's dressed. We don't have all day."

As soon as he had swished out of the tent, Clytemnestra sunk to the floor, taking Iphigenia into her arms.

"Are you hurt?" she asked, her voice strained. She gingerly took Iphigenia's face into her fingertips, turning her this way and that as she searched for any traces of wrongdoing. A particularly nasty gash dripped from Clytemnestra's forehead to Iphigenia's cheek, and Iphigenia wanted to weep as her mother licked her thumb before tenderly swiping away the red stain.

"No, mother," she whispered. "But you are."

"Don't worry about me," Clytemnestra said. Iset sank to the ground next to her. She gave Iphigenia a weak smile that didn't reach her eyes.

Iphigenia was conflicted. "I'm so sorry," Iphigenia murmured, heart aching. Her best friend in the entire world, witness to her murder. At least this way, she'd be able to apologize. "I'm sorry for everything."

"Don't worry about that," Iset said, and her fingers drifted down to the chains that bound Iphigenia. She dipped her head close, so that only Iphigenia and her mother could hear her whisper. There was the telltale glint of a key in her hand. "We're getting you out of here."

Iphigenia's pulse quickened. All night she'd been hoping for a way out to present itself, anything to escape this fate, and she'd come up empty handed. There were thousands of Greek soldiers stretched across miles of this seaside plain, the biggest army the world had ever seen. Every plan she'd thought of had been a suicide mission. Yet, Iphigenia found herself entranced by the faintest taste of hope as her hands were finally freed. She rubbed at her wrists before clamoring to her feet, her legs burning with pins and needles.

"Why are you helping me? After what I've done to you—"

"Because you're my friend, and I didn't do all that work teaching you for nothing. Now, go along with the preparations," Iset said, leading her over to where a maid stood with a wash basin. Her mother had her by the hand the entire time.

Things moved quickly after that. She was bathed, and expensive scents of sweet rush and marjoram were rubbed into her skin. Rouge was painted onto her cheeks and lips, and her eyes were lined with an expensive black pigment straight from Egypt, the very same she'd watched her mother carefully apply for the past sixteen years, and that streaked down her mother's cheeks now. She could have laughed. She always wanted to wear the thick pastes currently sitting on her face, and the day she was finally allowed was to be her last on earth.

Iphigenia held out her arms as two girls approached, a robe of bright saffron draped between them. On any other day, she would be impressed; the garment was threaded with fibers of scarlet, woven in a winding pattern that she longed to trace all day with her fingers. It was heartbreakingly beautiful; according to the attendants, it was the very same gown that her Aunt Helen had worn when she was wed to Uncle Menelaus. She wanted nothing more than to tear it to shreds.

As the fabric slipped onto her bare skin, she turned her head. Clytemnestra was already dressed, her black gown striking against the painted pallor of her skin. The maids had done an exceptional job of hiding the bruises from the night before. Iphigenia could almost imagine that this was a normal day back at home. If Clytemnestra felt any lingering pain, she did not show it as she strode over to her daughter, taking her back into her arms.

"I know what you did in the crypt," Clytemnestra whispered against her ear. When Iphigenia jerked in surprise, her mother only held her closer. "I'm not angry. Euthalia told me everything. I do not know the extent of the power you hold, or from where it even came, but use it, Iphigenia, by any means necessary. You must use it."

"I don't even know if I *have* any powers," Iphigenia replied, craning her neck to look at her mother properly. "I...I don't feel any different."

Clytemnestra stroked her hair. "Just try and focus. We'll handle the rest. It will come, I'm sure of it."

Iphigenia nodded against her mother's chest, a lump rising in her throat as she took a deep breath. The same scent she'd smelled her whole life wafted off her mother's skin, and tears pricked at her eyes as she tried to commit it to memory. If the plan worked, she didn't know when or if they'd ever see each other again, and if it didn't — it wouldn't be much help where she was going, but it gave her comfort nonetheless.

Over her mother's shoulder, she saw Iset furtively looking out of the mouth of the tent while exchanging hurried whispers with one of the younger maids, who immediately darted outside. Iset caught her looking and gave her a quick smile and a nod.

Relief flooded through Iphigenia as her mother led her to a straight backed chair. Whatever her friend had planned was working. She might live to see the sweet light of another day after all.

Clytemnestra took a comb inlaid with pearls out of a girl's hand before shooing her away.

"Let me have the honor," she said, giving the maid a tight lipped smile. "It is my daughter's wedding day, after all." She then began to run the teeth of the comb through Iphigenia's tangled locks. The tugging hurt, but Iphigenia paid it no mind. She knew Clytemnestra was being as gentle as she was able, and she wasn't about to deny her mother this, even if she were ripping her hair out from the root. She closed her eyes. *Powers.* It had been a week since she'd ventured into the crypt, and still no magic had presented itself to her. What would it even look like? Would she shoot lightning from her fingertips? Or would she sprout a pair of wings and fly away? Either option was laughable when the closest thing to it had been on the ridge, and that had only been the barest of tugs. She'd need far more than a gut feeling to survive this. *Imagine the frog,* she thought. *Imagine it, and jump.*

Iphigenia found herself so hyperfocused on recreating that pulling sensation that she barely noticed when her mother began massaging her scalp. She'd long ago finished detangling, having loosely braided a crown and leaving the rest to fall gently down her back and shoulders in waves. She could smell the lilies woven into her hair.

"Iphigenia," Clytemnestra whispered, her voice soft. "I should have told you this long before— I wanted to wait until you were ready."

"Tell me now," Iphigenia said, craning her neck up.

Clytemnestra was looking down at her, playing with a thin green stem, uncharacteristic. Clytemnestra never fidgeted.

"Agamemnon, he...Iphigenia, you weren't my first child. I should've known that not even him believing the lie was enough to protect you."

"What lie, mother?" Iphigenia's head was reeling.

Before Clytemnestra could answer, Iset was waving them over.

"He's here," she said, pointing outside.

Iphigenia peeked out. The guard from earlier was nowhere to be seen, but Lysander was striding towards the tent, a couple of his friends laughing and jostling each other at his side. "Lysander will smuggle you out. Don't worry about the rest — just survive."

Iset pulled her into a tight embrace. "Be safe," she said, and Iphigenia clutched at her back. Her oldest friend, rescuing her one last time. She'd promised herself that she wouldn't cry, but she couldn't stop the floodgates that opened onto her cheeks.

They broke apart, Iset holding her at arm's length. Iphigenia was struck with just how selfish she'd been the entire time she'd known Iset. She'd only ever thought about her own suffering, not even realizing how much the girl in front of her had lost, down even to her own freedom. Iphigenia was about to apologize one last time when the front flap of the tent was thrown wide, the weak light of dawn streaming inside. Three men strode inside, a particularly lanky one at their forefront.

"Lysander!" Iset exclaimed, ushering the young man in. He smiled down at her, his pimply visage as awkward as ever, before turning his attention to the rest of the solemn room, bemusement painted across his face. He looked absolutely comical in his too large armor, despite its upgrade to polished bronze. Iphigenia angrily wiped away the tears on her face. How was *he* supposed to help her?

"We don't have much time," Iset explained, kneeling down to secure a rucksack. "They'll be here in minutes."

Lysander looked like he was about to throw up, and he looked back to the men behind him, as if for reassurance. One of them gave him a curt nod, while the other mouthed "you've got this". He stepped forward, his hand extended as if to help Iset up. For a split second, Iphigenia turned to her mother to share a hopeful smile. The moment ended as quickly as it had started as the sick squelch of pierced flesh and a groan of agony pervaded the tent.

Lysander had whipped out his spear just as Iset had turned to him, driving it through her neck.

The room erupted into chaos. The maids were screaming, and Iphigenia's vision swam as she watched her friend sink to her knees, hands uselessly tugging at the spear she'd been impaled upon. Clytemnestra was pulling at her, trying to drag her away, and as she met her dearest friend's eyes — the only thing she could see in them was hollow anger.

"Just following orders," Lysander sneered before sharply twisting his spear. Iset looked as if she wanted to cry out, but only gurgles came forth. Lysander placed his boot upon her shoulder to gain enough leverage to withdraw it. An arc of hot blood spurted from the wound. Iset slumped over, her rapidly fading eyes still locked with Iphigenia's as she mouthed inaudible words. Then she went still.

"Now, the girl!" Lysander yelled, and his allies moved towards Iphigenia.

"No!" Clytemnestra threw herself in front of Iphigenia, arms spread wide. "She's but a child!"

Iphigenia felt as if she were underwater; she begged for the magic to come, for that strange energy to wash over her, but as she watched her mother slammed to the ground with bone shattering force, it was as good as trying to light a fire beneath the sea. Only her mother's piercing screams and curses cut through the many leagues separating her from the surface.

And then, she was being ripped away. The moment the soldiers laid their hands upon her, everything came into focus as if her head had finally crested the waves. Iphigenia yelled, kicking and clawing at the men as they dragged her from the warmth of the tent into the dewy morning.

Clytemnestra followed out of the tent, but was kicked back by Lysander. Iphigenia's last glimpse of her mother was the sight of her crumpled in the dirt. There was an unbearable screaming that had her wishing to clamp her ears — a moment later, and she realized it was coming from her.

The men rushed her away, running through the dusty paths of the camp. Nervous women peeked from behind tent walls, and no matter how loudly Iphigenia begged for help, no amount of desperation compelled them to do more than silently stare. There would be no aid here.

The women's camp disappeared, flowing into the warrior camp proper. Here, things were different. The men stood openly along the passageway, their mouths agape. Some joined in, creating an odd sort of procession. There were no flowers, no hymns to Hera, only leering eyes and the sound of Iphigenia screaming herself hoarse.

As the march continued, now sloping upwards away from the rocky seaside, every nerve in Iphigenia's body burned with adrenaline. Her original terror paled in comparison to the agony she felt as she was paraded to certain doom — how desperately she wished she could go back and slap herself for being blinded to the true danger, worried as she had been about a marriage that never was to have been.

"Hera, hear me! Hymen, hear me!" She began to pray aloud, appealing to the few gods she knew and then all the ones she didn't. Terror scorched its way through her. How was she about to die? She'd barely even lived.

Whether from an inability to change fate or pure apathy, no gods came down to save her. No Demeter, no Persephone — not even Artemis from the woods answered her pleas. Iphigenia screwed her eyes shut. Bile rose in her throat. She wanted to tear out of her own skin, just to get the bruising grip of the soldiers off of her.

They crested the hill. The marble altar stood there, its gleaming white surface already stained with wine-dark blood. Around it stood several men, and Iphigenia was horrified to recognize most of them. Odysseus, his back straight; Diomedes, who looked anywhere but at her; the priest Calchas, eyes wild and robes bloodied; Achilles, who was already weeping with Patroclus at his side; and her father, Agamemnon, King of Men.

He met her gaze, and something in Iphigenia broke. She snarled, and with all the power she could muster, she broke out of the grasp of the soldiers. She sprinted towards the men, hair and robes streaming behind her. She had nothing left to lose, and so she tore the gown her mother had painstakingly dressed her in from her body, baring herself for the whole of the army to see. There was an audible murmur from the crowd, and she was well aware of the countless eyes locked onto her as she turned her attention to Achilles, who was standing with a basket of wicker in his arms. "I'm sorry," he said, face flushed. "I tried, I can't—"

Iphigenia turned her attention away. Calchas was locked in a holy frenzy, yelling strange incantations heavenward. Diomedes had stepped away entirely, shaking his head. There was only one left who could stop this.

Agamemnon looked down at her, his normally narrow eyes wide with what had to be shock. His nostrils flared as Iphigenia slid towards him, bare skin to the ground as she wrapped her arms around his legs. If she had to beg, so be it.

They held each other's gaze for what seemed like an eternity, both father and daughter unwavering. To Iphigenia, Agamemnon looked older than he ever had, the lines in his face long and deep. And then, he sighed. Had she reached him?

"It must be done," Agamemnon said, and Iphigenia choked with rage. She remembered her mother's plea then; something clicked within her. Liquid fire flooded her veins and she was joined in her fury by a cacophony of voices howling in her head. The words, foreign to her tongue, began flowing out of her before she even knew she was saying them — they spilled like hot blood, and she could feel their power rippling through her and into the ground. There was a terrible tremor, and then the panicked shouts of men.

"Curse you, Agamemnon, curse you, curse the poisonous fruit from your loins, and curse every man who stands with you." That much, she understood, for those words came not from that mysterious energy, but from her own heart.

Agamemnon's own enraged voice joined the din, and just as Iphigenia began to rise, defying the very rules of nature itself, rough fingers jammed a gag into her mouth. Still, she bitterly fought, clawing at any who came near. There was a great keening sound, and out of the corner of her eye she saw the ground beneath them beginning to split apart. Someone caught hold of her wrists, and before she knew what was happening they'd been bound behind her back and something silky was forced over her eyes and knotted tight. The flow of power dampened and then ceased as she was bodily lifted and slammed onto the altar. The men handling her were so hurried in their brutality that her skull cracked against the marble. Searing pain exploded from behind her eyes; and then there was a burning knife plunging into the hollow of her throat, ripping its way down into her chest. As the world went dark, the last thing she felt was the stirrings of an ice cold breeze.

X

sleep thou, in the bosom of thy sweetheart

The world was black. She was in a void, and she *was* the void; the void knew nothing but her, and she knew nothing but the void. She drifted, no regard to time or place or substance.

Light sliced the vacuum like a blade, and the void began to recede. Flashes of greenery, a smattering of blue, the ripple of sunshine on a pond. Then back to nothingness. It was cyclic, an endless alternating of nothing and of grass between her teeth, of unexistence and a body that felt like it didn't belong to her, of oblivion and a neck that couldn't crane towards the sky. Push and pull, pain the only constant.

During those brief moments of actuality, she trampled wildflowers recklessly, drank from ponds under the cover of darkness lest she catch a glance of her reflection. She stumbled, blind and voiceless, yet understanding more than she ever had. All throughout, voices called to her. Calls to come home. Calls of thanks, as if she gave her life willingly. Loudest of all were the calls for vengeance, the ones that had her smashing her head against trees until her vision was clouded by red and the void beckoned once again.

A ripple in the pattern, and the voice of vengeance, preternatural in its familiarity, cut through all the others.

"You'll soon awaken. Let me show you what waits."

Another ripple, and images materialized. She saw her younger sister, impossibly tall, dressed all in black and kneeling outside a tomb. She witnessed the lazy drift of hot embers floating up from a ruined city. She held the hand of a dark haired youth with wild eyes as a pillar drenched in blood collapsed into the sea. On hands and knees, she climbed a pile of bodies so high that she'd thought them a mountain and their blood a trickling spring. She saw her hands wrapped around a slender throat. She stood over the corpses of two women, one a dear friend and the other unknown, their hands joined. The one familiar to her sat up and she went to her, bowing her head to beg for forgiveness. Dead lips met her ear.

"And now let me show you the past, why you must walk the path laid out for you."

Bright sunlight threatened to blind her, and she cast a hand far too large to be her own over her eyes. She looked down. She was dressed in finer robes than she'd ever seen anyone in, more grand then even her father's. She stood tall, and at her side a boy hardly older than Orestes looked up at her with a toothy grin. His tiny hand slipped into hers, and she was unable to stop herself to even ask who he was before they walked through a roughly hewn archway leading into the side of a mountain.

She was covered in blood, hacking away at that same little boy until his limbs resembled no more than the choicest cuts of lamb. The axe was heavy in her hands and she threw it to the straw lined floor, not in horror, but in triumph. After rubbing each cut with a marinade of the choicest herbs, she took the whole bundle of flesh and dumped it into the eagerly boiling cauldron behind her. As the meal cooked, she inhaled deeply. Her hunger would soon be satisfied.

The scene changed. She was now in a massive room, gilded and heavily perfumed. She hummed as she set a great table, ladling her steaming stew into shining black bowls. As she served the last one, she heard voices approach, and she smiled, taking her own place at the table, the treasure in her pocket almost thrumming with energy. When they ate, she would as well, and would prove herself to have bested them. If they would deny her her birthright, she would simply have to take it.

She knew who she was by this point, and she was helpless to stop it. She was Tantalus, and now she was screaming, throat burning and stomach threatening to twist in upon itself. The water pooled around her ankles was cool and smelled so sweetly, and yet each time she leaned down for a drink—just a sip to relieve the rawness in her throat and the cracked landscape of her lips—it rushed away as if sucked up by some invisible force. Above her, tree branches sagged with the fragrant heaviness of their fruit. The juice from an overripe peach dripped onto her face, and as she reached high above her head for just a morsel, even the smallest fig, the branches danced away. She sank to her knees and wept.

That all encompassing darkness returned. She had no idea how long its heavy weight sat upon her before her senses returned. She was clapping a young man on his shoulder, the young boy she had once led to his death, the same boy who's flesh had passed her lips, and his shoulder was unnaturally hard and cold, as if it were carved from marble and covered by lacquer rather than skin. Pelops, she thought, and at the same time, wondered; if not he, who was she?

She and Pelops stood on a wide beach, a nearby ship preparing to depart. She embraced him and wished him luck and fortune for all his descendants. The young man smiled at her and as he walked away, she felt a deep apprehension drop into her stomach. She could only wish that she knew the reason why.

Day became night, and she was holding her little son in her lap tight as her sister screamed and tore at her hair. She'd come all the way home from far off Greece with none of her many children to show for it, nor her husband, cursing Artemis and Apollo with every breath.

"You," she gasped in between screaming fits. "She's punished me because of *you*."

She looked between her sister and her son before setting her face into a hard line. "I'll make it right, Niobe," she whispered.

She was then running through a forest, chasing a mighty stag as her hounds ran ahead. Her heart thundered in her chest as she lined up her bow for a perfect shot, straight and true. The deer collapsed, and she punched a fist in triumph.

That same night, she sat in front of a fire, the choicest part of the deer sizzling on a spit. She'd already fed her dogs a sizable portion; now, it was her turn to partake. She thought of the little boy at home; he would make a good and just king. Her knuckles were white with tension as they gripped her knees.

The meat finished. She took it off the spit with trembling hands, and greedily tore into it, juices running down her chin into her beard. It was delicious, and it was hers. All hers.

She felt her presence before she saw her.

"Why do you choose not to honor me, who guided your arrow to the beast's heart?"

She felt herself drop the meat and turn, and she found herself face to face with Artemis, who looked no different than she'd had that very morning, before she knew. She was sick to think of the way they'd laughed together, when Artemis had already slaughtered her nieces and nephews weeks ago.

"You know why," she heard herself say, deep voice rumbling with anger. "For my sister."

"So you dishonor me for your sister, who dishonored us both with her hubris? After all I have done for you?" Artemis sneered, stalking up to her and shoving her to the ground.

"You killed innocents, goddess. They were children." She was backing away now, crawling backwards across the forest floor. Artemis kept moving forward.

"My quarrel is not with you. Your sister thought she was above her station, and she had to pay. The same pride that destroyed your father destroyed her children, not I."

"You're wrong," she hissed. Artemis stopped and turned away.

"Fine. If I'm wrong, I'm wrong. But you can be right alone. Maybe one of your children will be a better choice."

"No! Leave my son out of this. You *owe* me."

"I owe you nothing, Broteas. I am your patron no longer."

She pounded the earth with her fist as the goddess melded back into the night.

* * *

She stood at the edge of the flames, willing herself to turn away. Instead, she stepped into them as casually as if she was taking an evening stroll. Her son called out to her in panic, but she ignored him, letting the fire latch onto her skin and melt it all away. This, at least, should be enough pittance to keep the goddess from her children. Right?

* * *

And then she was face to face with herself. Curious how now is the time that Iphigenia remembered at last who she had been.

Then the woman who she thought was her spoke, and Iphigenia realized she was looking at her mother, decades younger, her wedding veil pushed back to reveal a woman so blindingly radiant with a happiness that Iphigenia had never seen in her entire sixteen years.

"Atys," Clytemnestra whispered, placing her head on her chest. "I've waited for this day for so long."

"As have I," Iphigenia heard herself say. Inside, she was confused. Agamemnon had never gone by Atys.

Before she could question it further, she was seated on a dark veranda with her mother, laughing with mirth as she bounced the baby in her lap.

"Are you certain?"

"Certain," Clytemnestra said, flushed with joy. She patted her belly gently, the barest hint of curvature beginning to show. She was far too beautiful — but the baby in her lap was a *boy*, and Electra shouldn't have been born for another three years. Something was terribly wrong here.

Iphigenia's suspicions were confirmed when she next transitioned, a spear in her hands and a spear in her gut causing white hot pain so fierce her vision went blurry. Her mother's screaming filled the room, and as she looked up for the final time, she found herself face to face with a bearded man wearing her father's peacock plumed helm.

"Agamemnon," she spat, blood-coated saliva spraying. "You traitorous bastard."

Her cousin—*no, my father*—drove the spear deeper and twisted, causing her to cry out in pain. *How many times will you kill me?*

"Apologies, cousin, but I can have no rivals for the throne."

He then turned away, and from her fading vision, she watched as Agamemnon wrestled the wailing baby boy out of Clytemnestra's arms. There was a terrible pause as he considered the child. Did he see any family resemblance?

"A boy, isn't it?"

Agamemnon's words were soft, but his muscles were taut with deadly intent as he hurled the child from the veranda down to the rocks below. Her mother's weeping was the last thing she heard before that terrible blackness overwhelmed her once more.

Iset's voice rang through the void, and somehow she knew that this would be the last time.

"I showed you the path to freedom. A god walks within you. Now you must repay me in blood."

"How?" Iphigenia responded. Hazy memories of those last few hours at Aulis pierced her like arrows. She'd only been sacrificed once; Iset had sacrificed her dignity, her freedom, her life, all for her sake.

"Wake up and end this cycle. Avenge them. Avenge yourself. Avenge *me*."

The path of the blade had never been more clear.

XI

with divine countenance smiling

Sensation was the first mystery. It always had been, ever since that moment all those years ago that she discovered that she was alone in her pain and always would be. Her mother hadn't been looking; Clytemnestra had been talking to a slave about some trivial matter, and Iphigenia had been toddling behind her, unnoticed as she attempted to scale an outcropping of one of Mycenae's massive walls. When she'd slipped off with hardly a gasp, dashing her head firmly against the hard packed dirt of the palace courtyard, she'd immediately looked for her mother, to see if she'd seen, if she'd felt what she'd felt. When Clytemnestra didn't turn, scoop her into her arms to fret over her frantically, she wailed, not from the pain, but from the sharp realization that her mother hadn't felt that hard jolt against her own skull. Only then did Clytemnestra turn to her, gently prodding at the spot on her skull where a lump was already swelling into existence. It had been too late, of course; that magical hold of infancy, that enduring myth of being one with the mother, had been extinguished forever.

Nothing had come close to that blinding realization of sentience until this moment. She was three years old again, sobbing against her mother's skirts as she realized that she was alone in each and every feeling. There had been blistering pain, and then nothing — and then feeling returned, flooding her nerves as if a great dam had failed, releasing its violent deluge onto an unsuspecting valley. The curse of consciousness had reared its ugly head again. Everything ached, every part of her rebelling against life itself. She couldn't move, couldn't see, but damn if she could *feel*. Her mouth was heavy with the taste of salt; her jaw ached with its gritty weight. It was bitter, and it was even more unbearable than the sharp pain at her throat. Spitting provided no relief — it was as if it were cemented in her mouth, all the way back to her tonsils and up into her sinuses. She longed for water to wash it away, to wash *her* away, anything to escape the suffocating pain, but there was no trickle of a stream, nor roaring of a river. Her only companion was the soft melody of birdsong.

She must be Tantalus reborn, the way her suffering yet endured. The unfortunate nature of her blood had not been lost on Iphigenia; it had always been in the background, on her walls, in the songs of the maids and the prayers of the priests, but for her to be the next Atreid to bear the family curse? It had all been over, finished, and yet here she was, breathing the air of what had to be some fresh agony. She had offended no gods, wronged no man, and yet still the sins of her ancestors had not even allowed for the small kindness that would have been oblivion.

Something warm pressed at her lips, its heady scent fragrant with and sweet. She parted her mouth hoping to quench the burning thirst, but as the bowl tipped and liquid began to flow, she was met with something far more delicious than water. The first taste was electric; passion and desire danced on her tongue in ways that rivaled Aphrodite's most tender charms. The liquid hummed as it passed from her lips to her throat and beyond, warming her better than the finest wines the vineyards could offer. All traces of salt were washed away.

She was gulping now, greedily sucking the drink down. Every synapse and vein in her body was desperately screaming for more, more, *more*. A hand squeezed her shoulder.

"Iphigenia," a woman's voice murmured, and then the bowl was removed. The utterance of her name, something she'd been dangerously close to forgetting, went nearly unnoticed. The bowl was the more pressing issue here. Iphigenia whined, lifting her head in an effort to reunite with the most intoxicating beverage she'd ever had the pleasure of imbibing.

"Give it back," she gasped, voice hoarse. She longed to take it into her own hands, to drain the bowl dry, to lick at the rim until it gleamed.

A hand stroked her face, and she was suddenly aware she lay cradled in the crook of a woman's thighs, her arms bound behind her back.

"Too much, too soon," the same voice from before replied, just above her. "Any more and it might drive you mad."

Something cold and sharp pressed against Iphigenia's leg, and she jerked, the fear of further bloodshed sobering her. Instead, there was the sound of fabric being sheared, and suddenly she had usage of her arms again. As blood flowed hot into her limbs, Iphigenia immediately set to pawing at her face to snatch away the dry rotted fabric tied tight around her eyes.

She looked at the tattered remnants of the fabric, a bundle of pale orange bunched up in her hands. They'd blinded her with her own veil. She let it slide from her grasp and turned her gaze skyward. Instead of her father looming over her, she was greeted by a thick green canopy of trees with gray clouds breaking in through their gaps. A woman stared down at her, her bright eyes shining with concern but, strangely enough, brimming with triumph as well. Freckles painted her cheeks, and despite the lack of sunlight, a twinkling silver circlet sat upon her dark hair.

"This can't be real," Iphigenia rasped. She felt what little strength she'd gained slipping right back out of her. She lay here, alive, in the lap of a *goddess* — the very same one that had threatened her father.

"This is as real as real can be," Artemis murmured, and then there was a slender hand on Iphigenia's cheek. "Do you know who you are? Do you remember?"

She wished she didn't. Iphigenia wanted to scream, to pull away. Something terrifying lurked beneath the visage of the woman before her, no matter how gentle her words or soft her caresses. Still, it wasn't as if she had the strength to fully express her fear. Despite her somehow still drawing breath, she was exhausted. It took all her energy to even force out the few words she'd uttered, let alone to get up and flee. She settled for the one thing she could manage.

"How?" she asked.

"Let me show you.

The tender hand on her cheek moved over her eyes, encasing them back into that suffocating darkness. When she opened them again, she was floating; bodiless, as light as the open blue sky surrounding her. She looked down at where her hands should be, and saw nothing. An attempt at a flex of fingers yielding nothing — sensation had fled just as quickly as it had reappeared. Maybe this was death at last?

"Forgive me," and to what she assumed to be her right (it was hard to tell, considering her sudden lack of a physical form), hovered Artemis, as resplendent as she'd been that night in the woods. "The conjuring of sights is my twin's forte, not mine. Don't be afraid; your body is safe where you awoke."

It could hardly be called a reassurance. Iphigenia was sure she'd heave if she had the stomach to do so, but something far more dizzying than a lack of a body lay below the pair of them.

It was a vivid vision of a vivisection; rivulets of blood raced from pale flesh onto even paler marble. Even from here, the torn ligaments and tattered skin made a horrid sight. It was repulsive, and only became more so when Iphigenia realized just whose battered, broken body she was gazing down at.

There she lay on that hilltop altar, surrounded by hundreds of silent men. The wind howled as they gazed at her still form. An awful gash ran from her neck down her chest and into her abdomen. The gore piled at one man's feet, and she seethed. Agamemnon stared not at the corpse of his daughter, the one he'd lured to her own demise, but eastward.

Towards Troy, Iphigenia bitterly thought.

"Am I dead?" Iphigenia asked after a long silence.

"No. Far from it."

"I don't understand."

"Look," Artemis said, pointing down at the altar.

The girl's body seemed to flicker in the sunlight, her mangled body shifting between itself and that of a great doe. The deer's eyes were glassy with the film of death.

"I took you —" Artemis paused, like she was struggling to find the proper words. "I wasn't expecting you to be in that state. I was going to set you in the stars, but something in you still clung to life. I traded that doe's life for yours, and preserved you in its form. Those men will go believing they took your life there. Us gods, we can enchant the eyes to see only what we allow — whether it be in slumber or a waking dream."

Waking dream. Hazy memories of her own dreamlike state in a body that was not her own came unbidden to Iphigenia. *More like waking nightmare.* She scowled. "And who's to say that this isn't an enchantment itself? That you're just showing me illusions?"

"Not an illusion, but a memory. I will *never* lie to you," Artemis said. "It's the least I owe you."

Iphigenia bristled. She wanted to strike her, to lash out, to make her feel even a tenth of the pain she was feeling. Her life had been stolen in the name of this goddess, all for Agamemnon's ambition, but she was supposed to be satisfied with simple assurances of truthfulness?

The men were leaving the altar now, streaming towards the beach and the ships awaiting them in the channel. Only a few remained to clean up as the wind whipped at their hair and clothes. The funeral pyre was already ablaze, bright sparks jumping in the sunshine. Within Iphigenia, rage frothed like the foamy surf that the men were splashing into with abandon. How dare they?

Artemis seemed to sense her discomfort. "They'll say you went bravely to the altar, that you made the choice to die for your countrymen with dignity."

"They'll speak only lies. There was no choice," Iphigenia spat. She averted her eyes from the scene below. She couldn't bear to watch them heave the doe that looked like her onto the flames with all the other spent corpses, to watch as its flesh contributed to the black smoke already choking the air. To those men, she'd been just another sheep or goat to sacrifice in the name of war, in the name of glory in bloodshed. She wanted them dead — if only she could be the one to do it. A fantasy of tearing out their throats with her own teeth came unbidden.

The world changed. Another beach, another camp, but the sea had mirrored itself, and a towering citadel rose out of the distant plain. Tents once again littered the camp, but they were fewer and farther in between. Men lay moaning on makeshift pallets, grievous wounds bleeding out onto the sand. A smug satisfaction flooded into Iphigenia. *Good*, she thought. *Let them suffer.*

The sound of jeers redirected her attention, and Iphigenia felt her blood run cold. Her father was being teased by his men as he dragged a girl towards his tent, a girl that looked so similar to her that they could be twins.

"This is not a memory, but a vision across the sea," Artemis spoke, her voice solemn. Iphigenia watched in stunned silence as her father and the girl disappeared for a time. When they emerged, Agamemnon was readjusting his belt. He didn't bother sparing a glance to the bitterly sobbing girl next to him.

"*This* is what my blood has wrought?" Iphigenia shut her eyes, unable to watch as the girl collapsed at the feet of several women who looked as if they knew all too well what she'd just endured.

When she opened her eyes again, they had returned to the forest, the blue skies of Aulis replaced by leafy green. She was firmly back in her body; the aches and pains were evidence enough.

"I want to see my mother," she said, trying to prop herself up. "Show her to me."

"Calm down. The nectar has healed you far faster than even I could have imagined, but you're still weak. Do you have any idea how long you've lain here?"

"I don't care. I need to see her." The last she'd seen of her mother, she'd been knocked unconscious in the dirt. Iphigenia had to somehow get a message to her, one that let her mother know she yet lived.

"Watch yourself. I like you, Iphigenia, and I saved you for a reason, but do not forget who you're talking to."

Iphigenia slunk out of the goddess' lap and onto the forest floor. She hadn't forgotten. On the contrary, she recognized the goddess for who she truly was. Agamemnon may have committed the crime, but she'd been the arbiter of the punishment.

She struggled to her knees, wheezing with the exertion of it. It was as if she'd somehow aged a hundred years.

Artemis stood and placed a hand on her bare shoulder. "Calm down. Everything in its due time. You need to rest."

"I don't want—" and before she could say anything more, a bowl of that intoxicating liquid was being coaxed into her hands. Iphigenia couldn't help herself: she immediately set to drinking. The liquid felt like strength itself, warming all the aches, little and great, within her. When the bowl was finished, she felt her eyes growing heavy as if she'd just downed a *kylix* of rather potent wine. In front of her, Artemis stood with open arms. She glanced between the goddess and the ground and sighed, easing her way into the embrace. The two of them descended slowly to the grass; as they did so, Iphigenia was convinced she heard Artemis hum triumphantly.

A finger traced its way down her cheek, and though she longed to lean in to the comfort, Iphigenia tugged her head away. "Sleep. We will talk more when you're in a better state. You can trust me." As sleep overwhelmed Iphigenia's senses, her last thought was that she wasn't sure if she could even trust herself.

* * *

"This is my place," Artemis said, placing a hand on a crumbling stone pillar while looking up at it fondly. "It's one of my most sacred. My happiest days were spent right here."

Iphigenia ignored her, arms wrapped around her knees as she gazed into the fire. Her lips felt numb and her limbs buzzed as if she'd held them in one position for far too long. Yellow and red flames jumped, and though the heat's radiance felt like the rays of the sun, she'd never been more cold. Waking up not to Electra's familiar grumbling, but to the rustling of the creatures of the forest had been a shock, but not as great as the remembrance of just what had brought her to this place. It sickened her to think about longer than a few seconds, all the blood and gore and her mother and *Iset*, poor Iset ran through with a spear, never to see the light of her homeland again. Regret coursed through her at the way she'd treated her — and now she would never have the opportunity to properly apologize. How could she have *ever* atoned though?

She wracked her mind for memories of that time in between, when she'd sworn she'd heard Iset's voice, the only distinct one among the multitude. No matter how desperately she tried to hang onto those memories, they were disappearing as swiftly as the winter sun. The only thing that remained was an overwhelming lust for blood, for eradication. Is *that* what Iset would have wanted? Iphigenia snapped her head up as a terrible trembling struck up in her. She needed to ground herself, find something real to focus on.

When she'd first awoken, she hadn't had a chance to get a decent look at the clearing they were now in, but after her forced slumber, she realized that she had been here before. There was the carved stone of an altar, and just behind it, a rushing creek, its rocks worn smooth by the force of its current. Artemis had brought her to the very same place Agamemnon had confronted the goddess.

Artemis had built a fire and somehow procured the material to construct a small shelter. Fresh game roasted over the flames. She had even laid out a chiton smelling of sweet flowers and new grass next to her.

Iphigenia had hastily thrown it over her head as soon as she'd noticed it; the heat may have finally broken, and it wasn't particularly cold, but Iphigenia was loath to reveal any more of herself to the goddess than she had to. She'd noticed the way the other woman constantly sneaked peeks at her; it wasn't dissimilar from the way she herself had looked at the various serving girls throughout the palace. Amazement, maybe, sometimes jealousy, but there was always something else, lurking just beneath the surface. Iphigenia had blushed hot with shame as it dawned on her what she'd inflicted on those poor girls was her own clumsy desire.

Now it was Iphigenia's turn to stare as Artemis poked at the rabbits cooking on the spit. She couldn't figure her out. Artemis was the one who had basically ordered Agamemnon to kill her. Why had she let her live, and more importantly, why was she treating her with such tenderness?

Artemis must have noticed her staring. She gave Iphigenia a small smile and a wave. Iphigenia tore her eyes away. They weren't friends.

"Tell me what you want," Artemis said, drawing near. "Is the fire too hot? Are the clothes not to your liking?"

"I *need* my mother," she mumbled, drawing the rough blanket tighter around herself. This wasn't a silly sleepover like the ones she, Electra, and her cousin Hermione had had — she was this goddess' captive. "I need her, and Electra, and little Orestes too." She thought back to Mycenae's great walls, and the incredible hustle and bustle they contained. "I want the loom, and Iset's songs, and the chickens pecking in the dirt." She wanted the familiar routines, the daily flutter of the birds living in her wall, the constant tripping over her siblings underfoot, the daily lectures from Sitamun. She wanted her walks through the forests, and her chest of herbs and draughts, and above all she just wanted to be where she understood how the world worked. "When will you take me back to them?"

Artemis' smile had faltered, and she spoke a single word as if her mouth had been stuffed with reeds. "Can't."

Iphigenia had figured as much, but to hear it voiced so callously, as if it were a comment about the weather — it was too much. The tears came hot and fast. "I want to go home!" She began furiously wiping at her eyes, fighting against the ugly sobs that threatened to fill the grove. The goddess was not and would not be her savior. She forced herself to stand.

"Where are you going?" Artemis asked, eyes narrowing.

"Home," Iphigenia wheezed, heading towards the slope. Her body still ached, and her limbs were heavy with weakness, but damn it all if she weren't going to get out of here. Just up the ridge and down again, and she'd be at the road. They weren't far from Aulis. If she was lucky, the caravan may have even stopped by the riverside again for their return to Mycenae. There'd surely be no singing or dancing, not after what had happened, but the mass of people would be impossible to miss. "My mother, she needs me. I've served my purpose. Whatever quarrel you have with my father is resolved."

Artemis sidled up to her, a hand on her arm. "You can't leave, Iphigenia. Your home is with me now. That was the deal."

"I have to go," Iphigenia said, shrugging off the goddess' hand. "Father got his wind, you got your revenge, but mother—"

"Your mother wouldn't survive seeing you like this," Artemis interrupted, catching Iphigenia by her sleeve. "She would think you some evil shade, a trick sent to torment her, and she would perish where she stood."

Bullshit, Iphigenia thought. She wanted to argue that Clytemnestra was the strongest woman she'd ever met, that she could withstand anything, but she settled on trying to wrench her arm away. The goddess' grip was steadfast. "Please. Let me go."

"I can't let you go back there. Not now."

"Then when?" Iphigenia snapped. If she just made it to the top of the ridge, one shout would be enough to alert the guards...

"Iphigenia, just how long do you think you've been asleep?"

Iphigenia thought back to that hazy time, the mishmash of images, the dreams she was quickly forgetting.

"I don't know, maybe a week?" That didn't account for the men already being at Troy. It would take them nearly a month to reach the opposite shores, even with the wind on their side. Even as horror began to strike at her heart, she couldn't resist inflecting her next words with heavy sarcasm. "Why don't you tell me, all knowing goddess, the reason I can't leave?"

Artemis sighed, dropping her arm at last.

"I heard your prayers, and I endeavored to save you from your fate — as other girls have been saved."

"And what does that mean?"

"You really are an agnostic, aren't you?" Artemis said, her eyebrow raised, before continuing. "I knew what your father intended to do at Troy, and I developed my plan from there. I told him that you were to be consecrated as a priestess in my temple and he refused. He said you were too good of a bargaining tool, a potential replacement for Helen, even. You *do* share a resemblance. Because of his refusal, I had the wind stopped. If you weren't going to be mine, I told him, then none would have you.

"I've already told you that I was going to set you in the stars. Your death would've been unfortunate, but it would have appeased both your wishes and the fates. I don't know why you didn't perish on that altar, but here we are, nearly ten years later. The world has moved on without you."

Ten *years?* "You've ruined me," Iphigenia wailed, dropping to the ground limply.

"I've saved you," Artemis replied, dropping into a low crouch next to her. "Why can't you see that?"

Iphigenia closed her eyes, but she couldn't stop the hot rush of vomit traveling up her esophagus and splashing onto the forest floor. Behind the darkness of her eyelids, the only thing she could see was her broken mother collapsed in the dust, a spear cutting a once vibrant life to ribbons, a father's frigid stare, and an even colder corpse.

XII

my ears hear nothing but sounds of winds roaring, and all is blackness

Time didn't feel real. Hours bled into days, and the leaves on the trees began to shake off their greenery for blazing orange. Iphigenia didn't know if she'd been there a week or a month; if it weren't for Artemis leaving the grove twice a day, once just prior to dawn and again at noon, she would have given up marking time entirely.

The nectar didn't help. That delicious drink Artemis had fed her became Iphigenia's sole reason for living. It allowed her to sleep, and with sleep came blissful numbness. Each time she opened her eyes, she begged for even the tiniest taste. Artemis would acquiesce, though she wore a grimace each time she allowed her to drink from her bowl.

Iphigenia didn't care. She was out of options — though strength had steadily returned to her body, it wasn't as if she could escape. She could conceive of no plan that would not result in her being skewered through the heart with an arrow. Every potential idea led to the same bloody fate. At least the nectar quieted her thoughts. One could not be devastated by fruitless hope if one felt nothing at all.

Even when she had the clarity of mind to do more than the drink and sleep, magic was too painful to practice.

"Iset, what would you have me do?" Iphigenia murmured, holding her head in her hands. A meager spread of foraged herbs sat in front of her. It was the best she could do; it wasn't like she could venture off into the forest proper without Artemis breathing down her neck, nor did she have Iset to procure some cardamom or coriander from the palace kitchens. A sudden pang of guilt struck her, and she scattered the herbs from her with an angry flourish of her arm. Here was Iset, *dead*, and still all she could think about was how she no longer had easy access to kitchen spices. Self-loathing barely began to describe it.

Artemis didn't bother her. She brought her fresh game and roasted nuts every day (that she barely picked at — something about venison made her stomach do flip flops), and occasionally asked how she was doing (it would be rude to respond "terrible", so Iphigenia rarely responded at all), but other than that, the goddess rarely ventured to the little corner of the grove that Iphigenia had staked out for herself. Instead, she sat atop the crumbling ruins nearest to the waterfall for a few hours each day, back turned to Iphigenia. She'd sit impossibly still until the sun rose to its highest point in the sky, then she'd spring up like a startled rabbit and dart off into the forest proper. The first few times this had happened, Iphigenia had been afraid. Was she just being abandoned in this place then? But Artemis always returned just as the sun was sinking below the trees. Iphigenia didn't ask where she'd been, and the goddess didn't seem to be willing to share either.

Everything changed the day Iphigenia awoke to a hand gently shaking her shoulder. She recoiled like she had been burned. Not since that first day had she allowed the goddess to place a hand on her. Artemis was standing above her, a dejected expression marring her otherwise ethereal features.

"You hate me," she said simply.

Iphigenia considered her next words carefully. No matter how much she wanted to snap that the goddess was entirely right on that one, the tales of mortals suffering tremendous punishments for disrespecting the gods loomed large in her mind. Niobe had taunted, and she had suffered for it — she'd somehow been a witness to that first hand. But Iphigenia had no children — what could be a worse punishment than the one she was already in?

"You've given me no reason to feel otherwise." There. That should be neutral enough.

There was a crinkle in the goddess' brow. "But I've tried so hard to make you comfortable?"

"How could I ever be comfortable when I'm your captive?"

"You're not my captive, I rescued you! What can I do to convince you of the truth?"

"Let me return home."

"That was never to be your destiny. I've consulted the fates, Iphigenia. It's not to be."

Fate. Iphigenia wanted to scoff. Fate had done nothing but bring destruction and suffering. A memory of Achilles that night at the beach came to her unbidden. His words to her, of his desire for a world without the burden of destiny, sparked an idea.

"Let me write my own destiny," Iphigenia said quickly, clamoring to her feet in what felt like the first time in weeks. "I want to fight."

"I'm not much for wrestling, but I think there may be a few wood nymphs—"

"In Troy. Send me into combat."

Iphigenia watched with a detached sort of glee as Artemis' expression collapsed into confusion. She'd finally cracked her.

"What? Why would you *ever* want to go to that massacre?"

"I hate them. My father's men deserve to die, and I want to help."

"You don't know what you're asking of me. War is violent, bloody, destructive of everything beautiful."

"I know *exactly* what that's like. Send me."

"You've never even held a real weapon."

"You have. Train me."

Artemis bit her lip. For a moment, it looked as if she were seriously considering Iphigenia's request.

Then: "No. I've seen the battlefield, and I've fought against the very men you seek to destroy. The weakest of them would eviscerate you."

"But I have magic—"

"Magic that you've barely begun to understand, let alone control. You're not ready."

"Why *can't* I control it?" Iphigenia kicked a log, unable to help the furious tears that rose to her eyes. She didn't want to admit it, but Artemis was right. Despite all her trying, she'd been unable to replicate summoning the entity she'd once communicated with or call forth the magic she'd almost produced when she was being sacrificed. "Can't you tell me anything?"

"That answer lies with the Fates alone. Please understand me. I don't want you to suffer any more than you must."

"How could I ever understand you?" Here was a deity, older than the rocks worn smooth by the swift running creek, asking her to understand her?

Artemis let out a short laugh, raising her arms above her head. "It wouldn't be wise to continue to test me, Iphigenia. Your fate was cemented that day in Aulis. It's forever out of my hands."

Iphigenia growled, the throaty noise surprising even herself. "Shut *up* about fate. I haven't forgotten how I got here, and just who orchestrated that. Fate has nothing to do with *choice*."

Artemis clamored to her feet, surging towards Iphigenia. Even though she stood almost a full head shorter than she, the goddess was still imposing. Would she strike her? Iphigenia found herself hoping she would. Then Artemis could finally drop the self-righteous act.

"I had to take what was owed to me, Iphigenia."

"Owed? Am I property now?" Tears of rage welled at the corners of Iphigenia's eyes, blurring her vision. "I prayed for so many years just so I wouldn't be treated like a piece of property, just another shining trinket in my father and inevitably my husband's household, and you say you saved me from that. Yet here you are, treating me the same?"

It was almost comical. If her cheeks weren't damp from hot tears, Iphigenia would laugh until her sides ripped.

Artemis stared at her, eyes wide and nostrils flared. Was it anger? Or fear? Iphigenia thought she was finally looking at her like the human being she was.

Artemis shook her head. "I'm...sorry. I can't give you what you want."

Then Artemis was embracing her. Iphigenia was about to push her back when she spoke. "I'm sorry," she repeated, and this time, there was a heaviness to her voice reminiscent of one half caught in a sob. "You have every right to hate me." Iphigenia couldn't help but pat the goddess' back awkwardly. The irony of her having to be the one to console was not lost on her. "I won't have your blood on my hands again. I can only offer you a place among my huntresses."

"How?" Iphigenia breathed, well aware of the warm breath against her neck. She couldn't help the pounding in her chest as the goddess whispered in her ear.

"I'll teach you to be wild."

* * *

It was as if dusk had struck at noon as Iphigenia walked up the slope Artemis had led her to. Trees towered skyward, their branches weighed down with leaves the deep emerald of late summer. Iphigenia winced every time a rock pushed painfully against the sole of her thin sandals. Still, she had to watch her footing; dead pine needles littered the forest floor, making for a very slippery trek. She tried to keep her balance by following a meandering goat path. Ahead of Iphigenia, Artemis paced. In her hand was a great silver bow glinting in the sunlight, as long as she was tall.

"Light on your feet now," the goddess said, her voice barely above a whisper. "They may be mine, but it is because of that these creatures retain their ferocity." Pride was clearly evident in her tone despite its softness.

Iphigenia nodded, mouth slightly open in wonder. Artemis had changed; gone was the almost self-flagellating attitude she had espoused back down in that clearing. Now, the goddess was all hard angles and calculating glances — there was no trace of that former gentleness, and Iphigenia found herself almost missing it. The huntress had emerged at last. Still, this deadly precision was preferable to the alternative. A single moment more of being analyzed and fussed over like a sickly infant and Iphigenia might've risked it all and hit the goddess.

"Here," Artemis said, striding over to a fallen cedar parallel to the path. It had been massive; its trunk stretched at least as long as the walls of Mycenae's *megaron* were tall. Its branches were still thick with green needles, and Iphigenia watched as Artemis dropped to her haunches and made her way amongst them. She turned her gaze up towards Iphigenia expectantly.

"Are you coming in, or are you going to scare off all the game?"

Frowning, Iphigenia tenderly picked her way into the tree, wincing when the needles pricked at her skin. This was ridiculous. She'd been dragged halfway up a mountain just to hide in a half dead tree? She fished out a large knife from the thin bag of hunting supplies she carried on her shoulder. She checked out her reflection; ultimately unchanged from those days at Mycenae, save for the deep dark circles beneath her eyes.

"Our prey won't be able to see us here, as long as you stay *still.*" There was a certain edge to Artemis' voice.

Rolling her eyes, Iphigenia slipped the knife against her belt. Was there no pleasing this woman?

"The art of the bow is sacred to me above all — more sacred even than the beasts of the earth and the daughters of men. There is beauty in it, Iphigenia. Choosing your target, tracing its every movement, and finally, being the arbiter of their ultimate destiny by virtue of your arrow's trajectory alone —" There was a rustle in the trees just across the path. Artemis' cheeks were flushed as she angled her bow. "It's the closest you'll ever get to the sublime."

A hare hopped into view, its beady eyes moving rapidly in all directions. The air hissed as Iphigenia blinked, and when she opened her eyes again, a silver feathered arrow had embedded itself straight through the creature's skull.

She turned to look at Artemis. The goddess' chest swelled as she inhaled deeply, a smile gracing her features for the first time that day.

"That's lunch. Now, together we'll take dinner."

"Together?" Iphigenia asked, and before she could protest, Artemis was bundling the bow and an arrow into her hands.

"Together. I promised you — I will teach you myself," Artemis said firmly.

Iphigenia knew her mouth was hanging open in astonishment, but she couldn't help it. The silvery wood of the bow was warm against her palms, and impossibly light. Here was a goddess' own weapon, in her decidedly very mortal hands. As far as she'd been aware, only the greatest heroes had ever been allowed to use the arms of the gods. She traced a finger along the bowstring; this portion was frigid, a stark contrast from the heat of the day and the wood it was bound to.

"I've never used a bow," she whispered, still fascinated with the weapon. "You trust me with this?"

"It would make no difference if you had used one a thousand times; this is *my* bow." Artemis placed a hand on Iphigenia's, and this time, Iphigenia did not shrug away. "The only ones able to successfully wield it are those in my favor, and among them, those who refuse to hesitate."

Before Iphigenia could question just exactly what Artemis' favor meant, the goddess was shushing her. "Listen."

There was a scraping noise ringing through the forest. Iphigenia looked up. Directly across from them, mere feet from the fallen hare, a stag was furiously rubbing its antlers against the trunk of a pine. They were red with slivers of gore, as if the creature was trying to slough away the evidence of a slaughter.

She hadn't even heard the deer approach. Artemis had drawn so close to her side that she could hear the rise and fall of every minute breath she took. Butterflies exploded in her stomach as a hand settled on her lower back. The goddess' words were warm in her ear as she whispered, "Let the bow guide you, and shoot true."

Iphigenia raised the bow, notching one of the silvery arrows. As she aimed, a queasiness rose in her throat. Despite the pang of kinship she felt for the creature, only one thought churned through her: what would happen if she missed? This creature was clearly deadly, a mere step below rabid. She hated to think of just how large the animal it had attacked would have had to be to produce that much carnage. It would make quick work of her if given the chance.

Her breath hitched. The stag snapped its head up, staring directly at her and Artemis' blind.

She let the arrow loose.

It struck, but the wound was nowhere near mortal. The deer gave a howl of pain before it twisted away, crashing through the undergrowth in its mad dash to flee. *No*, Iphigenia thought, throwing the bow to the ground. *I can't fail her now.*

"Come back!"

She could hear Artemis yelling, but it was in vain. Instead, she whipped out the blade she'd been playing with moments before. She had to finish the job.

The deer was losing blood fast. Red splatters were bright against the brown of the fallen pine needles. Tracking the creature should be a cinch. Her breath came in hard little spurts as she raced up the mountain.

The mouth of a cave came into view; the blood pooled at the entrance. *Excellent*, Iphigenia thought. *I have it cornered.*

Just as she took the first tentative step inside, she noticed two things. First, the deer had collapsed into a bloody mess on the cave floor. Second, and infinitely more important, a hulking mass of brown fur stood over it, pawing at its mangled corpse. The creature was impossibly large, standing on four legs. Iphigenia held her breath, praying the bear wouldn't notice as she took delicate steps backwards.

Then her balance failed her as her sandal slipped against the needle strewn ground. The bear turned, its eyes locking onto her as it gave a low growl before rearing back on its hind legs and roaring. It was all Iphigenia could do to scramble to her feet and run as it dropped back onto all fours and thundered towards her. She crashed through the underbrush as the bear effortlessly gained on her. The lessons Artemis had taught her about the creatures of the forest had slipped her mind, replaced by pure panic.

Hot breath was on her neck. She was going to die, and there would be no miraculous rescue this time, no god descending from the sky to scoop her from the arms of her would be murderer.

Then she was muttering in that strange language so unfamiliar to her ears, the same as that day on the altar. White hot dizzying pain assaulted her senses. The sound of howling voices rang in her head, rising and rising in volume until it was as if they waged battle inside of her own skull; she crashed to the ground with her hands over her ears, but no amount of trying to block out the noise could cease the clamor of clanging swords and desperate war cries.

It was a long time before she came back to reality. The forest was silent, save for her own ragged breaths. The first thing she noticed was the fact that she had *not* been ripped apart. The second, which was almost more distressing, was that the bear *had*. All around her was bright red gore — the creature's flesh had been sundered into chunks of sinew and pulp. If she didn't already know what it had been, she never could've narrowed it down to having been a bear. Iphigenia raised a trembling hand to her face. It came back painted in red that almost certainly wasn't hers. She tried to rise to her feet, but a great hot weight bound her to the ground.

And then, a strangled noise. Iphigenia looked over her shoulder, to see Artemis staring at her, body rigid and a hand against her mouth.

Neither of them spoke. The forest seemed to stretch between them as they held each other in a wordless stare. Iphigenia felt a chill at her knees, cutting through the heat on her back. She looked down to see that she'd collapsed onto the bank of a trickling stream. Rippling in the water was her reflection, and she leaned into get a closer look. The same face that had stared at her in the blade met her gaze, but as beads of red dripped into and distorted the image, she realized she had far more to contend with than dark circles. Shrouded on her shoulders was the stinking pelt of the bear, her head safely encased in its maw.

* * *

Iphigenia scrubbed furiously at her hair, but no matter how many times she dunked her head into the cool stream's water, the water refused to run away clean. As the little pink trails rushed away from her spot on the bank, she inspected her hands. Her nails were still caked with gore underneath and around their edges.

She wished the water was deep enough for her to disappear beneath. Instead, it was barely knee height. Across from her on the bank were her clothes, stained beyond repair, and the bear skin itself, strung up between two trees. From where she was standing, she could see the heavy damage that had been inflicted on the pelt. Score marks and slashes littered it, as if swords had been plunged deep. She shivered, but it had nothing to do with the chill of the stream.

Iphigenia got down to her knees, ignoring the way the rocks of the stream bed scraped against them, and plunged her face into the water and screamed. The beast could have killed her — *she* should be the one in pieces across the forest floor, not the bear. And yet, here she was, healthy and whole. That awful power, the one she'd felt when the spirit came, the stirrings of which she felt when she was being dragged to the altar before she was gagged — it had been what had saved her. But why couldn't she control it?

Something in the air behind her changed; someone was here. Iphigenia wrenched her head from the water, sucking in a breath so deep it made her chest ache. She'd been under for longer than she thought. When she saw the way Artemis was looking down at her with her arms crossed, she almost dived right back in.

"We need to talk. Now."

"Here? Like this?" Iphigenia's face reddened as she mirrored the goddess' pose to cover her chest.

"It's nothing I haven't seen before." Artemis kept her gaze locked on Iphigenia. "But I will wait for you. Be swift." She turned on her heel, stalking back towards camp just beyond the dense thicket of bushes and trees.

Iphigenia wanted to scream again, but her embarrassment at her nudity was overshadowed by unease at the expression Artemis had held during their brief conversation. The goddess' eyes had been streaked with red — she'd been crying. The thought of the goddess of the moon weeping like a common maiden made something in Iphigenia's chest ache.

Iphigenia rose out of the water, abandoning her efforts to clean her hair. She threw on the pale blue *chlamys* Artemis had left for her — the short garment would have to do until something better could be fashioned. It was breezy, but the day was steadily growing warmer as morning rolled into afternoon.

She came upon Artemis just off the narrow trail. She was seated on a fallen tree, body poised in the lotus position and eyes closed as if she were meditating. Iphigenia approached, and when the goddess did not look up, she gingerly took a seat on the same log a few spaces down. She was still dripping, and getting her wet would probably provoke Artemis' ire to a tipping point, judging by the deep breaths she was taking with balled fists.

"Do you have any idea of what you did on that mountain today, Iphigenia?" Artemis' voice was terse. Iphigenia knew she'd have to choose her next words carefully. For whatever reason, she held great favor with Artemis, but this was still an ancient and nigh primordial deity she was dealing with; at this point, Iphigenia knew better than anybody that Artemis would have no qualms about expressing her wrath.

"No," she replied softly.

Artemis' eyes remained closed. "Has it happened before?"

"The sensation? Yes. The bear—" at the mention of the bear, Artemis flinched, "no."

"A sensation? I see."

The flinch did not go unnoticed by Iphigenia, and guilt tugged at her. Despite being the goddess of the hunt, Artemis had made it very clear that she never wanted any of the creatures of the forest to suffer needlessly. She was positive that the bear's death had been anything but painless.

"Listen, I didn't mean for it to face any harm—"

"I think I understand why what happened at Aulis did not kill you. This magic that you speak of is more than a simple party trick. Something far older protected you, and is with you even now."

"What are you saying?" Iphigenia breathed.

"What happened today has almost certainly confirmed it for me; Iphigenia, the stirrings of divinity are within you."

Iphigenia felt a strike of adrenaline in her chest, but not surprise. The specter at the gorge, the blackouts, the dreams where she couldn't tell past from future and fiction from reality? All that dabbling in Egyptian magic had consequences, as Iset had warned her time and time again, and now they'd finally come to roost. At the same time however, she was confused. As far as she knew, both her parents were mortal — how on Earth could she be even *close* to divine?

"Explain," she whispered, thoughts racing.

"I would if I could," Artemis replied, "but it makes little sense to me. Do you remember just after I rescued you? What happened at that moment?"

Iphigenia looked away. Every time she thought back to the sacrifice, when harsh metal had plunged into her skin, cold terror flooded every part of her. What had happened afterward was a haze of pain and fogginess. All she could recall was the taste of something finer than the sweetest honeyed wine on her lips, and a soft embrace.

"I remember drinking that drink."

"I fed you ambrosia, a small amount, just enough to keep you alive through the trauma — I've done it a hundred times before with my other girls— but you were different. What was a normal medicinal dose resulted in your skin taking on a glow like none I'd ever seen before, and I had to wrench the cup away from you. You've been begging for it ever since — that's normal. What isn't normal is the fact you haven't burned your mind to ash from its effects."

Artemis came closer, placing one hand on Iphigenia's cheek and another on her waist, her touch akin to that of a lover. Iphigenia's eyebrows raised in shock.

"There's something strange about you, Iphigenia of Mycenae, stranger than I originally realized. You remind me of a woman I once knew..."

Iphigenia's heart raced. Artemis's hand, touching her — it was electric. And yet...

Niobe. *Broteas.* Images of the goddesses cruelty flashed in cruel juxtaposition with the tenderness she was expressing.

She pushed her hand down, gentle but firm. "That's not enough. I need answers."

"You will have them." Instantly, Artemis separated from her. Gone was the warmth in her gaze and the gentleness of her touch. Now, her movements were defined by a sort of cold detachment. Iphigenia was reminded of the attitude her mother would take on when arranging negotiations in her father's absence.

"Who was she, this woman that I remind you of?" It would be best to start simple. Bringing up the gory interactions the goddess had had with her family might not be for the best, considering how close she was to being allowed to go to Troy.

"I...made a mistake, once. I've realized today that I'm dangerously close to repeating that recklessness. I won't allow you to suffer the same fate."

The sharp screech of a bird broke the moment. Iphigenia looked up to see an eagle flying in a lazy circle overhead. Its sole visible eye seemed to peer down at her hungrily.

"And there's your evidence," Artemis said coldly, rising to her feet. She didn't bother extending a hand to help Iphigenia up as she glared at the sky. "You may not be ready for war, but your safety among my huntresses is guaranteed. It's time to go."

XIII

now rose the moon, full and argentine, while round stood the maidens, as at a shrine

The chariot landed with a jarring bounce. As far as Iphigenia was concerned, the harsh jolt against her spine was the best feeling in the world. Her teeth were clattering fiercely in her skull as she pulled at the damp chlamys clinging to her skin; the clouds had been as cold as they were wet. Her stomach roiled with queasiness; hurling over the side of the chariot was looking like a very attractive prospect at the moment. Soaring in the sky was strictly for the birds, she decided.

"I don't see how you do it," she murmured, giving the goddess at the reins a sidelong glance. Artemis was beaming, dark hair windswept over her face. There was a rosiness to her cheeks that hadn't been present during their time in the grove, and Iphigenia swore that the woman in front of her had been laughing the whole way, inaudible over the roar of the wind.

Artemis flashed her a radiant smile. "One only has to look over the edge to understand. Arcadia is beautiful this time of year."

She's beautiful, Iphigenia briefly thought before mentally kicking herself. This woman was her captor, and above that, an actual goddess, not some object to idolize. That didn't even take Iset into account. Guilt bled anew from within her as she descended from the chariot onto firm ground. She'd treated Iset as less than her equal, denied her full autonomy, used her, and even kissed her against her will. After all she'd done, her friend had still stood by her, and what had it gotten her but a severed throat? So no, she had no right to indulge in the same ruinous desires that had led her to disrespecting her only friend so badly.

If Artemis noticed Iphigenia's mood suddenly souring even further, she didn't comment on it. Instead, she gestured ahead.

They had landed in a wildflower meadow. Despite the overcast sky above, bright violets and yellow daisies danced in vivid hues. A few olive trees sprouted up from the sea of flowers. Just beyond the thickest copse of flowers rose a hill, and Iphigenia could see tendrils of smoke curling in the air.

"Ah, it's more conspicuous than I would have chosen, but at least the air is sweet," Artemis said as she gave the deer at the head of the pack pulling the chariot a firm pat on the rump. The deer dipped its head in a pantomime of a bow before leading its brethren back into the sky with a leap.

Before Iphigenia knew it, the goddess was halfway up the hill. She fumbled to catch up, still half paying attention to the chariot's flight. Guilt was rapidly being replaced by trepidation as they walked. Who stood at the top of that hill? She thought of the images of the huntresses carved onto the temple back home, one's she'd never paid much attention to. Were they already up there, throwing their heads back and singing boldly to the sky? Images of twirling nude women danced in her mind. The idea of joining a group like that — one where she'd be expected to shed her clothes in front of *her* — had her picking at her hands in anxiety.

When they crested the hill, she was surprised to find her fantasies were just that. Instead of a cohort of nimble young maidens, a gang of gruff looking girls was loosely gathered amongst a collection of tents. They were far from what Iphigenia had imagined; yes, they were still very obviously somewhere around her age, but instead of out-right nudity, they were clothed in an assortment of animal pelts and rough spun tunics. Instead of supple limbs, their arms were well toned, muscular even — she could sense the strength in them as one of the girls swung an axe against a stump. A pair of women were up to their elbows in gore as they gutted a freshly slain deer, while another couple were busy stringing up a skinned boar over the fire. The ones who weren't actively working were clearly engaging in leisure; instead of hymnals, bawdy songs coasted across the air while a particularly rowdy group had set to holding a wrestling match on the grass. Several of them were passing around a heavy looking amphora, each taking long draughts out of it.

Iphigenia stood stock still. These women were the retinue of huntresses praised in temples the world over? Could they even be considered women?

"If you think they're bad, you should see the maenads," Artemis said, taking Iphigenia by the arm and moving forward.

Iphigenia didn't even have time to ask just what a maenad was before she was thrust into full view of the women gathered there. The chatter and singing died down the instant the women saw who had stepped into their throng. The drink was quickly stashed away as the women sheepishly stood in greeting.

One by one, the women paused in their activities to face Artemis, and Iphigenia felt their eyes scrutinizing her by association. As they'd boarded the chariot, Artemis had said she'd informed them of her im-pending arrival, but she hadn't said anything about how the huntresses actually felt about it. Then the murmurs began.

"This is her?"

"She seems a bit scrawny."

"How long has she been asleep again? Because we get up before dawn — you know we don't do wake up calls."

"If you would all please calm down," Artemis interrupted, drag-ging Iphigenia in front of her. Iphigenia couldn't help the tremble as the goddess' fingers lightly gripped her shoulders. "This is Iphigenia, Princess of Mycenae and the newest addition to our band. She's already proven herself twice over. Treat her as you would treat each other."

The women were skeptical, looking at each other with raised eyebrows. Then Artemis flung her arms wide, a broad grin splashed across her face. "Why do you all look so glum? Let's celebrate both my return and our new addition. I can update you all on what goes on at Troy while we drink."

That worked. A roar rose up among the women and they crowded around Artemis, lifting the goddess onto their shoulders. Iphigenia struggled to keep her footing as she was jostled by the throng.

"Yeah!"

"A round all around!"

As the women carted Artemis off into the center of the campsite, Iphigenia found herself alone for the first time in weeks. Instead of relief, she felt more like a boat without an oar, left to float aimlessly on a windless sea.

* * *

Iphigenia pushed away the amphora offered to her. "No, thank you," she said softly. She was sandwiched uncomfortably between two strange girls on a log. The revelry had gone on into the night, the gray pallor of the sky having been replaced by dark mist.

"What? Too stuck up to try a little drink?"

Iphigenia said nothing, and the girl who'd been trying to get her to drink scoffed as she stood to leave. "I wouldn't want to sit with me, either," she murmured.

There's a snicker next to her, and Iphigenia looked up from her knees. The other girl is still there, a lopsided grin plastered across her face. She was probably around Iphigenia's age, if not a bit older. Dark eyes and skin and even darker hair all done up in intricate little braids shone against the brightness of the campfire. *She's pretty,* Iphigenia thought.

The girl laughed again, this one a full on guffaw.

"Did I say that aloud?"

"I'll let you figure that one out," the girl said. "Our lady sent word ahead about you. Said you'd be, ah, *unaccustomed* to our ways."

Iphigenia looked out again at the campsite. Two women were quickly draining large amphorae while surrounded by a cheering and increasingly inebriated crowd. "Aw, come on, Zoe, grow a pair of tits and *drink*," someone yelled as one of the women wobbled dangerously, amphora clutched tight. There was a roar of laughter as she stuck her head inside the large pot and heaved.

"You could say that," Iphigenia said, careful to keep her tone neutral.

The girl laughed again before clapping a hand on Iphigenia's shoulder.

She shrank back, but the girl just shrugged and removed her hand.

"No touching, got it. I'm Beroe."

"Beroe," Iphigenia repeated, feeling the name around in her mouth. The simplicity with which Beroe had retracted her touch had made her feel warm, almost trusting. Was it really that easy to respect someone's boundaries? She didn't know whether to thank Beroe or curse at her for making her feel even more ashamed of her earlier actions.

"They say you're a princess," Beroe continues, her mouth still curled in a grin. "That you're spoiled."

Spoiled. *More like spoiled goods*, Iphigenia thought.

"I'm no one and nothing."

"Then there's plenty of room to be my friend. Here." And instead of wine, Beroe was pressing a bit of dried meat and a water skin into Iphigenia's hands. When Iphigenia looked up at her quizzically, she just smiled that dazzling smile once again.

"Eat well, and don't let them get to your head, Princess of Nothing."

Iphigenia watched as Beroe joined the throng, and as she nibbled at the food she'd been gifted, she realized she hadn't even told the girl her name.

"Iphigenia!" She looked up. There was Artemis, hands on her hips and a flush on her cheeks. "Come — my huntresses want to meet the real you."

"The real me?" It was a funny question, one she herself didn't have the answer to. Girl or ghost? Witch or wraith, not worth the air she somehow breathed? Princess or pariah? Manipulator or victim?

"Yes," Artemis said, swaying slightly.

"Are you drunk?"

"Probably."

"Goddesses can get drunk?"

"If we couldn't, do you think Dionysus would be anywhere *near* as popular?"

"Who?"

"Never mind. Come." Artemis was walking away, towards the source of the most rambunctious noise. *Even her stumbling is elegant*, Iphigenia thought as she stood to follow.

As soon as Iphigenia stepped into their midst, the once wild party went silent. She felt eyes following her every motion as she gently lowered herself to sit by the fire. Artemis, for what it was worth, either didn't notice or just didn't care that her huntresses had suddenly lost all their previous mirth.

"Another drink, Crino," she said, waving her hand at a girl holding a massive amphora. The girl wordlessly passed the container to Artemis, who brought it to her lips happily. Meanwhile, Crino only had eyes for Iphigenia, it seemed.

"How are you alive?"

Those four little words were all it took to open the floodgates.

"Where have you been?"

"I heard you killed ten men."

"I heard fifteen!"

Iphigenia shrank back, even as the other women kept coming closer. She whipped her head around; Artemis was paying zero attention, her head almost entirely engulfed by the clay jar of wine.

"Help me," Iphigenia hissed, tugging at Artemis' chiton. She was shocked when her hand was swatted away.

"Help yourself." Artemis' voice was distorted by the echo of the amphora, but her words were unmistakable. "Huntresses hold their own. Unless you're not a huntress?"

The subtext was plain — if she was not fit to be a huntress, how could she even entertain the thought of fighting in Troy? She took a deep breath.

"I'm only alive because of the actions of my friend. She taught me everything, and I never appreciated it. I've never taken a life aside from hers — she lived and died for my sake, and that is how I stand here before you all." Iphigenia made no motions to wipe away the solitary tear sliding down her face. "Her name was Iset."

The campfire had gone eerily silent. Iphigenia didn't care. She'd said her piece; if they didn't like it, there was nothing stopping her from going back to drinking ambrosia day in and day out.

There was a warm presence at her shoulder. Beroe had taken hold of her elbow, pulling her to sit down.

"You don't have to talk if you don't want to. But if you do...we're here to listen."

The other huntresses nodded, settling down upon the ground in a half moon around her.

The tears fell in earnest now. "I — thank you. I guess I'll start from the beginning."

The tale came easy to her somehow. Iphigenia noticed that Artemis was conspicuously absent as she spilled her life story. Yet, surrounded by these women with concern in their eyes, she found herself uncaring.

XIV

a subtle fire races

Autumn froze into winter, and before she knew what had occurred, balmy spring had thawed both the frost from the trees and the ice from Iphigenia's heart. Life among the huntresses, as spartan as it may have been, had seemed to have cleared the fog that had settled in Iphigenia's mind since she had awoken in the lap of a goddess. Here, no one expected her to be perfectly polished from dawn to dusk, she never had to endure the pins and pricks of weaving, and certainly no one expected her to adorn herself with bridal veils, ruse or not. No, amongst Artemis' divine huntresses, Iphigenia could wear her hair as wild as she willed, spend every waking moment mapping the forest, and learn whatever skill she wished, gender a non-factor. It was Mycenae's foil in the truest sense; there, a woman had been restricted to the study of weaving, child rearing, and not much else. Free from those restrictions, acquisition of knowledge enamored her to her new comrades. Languages of far off peoples flowed from her tongue, she could filet a fish in under five minutes, and, at her own insistence, the other women had taught her the ways of battle with blades, bows, and playful grapples that had her bubbling forth with laughter even as they tossed her about like a child's doll.

Her body had changed with her mood. Many afternoons spent chopping wood resulted in callouses dotting her once smooth palms. The muscles in her arms and legs had grown toned with well earned muscle. Even her height, once barely three wine casks tall, had increased, something she'd once considered out of the realm of possibility.

The longing for ambrosia had ceased, replaced by magic's lure burning anew. She threw herself fully into studies of a different sort, using only what Iset had taught her and the sparse resources growing near their rotational campsites. By day, Iphigenia grew strong in body, and by night, with the light of the moon as her only instructor, she grew strong in witchcraft.

Though life had radically improved, confusion still plagued Iphigenia. How had she reduced that bear to little more than fleshy pulp? What had Artemis meant by stirrings of divinity? And why couldn't she be sated with things as they were? Considering what had awaited her on that altar, Iphigenia had nothing to complain about. She should be *happy*, not still questioning things that she was still unsure if she even wanted the answers to.

She frowned as giggles cut through her brooding. Looking up from her mortar, she spotted the source: a pair of huntresses cuddled up against a tree not ten paces from her. Iphigenia blushed furiously as she tried (and failed) not to stare. How could they be so *open* about such a thing?

"Hey, Iphigenia!" One of the girls, Crino, waved her over. Zoe, another huntress, lay with her head in her lap. They both grinned up at her as she set her pestle down with cautious resignation.

Memories of a long ago afternoon came unbidden, of a time when her own head was cradled atop a goddess' thighs. That goddess had been one and the same with the one who had saved her, nursed her back to health, and released her into this wild gang of unabashed girls. The very same goddess, who, moons and moons ago, had claimed the blood of the gods flowed through Iphigenia's own veins. And yet, she hadn't seen that goddess in weeks, let alone spoken to her. Iphigenia wanted nothing more than to show Artemis all the wondrous things she'd learned and done — perhaps they would be enough to convince her to train her, to make her worthy for combat at Troy. Iphigenia would even settle for a warm pat on the head at this point, no matter how patronizing it would be. Yet it was as if Artemis was smoke slipping between her fingers, dissipating every time she even got within earshot of her. Here in this divine sisterhood, she'd never felt more abandoned.

"I hope you're proud of me," Iphigenia whispered to herself as she glared down at the bowl of ground herbs in her hand.

"Uh, we're plenty proud of your little hangover cure, but are you coming over here or not?"

Iphigenia jerked her head up, flush staining her cheeks anew. She'd forgotten where she was. Sheepishly, she made her way to the tree, trying to look anywhere but the scene in front of her.

"What?"

"Sit, sit," Crino said, still grinning. "I want to tell you, not the whole forest."

Iphigenia gingerly sat on the ground, a *respectable* distance from the couple.

"How good are you at making slippery things?"

"What?" Iphigenia repeated. They'd lost her.

"Maybe the consistency of olive oil but without an olive press since, you know, we're kinda mobile?"

Scrunching her nose, Iphigenia considered the question. She certainly could make a little olive oil with just her mortar and pestle. "I can get started right now. How much do you need?"

Crino and Zoe looked from her to each other and back again. They then burst into raucous laughter.

"How much do you *think* we need?"

"I think," Iphigenia began, standing, "that the two of you are playing a very annoying joke."

"No," Zoe moaned, rolling out of Crino's lap. "We really do need your help."

"Then what's so funny about oil?"

Just as the two girls were descending into another fit of laughter, Beroe appeared from behind a tent.

"Oh, leave her alone, you two."

Iphigenia sidled up to the newcomer, ecstatic at last to see someone with an iota of common sense. She found herself gravitating towards the pretty girl in times of uncertainty, and that was true even now.

"Beroe, what are they going on about?"

"Do you really want to know?"

"If I didn't, I wouldn't have asked."

"It's a sex thing."

"*Oh.*"

Just as she was about to melt into the ground out of sheer embarrassment, there was a shout. Iphigenia looked to the sky to see Artemis' silver chariot descending in tight circles. She drew even closer to Beroe as the source of her primary grievance slipped slowly down from the clouds.

The goddess hadn't just made herself scarce to Iphigenia; the rest of the huntresses had seen very little of her as well. First, she'd claimed to have been spending time with the forest, unadulterated by the influence of humans. Iphigenia supposed that had been fair; the wilderness *was* the domain of the goddess of the hunt. That was before the excursions had begun. Artemis claimed that they were just flyovers to see how the war fared at Troy. However, what were overnight trips soon morphed into days, and before long, the days had stretched into weeks at time.

Each time Artemis returned, her irritability was that much more obvious. Gone were the days of dancing with everyone at their nightly revels, as she had done in the earliest days of Iphigenia's stay with the huntresses. No, instead the goddess now preferred to watch in sullen silence as the group of women twirled half heartedly. When one of the huntresses, a former Thracian named Hyale, asked why Artemis neglected to join them, the goddess had simply stood, taken her bow in hand, and declared that she was going for a nocturnal hunt, and none were to join her. For one who delighted in bringing as many girls as possible on her hunts, that had been the utmost oddity.

That had all been a month ago, and this was the first time the goddess had walked among them since. Her herd of deer grazed silently as she leapt down from her chariot.

"I have an announcement to make." Iphigenia's heart beat in double time as she laid eyes on the source of her frustrations. Artemis was decked in that curious attire that Iphigenia had come to realize was distinctly Trojan; when she bothered to return to the huntresses, Artemis would arrive from the warfront arrayed in the furs of animals unrecognizable, and this time was no different. Today was a departure from the norm, however; she also wore a tasseled headdress. Iphigenia scowled. Hadn't Artemis once told her, in the days before the bear, that crowns were the symbols of those in love with power for power's sake? The glittering gold swayed with her head as she tilted it towards the chariot.

A brief pause, and then out of the chariot rose a young man, a full head taller than the tallest among them. His sable hair was cropped short, save for disgustingly long, skinny braid at the base of his skull. His dress was similar to that of Artemis, save for the addition of a bronze breastplate. He kept his gaze locked towards his own feet, and Iphigenia watched the slight tremble in the way he held his bow between his palms. A heavy murmur erupted as several of the huntresses not so subtly reached for their weapons.

Artemis raised her hand. "Calm yourselves. This is Skymandrios, and he is here for training to be my champion amongst the Trojans."

There was a cough, and then Zoe stepped forward, her long tipped spear already in hand.

"Champion? Goddess, I mean no disrespect, but who is _he_ compared to any of us?"

"There is no argument to be had," Artemis responded. "Skymandrios is a guest, and he is to be treated as such."

"But—"

"I'm well aware of the obvious," Artemis said dryly. "He'll go nowhere alone; I think he'll be far too exhausted to even consider trying anything." There was a dark edge in Artemis' voice, and Skymandrios shuffled nervously in place. "You are all dismissed."

* * *

Over the next week, a dark pallor hung over the camp. There was heavy brooding amongst all the huntresses, and Skymandrios was the victim of many a glare as he sat apart from them at meal times. It didn't alleviate even when Skymandrios disappeared with Artemis into the forests before dawn could alight upon the rocky crags that they had camped upon, nor when he returned far after the moon had risen in the sky, limping and covered in the gore of various animals. Artemis, for what it was worth, always returned with nary a hair out of place, and often with a boar slung across her shoulders. But not even this peace offering could appease the ire of the huntresses, who took the offering in cold silence. Iphigenia was still apprehensive of the goddess; she had intimate knowledge of the misfortune she was capable of bringing upon those who disrespected her, but all Artemis had done was shake her head at her followers before murmuring to Skymandrios as they passed morsels of meat around the circle.

Iphigenia was not unaffected by the sudden intrusion into their midst. Her stomach dropped like a sack of rocks cast into the sea every time she saw Artemis disappear into the tree line with that boy trailing at her heels. *It should be me*, she thought as she bitterly scrubbed the laundry in the creek, not some nobody from that godsforsaken plain. She may be just a girl, but the goddess clearly saw her as more than such; otherwise, she wouldn't have rescued her from the pyre now, wouldn't she? Iphigenia would give nearly anything to be fighting on that field on behalf of the goddess against the men who'd used her very blood to get there. She deserved to be racing through the fields at the goddess' side, learning to loose arrows with the deadliest precision from one whose skill could only be compared to that of the sun god Apollo, her twin.

There was a cough as a weight settled next to her. She looked up, surprised to see Beroe; had she really been so deep in thought that she hadn't heard her approach?

Her eyes shone with a twinkling glow that Iphigenia had only seen on Artemis herself, and the girl's limbs were as graceful as they were long. Even her skin was unmarred, bronze and shining as brightly as her ebony hair tied up in intricate braids. All the other huntresses were varying forms of dirty, exposed as they were to the elements, but the filth of the ground never seemed to touch Beroe as she went about doing her daily duties. Even Artemis emerged from the woods covered in dirt and blood from time to time, but Beroe remained uncorrupted. Still, none of the other girls treated her any differently to themselves, and Iphigenia had committed to do so as well. While the others treated Iphigenia well, Beroe had been the only one of them to treat her as if she'd joined them as naturally as anyone else.

"How are you feeling?" Beroe asked in that sweet low voice of hers, placing a hand on Iphigenia's knee.

"How am I feeling?" Iphigenia felt a tingle up her spine at the contact, and she met Beroe's eyes shyly. The older girl was smiling gently.

"Everyone else is so angry, so I assumed you must be—"

"I'm not mad," Iphigenia quickly interrupted, shaking her head. Bitter, maybe, and lonely above all else, but anger? Anger to her was broken pottery and harsh words spat across empty halls, blackened eyes and bruised flesh. Skymandrios' presence may have been upsetting, but she was the furthest thing from angry.

"Oh?" Beroe's voice was soft, and Iphigenia could hear the smirk in it even if the girl's lips did not betray her. "The fact that she spends all the hours of her days with him and not *you* doesn't bother you?"

"I didn't say that," Iphigenia responded, feeling a strange sensation beginning in her chest.

"Then why do you brood so darkly, as if he'd snatched her out of your arms himself?"

"She was never in my arms, no matter how much I'd wanted her to be," Iphigenia spat, glowering at the fire. The flames flickered and jumped, striking pieces of white hot wood with each crackle.

"Aha, there it is," Beroe laughed, and Iphigenia whipped her head around to see the girl winking at her. "I see what your problem is now."

"I don't have a problem."

"You're *jealous* of him. You wish that were you she was teaching to string a bow, how to kill—"

"What do you care for?" Iphigenia snapped, beginning to grow cross. An interrogation on her feelings of all things was the last thing she wanted right now.

"Is it a crime to care for a friend?" Beroe laughed again, drawing closer. "You glare at the trees all day waiting for her to return and you stay up all night muttering to yourself."

Iphigenia looked up sharply. None of the huntresses, not even Beroe, were supposed to know the true extent of her magic. She hardly understood it herself; she didn't need to confuse the waters any further. As far as they knew, she was simply a talented healer who'd called upon the gods to rescue her.

"What have you seen?"

"Nothing but a woman who is setting herself up for a mental breakdown."

Iphigenia felt a rising ache in her temples. Beroe was sweet, but this was getting ridiculous.

Beroe turned from Iphigenia then, directing her attention to the water. "Artemis haunts you, doesn't she? You long to understand her, and she pushes you away, and so you return the favor to us huntresses in kind. We're worried about you, Iphigenia."

"The last person who worried about me got herself killed," Iphigenia snapped. "So don't."

Beroe voice was calm as she tossed a pebble into the stream. "If you really don't want any of us worrying about you, why don't you leave? No one's stopping you."

"I can't leave."

"Why?"

Iphigenia stood suddenly, kicking over the laundry basket. She couldn't find it in her to care that the linens had fallen right into the mud. "Isn't it obvious? It's because of *her*, because she's a goddess and I've been cursed to suffer for crimes I didn't even commit. Is that what you wanted to hear? Did the others put you up to this just to torment me?"

Beroe still sat with her hands folded as if Iphigenia had never had her outburst at all. "The exact opposite, actually. I like you, Iphigenia. We're not that different."

"What are you talking about?"

"I wasn't always a huntress," Beroe said, and she tilted her gaze skywards. The stars twinkled in and out of the sky as dark clouds floated across them. "I never would have imagined I could be my true self, let alone be around people who accepted me."

"Your true self?" Iphigenia sat back down. As pestering as the girl had been tonight, Iphigenia did have a certain fondness for the only one among the huntresses she could really call a friend. She didn't really want her to go.

"Have you ever felt, ah, *constricted*, by what someone else wants you to be and who you really are?"

She could discuss the role she'd been practically bred for, to be a broodmare and a bargaining tool, but the only thing that fell out Iphigenia's mouth was a pathetic mumble of "I think I was a deer for a little while."

There was no malice in Beroe's tinkling laughter.

"Shut up," Iphigenia pouted, lightly punching Beroe on her arm.

"I'll keep it brief. I wasn't who my parents wanted me to be. Of course, I looked the part, but I never felt like it, and I certainly didn't act it."

"Who did they want you to be?"

"Their son."

Suddenly, a lot of things about Beroe were beginning to make an incredible amount of sense.

"Everything was wrong about me, from the sound of my voice to the shape of my hands. I refused to look in mirrors. I wanted to weave with my mother but I was forced into the forge with my father. He hated me," she said with a wry grin on her face. "I was his only child, and I had turned out like *that*. Then the army came calling and he saw his out. I saw mine too. I wasn't joining the army, and I wasn't going to be their son any longer either." There was a heavy silence.

"That's awful...but how?"

Beroe brought both her hands to her neck, pantomiming the act of choking herself accompanied by full sound effects. Any other conversation, and Iphigenia might've laughed.

"There are no expectations dictating who the dead should be. I happened to see the goddess in the same pool I intended on drowning myself in. She was bathing; I'd heard the stories of what she'd done to men who'd gazed upon her. My job had been made that much easier."

"What did she do to you?" Iphigenia's throat was suddenly hoarse.

"She *made* me," Beroe responded, twisting two of her braids together as she smiled. "She saw me, said she knew who I truly was, and told me I was precious to her, and would be forevermore. Then she invited me into the water, and when I came up for air, I was changed. I was finally myself, with a new body, a new name, a new history. Most importantly, she gave me a new future."

"Why are you telling me this?" Iphigenia asked. Despite their friendship, this seemed like a deeply personal tale, not one you'd regale to someone you'd only known a matter of weeks. Beroe laughed again, taking Iphigenia's hand into her own. This time, Iphigenia did not let go.

"I'm telling you because despite everything, I'm happy, and you can be too."

"How could I ever pretend to be happy when she won't even look at me?"

"She pushes you away because she can't bear to lose you."

"How do you know?" Iphigenia asked, all annoyance cast aside. This was an insight into Artemis that she hadn't expected.

"Even goddesses need someone to confide in. Who do you think told me?"

That ever familiar sensation of guilt hit Iphigenia like a shield to the face. She ought to be happy. She had good food, better company, and a purpose. She had her life. Still, she couldn't escape the pain of *desire* — the desire for answers, for revenge, for silver eyes focused on her and her alone.

"Could I confide in you, then?"

"Always."

Iphigenia took a long, trembling breath. "I want her," and then the words were spilling out of her mouth unbidden, as fast as the stream trickling past them. "I want her as much as I hate her. She ruined me, and she continues to ruin me every day when all I want is for her to look at me like she used to."

"And what do you plan on doing about it?"

Iphigenia took a long hard look at Beroe. There was a subtle flush building up beneath the brown of her cheeks, despite the somewhat neutral smile the girl was wearing. She was playing coy, and Iphigenia knew she was being charmed, but suddenly her palms were sweaty and she was just so upset and Artemis hadn't spoken to her in *weeks*— Iphigenia kissed her.

It was different than it had been with Iset. Warm, welcoming, wanted. She could feel Beroe's lips against hers in that ever present smile, and before she could pull back, there was a hand on her cheek and one on her thigh.

"Is this what you want?" Beroe whispered against her mouth, and it took everything in Iphigenia to not nod like an overeager child offered a honeycomb to snack on.

"Yes, but I don't know how," Iphigenia replied, her heart thundering in her chest. She'd never done more than kiss, and even then, those had been chaste compared to the way Beroe ran her tongue across her bottom lip. She barely knew the theory behind laying with men; when it came to other women, she was clueless.

"I'll show you. Don't worry about anything, just feel."

"But the others—"

"*Aren't* thinking about us right now," Beroe said with an air of finality. Indeed, the sounds of the other huntresses grumbling about how Skymandrios used far too many of their arrows was ever present, but also distant— now that the fire was out, no one would be venturing to this lonely copse of trees.

"Iphigenia, if you don't want to, we don't have to," Beroe said, her expression gentle. "I don't want to pressure you—"

"I do want to," Iphigenia quickly said, her face flushed. "It's just—"

"You feel like it'd be betraying her."

Define betrayal, Iphigenia thought to herself ruefully. "Something like that."

"You know she's only training him, right? No more, no less?"

"I know, but..."

"It's no use pining endlessly, Iphigenia. Desire isn't a crime, and neither is expressing it. Let your heart guide you and live for yourself."

Iphigenia took a deep breath, and then placed her hand on Beroe' shoulder, plunging back in. Kissing the other girl was like swimming in the coolest of streams on summer's hottest day, and Iphigenia's mind had never been clearer. She knew what she wanted to do, regardless of the consequences. She would allow herself to feel, even if it were just for a few fleeting hours. She held Beroe, despite knowing that she might as well have been trying to hold water in her hands.

* * *

She was wandering, the obsidian path below her feet unforgiving in its frigidity. The ever-looming dark loomed at her back, and she fled from its caress, frightened. When it left her not, fear morphed into rage, and her rage became flame, and her flame struck a torch into brilliant light.

Light. Plunged into stiff flesh, unyielding sinew and bone. Overwhelming heat, fat black flies crawling over her skin, and more men than she'd ever seen in her life shouting, their eyes trained on she alone. She longed to call out to them, to reassure them, but her muscles wouldn't cooperate, her tongue wouldn't unlash—

Pressure, then pain, blooming at the back of her skull. If not for the heavy helm, her brains would be leaking down her back. This, finally, was what granted her the strength to turn.

There. A young man, hardly old enough to grace this plain, his arms trembling violently even as he notched his bow to strike again. No matter. This would be quick work.

She thundered toward the youth, unable to help the stretch of her mouth into a wild grin. He was running, the poor whelp, full on sprinting away. As she gained on him, she could hear his cries for mercy, his degrading little pleas. How pathetic, *she thought, aiming her spear. It arced through the sky like the holiest of eagles, blessed by Zeus on high.*

Her aim struck true. As her spear impaled the tender space between his shoulder blades, the boy dropped like a sack of grain. She jogged up to him eagerly.

Still the coward begged, though his voice was far weaker. She would fix that. The spear was warm from the sun as she drove it deeper into him, until flesh gave way to the dust of the ground. Roiling pleasure, so similar to that brought on by Beroe's touch, made her shiver even as the boy's voice faded and the crowd's raised in cheers. Then came the strike of another arrow against her breastplate and already she was turning, seeking her next target —

* * *

Iphigenia awoke with leaves in her hair, an unbearably dry throat, and the broadest smile she'd worn in weeks. Long after the moon had set, Beroe had left her with the world's chastest kiss and a wink, and as she'd settled off to sleep on her thin wool mat, the only emotion that had graced her mind was a deep sense of contentment that had followed her into the dawn. She'd slept soundly; she couldn't even remember if she'd dreamed or not.

What she'd shared with Beroe wasn't love, she was certain, but a sort of communion, a deep seated kinship made manifest. Why had this ever been denied to her? To anybody? What was wrong with that?

The sound of arguing cut through both Iphigenia's happy thoughts and the trees like an axe. She clamored to her feet and rushed through the camp to the central fire. Many of the huntresses had already gathered there, clutching each other. In the center of them stood Artemis, her normally calm features transformed by rage.

"Are you all happy now? Glad to have gotten what you wanted?"

"My lady, we—"

"I don't want to hear it, Evadne," Artemis snapped, and Iphigenia prayed that that rage would not be turned upon her for what she had done in the small hours of the morning. There was no rule against it — quite the contrary, judging by the near incessant flirting she witnessed amongst the others day in and day out — but her tryst with Beroe, while sublime in the moment, now felt like she'd transgressed over an unspoken line.

"I am championless — Skymandrios was slain yesterday. Despite my best efforts, that bastard Menelaus ran him through with a spear. Again, I ask you all, are you happy?"

At the mention of her uncle, Iphigenia twitched. So, he still lived. Unfortunate.

There was a hush among the crowd; Artemis glared at them all as she continued. "I chose Skymandrios not only for his hunting prowess, but because his death was always a possibility. This is *war*. I am loath to lose any of you. Not one of you respected my decision, not even those of you dearest to me." And to Iphigenia, it seemed the goddess was looking directly at her as she said this. She dipped her head, shame flooding her veins. "And because of this, I am leaving you for a time. My allies within Troy need me more than ever. You are free to move on to wherever the hunt is freshest. I will rejoin you when the time is right."

Protest erupted amongst the women, but was snuffed out as quickly as it had begun when Artemis raised her hand. "I will not hear your arguing. Perhaps if you had saved it the first time, had helped me train him rather than criticize, Skymandrios would still be fighting on my behalf today, and I would not have to go."

With those words, Artemis walked away from the camp towards the flat outcropping of rock that separated the cliffside from the sprawling valley below. There, her chariot awaited, its silvery stags clopping their hooves against the gray stone. While the rest of the huntresses grumbled and made to pack their things, Iphigenia broke off from them.

"Wait," she exclaimed. Artemis already had one leg inside the vehicle, and the deer were already turning eastward.

"What?" The goddess' voice was clipped, as if she were moments away from sniping Iphigenia with one of her arrows. Maybe she was, Iphigenia thought briefly, judging by the way those piercing silver eyes had narrowed.

Now that she was before her, the words dried up in Iphigenia's throat. Visions of the night before flashed through her mind as she sought the right thing to say.

"I just want to— I…" her voice trailed off. Guilt mingled with shame; she had been jealous of the attention Artemis had been lavishing on the boy, but she had never wanted him to die, had she?

"We'll talk when I return," Artemis said tersely. Iphigenia was about to turn away, dejected, when the memories of Beroe' words struck her. Why shouldn't she ask for what she wanted?

"You're in need of a champion."

"I'm in need of *loyalty*, something I seem to be severely lacking."

"Let me be your champion. I came to be with your huntresses; you've seen what I can do. Train me, properly, and I promise you, I'll bring you glory at Troy." Iphigenia thought of the bear she'd torn apart. "One hundred Greek men, slain by my hand."

"I told you—"—

"And I'm telling *you*," Iphigenia interrupted, forcing her way onto the chariot. "I want to go to Troy. I've seen what the Greeks have wrought, endured it even, and I'm not impressed."

"Iphigenia, you don't know what you're asking."

"But I do," she replied, stepping close enough that Artemis would have nowhere to flee. Beroe' words came to mind yet again. *Live for yourself.* "The world is changing, being remade right before our eyes. I want to make sure it becomes a place where what happened to me, what happens to girls everywhere, never happens again. I'm willing to kill for that world."

"And your life, Iphigenia?"

"My life is mine to lose. No one else's."

Artemis was silent.

"One last test," she murmured. "If you pass, I'll let you go to Troy with my full blessing."

"Of course," Iphigenia said through gritted teeth. "What trial must you make me suffer now?"

"Conquer that which has never been conquered." Before Iphigenia could even ask what that meant, Artemis had shoved past her to fiddle with the reins. "We leave immediately."

The chariot rose jerkily, and Iphigenia struggled to hold her footing as her stomach lurched. Gone were the smooth movements that had defined the first ride she'd taken in this vehicle; Artemis' knuckles were pale as she pulled tight the thin cords binding her to the deer. As they rose into the sky, and the camp of the huntresses shrank further from sight, Iphigenia couldn't shake the notion that this would be the last time her eyes fell upon it. She shook the sudden wave of sadness from her shoulders. She'd spent a year with them, growing and learning. It was time to stand on her own.

She'd come of age through blood once already. This time, it wouldn't be her own.

XV

and all my body is seized with trembling

"You'll need to watch your back at all times, but more than that, watch its teeth. They call it *androphagos*," Artemis said, pushing the low hanging branches aside as she made her way down the path. "Lucky for us, however, we're women."

Iphigenia didn't laugh. She was armed with only a bow, a rather large stick she'd picked up along the way, and a couple of poisons that she barely understood herself. *Androphagos.* Woman or not, she didn't like her odds against something called a man-eater. Her heart thundered in her ears as she and the goddess began to descend, the dirt path growing wilder the further they went. Eventually, it totally disappeared, and they were blindly hacking their way through the underbrush.

"How do you know we're going the right way?" Iphigenia asked, pausing to lean against a tree. Artemis stopped as well, raising an eyebrow before deadpanning "Are you seriously asking the Goddess of the Hunt how she knows where a beast is?"

"It was just a question," Iphigenia said, turning away. "You don't have to be so snarky."

Artemis gave her a cool glare. "And you don't have to be so cheeky. Remember who you're dealing with, mortal." She began hacking away again, and to Iphigenia, it looked as if she were doing so a bit more violently than before. She rolled a few choice words around in her mouth before deciding to save them, opting instead to follow in strained silence.

Eventually, the rocks grew mossy and the sound of running water arose. Artemis motioned for Iphigenia to keep silent as they emerged from the forest into a clearing. The trees had thinned, and in their place was a babbling creek bordered on each side by a mossy bank. The sky above, finally revealed, was striking, fluffy clouds awash in the pink flush of early evening, coated in a golden haze. What drew Iphigenia's immediate attention was not the simple beauty of the brook, nor the explosion of color above, but the gaping maw directly across from them. Looking almost as if it had been scooped out of the hillside opposite the creek stood a cave entrance, pitch black. When Iphigenia took a step forward to see better, she almost took it right back. Scattered all around the bushes just outside of it were little piles of neatly arranged bones, bleached by the sun.

"Are those..." she hesitantly whispered, clutching at her stick a little more firmly.

Artemis nodded solemnly, before sloshing across the water. When she reached the other side and saw that Iphigenia had not followed, she motioned her over.

Iphigenia shook her head, eyes still locked on the bones. She recognized the delicate wing of a bird, the spine of a deer, but a jaw bone stood out most of all, very human looking teeth still attached.

She didn't realize she'd been trembling until she found her arm in Artemis' grip as she dragged her across the creek. Water splashed up onto her bare legs, and the cold shock of it brought her back to reality, and she wrenched her arm away.

"Maybe we should turn back," Iphigenia said, looking back across the water from where they'd come.

"You expect to fight at Troy, but can't handle this?" Artemis seethed, voice low.

"Do you not see those?" Iphigenia said, jerking a thumb at the cave entrance. Anger joined fear in the pit of her stomach. "You might be immortal, but I'm not!"

Artemis wheeled around, and the force with which she shoved Iphigenia against a tree had the latter gasping for breath. "Damn straight you're not immortal. That's exactly why I didn't want you to come. You're just a silly little privileged brat who thinks she knows what she's doing. You don't belong here, and you certainly don't belong on the battlefield. You're right. Let's go back."

Pressed against her as she was, Iphigenia could see her own face reflected in the goddess' scowling eyes. The pathetic, almost fearful expression on her own face made something in Iphigenia snap. Suddenly, the scattered piles of bones meant nothing to her.

"No," Iphigenia growled. Feeling brave, she grasped Artemis' hand, removing it from her shoulder. "I'm more than just some pretty trinket. I'll kill it, and then I'm going to Troy."

Artemis glanced at their joined hands. "Your funeral," she said, and if Iphigenia wasn't paying attention, she might not have noticed the near imperceptible tremble in the goddess' voice.

And with that, Artemis stalked off towards the cave. Iphigenia took a deep breath. If she could've gotten away with it, she would've gone back to the creek and picked out a nice smooth rock to hurl at the back of Artemis' head. She was sure Artemis wouldn't hesitate to have her torn apart by wild dogs or something equally heinous though, and so she begrudgingly set off after the goddess.

When she'd caught up, Artemis was slipping her sandals off and abandoning them next to one of the piles. She gestured for Iphigenia to do the same, putting a finger to her lips before pointing at her shoes. Iphigenia shrugged before kicking off her own leather sandals and following Artemis into the cave.

As soon as she entered the cave, darkness washed over her. It was as if the sun outside had been swallowed up. The dank scent of decay was thick here, and Iphigenia suddenly found herself wishing for her long ago discarded veil, just as some sort of barrier against the stench.

"Torch," Artemis muttered, and Iphigenia fumbled for the firestarter in her chiton pocket before placing the small flame against her stick. Scarlet embers crackled into life before the top was engulfed in a flame, illuminating the two women as they moved deeper into the cave.

It was a large chamber, much larger than the outside suggested. The ceiling stretched above them, and though their shadows jumped, they did not quite stretch so far as to allow them to see the top. Stalagmites jutted up from the pale stone floor like teeth, and the walls dripped with moisture. Iphigenia could not help but feel that they'd waded into the jaws of the beast itself.

The chamber branched into several different tunnels, some large enough for a giant to stroll through and others so small that Iphigenia would have to crawl on hands and knees to enter them. Artemis hummed for a moment before moving confidently towards one of the larger tunnels.

"This way," she whispered, not turning back. "Have a weapon ready, and I'll tell you when to deal the blow." Iphigenia followed, staying close as Artemis unsheathed her bow from its holster on her back.

The tunnel was still large, but definitely a step down from the main room. It stretched off into the darkness, and Iphigenia clung close to Artemis, bearing the torch high above both their heads. The sound of their bare feet slapping against the damp floor seemed to Iphigenia to be as loud as the crack of thunder, and she found herself taking much smaller footfalls. Artemis paid no heed, striding at a steady pace further into the tunnel. Iphigenia felt another wave of annoyance rush up her throat.

And then, the tunnel ended abruptly. They were in another chamber now, and this one made the tiny hairs on the back of Iphigenia's neck stand at full attention. She looked around wildly — then she saw it.

In the corner of the room, curled up tight, was a massive serpent.

The firelight glinted off its thick scales, and its trunk was as large as a chariot. A set of scarlet horns formed an awful crown atop its head.

Its eyes were thankfully shut as its length rhythmically expanded and contracted. From its mouth, which was just a thin slit, emanated the same rumbles she and Artemis had heard outside. It was terrifying even in obvious slumber. The thought of what it could do when awake made her knees falter so badly that she began to wobble. Then Artemis' hands were on her shoulders, steadying her as she whispered in her ear.

"All you have to do is stab it, right there through its head." She extended an arm towards the creature's diamond shaped head. "I'll be here, just in case." The goddess' bow glinted in the firelight.

Iphigenia took a breath and stepped forward. She could do this. It was just sleeping; heroes before her had tackled much stronger beasts at half her age without the assistance of a deity. She should consider herself lucky.

As she stepped into the serpent's nest of forest debris and what she hoped were the discarded bones of deer and not anything else, dagger poised, her eye was captured by a glint of white. A fang hung free from the mouth of the serpent, and from that fang dripped a steady stream of dark liquid. She thought back to her studies with Iset, and how the venom of live snakes was used in healing the wounds of their victims. Iset herself always carried a vial around her neck; the only reason she hadn't had any the day she died was because she'd used the last of her store in a botched attempt to save Timycha's life. If Iphigenia herself had carried some back on that awful day, Iset may have lived. Such an elixir from a beast of this caliber could prove invaluable...

Instead of driving her blade into the serpent, Iphigenia found herself exchanging her blade for her water skin, close to empty. She drained it, and then quietly sank to her knees in front of the creature, suddenly brave. She dared not turn around, for Artemis had to be pulling her hair out at this point. She held the container just below the fang, careful not to come into contact. Iphigenia felt a wry smile cross her lips as the skin began to fill with the curiously warm liquid.

And then, there was a presence at her side and she was being jerked up and away. She glared at Artemis, who was staring just as hard at her, nostrils flaring. Iphigenia shook her head and made to lean down again. Artemis then snatched the skin out of her hand, replacing it with the dagger. Iphigenia made to lunge for the container, but before she knew what was happening, she found herself slipping from the sudden movement combined with the slickness of the stone beneath her. The torch flew into the air and she hit the ground with a crash.

A moment's pause, and then a sickening hiss. Hot breath washed over her. The beast was awake, and its ruby red eyes were looking down right at her.

The dagger in her hand felt feeble as she raised it to defend herself, no matter how vainly it would be, but then she was being dragged to her feet and pulled away by Artemis. She'd be angry at this newest instance of the near constant dragging if it weren't for the leviathan lunging its lethal head at her.

They were running now, through the closest tunnel. Iphigenia cast a quick glance over her shoulder, and dread struck her heart when she saw that the creature was not slithering on its belly like she expected, but was instead moving incredibly fast towards them on multiple legs as if it were some sort of hellish centipede. She turned her head then and pumped her legs faster.

Luckily, Artemis had snatched up the torch, as the tunnel twisted and turned in such a way that without light, they would have slammed into one of its walls long before. It didn't help that it was not the one they'd come down.

The beast was gaining on them, and Iphigenia couldn't help but whimper as she felt hot breath on her heels. She was going to die here like a coward. Artemis had been right. She had no business even entertaining the thought of going to Troy.

"Here," Artemis gasped. Iphigenia squinted ahead to see a narrow opening in the stone near the ground. It would be a gamble if they'd even fit.

Iphigenia was just about to reach it when something wet wrapped around her leg. She looked down to see a fleshy red tongue encircling her ankle. She shrieked as it slammed her to the ground. In a panic, she began wildly hacking at the appendage with her knife. Just as she cut it off and the beast gave a hellish scream, Artemis was tugging her through the opening. Rocks cut at her sides as the two of them forced their way through. The whole tunnel began to quake, and Iphigenia didn't know what was more terrifying — being crushed to death or eaten alive by the creature that had forced them inside.

Then they were through, and the only thing on the other side was solid rock. It was impossibly dark without the light of the torch, as if they'd crawled into the realm of Hades. The beast smashed against their narrow hiding place, desperation evident in its frantic assault. Its snarls were joined by the low rumble of a collapsing tunnel.

"Wait," Artemis breathed. As if her word had been a spell, there was a keening whine accompanied by the thumping of dozens of feet as the beast settled down..

They were without light and no recourse was to be had to create any. The chamber they'd wriggled into was impossibly small, not even wide enough to extend her arms in any direction. Iphigenia felt a cold prickle at the back of her neck. This was too much like that long ago day in the coffin, like those moments on the altar when even her sight had been robbed from her. Artemis shifted against her, and something within her broke. Tiny gasps became great heaving struggles for breath. She thrashed uselessly against the sharp walls, cutting herself in the process yet not feeling the pain.

In the dark, she was no longer a trojan war hopeful. She wasn't even Iphigenia, the girl who'd been sacrificed and yet lived. She'd been reduced to a little girl quaking with terror from that universal childhood fear.

"Iphigenia, it can't reach us. Why do you weep?"

"Not — not that," Iphigenia choked. Desperate to escape, she began to squeeze her way out of the same gap they'd come through. She'd take her chances with the *androphagos*.

"No," Artemis pulled her close, trapping Iphigenia against her. "Stay — help will come soon."

She fought the goddess' hold. When Artemis' arms held steadfast, she resorted to kicking and scratching. When that too failed, she brought out her teeth. She was feral in her blindness, desperate to escape. Not even the metallic taste of blood could deter her.

A swooning sensation in her abdomen, and there the magic was. It came easier now than it ever had — she simply had to reach for it and it was there, ready to be wielded.

"No," Artemis gasped, and then a pair of hands were on her face, squeezing gently. "You'll crush us."

I don't care, Iphigenia wanted to say, but all that came out was a whimper. The voices were back, but she could direct them this time. She would raise the dead, have them tear this place stone from stone, just for a bit of light. A shout bubbled forth; she only had to say the word.

Lips pressed against hers, soft and open. A torrent of emotion thundered through Iphigenia, shock chief among them.

The magic faltered, then dimmed.

As Artemis separated from her, Iphigenia whimpered, drained suddenly. "Why?"

"Look up."

Trembling, Iphigenia tracked her gaze heavenward. There, in the ceiling, a sliver of light broke through. The pale light of the moon shone onto them.

"Better?" Artemis whispered.

Shame flooded Iphigenia's senses. She'd almost destroyed them both. "I'm sorry," she murmured, unable to meet Artemis' eyes.

"Don't be. You've just opened the path to our rescue," Artemis said, patting herself down. "Got anything that'll burn?"

Iphigenia sheepishly reached into her pockets. She'd stuffed them with a few healing salves before they'd left the chariot, along with a packet of dried herbs that she could use to make more, just in case. The thin cloth she wrapped the herbs in was flammable, but the herbs themselves ought to catch effortlessly. She passed the fragrant packet to Artemis, who gave it a whiff before raising an eyebrow at her.

"It's all I've got," Iphigenia said, suddenly defensive. What was wrong with her herbs?

"Whatever works for you, I guess," Artemis wryly mumbled, a small smile tugging at the corner of her mouth. With a strike of flint against stone, the bundle burst into warm, glorious light.

Iphigenia frowned. She had a feeling that there was something she wasn't being informed about here, like she was about to be on the receiving end of a particularly cruel joke.

"Alright," Artemis murmured as smoke began to waft up towards the ceiling. Iphigenia couldn't help but notice the gash on the goddess' arm, dripping golden blood. "All we have to do now is wait. He should come soon."

Iphigenia wanted to ask who "he" was, but judging by Artemis' sour expression, it was probably a question best not ventured. She watched as the smoke filtered out of the natural chimney. Still, it was not enough to prevent the chamber from filling with hazy vapor. Iphigenia found its scent to be pleasant, filling her with nostalgia for the spiced bathwater she'd enjoyed back at Mycenae. It was almost nice enough to make her believe she was sinking into those steamy waters, not recovering from a panic attack in a cramped subterranean chamber.

Iphigenia, calmed by the brightness of the flame, felt comfortable enough to venture a question.

"Why did you kiss me?" Iphigenia whispered, as if she were afraid someone would hear her question. A rush of daring overtook her, and she sought the goddess' hand in the dim light.

Artemis flicked her gaze down to their now interlaced fingers before locking eyes with Iphigenia, her gaze intense.

"Because," she began, thumb stroking Iphigenia's knuckle. "I had to calm you."

"We both know there's more to it."

"You remind me so much of *her*—" at this, Artemis cleared her throat, as if something particularly harsh was trapped within. "But you're so much more than a memory. You live and breathe despite everything."

"What do you mean?" she asked, looking up at Artemis. The goddess' eyes had welled up with tears.

"I have to tell you something," Artemis said, cradling Iphigenia against her. Iphigenia stiffened, but relaxed into the hold soon enough. "And I should have told you long before I'd even considered summoning my father."

Iphigenia took Artemis' hand in hers. "I'm listening," she replied.

Artemis took a deep breath. "The woman you remind me of. She's dead. She died because of something that I did. A long time ago, when I was barely older than you are now, my huntresses and I roamed the forests of Arcadia. I loved them all, but there was one who I loved above all the others. Kallisto, for among them, she was the most beautiful. She was the most talented hunter of her city, and when she came to us, she proved herself to be the best of my huntresses. No one has come closer to me in skill since her. Every day, she was by my side as we wandered the mountains and valleys, and every night, she was by my side as well. That's where I made my greatest mistake. I've not lain with anyone since," Artemis said softly, eyes downcast. "I was greedy, and possessive, and on a whim made her promise on pain of death that she'd never lay with anyone else. She laughed at me, swearing it, but I never would have harmed a hair on her head.

"Sometimes, she went on solo hunts. You know I don't allow that, but Kallisto was different. She was special. It was one of those times when she was all alone that everything went wrong.

"Power craves power, and my father was and is insatiable. He attacked her. He knew about her and I, and he used my own image to trick her, make her think it was I who approached her. I suspect it wasn't difficult to pull off. The only one who loathes more than I the fact that I take after him is my step mother, but we'll get to her.

"For a long time after, Kallisto hid from me. She wouldn't eat or bathe with us, and at night she'd sleep on her own. I thought she needed space, to clear her head like she always said, but the distance was killing me. So I finally confronted her, in front of everyone. It was another one of those times when she wouldn't get in the bath, and I was so sick of it and why wouldn't she just *talk* to me? I let my anger get the best of me and so I pushed her. Her clothes slipped and I saw the evidence of what my father had done. Before I could say anything, she had taken off into the woods. That was the final time I saw her before it happened.

"I raged. I cried. I didn't understand what had truly occurred; instead, I was caught up in my own selfish feelings. By the time I got up the courage to go after her, not out of concern but anger," at this, Artemis' voice hitched, "it was too late. I found my step mother in a grove, her hands bloodied, and beneath her was a bear, fur matted with blood. I yelled and pulled my bow, and both Hera and the bear turned to face me. When I saw the bear's eyes, *her eyes*, my blood went cold. There was no coming back from that sort of transformation.

"I didn't want to shoot her. It was the absolute last thing I desired. Hera said it would be the merciful thing to do—" at this, Artemis scoffed, "I was yelling and then Hera was on top of me screaming in my ear and Kallisto was in pain and crying out and I just couldn't think— before I knew what was even going on, I'd fired. Iphigenia, she was *so* scared in those last few moments. I held her and I tried to comfort her the best I could, but she knew she was dying and she knew I'd done it. She was afraid of me." Artemis was openly weeping now, an unnerving sight on one normally so stoic. "It wasn't fast, and it wasn't poetic. It was the worst thing I've ever done, and I hate myself for it."

Iphigenia felt her own eyes prickling.

"I had almost forgotten she had been with child, and I thought about letting it die with her, but I couldn't do that to him. My brother was just as much of a victim of our father as I, and so I did the rotten work and brought him into the world. I buried her while her son wailed, and then I set her image into the sky. If she couldn't be free with me, at the very least she could be free among the stars. I owed it to her.

"I abandoned the boy with some of her relatives, and then I built a temple at her burial mound. They say it's mine," Artemis paused momentarily to roughly paw at her eyes, "but it was for her. Everything I've done since has been for her."

The two women sat in silence. Iphigenia mulled over Artemis' words, and thought back to what the goddess had said to her father.

"You saved me, because of her?"

"Not really. I had an ulterior motive. I heard your prayers, and I wanted to make you a priestess, like I would with any other girl who'd asked. If I could save you, prevent you from suffering a future you desperately didn't want, fantastic. That's why I ordered Agamemnon to sacrifice you after he denied me your priesshood. If Agamemnon refused, then this whole war would have been avoided. I should've known better. If it weren't for the wind, he would've given you up for some alliance, or treasure. He'd never let you live for yourself. Fathers never do."

Iphigenia gave a shaky breath as she placed a trembling hand on the goddess' cheek, thumbing away still falling tears.

"Iphigenia, I kissed you because you came back. You were transformed by a god's own hand, just as Kallisto was, and yet you came back. I knew from the moment you opened your eyes that I wanted you to live, to be by my side."

"Then why have you been avoiding me?"

"I realized something after the incident with the bear. When you'd looked at me, covered in gore, I realized that I'd placed you on too high a pedestal, expected too much out of you, was too possessive of you. I disregarded your trauma. Worse than that, I'd firmly placed a target on your back. Zeus would take you from me, just as he'd taken my Kallisto. I needed to distance myself from you, make him see that you weren't special to me. I threw myself into fighting at Troy, to both clear my heart and my conscience."

"Is that why you've allowed me to go?"

"Yes. If I loved you, I had to protect you. Gods love stealing from other gods; my father can't take from me someone who was never mine."

"You love me?"

"Yes."

"Then let me make this decision," Iphigenia whispered. The flame had long ago died, entrenching them in near blackness once again. "Lay with me."

"You don't mean that. It's just the silphium talking."

"Silphium?"

Iphigenia watched as Artemis gestured towards the smoky haze filling the chamber. "You mean to tell me you don't know what this is?"

"Of course I know what it is. I take it for headaches; it's a medicinal herb."

"And an aphrodisiac."

"Oh." Heat flooded Iphigenia's cheeks. Then, "It doesn't matter. I — I've known for a long time. I want this."

"What about what I want? I don't want you to die," Artemis croaked, arms wrapped around herself. "I can't— not again."

"I won't die," Iphigenia's throat was hoarse. "Whatever it takes, I'll live."

"He'll kill you. If I touch you, my father will kill you."

"Look at me," Iphigenia said, tilting Artemis' cheek up. Her heart thundered in her chest. Was she really doing this? She should stop, say never mind, wait for help and pretend none of this ever happened. It would be easy enough to give up on both Artemis and her dream, living out the rest of her days inconspicuously amongst the huntresses. Then her eyes met broken ones swimming in tears.

No. She was through with letting fathers traumatize their daughters.

She pressed a soft kiss to Artemis' lips, chaste enough that Artemis could pull away if she needed to. There was a pause; then, reciprocation. Iphigenia deepened the kiss; Artemis' mouth against hers felt like soaring in the chariot, sensational, like drinking from the source of the ambrosia of the gods. A pleasurable heat bloomed throughout her body. It was only when hot tears began to soak her face that she broke the kiss.

"Your father could kill me regardless if you touched me or not. Can't you see it's all about control?" She brought Artemis' palm to her breast, struggling to keep her own breathing under control. Their bodies were already tangled in the narrow space; it was as if they were Aphrodite and Ares ensnared in a net of gold — but there was no shame as they began to move against each other, no jeering audience. "What happened to Kallisto wasn't your fault, and I won't watch you continue to drown yourself in guilt. I'm not her, and I never will be, but if you love me like you loved her—"

"I'll *show* you like I showed her," Artemis interrupted, moving her hand in a way that made Iphigenia shudder darkly. "Promise me, you'll live?"

"I'll cut down every man at Troy just to get back to you."

"Good." Eager hands made swift work of her chiton. "Make the waves pink with their blood."

* * *

Afterwards, they leaned against each other in silence, each other's breaths the only sound filling the hollow cave. To Iphigenia, she felt like she was floating in the space between dreaming and wakefulness, never fully belonging to either one. If it weren't for the hand intertwined with hers, she might've thought she'd died and been sent to Elysium.

She reached a hand up, caressing the goddess' face. "What are you thinking of?" she asked softly. She knew the goddess wasn't really present, not in the way that she was. She knew as much by the way she had sobbed Kallisto's name instead of hers halfway through the act. Iphigenia hadn't corrected her.

"Everything," Artemis whispered. "Everything, and nothing at all. If he harms you, if you die here—"

"If I die here," Iphigenia interrupted, "then I die happy." She caught Artemis' lips in a tender kiss, despite the lie that had just fallen from her own. Without her achieving her singular goal, her soul would go beyond the Styx restless. "Just know that."

Artemis took a deep, shuddering breath, and to Iphigenia, it seemed as if the goddess were about to utter something incredibly profound, but before she could, the cave began to shake violently. Iphigenia felt Artemis nestle her close, covering her head with her arms, but just as suddenly as they had begun, the tremors ended. There was a pause, and then the ceiling split open with a resounding crack, revealing the pink blush of dawn in all its rosy glory.

Above them, a man's head topped with shining gold hair poked into view, his brows furrowed.

"Ah. I've finally found you; I almost didn't check this accursed place," the man said, his voice sweet as honey dripping fresh from the comb. Half his torso hung from the gap in the ceiling; with his fine features and well muscled chest, he looked like an upside down statue.

As the man dropped a rope down into the cave, Iphigenia was shocked to see that the goddess was positively beaming at the radiant newcomer. "This place," she began softly, throwing a brief glance to Iphigenia, "is far from cursed. These caves, and the grove above, are sacred to me now."

The man's handsome face lit up briefly, and Iphigenia thought he was close to laughing, if not for the way his hands shook as he hung from the ceiling. Heavy bags were evident under his eyes, and there was a coolness in his gaze as he let his vision pass over her briefly.

"I apologize for my lack of introduction; I am Apollo, lord of music and light, and highly esteemed twin sibling of the goddess standing between us." Iphigenia gave a small nod, suddenly shy. She was aware of the similarity he shared with his sister in their potential for lethal behavior.

Artemis took her brother's hand into hers. "While I'm pleased to see you rather than him, where is our father?"

"Sitting on his high throne, laughing at the slaughter. He dispatched me in his stead, said he'd deal with *you* later." He jutted a finger at Iphigenia.

"Deal with me?"

"He'll do no such thing," Artemis murmured darkly. "Now, what of this slaughter?"

"Sister, I don't have long. There is tragedy at Troy this morning. One of my temples was defiled with the blood of one as dear to me as she to you. I don't know if my Troilus was targeted for being too pretty, or too bold, but he's dead. He was ambushed, chased to my altar, forced to beg for his life, then caught up by his shining hair and murdered. He *mutilated* him," the god murmured darkly, "and he shall pay one hundred times tenfold for this slight."

"Who?"

"Achilles."

Iphigenia's breath hitched. Achilles? Sweet, gentle Achilles, who'd almost been stoned to death for her sake? Achilles, who'd burned so bright despite the threats hanging over him? She'd known he was a warrior, had even seen a bit of that fabled rage in action, but a child murderer? She could scarcely believe it.

"I'll kill him myself," Iphigenia murmured, and Artemis' head swiveled to look at her in shock. "What? He was to be my husband — it's only right that I take his life."

"You don't have the troops——"

"But I know who does," Apollo interrupted, taking Iphigenia's hand in his free one. Iphigenia was surprised to find that, despite his gentle image, the god's hands were impossibly rough, more callouses than skin. "She holds troops, training, and a battle skill fit to rival Ares himself. My sister will help you convince her to aid you."

"Then let us make haste." Artemis said. Iphigenia cast a nervous glance back towards the crack that was all that remained of the cave entrance.

"Do not worry about the dragon," Apollo said, his voice tight. "I played my lyre; it shall sleep, and by the time it awakens, we shall all be gone, and it shall be loyal to my sister alone."

"Ah, you were always the better at diplomacy among the two of us."

"And you the better at vengeance, which I hope you will lend me for this wrong."

Iphigenia felt Artemis press a kiss to her cheek. The shameless display of affection sent butterflies to her stomach anew. "I shall, in the form of my champion. She has offered to fight for me in Troy."

For a moment, Iphigenia's heart soared. It sank almost immediately when she remembered the deal. "But I didn't slay the dragon?"

"That was never the challenge — I told you, conquer the unconquerable." The goddess gestured towards herself.

Confused, Iphigenia looked to Apollo. His face was blank for a moment as he met her gaze and then his sister's. Then it exploded in a smile.

"She's right. You've conquered her *heart*."

XVI

innumerable drinking cups thou drainest

"As long as you promise to yield to the Amazons, they shall embrace you as one of their own."

"Do you think their queen will agree to help me, then?"

"I am not sure." Artemis cast her gaze beyond the clouds. "Penthesilea's mood is as mercurial as that of a new flame; whether she'll catch on or be entirely turned off is beyond my knowledge."

Rosy dawn crowned the sky above them as the girl and the goddess sailed through the morning air, hundreds of feet above the sea. They'd left as soon as Apollo had dragged them from that cave, barely making time to adjust their embarrassingly askew clothes. Apollo wanted his revenge to be delivered swiftly, and Iphigenia had agreed. Blood should be repaid in blood, and it shouldn't take ten years to draw it.

Iphigenia looked over the edge; she could no longer fear things so banal as heights or the dark. In the near distance, deep blue waves were giving way to seaside cliffs. She knew her time with the goddess was quickly coming to an end.

"There," Artemis shouted, flicking the reins. Iphigenia followed her line of sight to see a wide river emptying out into the sea. "Follow this river, and we'll be at their door."

"Drop me here!" Iphigenia yelled over the roar of the wind.

"Why?"

"Please!"

Artemis wheeled the chariot around until the stags were descending in tight little circles. Their hooves skidded wildly against the loose gravel of their landing site, but they held firm.

"Why here?" Artemis repeated, her expression one of befuddlement even as Iphigenia hefted her rucksack on and hopped from the chariot. "It will take only a moment for me to take you the rest of the way."

"I can walk," Iphigenia replied, patting one of the stags on the rump gratefully. Of all the animals she'd encountered during her stint as a huntress, these creatures had been her favorite.

Artemis gingerly picked her way out of the chariot. "It will take you half the day to reach even the outskirts of their lands."

"And so it shall."

"You don't even know where to go."

"'Follow the river, and I'll be at their door.' Your words, not mine."

"But..."

Iphigenia took Artemis' hand in hers. It boggled her mind to think how much had changed between them in the night prior for even that simple act to happen. "I have to do this on my own."

"I know." Artemis' tone was the most dejected Iphigenia had ever heard it, and her resolve almost broke. The gravity of the fact that she may never see the goddess again was crushing, especially in the light of what they had shared mere hours before.

"I'm sorry," Iphigenia said, bringing Artemis' hand to her lips. "I won't let you down."

The crash of the waves almost drowned out Artemis' reply, but as she drew her in for an embrace as fierce as it was brief, her murmured words had been unmistakable. *"Come back to me."*

* * *

As the pink dew of morning faded, the day grew sweltering. Iphigenia's chiton clung to her back with sweat as she marched along the thin river. It would be easy to blame the change in climate, to attribute the heat to the lack of trees growing out of the dusty ground, but Iphigenia knew in her heart that it was the work of Apollo. She hadn't been able to even gaze at the god as he saw them off, so luminous he had been with rage. She found herself thinking of Troilus, the boy who had been killed, and wondering — had anyone been as angry for her? She shook her head; they couldn't have been. If they had, Agamemnon would not still draw breath. That was okay though. She'd start with Achilles, and then she'd seek out the head general of the Greeks and perform the delicious work of avenging her own life.

She trekked through the blistering heat with only the slight breeze wafting off the river for comfort. Though she was journeying to the capital of the Amazons, her thoughts were not of how she'd coerce Penthesilea to her cause. That would be the easy thing. No, with every step she took, she thought of the shores of Troy. There, thousands of soldiers gorged themselves on blood and glory, all of whom had been present at her sacrifice and had done nothing to stop it. Her father, who took girls who like her for prizes and left them sobbing messes, was at the helm of the multitude. And Achilles, the only one of the Greeks who'd had a heart that dark day in Aulis, lay in wait, a child killer and a coward.

After a while, she abandoned the river to get a better view from one of the slopes just above its banks. The land here was a far cry from the emerald forests she'd roamed with the huntresses; it was rolling, rocky, and just familiar enough to the low mountains of Mycenae that she had to fight the urge to sob more than once. As she trampled wildflowers underfoot, she steeled her resolve. *This is good,* she thought, even as she crossed a spring so similar to the *Perseia* that she could hold back hot tears no longer. *Remember it, and remember why you fight.*

Rubbing at her eyes, Iphigenia crested the top of a hill, and though her vision was bleary, she saw at last her goal, spread out beneath her.

A peninsula dotted with low wooden buildings stood in stark relief against the river bounding it on three sides, forming what had to be the home of the Amazons. As she peered down at it, Iphigenia found that the settlement, while vast, was as crudely built as that of the Greeks at Aulis. Palisades of trees still green with foliage formed the walls, and the sentry towers seemed to sway with the wind. It was as if it had been thrown together in a matter of days, rather than being the capital of legend.

From her high vantage point, she could see a couple of guards milling about the sole entrance. Their heavy bronze armor gleamed bright in the afternoon sunlight. As she peered closer, Iphigenia fought the urge to whistle in wonder. Despite all her time amongst the huntresses, the sight of women wearing armor and wielding weapons was still breathtaking. She'd have to proceed cautiously; woman herself or not, these warriors would defend their lifestyle tooth and nail. This wasn't a world that took kindly to people like them. She was positive if she misstepped, if she gave any semblance of a threat, they'd tear her apart.

It was with these thoughts in mind that Iphigenia stepped forward, and promptly crashed to the ground as a heavy pressure knocked the wind out of her.

"Don't move!" The knee in her back drove itself deeper as a sultry voice barked at her in Anatolian, the language Beroe had once taught her painstakingly. The kiss of cold metal at her neck had Iphigenia eager to obey. She splayed her hands out against the hard packed dust.

"State your purpose."

"I seek an audience with the Queen of the Amazons."

"Do you, now?" There was a dry curiosity in her captor's voice. "You come alone?"

"Yes." The knee was *really* starting to hurt now.

The ground became blue sky as Iphigenia was flipped onto her back as if she were a bag of grain. Straddling her hips sat a woman in a golden breastplate and greaves. A scarlet plumed helm rested upon her head, obscuring her face entirely. The blade that had been positioned against Iphigenia's neck was now visible, and it looked just as deadly as it had felt.

"Who sent you?"

"The goddess Artemis," Iphigenia breathed, feeling intensely bare under the glare of this wild woman atop her. "She's sent me as her champion to curry favor with the Queen."

The woman on top of her seemed to consider her words carefully. Then she hummed, removing her helm to reveal a toothy grin and the brightest green eyes Iphigenia had ever seen. "It's your lucky day, little stranger. The Queen you seek has you in her grasp."

"Why can't I speak with you now?"

"Anything worth having is worth earning, little stranger. You'll have to get in line like everyone else."

Iphigenia grimaced and turned, poised to further argue her case, but the knife at her back prodded deeper, and so she resumed the brisk pace the Queen had established.

It didn't take long for the two of them to reach the bottom of the hill, where the wood of the palisades rose out of the ground like a dense forest.

"Your city is magnificent," Iphigenia murmured, just as she'd been taught as a child on royal visits to neighboring city-states. Currying favor with the Queen while she still could would be the best move.

A low chuckle emanated from behind her. "My city? Stranger, these are merely the barracks. Themyscira's true glory lies onward, up the river. Hopefully you'll live to see it."

"What?"

Before Iphigenia could get another word out, she was being ushered into the gate. There, two women as heavily armored as the Queen saluted in perfect unison.

"Hail, Queen Penthesilea!"

"Alcipe, Myrina, I bring you another for the tournament. She should serve as good fodder for the new recruits."

Tournament? *Fodder?* No, this was *not* how this was supposed to go at all.

"Wait!" Iphigenia shouted as Penthesilea began to walk away. The woman paused without turning, the slight tilt of her head the only indication that she was listening.

"Tell me how to win."

"Wouldn't that be cheating? I don't know about the goddess Artemis, but *my* favor doesn't lie with cheaters."

"But every soldier has training — I've had none. Please — tell me anything."

"You're nothing if not persistent," Penthesilea laughed as she turned to face Iphigenia. "Fine. Impress them."

"What?"

"If you want to impress a Queen, you have to impress her people. Good luck, little stranger" the Queen finished with a wink as she turned on one heel and exited the battlements.

* * *

Iphigenia was doomed. She'd be going back to Artemis in shame, if at all. All around her, women worked out in the glistening sun. Some split larger than life logs with massive axes, while others raced, bare-foot and swift as horses. Others still sent javelins flying in perfect arcs through the sky. Iphigenia, though she'd gained a respectable bit of muscle during her time with the huntresses, couldn't hold a candle to the athletic nature of these women.

"Can you at least tell me what the sport of the tournament is going to be?"

"We decide with a toss of the dice. I hope it's wrestling," one of the women holding her arm tight says.

"Myrina, it's *always* wrestling," the woman holding Iphigenia's other arm, Alcipe, says, rolling her eyes.

"And with good reason! Wrestling brings the most blood."

Iphigenia was *definitely* doomed. As she was shoved with a certain finality into the training grounds, she began to think of just what she'd say to Artemis to explain how what was supposed to have been a covert assignment ended in her ass getting resounded kicked in the full light of the sun.

Then she saw it, leaning against a water trough. A bow, already strung, and a gleaming quiver of arrows next to it. Iphigenia looked from right to left — no one was near, as if this deadly instrument was no more than a discarded cloak. No, all the other women in this section of the field were focused on either hand to hand sparring or swordplay.

Damn it all, this was a sign. That bow was *hers.*

As soon as her fingers curled around the finely carved horn of the grip, snickers erupted.

"Of course the newcomer wields the coward's weapon," a cruel voice chuckled. Iphigenia glared at the woman twirling a spear in front of her. She was tall, angular, and, judging by the sneer on her face, not particularly pleasant.

"What's it to you what weapon I use?" she spat. It was unbearably hot, and she'd just walked dozens of leagues only to be held at knifepoint. She was not in the mood for any more petty posturing from anyone.

"This tournament determines who gets to be the first member of the Queen's new elite guard," the spearwoman seethed. "The bow is for cowards who are too afraid to meet their opponent one on one. Worse yet," and the woman smacked her hand against her breast plate, "bows aren't compatible with these. Can't shoot a thing with a tit in the way. We don't need any foreign riffraff who thinks otherwise slipping through the cracks and endangering our queen."

Iphigenia rose to her full height, balling her fists as she did so. Riffraff? If only she knew.

"Ah, a fighter now, are you? Good. Let's do this the old fashioned way," the woman said, dropping both her spear and her stance.

"Thermodosa, stop it! They're about to roll the dice!" A young woman ran in between Iphigenia and her opponent, flashing an apologetic smile. "Hi. I'm Harmothoe."

Iphigenia ignored the girl and glared into Thermodosa's cold gray eyes. "You, me, and whatever challenge the dice say."

"You're on."

* * *

There was an unnatural hush on the dirt of the arena. A woman dressed in loose robes, a priestess most likely, stood on a low platform. She prayed loudly, beating at her breast as she did so. Next to her, young girls beat drums, and Iphigenia could not deny the excitement in the air. She felt it too as the prayers rose in both volume and fervor. The gods were invoked — a tickle ran up her spine at the mention of Artemis — and then the priestess mentioned something that had her white knuckling the bow.

"And we pray to you, deity of everything in between. Bless the dice as they transition from unknown to realized."

"The bow," Iphigenia whispered. She could hardly hear the women giggling around her. It was like the priestess had whispered directly into her ear, seeking an answer that only she could give. The compulsion to respond had almost buckled her knees, and so she had.

The dice were tossed into the air. To Iphigenia, it was as if they hovered there, turning with the minutest of movements. She willed them to drop. They hit the dust, rolling once, twice, and then settled with finality. Everyone was silent as the priestess approached, bending low to observe the ivory pair.

"Twelve!" the priestess called, and there was a collective groan.

"What does it mean?" Iphigenia breathed, even though she already knew the answer.

"It will be a contest of archery," Harmothoe murmured, but Iphigenia didn't look at her. No, her eyes were only for Thermodosa, who clutched her spear so tightly that an unmistakable crack of splintering wood cut through the air.

* * *

The litter bearers were silent as they carried Iphigenia. Iphigenia itched to leap out of the sumptuously lined litter, to carry herself on her own two feet. She'd begged them to allow her to walk, but the priestess insisted one so honored by Artemis should be carried, lest the goddess of the moon strike ruin upon all of them for being inhospitable. At least she didn't have to wear the laurels. Instead, she clenched the circlet of green in her hand. It would serve as proof to Penthesilea that she was the champion, and nothing more. Anything else would feel like gloating, and she didn't need any further animosity from the Amazons. She was here to ask for their assistance, after all.

The trip was brief, but beautiful nonetheless. They left the barracks quietly, with none of the fanfare that was painfully apparent normally occurred after a tournament. Iphigenia was carried along the river as its calm current meandered in the opposite direction. The foliage was lush; Iphigenia would have killed for that sort of shade during her trek to the camp. Then they rounded a corner and Themyscira came into view.

If the barracks had been comparable to Aulis, then Themyscira was the Amazon's shining answer to Mycenae. Strong walls surrounded a lush city; the river ran directly under them, splitting the city into two equally populated districts. Rich green vines fat with flowers hung from every surface. The buildings stood tall, their heights reaching three and even four stories. The city's temples too were massive, towering constructions of marble carved with skilled hands.

While gorgeous, the infrastructure of the city was not what had captured Iphigenia's interest from her high seat. It was Themyscira's people that enthralled her. Unaccompanied, doing business, selling wares — nothing out of the ordinary, save for the fact that they were all *women*. She watched in slack jawed awe as women threw dice in the street and bartered with butchers. The huntresses had been one thing, and the Amazon soldiers' camp another, but this was *civilization*. Why couldn't she have been born here? Why had she never even heard of such a place?

As they approached a walled compound that could only be the palace, Iphigenia had a singular thought — an army that could support this city comprised entirely of free women would have to undeniably be world class, and therefore strong enough to take on the Greeks.

They passed through the palace gates into an open air courtyard. Lanterns were just being lit by women in loose robes, who paid them no mind as they happily gossiped amongst each other. At last, the litter was set down before a nondescript archway, covered only by a beaded curtain. One of the bearers cleared her throat.

"Your majesty, the champion has arrived."

"She may enter," replied a familiar voice.

Iphigenia gave an awkward nod to the litter bearers, who, without acknowledging her, turned and left. Hopefully that would be the extent of any awkwardness tonight. She passed through the curtain.

Expecting an ornate display of sumptuous silks and gilded furniture, Iphigenia was surprised to find that the room was sparsely furnished. It was incredibly different from anything she'd known at Mycenae; no deeply dyed curtains or detailed curtains resided here. There was a blazing hearth, of course, but the only thing that betrayed any signs of royal habitation was the massive lion's pelt spread across the floor. A simple bed rested low to the ground. It was joined by the only other piece of furniture, a basic table behind which Penthesilea stood, her hands splayed against dozens of wide open scrolls. She was far more relaxed than Iphigenia had expected: dressed in only a loose sage colored robe, she looked more like a lord's wife getting ready for bed than a Queen expecting an audience.

"So, it's you," she said, briefly looking up. Her jovial attitude from the woods was still evident as she smiled at Iphigenia, despite the dark circles beneath her eyes. "I'm not surprised. I watched from the battlements; your performance truly impressed me. Only one blessed by the gods could shatter even the stone behind the target. The job is yours, if you want it, but I doubt you came here to be part of my entourage. Now, what is it that you wish for, stranger? I promise you, we have no gilded fleeces, nor do we possess any winged horses, but—"

"An army," Iphigenia said, striding to the table. "I need your army, Queen Penthesilea, and I need you at its helm."

Penthesilea was all business now, straightening her shoulders before sharply responding, "Why? What land do you wish to conquer?"

"Not conquer, but rid of invaders. Queen, I need you to ally with the Trojans."

Penthesilea slammed her scroll shut. "Absolutely not."

"But I'm entitled to any request."

"Not that one. Do you have any idea the lengths I've had to go to keep my people out of that conflict, stranger?"

"Why? Aren't you a warrior race? What more could you want?"

"We are not warriors for the sake of being warriors, young one. We fight because otherwise, if other nations had their way, we would be reduced to less than a memory. They would enslave us, and there is no worse shame for an Amazon. We only strike if attacked."

"The Greeks will make their way south after they're finished with Troy," Iphigenia hissed. "Strike now, while they're encumbered."

"What drives you to do such a thing, stranger? You'd battle your own countrymen?"

"How do you know they're my countrymen?"

"Your Anatolian is atrocious, flavored by olive oil and the sea."

Iphigenia's heart hammered in her chest. Shit. Was it that obvious she was Greek? "They've done me a great wrong."

"They've done a lot of people wrong, but that doesn't mean you up and start a war with them. You're but a child," Penthesilea sighed as she collapsed into the chair by her desk. She steepled her fingers together wearily. "A child who has never even hefted the weight of a sword in combat — and yes, I can tell. I don't fault you for asking, but you must know this. War brings destruction, poverty, starvation. When Amazons get involved? Total annihilation."

"Why?" Iphigenia asked, approaching the desk. Total annihilation sounded pretty agreeable to her.

"Do you know who my father is? Lord Ares, God of War, listens even now, begging me to take up arms for your cause. He alone knows the true extent of the desolation I can bring."

"Then why deny him? Help me — make your father proud."

Penthesilea gestured towards the room's sole window, ignoring Iphigenia's question. "Look outside. My father's planet glows large with blood this time of year."

Iphigenia snuck a glance out of the portico. Overcast sky met her gaze.

"I see only clouds."

"Then the stars are in agreement; there will be no warmongering from the Amazons."

Iphigenia scoffed. "You just made that up."

"I cannot fulfill your wish," Penthesilea said, once again ignoring Iphigenia.

"If you have nothing else, I can offer you lodging and a victory feast tomorrow evening—"

"No, there is *one* thing you can do for me." Even as the words left her mouth, Iphigenia knew the idea was poison, anathema to everything she had become. Still, she'd seen the way the women of Themsiscrya had conducted themselves. Her last shot was far from being out of the realm of possibility. "Open your bed to me."

Penthesilea laughed, deep and long. When she finally noticed Iphigenia's stone faced silence, she stopped, wiping a tear from her face.

"You can't be serious, my little Greek?"

"I'm as serious as a summons from the lord of the dead himself," Iphigenia replied. "If I cannot convince you with my words, perhaps my mouth can woo you another way?"

At this, Penthesilea burst into another round of laughter. "If only all my pretty champions asked for this! I'd be a very happy Queen if they did." She winked at Iphigenia and stood, dropping her robe. Iphigenia flushed fiercely but did not avert her eyes. "Well? Shall we?"

* * *

Iphigenia struggled to keep her breath under control as she straddled the nude woman beneath her. This…was something almost entirely alien to her. Still, as she traced her fingers up and down taut muscle, she knew this was the way things must be, who *she* must be, if she was to get what she wanted.

The corpse beneath her did not protest as she slipped into its skin. Good — there was no time for insubordination when she had an army to lead.

XVII

in wild grief your mourning garments rend

The sound of crackling flames blended with that of crashing waves and boisterous laughter. Iphigenia lifted her gaze from the knees that weren't hers out towards the surf. There, the Amazons splashed, their armor long ago abandoned in the sand. They played with wild abandon, attempting to knock each other off each other's shoulders as if they were children out for day at the shore. For a brief moment, Iphigenia considered casting off her own chest plate and joining them; they'd certainly welcome her with open arms. Then, she remembered.

She'd committed a terrible transgression. Penthesilea, dead at the hands of the stranger wearing her face. Even if they won at Troy, she couldn't return to Themyscira and pretend nothing had ever happened. The Amazons, sooner or later, would figure out that she didn't have the first clue when it came to ruling a city, and then they'd know the truth. Iphigenia would have to come clean, and then they'd tear her apart. She certainly deserved to be run through with a dozen blades. It didn't matter though. For all intents and purposes, she was dead, her life a trade for Achaean passage to Troy. Every day beyond that still morning in Aulis had been a bonus. She'd go into this battle with no regrets.

"Queen Penthesilea!"

Right. That was her name now, wasn't it? Iphigenia grimaced, turning her attention away from the frolicking women. In another life, she could have been one of them.

Thermodosa stood before her, panting and chest swelled with pride.

"I've returned from scouting, my Queen. Troy is but a day's march away. We'll avenge our guest in no time. You'll hear the clash of swords and shields by this evening."

"Good. We'll need to arrive by night anyway, to circumvent the siege."

"Your strategy is excellent as always, my Queen."

Iphigenia nodded tersely. She didn't want to think about who she'd learned that particular tidbit from — the very man whose armies she was about to engage in combat.

She didn't know what she would do if she encountered Agamemnon. Would she immediately attack him? Or would she lay low, watch his movements, see if he ever gave an inkling of regret for the daughter he'd traded for the breeze? Would she spare the man who, despite forgetting she existed after the birth of Orestes, had ensured that she had the finest of educations, even going so far as to procure Iset, who had been so well versed in all things medicinal, even those that went beyond human understanding?

"If you see the King of the Greeks on our way in," Iphigenia began, trying with all her might to keep her voice even, "bring me his head, would you please?"

* * *

Just as the first pink tinges of dawn teased the horizon, Iphigenia led her forces to the gate of the fort at the base of Troy's massive wall. It had been unnervingly easy to slip through Mt. Ida's pass and up to the walls of Troy; the Greeks had been plastered, shouting praises to their gods as they drank themselves oblivious. It was just as well; she'd rather fight hungover soldiers than ones perfectly honed for battle. Honor was already out of the question.

The pair of Trojan soldiers guarding the gate were startled, pointing to the group and speaking quickly in a rough Anatolian dialect that Iphigenia was woefully unfamiliar with.

But Penthesilea would know, a small, guilt stricken voice in her head thought.

Luckily, she didn't have to make a fool of herself in an attempt to interpret. Antandre, the tallest of them, strode forward and began discoursing with the men in their language. The woman turned toward her, and with a start, Iphigenia realized she was looking to her for guidance.

"Tell them that we Amazons," Iphigenia began, "are here to provide aid to King Priam. A Greek spy has infiltrated Themyscira and killed an honored guest. We remain neutral no longer." The lie fell easily from her lips. It wasn't hard to come up with; her own body had been slumped over in Penthesilea's bedchamber, even as she walked within Penthesilea's own. Inventing a Greek assassin had been child's play; she'd simply told the rest of the Amazons that she'd chased him out of the city and off of a cliff. Convincing them to march on the Greeks after that had been easy. It was simply the hospitable thing to do, after all.

Apparently her words had been the correct ones; the guards stepped aside and pointed their spears to a massive rope ladder hanging against the far wall. Iphigenia squinted up, shielding her eyes from the intense light of the rising sun. There, at the apex of the wall, was a tent draped in purple and gold, and there she knew Priam would be. From that vantage point, he would have been able to see them coming — and yet, he'd not raised an alarm. How much did he already know?

As Iphigenia and her twelve moved past the pair of guards, she noticed them regarding their little group, and her in particular, as if they were some sort of beings straight from myth. At this point, though, she supposed that wasn't too far off. One could only cheat death so many times, could only consort with so many gods, before one might as well meld into the realm of fantasy.

The ladder was an easy climb. Iphigenia appreciated its simplicity; at any time, the Trojans could use it to access their city, but if things were to spiral so badly that the wall was overrun by the Greeks, the ladder could be up in smoke in a matter of seconds.

The moment she crested the wall, the bitter sound of weeping hit her.

Soldiers reached out to help her and the rest of her troop, but Iphigenia shrugged them off, just as the rest of the Amazons proceeded to do.

"Priam," Iphigenia barked, pulling herself to her full height. That, the soldiers understood, and they waved their spears towards the tent, the source of that bitter crying.

Iphigenia ducked her head in. Instead of a woman, as she'd expected by the wailing, she was surprised to see only a wizened old man, seated with a dozen toy horses at his feet. Red rimmed eyes met hers.

"So, it's you," he said in the Anatolian of the Amazons, his tears staunched for a moment as he dabbed at his face. "Come to finally destroy me, Penthesilea? To take your revenge? I suppose I deserve it."

"No," Iphigenia breathed, sinking to her knees across from the man. Priam, King of Troy, laid so low that he'd resorted to playing with children's toys and sobbing like a woman. This was the man who'd refused to return her aunt Helen, even when the threat of one hundred thousand men at his doorstop loomed? "I'm here to fight. For you."

Priam laughed, and though he threw his head back, there was no mirth in it.

"The fighting is over. My son, my beautiful Hector, is dead, and there will be no combat until he is buried. And even then, all is lost." Priam sadly gestured to the horses. "These were his, you know. Hector, who only ever wanted to love his horses, put his life on the line for his people. And now my boy is gone."

"By whose hand was he slain?" Iphigenia asked, trying to hold down the nervous energy lest it showed in her voice.

"Who other's than Achilles? Only by the grace of the gods was my son's body preserved — the things that man did to it..." Priam shuddered, then began weeping again in earnest.

"I'll avenge him," Iphigenia said. "Allow me to fight for you, Priam, and I shall have Achilles' head at your feet."

"Why? Why engage in this fruitless aim?"

"Because I want something from you, Priam. If we win, I want all women captured from the Greeks to have full agency over where their fate lies. Many are without families or futures, and the Amazons will welcome them with open arms."

"But — those are *our* women. I cannot accept those terms; they must be returned to Troy, to their husbands and fathers."

"What husbands and fathers, Priam? One has no need for women when all your men have perished in battle."

"Still..."

"You owe me, Priam. The only reason that the Amazons have not allied with the Greeks to batter at your doors is because we find them twice as repulsive as you all. I have not forgotten your youthful indiscretion against us." In truth, Iphigenia knew nothing about it. As she'd scoured Penthesilea's documents in a state of panic, she'd found evidence of a war with the Trojans, fought in her host's youth. It had been a resounding defeat, and there'd been a trade embargo with the Trojans ever since.

"Fine! You may try. The truce ends tomorrow at dawn; Hector's funeral games finish tonight. I suggest you prepare for any last rites there. I know I shall."

* * *

The last embers of Hector's funeral pyre drifted up towards the stars as Iphigenia and her troop readied themselves for battle. It had burned bright and quick. *Fitting for a hero prince*, she supposed. Rosy fingered dawn had yet to creep over the horizon.

Penthesilea's words came to Iphigenia's mind as she ghosted the edge of a blade with a finger. Beads of blood welled up; the bronze sword was impossibly sharp. No, she'd never lifted a blade, had never really considered using anything but a bow, but today? Today would be a day for firsts. She would wield Penthesilea's own sword, taken from the Themysciran armory, and hope that wielding it would make the afterlife that much easier for the woman whose body she had stolen.

"It would not."

Iphigenia whipped her head around. All of her contingent were focused on readying their weapons and donning their armor; not one of them was paying her the faintest bit of attention.

"None of them have spoken to you, and nor should they," the same voice sneered. *"We normally behead thieves in Themyscyra."*

Iphigenia lifted the sword. "If this is a joke," she murmured darkly, "I suggest you quit it."

Thermodosa quirked an eyebrow at her, but it was from within her own mind, Iphigenia realized, that the voice spoke again, its timbre disturbingly familiar.

"No more a joke than the trespass you've committed against me."

"Penthesilea," she breathed, careful not to allow anyone else to hear.

"The one and true only. You may have incapacitated me, witch, but I still live."

"How?"

"Your will is weak, nothing compared to mine."

"What does that even mean?"

"That you're caught between two worlds, that you're indecisive and cowardly. You won't commit to either, and therefore you won't act."

"Is *this* not acting?"

"This is foolish. This is suicide. This is you breaking the rules of nature for a selfish genocide that will never *come to fruition."*

Iphigenia grasped the sword, only to promptly drop it through no effort of her own. She grimaced.

"So you won't help me."

"I never said that. Warfare is my domain, and I intend to retain the last shred of my honor, thank you very much, usurper."

The men gave them a wide berth as they marched down to the plain. Distrust and doubt was plain beneath their plumed helms, at least the ones brave enough to chance a glance at them.

It's inevitable, Penthesilea whispered in her mind. *We are unnatural to them. Ignore it.*

"Doing my best," Iphigenia murmured.

"What was that, my queen?" Thermodosa said, running to march at Iphigenia's side.

"Nothing. Listen," she said, quickly changing the subject. "Do you hear that? Have we reached the sea?" The faint sound of roaring was evident.

Thermodosa cocked her head to the side. "Perhaps?"

Then their little troop crested one of the man-made levees separating the sea plain from the farmland just below Troy's citadel, and the source of the sound was revealed.

Tens of thousands of men greeted them, their voices so loud that they drowned even the crash of the waves. They rushed forward like ants descending on a carcass. The Trojans responded in kind with war cries of their own, with the cavalry rushing forward on their broad horses.

"Push them back to the sea!" Iphigenia shouted, raising her sword high. "Drown them in the waters that brought forth their hateful forms!" The battle began in earnest as she and her contingent strode forth into the fray, voices raised high in war song.

Bloodlust, Iphigenia found, became her. She sliced through her countrymen with glee, relishing in the transmutation of sinew into splatters. Her sword sang a sick hymn as she hacked with abandon just shy of reckless, if not for its deadly precision. She didn't even pause when gore splattered against her greaves, nor when the sharpness of her blade began to dull after severing so much bone. Something in her should be disgusted. She should be trembling like a newborn fawn, but the only sensation that dominated her emotions was pure, undiluted euphoria.

192 | J. DONAI

Fields scorched dry by the heat of the sun became muddy with blood. Iphigenia struggled not to slip in it even as she drove her spear through the belly of a youth, his steaming innards adding to the mess on the ground. Next to her, Harmothoe bashed in the brains of a grown man with her mace. Iphigenia beamed with pride. There was a whoop from Antandre as the foam of the surf began to crash against her ankles. And looking around, Iphigenia realized that they'd done it — in all the years of this war, it was their troop that had finally forced the Greeks into a corner. The water turned pink as both they and the Trojans renewed their attacks in earnest. Iphigenia gave the strongest rallying cry she could muster, and her Amazons responded with such fervor that she almost wept. In that moment, she and Penthesilea were truly one.

Then the waves, once frothy pink with blood, stilled. Iphigenia whipped her head around in confusion as the Trojans began to retreat.

"What are you doing?" She screamed, raising her sword arm high. "We're *winning*."

Iphigenia grit her teeth. No matter; she didn't really need the Trojans. She had the blessing of a god, the body of a warrior, and the will of a witch driving her forward. She tuned out the sound of Thermodosa's panicked pleas and swung onto an abandoned horse. Its hooves beat against the sand to the same tempo as the heartbeat thumping through her ears as she approached the line of Greek soldiers.

Then, as she crested a dune, she spotted him. He was a black mass sitting astride a gleaming stallion, his hair a tangled mess as he barked orders to the bloody maelstrom of warriors surrounding him. Agamemnon, self proclaimed King of Men, the man who'd once called himself her father, was a mere javelin's toss away.

Iphigenia let loose a war cry, raw and feral from a throat that was not hers. She would pursue him, tear the head from his shoulders, and drink the blood that would pour from the fount of his neck. She would desecrate his body before his men and let them know that their king was less than nothing. Ten long years of waiting, all for this moment.

As she spurred her horse on, Iphigenia cast her gaze to the sky. *Do you see me? Will you be a witness to my revenge? I hope jealousy is curdling the innards of all the other gods.* She was Artemis' champion and she was going to prove before her and all the others of the pantheon that she was the best of them all.

Dark eyes met hers across the sand. Did Agamemnon recognize her? She hoped he alone out of the thousands present did, so that he would know just who was disemboweling him. As she raised her sword, the sound of a thousand horns exploded across the battlefield and a soldier, seemingly conjured from nowhere, stepped into her path.

The one who stood between Iphigenia and her revenge was dressed in armor so bright that she had to shield her eyes. From beneath their helm, hair like flames hung to their shoulders. They were slender framed, strong calved, and striding straight towards her.

This is fate, Iphigenia realized. Of course this would be the one person she needed to eliminate if she was to enact her vengeance. The soldier, who once upon a time, she'd been forced from everything she'd ever known to marry. The lone soul among the Greeks who'd had the humanity to weep for her. *Achilles.* She leapt from her horse, even as the Trojans raced back to the battlements.

They met as if drawn by magnetism, exchanging blows the second they come into contact. Iphigenia wondered as she slashed and parried — was there any degree of recognition? Did Achilles remember the promise, broken despite it all?

They fought with a total disregard for their surroundings. Iphigenia knew that her movements were all Penthesilea now — she may have had anger fueling her, but Achilles was no common foot soldier. Only an expert warrior could begin to have a shred of hope against the ferocity held in those fierce green eyes. They traded blow after blow, clash after clash, and both armies ceased action to watch as the sun arced from high noon to sunset.

At last, Iphigenia's energy began to wane, even as her opponent's churned unwavering. Why? What was so special about the general of the Myrmidons? *Don't fall to the ground,* Iphigenia desperately thought as she grappled with the foe that was once her only ally among the enemy.

She shouted for help, scanning the faces of the crowd that had silently surrounded them for any of her Amazons, to see if any of them could render aid in this battle that she was rapidly losing. The only expressions that met hers were hidden by thick beards. Seething, she cast her gaze away from them and towards the ground.

Among the countless bodies lay her Amazons. Antandre, with a spear through her chest. Harmothoe's corpse was face down in the dirt, a massive crater where the back of her skull should be. Derinoe's head lay a handsome ten meters from her body. Even Thermodosa had perished; her eyes gazed unseeingly at the sky's waning light. The twelve that she'd rallied, journeyed with, pretended to have known for decades? All of them were dead, never again to walk the Earth. She'd called them all here, used nefarious means to accomplish it, and now they were all dead for her sake. She didn't know if it was her doing or a response from deep within Penthesilea, but Iphigenia, for the first time, faltered.

As cold bronze sliced through the back of both her heels, Iphigenia refused to stifle the cry of pain that fell from her lips. She collapsed to the ground like a bag of rocks cast into the sea, unable to support herself any longer. A triumphant shout rose from the Greeks amidst the sound of approaching armor.

A blade slipped below her chin to tilt her head up, and she bared her teeth, prepared to meet Achilles with the most ferocity she could drum up. Everyone else may be dead, but she'd be damned if Achilles didn't leave this place knowing he'd been in a fight.

Instead, she was surprised to see not anger, but immense grief as slightly unfocused green eyes met hers.

"You," he mumbled, and for a moment, Iphigenia believed he'd somehow recognized her, seen through her glamor. The sword was cast to the side as Achilles dropped his full weight onto her, pinning her to the ground. Iphigenia screamed, the wounds in her legs sending crackling agony up her spine.

"No one ever told me that one like you walked this earth," he said, fat tears rolling down his blood spattered cheeks. They splashed one by one onto Iphigenia's face. "One so brave, so beautiful, so *deadly*. And now I must kill you. How many times must the gods curse me?"

Iphigenia struggled to pull away, raise her sword, do *anything*, but Achilles did not budge as he roughly took her shoulders in hand and half raised her from the ground.

"Here! Right here, your proof!" Iphigenia didn't know if Achilles was yelling at the soldiers surrounding them or the heavens themselves, but as she was shaken like a rag doll, a terrifying realization struck her — she was going to die here, on the sandy plain of Troy. One name swirled in her mind like a mantra — *Artemis*. She would be watching from lofty Olympus as Iphigenia broke her promise.

Hands encircled her neck, bearing down with bruising force. Pink waves soaked the two of them as she gasped for breath and his tears fell onto her thrashing form.

Spots clouded Iphigenia's vision. There was no breaking Achilles' hold, and so she did the only thing left to her. Iphigenia weakly raised her arm, fingers seeking the face of her former friend. When they found his cheek, Achilles stilled, his green eyes wide. As he leaned into her touch, Iphigenia couldn't help but wonder — was there still a spark of compassion, of humanity, within the warrior before her?

"They've ruined you," Iphigenia struggled to whisper. Her windpipe had been crushed. "You were a wondrous balm to me, and they've ruined you."

"I could have *been* you," Achilles seethed. At those words, Iphigenia couldn't help but think of Beroe. An acute realization struck her. She was just about to speak, to affirm Achilles that *she* still could be, when the same chill that had sliced her ankles open was thrust beneath her armor, piercing her just below her ribcage.

Blood roared in her ears even as it ebbed out of her. She watched, dazed, as Achilles stood. The soldier before her wiped away tears with one hand and with the other, fumbled with a belt. As she choked on her own blood, Iphigenia realized what Achilles intended to do as she lay dying. She would not, could not, allow her last sight to be *that*. She cast her rapidly fading vision to the sky where, high above her, an eagle soared on broad wings. *So, the Lord of the Skies finally makes his appearance.* Zeus was too late. He could influence Achilles all he wanted, but he would not succeed in using her to harm Artemis as he had used Kallisto. With oblivion swiftly overtaking her, Iphigenia laughed, even as Achilles continued to weep. Even in death, she'd secured the smallest of victories.

XVIII

let buffeting winds bear it
and all care away

The acrid taste of brine flooded Iphigenia's mouth.

Am I on the banks of the Styx? If so, good. She deserved to wait by the riverside forever, no one left to pay her way by the ferryman. Then pain, bright and sharp, rocketed through her form as memories of Troy's wide plain spirited back to her.

She was alive. Somehow, miraculously, she'd survived the assault at Troy. There was no telling how much sea water she'd ingested, or how long she'd languished in the waves. It could have been moments, or she could have suffered another decade long slumber. The only thing she knew was that she somehow, some way, was alive. The guilt was proof enough.

Since she lived, that meant that Penthesilea must be truly dead, her corpse abandoned on a blood soaked beach to be desecrated by the Greeks. The image of Achilles rubbing furiously at his genitals while he wept over her, the last thing she'd seen with those eyes that weren't her own, was burned into her mind. Iphigenia couldn't stop herself as she vomited onto the beach.

They should've won. They had been winning, but Achilles...his strength had been unnatural, even more so than the circumstances that had led them to meet again. No longer was he the slender, effeminate youth that had desperately cried at her sacrifice. No, he'd become something far darker, a being unhinged by grief. Twisted beyond recognition.

Though, she supposed, she couldn't talk. The bodies of the Amazons, mutilated and ruined, were at the forefront of her mind. Who would protect that glorious city of women now? No, Iphigenia could not judge when she'd become just as monstrous as Achilles.

All the fight had fled from her body. A desperate dream of revenge had caused her to throw away her second chance at life, and now she was here. Alone. She rolled onto her back, ignoring the rocks now digging into her spine.

"Help me," she whispered, searching the pitch sky for the moon. When the horizon revealed only dense clouds, she knew. Iphigenia couldn't help the tears that ran down her face, mingling with the sea. So, that was how things were going to be.

She couldn't lay there forever, no matter how much she wanted to. Eventually, she climbed to her feet shakily and scanned her surroundings as best she could despite the darkness. A few stars provided enough light to see that she was in a land where thin scrub was the main vegetation, and that the beach she'd washed up on was at the base of a small cliff. For a moment, she considered climbing it. Then she looked down the beach.

In the distance, the light from what could only be campfires twinkled. Other humans...it would be a risk, considering she had no idea where she was, but what did she have to lose at this point? She sighed, pushing her sopping wet hair out of her face. There was nothing else to be done but to move forward.

The walk was long and arduous. A strong wind kicked up, bringing with its howls a heavy chill. Iphigenia longed for the warmth of her pelt, a cloak, or at the very least, a friendly arm draped over her shoulder. She had been nude when she'd possessed Penthesilea, and so she was nude now.

As she trudged along the beach, rocks sharply cutting into the soles of her feet, she came upon a sturdy piece of driftwood. Iphigenia felt the faintest spark of hope at the sight of it. At the very least, she'd have a torch to guide her path through the darkness. She grimaced as bittersweet memories of wielding a torch in a cave not too long ago hit her like a shield to the face. It would be best to pretend that that little indiscretion had never occurred — gods were fickle beings. What had occurred between her and Artemis was over now. She'd failed in her quest, and in doing so, she'd lost the goddess' favor. The hidden moon said as much.

Her calves burned, and her stomach twinged with hunger, but Iphigenia pushed on. She was unsure if she did so out of necessity or pure spite. The beach disappeared, transitioning to the rocky soil and dry grass of a barren plain. She trudged across it, marveling at its desolation. Empty save for a few collapsed silos, this blackened former farmland perfectly reflected the roiling despair in her heart. This was where she belonged, where she deserved to be. This land would be her penance.

As the source of the flames, a low rock wall, came into proper view, Iphigenia slowed her pace. A naked woman approaching under the cover of night was suspicious at best. Any people with the tenacity to still be alive in this land would shoot first and ask questions later, and that was if she was lucky.

Iphigenia peered up on top of the wall. Instead of armored sentries, she saw only a couple of shepherd boys dozing off on each other's shoulders. They were scrawny little things; the clear impact of far too many missed meals. The wall they sat upon was in incredible disrepair. Some portions were half collapsed while others had been completely dismantled, their bricks hauled off to gods know where. Between that, and the razed fields outside the walls, things did not bode well for Iphigenia being able to catch a warm meal. Nevertheless, she cleared her throat.

Two of the boys awakened with a jolt; the third dozed on, oblivious, until the leanest of the trio elbowed him harshly in the ribs.

Iphigenia opened her arms wide. The boys were frazzled as they whispered amongst each other while giving her wide eyed glances. She strained to hear what they were saying, but it was nigh impossible to parse out even a syllable over the roaring of the wind.

"Excuse me," she said, growing frustrated. If the boys were just going to chatter uselessly among themselves, she'd push past them and find an actual adult to speak to.

The sound of her voice seemed to have done something, however; the boys sprang into action. The sleepy one turned on his heel and dashed beyond the walls into the town proper, the big one collapsed onto the ground, arms covering his head and screaming unintelligibly, and the lean one, the obvious ringleader, leveled a staff at her, the long piece of wood trembling between his fingers.

"I mean no harm—" Iphigenia began, but the boy stepped forward, thrusting his weapon at her and snarling. Through the dark, Iphigenia could see that his eyes were wild with panic — he barked something at her, and she realized with a start that he was not speaking Greek, nor Anatolian, but one of the foreign languages her father had offhandedly mentioned a few times. Barbarian tongues, he'd called them, and her mother had only given him cold glares from across the dinner table in return. Inwardly, Iphigenia groaned. She knew not what land she was even in, let alone the tongue the boy before her was shouting at her— she'd have to find another way to communicate.

She stepped closer to the boy, and therefore closer to the campfire flickering against the wall. Perhaps the light would better illuminate her, and therefore her womanhood, showing that she wasn't a threat, and that would calm the boy?

Her motion seemed to have the opposite effect, however. He lunged for her, and Iphigenia had to leap out of his path. He kept coming. Despite his size, the boy was incredibly tenacious, relentless in his attacks. If he'd been just a few years older, he would have been indistinguishable from the countless men she'd cut down at Troy.

"I don't want to hurt you!" she yelled, taking several steps back towards the way she'd come. Killing a youth in an unfamiliar land was a one way ticket to her head on a pike, guaranteed. Running was her only real option here. The boy was about to strike again, his muscles tensed, but there was a great clamor just beyond the wall, and then a shout. The boy snapped his head to look back, and Iphigenia followed suit. Clamoring over the wall was a pale faced, red haired man dressed in threadbare furs. He was young, his beard barely more than a patchwork of ginger fuzz, and yet, Iphigenia could recognize the aura of royalty anywhere. *Perks of growing up steeped in it*, she supposed.

The man rushed up to them, concern evident in his heavily lidded eyes, and trailing behind him was the sleepy boy, much more awake at this point. He pointed at her and said something in the same harsh language to the boy with the staff, who nodded furiously before dropping his weapon. The man then looked her up and down, peering at her with suspicion. He stepped closer, and Iphigenia took a step back of her own, cautious. The gleaming dagger hanging off the man's belt had not escaped her attention; it was undoubtedly more deadly than the wooden staff of a child.

The man inhaled sharply, and Iphigenia was about to flee, take her chances sleeping back on the beach, when the man spoke.

"The sea?" the man said, his Greek garbled and heavily accented, but Greek all the same. He waved his hands as if he were trying to conjure his next words from the air. "You come from the sea?"

"Yes?" she ventured cautiously. Hopefully reeking like salt and fish wasn't a capital offense among these people. At that moment, the cloud overhead shifted, and the full gleam of the moon shined down upon her, casting a pallid glow on her clammy skin. So she hadn't been completely abandoned after all.

The man and the boys looked at each other, mouths agape, before turning towards her, beaming. The man gathered Iphigenia up in an embrace before she even knew what was happening, mumbling one word over and over amid laughter. Her first instinct was to tear out of his arms and dash for the hills, but Iphigenia quickly realized that instead of any kind of lasciviousness, the man's grip was light, almost reverent — she let out a soft gasp when she realized the Greek word he was desperately repeating like a prayer was referring to her.

Savior.

* * *

Before she was aware it was even happening, the red haired man had offered her his cloak and Iphigenia was being rushed under the cover of darkness into the town beyond the wall. She couldn't understand a lick of anything her escorts were excitedly babbling about, but it was clear from the lively tone of their chatter that their mood had shifted for the better significantly. She glanced from them to the moon above, shining and full. Savior. She rolled the word around on her tongue, trying it out. Judging by what she saw around her, this city certainly needed one.

Their path was lined with the ruins of burned buildings and collapsed market stalls. Hastily constructed lean-tos were supported against half collapsed walls. Occasionally, the crunch of a discarded arrow snapping in two beneath their feet would ring out. A few open campfires illuminated their surroundings, and Iphigenia noticed that the shadowy figures huddled around them looked particularly forlorn as they held their hands out for a hint of warmth.

Iphigenia thought about asking for details of what had happened here, but decided against it. She didn't want to break the mood of her hosts. They clearly hadn't had very much to be happy about in quite some time, and the red-haired man's Greek was so broken that he most likely wouldn't be able to answer her question fully, if he even understood it in the first place.

They continued their trek, and before she knew it, Iphigenia was being led up the steps of a small temple. It too had seen its fair share of the destruction, with its painted frescoes irreparably damaged and chunks of broken marble littering the ground surrounding it. Still, it alone of this town's buildings stood fast, its modest columns standing tall.

The man murmured something to the boys. Whatever it was, it caused them to dash away. Iphigenia was about to say something when the man gave an excited shout.

Moments later, a wizened old woman hobbled out of the temple's entrance, a candle in one hand and a cane in the other. Her tiny form was dressed in heavy purple robes, a large gold medallion dangling from her neck. Her eyes drifted over to Iphigenia, and she could see that they were cloudy with cataracts even from this distance. If she wasn't blind, she was very near to it.

The old woman smiled toothlessly, and Iphigenia was just about to raise her hand in greeting when the wrinkled crone crumpled to the ground. The red haired man gave an excited whoop as Iphigenia rushed to the woman's side, cradling her head in her arms. She pressed a finger to the side of the woman's neck, but felt nothing. Dead, just like that. She looked up at the man in confusion as he laughed happily. He crouched next to the two, plucked the heavy gold medallion hanging from the woman's neck off of her, and slipped it over Iphigenia's head.

"Savior!" the man repeated, while Iphigenia stared at him, her mouth agape, the woman's corpse still warm in her arms.

* * *

Iphigenia sat on her knees in the main hall of the temple as the red-haired man poured her a cup of wine. From deep within the temple, a single girl had appeared, maybe ten at the oldest. She'd brought her a gown. Iphigenia had hastily thrown it over her head, highly conscious of her state of undress around so many people. The girl's eyes didn't leave her as she set out loaves of bread and a pot of thin broth, and from behind an altar, procured a small jar of wine and a set of cups. Afterwards, she'd run off, but Iphigenia could still feel her eyes on her, despite the apparent solitude.

Iphigenia's appetite, once ravenous, had disappeared entirely. Thoughts of the dead old woman, whose corpse had been carried to a small chamber just off the hall by the man, tamped down any desire to eat. Still, it would be rude to deny the gift of hospitality from those so obviously food insecure—it clearly meant a lot to the man that she ate. So she nibbled at the hard bread and thin broth offered to her.

The man pointed to himself. "I am king of this place. This land is Tauris, and my name is Thoas." Now that they were out of the noise of the wind and the man had calmed himself, Iphigenia could understand his Greek much better. Then he spoke again, that same strange language. Iphigenia realized quickly that he was trying to teach her a bit of it, and so she repeated him in both Greek and his own language. He beamed, filling her cup again.

"Your name?"

Thoas' Greek wasn't great, but Iphigenia understood his question perfectly. She could tell him the truth, of course. She could forget that she'd ever lived and loved among the huntresses, could begin to rebuild her life here. Just as she was about to respond, a moonbeam fell into her lap from the open window.

Iphigenia thought of just how far she'd come from that little girl who'd never even left the mountains surrounding her home. She'd roamed the forests with a goddess at her side, jumped across the wine dark sea, killed dozens of battle seasoned soldiers, suffered two terrible deaths, and had somehow survived to walk among the living again. What would Iset, who had been taken so far from home and had been stripped of everything, even her name, say? This was her frog on the lotus leaf moment, she realized as she looked at the expectant face gazing back at her. The Egyptian word for frog, taught to her by Iset on a muggy summer's day many years ago, floated in her mind. She would leap. "Call me Hecate," she breathed, warmth flowing into her cheeks.

"Hecate...prophecy...that's what the prophecy said. New priestess. Our savior from the Greeks."

Savior from the Greeks? The razed lands and destroyed buildings suddenly made quite a bit of sense to Iphigenia. Achaean scouting parties, in search of resources, must have discovered this place and raided it for all it was worth. She couldn't help the pang of anger that tore through her. How many lives were going to be destroyed?

Thoas stood and clapped his hands. Immediately, the girls flooded back into the main hall of the temple. In no time at all, she was being ushered through narrow halls. Iphigenia wondered if she was hallucinating everything, if this was just an extended dream brought on by a dying brain, but the weight of the medallion around her neck proof enough that she lived. By the time she was set up for the night in a tiny alcove bedroom deep within the temple, she wanted nothing more than to curl up in the bed and sleep for the next ten years. Iphigenia was about to collapse on the straw mattress to do just that when she caught a sight of a fine nightgown laid out on the bed, one much too small for her, alongside a cup of half drunken wine. With a wave of queasiness, she realized that the room she had been so hastily deposited in had belonged to the old woman, now dead. The floor was going to have to do.

* * *

There was a gentle knocking at the door, and Iphigenia rose to her feet, groggy with the last tendrils of sleep's embrace. Her back was killing her; she lamented that she was no longer in the forest where the bark of the willow tree was as easy to find as her own two feet. She wondered if there was a healer anywhere in this town who would be willing to provide her with some so that she could whip up a painkiller. Wrapping herself in the blanket she'd slept on, she answered the door with a barely-concealed yawn.

A group of young women greeted her, all trying and failing to hide their wide-eyed expressions. Among them was the girl from last night. Iphigenia supposed that she must have told her friends about the stranger in the temple. Curiosity tinged with the faintest hint of fear was written plain as day on these girls' faces, none of whom looked a day over fourteen. Iphigenia, remembering her own not so distant youth, gave them a small smile and stepped aside, ushering them into the room with a wave. The girls trotted in with a pot of steamy water, a stack of fresh linens, and a bundle of clothes that looked like they'd been spun off the loom that very morning.

As they busied themselves around the room, Iphigenia longed to tell them thank you, that she could take it from there, but when she tried to communicate with a miserable attempt at rudimentary sign language, the girls only stared at her blankly.

She sighed, shrugging before she allowed them to bathe and dress her. Despite years of being the sole one responsible for her hygiene, the motions of being attended to came back to her as if she'd never lived wild in the woods at all. There wasn't much difference between being a princess and a priestess after all, she mused as soap was rinsed out of her hair.

After she was dry and dressed in the comfortable fur-lined robes that seemed to be the primary fashion of the people of this land, the girls led her out of the temple and into the bright light of the midday sun.

King Thoas was already waiting for her at the bottom of the marble stairs. He broke out into a wide smile when Iphigenia descended. The girls curtsied to him and then her before scattering. Iphigenia presumed they could hardly wait to gossip amongst themselves about the strange woman who'd walked out of the sea.

"Good to see you!" the king exclaimed, thumping Iphigenia heartily on the back. She stumbled forward. For a man, and especially for a man of his rank, Thoas was incredibly familiar with her. Iphigenia was unsure of whether she should be amused or uncomfortable.

"Good to see you too," she replied carefully, settling on feeling something in between.

Thoas was positively humming with excitement, bouncing on his heels. "Busy day ahead," he said, waving his arm at the buildings around them. "Let me show you Tauris. Your new home."

Home. Iphigenia could have laughed. Whatever. She could put up with a simple tour for a few hours.

Not even an hour later, and the tour had become the furthest thing from simple. What started as a few eyes peeking nervously from burned out buildings had amassed into a crowd following at their heels. They shouted praises at the two of them as they walked through ruined streets. The king pretended to be oblivious to his people's adoration, even as they kissed the ground the two of them walked on. Iphigenia wanted to close in on herself. It was far too many eyes on her, and she longed to slam her hands over her ears and screw her eyes shut until it all went away. Instead, she forced a smile and gave a half-hearted wave, all while Thoas chattered away aimlessly in broken Greek about blessing the sole grain silo and caring for widows.

Finally, they circled back to the temple, now bathed in the reddish glow of early evening. The townspeople followed, gathering as Iphigenia stood uneasily at Thoas' side as he issued some sort of proclamation. There was no understanding the full content of his words, but she could pick up bits and pieces. *Hecate, priestess,* and *Artemis* stood out to her the most, and she couldn't help but grin ruefully, thinking back to that day when she'd begged the high priestess of Mycenae to let her join them. Life was determined to foist irony upon irony onto her, it seemed.

Then Thoas said the word that the boy from the night before had screamed at her as he tried to gore her: Taurian for 'Greek,' she supposed. That got a resounding cry of anger out of the crowd until Thoas calmed them, gesturing towards Iphigenia with a twinkle in his eyes. She gave a brief bow, and then, as she was rising out of it, she caught sight of a woman standing just apart from the crowd. She was dark haired and unveiled, and despite the night's encroaching chill, her arms were bare, adorned only by gold bangles that caught the last rays of the sun. Even from this distance, Iphigenia could see that the woman was staring at her with an intensity the likes of which she'd never seen before, as if she could see into the very depths of her soul, and for the first time since she'd approached the walls of Tauris, she was afraid. Even as Thoas led her into the temple and away from the roar of the crowd, she could still feel the gaze of the woman hot upon her back.

She was almost relieved when they passed through a heavy door at the back of the hall, one she'd somehow missed the night before. This new room was smaller than the main hall, but was much more ornate. The walls were patterned with gold, a far cry from the shanty town just outside. This wasn't what had Iphigenia breaking out into a cold sweat, however.

In the center of the room stood a life size statue of a goddess, her goddess. The stone depiction of Artemis was uncanny in its resemblance to the real thing, and Iphigenia had to tamp down the urge to ask it *why*. Why here? Why *her*? Beside her, Thoas had sunk to his knees in supplication, and Iphigenia hesitantly followed, not taking her eyes off the effigy for a second. It seemed to be taunting her, standing there in its unyielding, rock-hard impassivity.

The prayers were brief, and then they were outside again, on the other side of the temple from the one they had entered. This portico faced the sea, which shone in the distance. Iphigenia inhaled the brackish air before surveying the scene before her.

The crowd here was much smaller than the first, and as Iphigenia's eyes searched the assembly gathered there for the strange woman, she caught sight of something that nearly made her knees buckle.

Just steps away from the bottom of the portico stood a gleaming white altar, painstakingly carved with scenes of leaping does and ravaging bears. To Iphigenia, it may as well have been the altar she'd been forced upon all those years ago. Bile hot with panic rose in her throat, and she wheeled her head around in terror, the roar of the wind and the salt of the sea assaulting her senses as she felt the bruising crush of hands around her arms.

But there was no Achilles here, nor Calchas; Diomedes was not there staring off into the distance, nor Odysseus weaving lies into the ears of any who would listen. Not even Agamemnon darkened these steps; there was only Thoas, escorting her down the stairs, face shining with excitement as he called her his priestess of the highest order.

Thoas gave a quick command to a young man, who sprinted away. Moments later, another man was dragged before them, chains clamped tight around his arms and legs. He was a brute, haggard and broad, and it took no less than four struggling boys to wrangle him into submission. He snarled like a caged beast, face ruddy— and then, Iphigenia's eyes met his.

All color drained from his face. He screamed, and Iphigenia, through her mounting terror, realized that the man was speaking Greek, and not only that, but that she also knew his voice. His hair and beard may be wild, and he may have bulked up considerably since their last encounter, but Iphigenia would know this treacherous coward anywhere.

Begging for his life at her feet was Lysander, the murderer of her closest friend and betrayer of them all. Fear became fury, and as Thoas eagerly pressed a blade into her hands, Iphigenia graciously accepted it. She watched with a churning pleasure as Lysander was thrown onto the altar with less ceremony than a common lamb. Iphigenia couldn't help the wild pounding in her heart as the girls from that morning, so young and sweet, trotted forward and anointed Lysander with heady herbs and fragrant oils. As Lysander began to weep, calling for his mother, Iphigenia thought she heard one of the girls say something about continuing their game of marbles.

Then, they were alone. The crowd and the king were still there, of course, but as Iphigenia stood over Lysander, they might as well have been the only two on the planet. She carefully peered down into his face. There was no remorse there, only the familiar, all-encompassing terror of one who knew they were mere seconds from oblivion. Then, her name, her true name, slipped out of Lysander's mouth in a low moan. Her eyebrows rose in surprise. So, they hadn't forgotten about her after all.

She plunged the blade in anyway, twisting deep.

XIX

to me thou didst seem a small and ungraceful child

Iphigenia's hands shook as she sat on the bed in silence, back in her chamber. The roar of the crowd still rang in her ears, but not as loudly as her racing thoughts. She'd heard of barbaric tribes that practiced human sacrifice, but she'd never imagined Artemis would be so spiteful as to deposit her onto the shores of one. Only the cruelest of goddesses would wrench open wounds still raw by having her pantomime her own trauma.

She stood, pouring a cup of water. Some sloshed down her chest as she greedily gulped it down. Being amongst those who would serve up living, breathing people to the gods so nonchalantly was not what had her ready to tear her hair from her scalp. No, it was the fact that as she'd driven the knife deep into Lysander's chest as if she'd been coring an apple, the only emotion she'd felt was a deep, roiling pleasure. Wrenching the life from the man like he was no more than a common pig had felt *good*. Killing in on the battlefield was one thing, but this was far different than the heat of combat. The bastard had deserved it, that much was certain, but she wasn't capable of cold blooded murder, she *couldn't* be — and yet she was, and she did, and she wanted to do it again.

As Iphigenia looked down at her hands, she envisioned blood coating them, despite having scrubbed them in the temple's purifying waters after the act.

There was a curt knock at the door.

"Go away," Iphigenia said. King or not, she had no patience for Thoas and his unending enthusiasm right now.

The visitor knocked again, and Iphigenia hurled the clay pitcher of water against the wall, shattering it.

"I said leave me alone!" she spat as water spread across the floor.

"And I think you should let me in," a female voice, decidedly not Thoas, replied in Greek as impeccable as Iphigenia's own. Her voice was smoky, and Iphigenia found herself suddenly soothed as curiosity cut through her rage. She opened the door with a slight huff.

She was startled to see the woman from the crowd standing on the other side, staring with that same burning intensity as she had before. This closely, Iphigenia could see that the woman held a definite resemblance to the people of Tauris with her fair skin and the shape of her jaw, but the similarities ended there. She towered over Iphigenia, as tall as any male warrior, and her build was that of a woman who had borne children and wasn't afraid to hide it. The woman's eyes were her most striking feature — feline, but not like some common house cat. No, as she stared down the woman, Iphigenia only saw the cunning of a lion in those icy blue eyes, the likes of which she'd never seen within Mycenae's walls.

"What do you want?" Iphigenia asked, suspicion heavy in her voice.

The woman flashed her teeth at Iphigenia in the barest of smiles. "Just want to talk."

"And why would I want to do that?" Iphigenia felt the onset of a headache. The woman was certainly intriguing, to say the least, but she was far from being in the mood. "I don't know you."

The woman leaned in close, and a wave of cedar entwined with lavender washed over Iphigenia. The woman's breath tickled her ear as she spoke.

"I'm glad you don't; it gives us even more of an excuse to chat. You and I? We could make beautiful poetry together."

Really? Was she being come onto? Since when did they let common *pornai* into temples, let alone the temple of Artemis? These people truly must be barbarians. Then again, taking another look at the woman's glossy black hair and the plumpness of her lips, Iphigenia could not help but think barbarism couldn't be that bad.

"I know nothing of poetry," Iphigenia breathed, taking a step back despite her sudden compulsion to move in closer.

"Ah, but you do," the woman tutted, taking one of Iphigenia's hands into hers and tracing the lines on her palm. "There is nothing more poetic than being destroyed by one of your own kinsmen." There was something forlorn about the way the woman spoke, as if she were speaking more to herself than Iphigenia. "But of course, you already know that better than anybody, Iphigenia of Mycenae."

And before Iphigenia could respond, the woman was gone, her footsteps echoing through the temple like the claxon bells of alarm ringing in Iphigenia's head. She'd told not one Taurian her true name.

* * *

For the next week, Iphigenia's days were almost entirely taken up by various ritualistic lessons and duties, ranging from the precise amount of salt to add to the purifying water to just how many incisions should be made in a lamb's flank before placing it on the pyre (three). It was all fascinating — the precision required was a far cry from the haphazard religious rites she'd been made to perform in Mycenae, done simply to keep the gods at bay. Here, the Taurians seemed to take pride in their rituals, finding inherent beauty within them.

Luckily, the human sacrifice portion was a rarity, only to be done when some poor Greek speaking soul washed up on their lands. Despite the uneasiness she felt with the sacrificial act, Iphigenia excelled at all the other aspects of priesthood. All things considered, she had it made; she was fed, adored, and best of all, lived and breathed. Still, she couldn't help but lament the lack of time she had to find out anything about the woman with the strange eyes.

She'd asked the girls as best she could despite the language barrier (they were to be her permanent attendants, she'd discovered) but they had all shaken their heads in confusion. She'd tried a game of charades with one of the guard boys, and he'd seemed to understand her, but when the light of understanding bloomed across his face, he'd just made the sign against evil and waved her away. She even tried some of the old widows of the town, who'd fawned over her with such adoration when they'd first met her. They at once knew who she was talking about; their warm expressions dissolved instantaneously into ones of warning, and they babbled at her in their language as they piled heavy strings of ceramic beads around her neck. Iphigenia had picked up a few words of Taurian by this point; she caught *protection* and *wickedness* before she was ushered into one of the old women's hovels and stuffed full of pastries. When she tried to ask more questions, they only hushed her and shoveled more onto her plate.

It wasn't until she went to Thoas himself that she found her answer. That night, they dined together in his house, a simple construction of stone and thatch, which Iphigenia had gathered was to be a weekly custom. Soup and bread with wine was the fare as always, but tonight, Iphigenia saw the large red clay amphora with its scenes of tigers wrestling with vines in a different light. She cast her eyes directly across the table. Thoas had already filled his cup to the brim.

He was prattling on about the harvest rites of last fall and how abysmal the following growing season had been when Iphigenia raised a hand. Thoas grinned at her and leaned forward, sloshing his wine a touch. His eagerness was rather endearing, despite its unnaturalness. Never had a man given her thoughts the time of day. And yet, Thoas clung to her every word, as if the gods themselves were whispering into his ear through her.

Iphigenia cleared her throat. She would have to word this carefully.

"Your highness—"

"Thoas!" he interrupted, face shining with mirth. "We are friends!" Ah. So the wine was already hard at work. Good.

"Yes, Thoas then. I want to learn more about your people. I've met so many, but that can't have been everybody?"

The king began to blabber about fishermen and merchants, ex-warriors and midwives, and as Iphigenia listened carefully, she realized none of them were even close to matching the description of the woman. She was going to have to be a little more heavy handed.

"What about criminals? Is there a jail here?" It was worth mentioning. Perhaps the woman had escaped, although she had been rather sumptuously dressed for a convict.

"All are sent to you! Only Greeks commit crimes here. Us Taurians stick together." Thoas' cheeks held a faint pink tint to them, and Iphigenia, growing increasingly frustrated, decided to strike.

"A woman," she said, gripping her own cup of well watered wine tightly. "Can you tell me anything about this woman that everyone's so afraid of?"

Thoas' expression darkened, and he set his cup down, his once jovial attitude now somber.

"You mean Medea."

"Medea." Iphigenia rolled the name around in her mouth. It was blunt, but somehow lyrical, and it held a certain weight to it. It suited the woman, she supposed.

"Don't talk to her. Evil woman."

Iphigenia felt it prudent to not announce that she'd been solicited in the temple by this Medea character. "Why is she here? She is foreign, is she not?"

"Yes, and no. Complicated. She helped us. All the men, dead. If not for her, Taurus would be only slaves." Thoas laced his long fingers together, sober now in his appearance. "But she's dangerous."

"Dangerous how?" Iphigenia breathed, leaning forward on her elbows. There was a chill breeze in the hall, no doubt from an improperly latched window, but she paid it no mind. Excitement warmed her skin.

"Does it matter?" Thoas asked, scowling.

"Please."

"Witchcraft." The king looked as if something particularly foul had been swimming in his soup. "Witchcraft and treachery. Beware of her."

Iphigenia nodded, sipping deeply from her cup to hide her growing smile.

* * *

Night had been well established by the time Iphigenia slid out of the temple. It hadn't been hard; save for one of the silly youths dozing off out front, she was unguarded. Grown men were a scarcity in these parts, which was an apparent source of stress for the maidens and mothers of this land. Iphigenia figured them rather lucky, but kept that thought to herself as she flung herself over the stone planters serving as a makeshift fence.

The streets were blessedly empty at this late hour. Iphigenia crept through them with ease, making a beeline for one of the great gaps in the city walls. Picking her way over the rubble was simple — her years spent scaling trees and traversing cliff faces had made her incredibly nimble. Still, as her foot caused a loose rock to tumble to the ground, she moved with caution. It was a miracle that any of the wall was still standing; it wouldn't bode well for her to finish with a thoughtless movement what the invaders had started.

Outside the city, the countryside was pitch black. The moon, absent entirely, wouldn't be illuminating her path tonight, but it was no matter. Iphigenia drew a flint firestarter out of the folds of her chiton, along with one of the smaller torches she'd taken from the temple. Creeping through the dark bearing nothing but a torch was starting to become a habit for her, it seemed, but Iphigenia didn't mind. Being able to go wherever she desired aided by the light of her own creation was an amazingly liberating experience, and she felt confidence bloom in her chest. She'd find the lair of this Medea, and then she'd get her answers.

Iphigenia hugged the wall as she walked, scanning the darkness for any anomalies. Thoas had made it seem like this Medea lived too close for his comfort; Iphigenia wondered if her home perhaps shared a wall with the city directly. She'd seen it done at Mycenae, and again at Aulis (although those had been hastily-constructed shacks for the late arriving Myrmidons). It would certainly make her quest easier if Medea had followed those trends.

The city itself wasn't large. Iphigenia figured she could circumvent it three or four times before the sun rose. She was slowing down to take more of the night in when the sound of a yip reverberated through the night. She waved her torch in the direction the sound had come, and was greeted by a series of loud barks and howls.

"Fuck," she whispered, looking up at the wall. Of course she was at the section with no gaps or footholds to even scramble up. This was bad. Memories of her head in Artemis' lap as the goddess relegated how she'd had a man ripped limb from limb by his own dogs raced through her mind as she rapidly began to walk back the way she'd came. Every nerve in her body screamed at her to run, to break into a sprint as fast as her legs could carry her, but she held her pace. If she'd learned one thing from her time in the wilderness, it was that she was always to play the hunter, never the prey.

It was with that thought in mind that Iphigenia stopped, turning to face the night. Why should she flee? She'd survived this far, hadn't she? Power hummed from her core to her fingertips, and she held the torch high as she waited with bated breath. At last, she was about to see what she could *really* do.

Just as the dogs came into sight, emaciated and covered in matted fur, the ground slipped away beneath Iphigenia's feet. She yelped as if she were one of the dogs while she fell beneath the earth, landing in a hard crumple.

Her chest was still pounding with adrenaline when she realized that she was on solid ground again, thanks to a sharp pang in her ankle. She'd landed hard on it, but as she rubbed it gingerly, she was thankful to find it wasn't broken. She then turned her attention to the place she'd fallen into.

It was a room, dimly lit, and it was filled with some of the strangest things she'd seen yet. Great big bubbling cauldrons, plucked chickens dangling headless from the ceiling amidst dried herbs, a cross-looking woman waving a pale hand in front of her face...her head snapped back in front of her once she realized who she was looking at.

"I've found you!"

The woman, Medea, snorted. "Found me? More like I rescued you. Those beasts would have devoured you and come begging at my door for seconds."

Iphigenia clamored to her feet, ignoring her ankle's protests. So this woman was the one who Thoas and the others feared so much. "You didn't save me from anything. You only dragged me down here." She pointed up. There, a wooden trap door shook from the force of the dogs scratching and pawing at it.

Medea laughed again. "Don't let your dear king hear that. He'd throw a fit if he knew I'd dragged his sweet new priestess into the witch's lair. Now tell me: what are you doing here?"

"You told me to come!" Iphigenia was quickly growing frustrated. Mind games were the *last* things she wanted to play. "Tell me how you know me, Medea." She spoke the name slowly, as if she were swirling a particularly vintage wine in her mouth.

The woman before her, Medea, had the audacity to look shocked for the briefest moment before her expression shifted to one of suspicion.

"How do you know my name?" she slowly asked, every syllable carefully enunciated.

"You first," Iphigenia countered, determined not to waver.

The two women stared at each other for a long interlude, Iphigenia glaring up at the woman who towered over her, before Medea broke first. She shook her head, a sad smile slipping across her lips.

"It's clear you know my name and my name alone."

"That's not true."

"You of all people would be the last to darken my doorstep if you knew. I call your bluff."

Iphigenia could only glare in affronted silence as she searched for sufficient words to counter with. "Your reputation precedes you. I've heard your story."

"You've heard the tail end of my "story". There's no need to treat me so coldly based on what you've heard up there." Medea waved her hand skywards. "I didn't have you pegged to be one so swayed by public opinion, princess." Medea stressed her former title, and the word alone was like a sword to Iphigenia's soul.

"Don't call me that."

"Of course," Medea said, but Iphigenia could sense a smugness behind those words. Still, the woman extended a hand towards her. When she didn't take it, she could tell she'd upset the woman by her frown. "Come, let me help you. Didn't you come all this way just to talk with me?"

"I did."

"Then come, sit. I'll make you a drink. *They* may bite," Medea admitted, glancing up to where the dogs had settled into a series of sniffing and pawing, "but I don't."

* * *

And so, Iphigenia found herself curled up on a plush *kline*, a mug of spiced wine keeping her palms warm. The chamber glowed with the soft light of wax candles, and it was quite warm despite the chill of the outdoors and its subterranean nature. As Medea floated around the room lighting additional torches, Iphigenia took the opportunity to get a closer look at the place. Shelves laden with all kinds of bottles and amphorae lined the walls. Pungent herbs, both dried and fresh, permeated the chamber with their heady odors. Iphigenia's thoughts were transported back to those quiet afternoons she'd spent at home, picking herbs to bring to her chambers and grind. Those memories, accompanied by the wine, had her oddly comforted despite the utter strangeness of the space.

"I saw what you tried to pull up there." Medea dragged over a chair to sit upon. She settled into it gingerly, as if something ailed her. Iphigenia was reminded of how her nurse used to have trouble with her knees, but Medea looked whole and hearty, nothing like the wizened woman so old that she'd been her mother's nurse as well.

"What? Scaring off a few pups?"

"Don't be coy. Iphigenia, those dogs have been starving for weeks, just waiting for an easy meal to make its way out of those walls. No torch would have held them off."

Ah, so her bluff had been called. Iphigenia could sense that Medea was trying to direct the conversation in a direction she wasn't quite so sure she wanted to go yet. Two could play at that game, however, she realized with a shock at hearing a sound she thought she'd never hear again repeated so soon.

"Why do you call me that?"

"It's your name, is it not?" Medea smiled, her sharp incisors gleaming white in the dim lighting.

Iphigenia hesitated. She hadn't told anyone in Tauris her name; most people just called her Priestess, or in the case of Thoas and his court, Hecate. There was power in knowing a name, and Iphigenia was intimately acquainted with just how much ruin that could bring. Just how much did this Medea woman really know about her, and was it a good idea to reveal any more? The rumors surrounding her were not kind, but something about her had Iphigenia unwilling to lie, either. This woman would not harm her.

She settled on the easiest response. "Yes."

There was no gloating nor smirking; Medea nodded as if it were the most obvious thing in the world. "Iphigenia...it means 'forcefully born,' correct?"

"Born from strength."

"Your mother chose well. It would take an extraordinarily strong woman to birth one such as yourself."

The mention of her mother was like Achilles' blade in her chest all over again. When was the last time Iphigenia had thought of her? She tamped down the feelings of guilt with a hearty swig of her wine.

"Let's not talk about my mother. Why did you lead me here? How do you know me?" Iphigenia waved an arm at their surroundings, all cold stone walls and dangling leafy herbs.

"I thought it was plain."

"It's not. Explain, or I'm leaving."

"How? The dogs—"

"I'll take care of them."

Medea was grinning now, her teeth shining brightly in the dim light. "You're but a girl—"

"Woman."

"Just a woman. They'll shred you."

Iphigenia felt a headache blooming into existence, and she stood to leave. A ladder leaned against one of the walls. Taking her chances outside would be better than this nonsense. Thoas and the villagers were right. She should have never wasted her time with this madwoman.

"Wait!" Medea lunged for Iphigenia's wrist. Cold fingers met warm skin, and it was as if Iphigenia had been stung by a dozen honeybees. She turned, wide eyed at the contact, to find Medea stark still, a litany of words both unintelligible and at the same time hers, her secret words, spilling out of her mouth so rapidly that she almost seemed to choke on them. The meaning was clear, even if the exact incantations weren't *I know what you are.*

"Who are you?" Iphigenia whispered.

Medea relaxed, her expression amused once again. "You really don't know?"

Iphigenia shook her head wordlessly. Medea tutted, then placed a hand on her cheek.

"I'm everything you once were, and everything you're going to be."

XX

upon a soft cushion I dispose my limbs

Iphigenia's days were split between the hustle and bustle of learning how to run a temple and retreating to Medea's chambers for lessons of a different lean. The butcher taught her just where to stab a man to snuff the life out of him in an instant, while Medea showed her how to drag out the same act so that he would writhe in agony for as long as she desired. The junior priestesses instructed her in drawing water from the sacred well; Medea demonstrated how to draw the blood from a person's heart up and out through their eyes and ears with a mere whisper. The sailors pointed out how to map the stars to time her sacrifices most auspiciously; Medea pointed out those gleaming pinpricks that held an entrance to the land of the dead beneath them. By day, Hecate learned who she was to become, and by night, Iphigenia learned who she had always had the potential to be.

"You're the most selfish creature I've ever had the displeasure to meet," Medea said one bitterly cold evening.

Iphigenia looked up sharply from her meditation. Medea's eyes, those odd eyes so pale they were nearly gold, were trained on her with a dry smile.

Why was Medea interrupting her so unprompted? Wasn't she the one who had said total focus was important to perfecting the act of bodily possession? According to her, she'd gotten lucky with Penthesilea. Any other novice would have been subsumed into their host's consciousness, lost forever. "Excuse me?"

"You heard me. I'm just unable to wrap my head around it. The Greeks kept you fed, taught you to ride a horse, and you can *read*. That's a life any girl would envy, but that wasn't enough for you."

Medea's smile had far too many teeth in it. Iphigenia, uneasy, drew her shawl tighter around herself.

"What are you trying to imply?" She couldn't hide the suspicion from her tone. Medea, no matter how helpful, was still a relative stranger to her.

"I'm merely admiring your egocentrism. I think it's a quality severely lacking amongst your peers."

"Plain language, please."

"Who did you con into teaching you? From where did you obtain your power?"

Iphigenia laughed. "If I had any true power, I wouldn't be here."

"Don't play me for a fool," Medea said, standing. "You know the art of witchcraft. Divine blood, both inherited and stolen, courses through your veins. I'd wager you're over halfway to being a goddess, at this point. Now, who taught you, and for the sake of the gods, *why?*"

A goddess. It made sense, didn't it? The dreams, the headaches, the sheer energy coursing through her? The feats she'd accomplished?

Memory circled back to a dream, hazy and half-forgotten, of a son stealing from his father, of a hunter walking into the flames in rejection of divinity, of a father that should have been hers dead at the feet of the man who called himself King of Men.

"She was Egyptian," Iphigenia began, unable to meet Medea's eyes. Iset had been dead now for more years than she'd even been alive. "She was bound to my household as a slave. I begged her to teach me magic, to help me become something more than myself."

"And despite your cruel mistreatment of her autonomy, she saw fit to allow a god to walk within you."

Why would she do that? Iphigenia thought of all Iset's midnight tirades, spoken in total confidence. Of how she wept for her dead countrymen, for the home and culture she'd never be able to return to. Iphigenia had nodded along at the time, uncomfortable in her complicity but not uncomfortable enough to do something about it. She'd been a coward, and yet, somehow, Iset had seen fit to help her. There could only be one reason.

"She wanted me to avenge her, to right the wrong my people had done to hers."

"And did you know this at the time?"

"No."

"Ah, a manipulator. I wish I could have met her."

"I deserved it for what I forced her to endure. If this is the only way I can repay her, so be it."

"Can you, though?"

Iphigenia thought of the bodies splayed on the shores of Troy, including Lysander's corpse, his skeleton bleached clean by the cleansing light of the sun. She flexed her fingers; she could still see the blood.

"I've already begun."

* * *

The temple girls didn't seem to mind her quick departures once the sun had begun to sink below the horizon; on the contrary, they all seemed to breathe a collective sigh of relief each time she dashed off with barely a goodbye. Iphigenia knew they were afraid of her. A foreign woman, born from the lands of the people who'd destroyed their country, and one who spent all her time practicing to cut throats while taking her leisure beneath the earth with one whose name they were loath to mention? Damn straight they were afraid. If the situation were to be reversed, she knew she'd be just as terrified.

Iphigenia was positive Thoas knew about her nightly strolls to Medea's chambers, but whether out of apathy or fear, he'd said nothing about it during their weekly dinners. He only asked how her training was going, in between excitedly remarking on how fat the livestock had grown despite the bitter weather and meager stores of grain.

Soon enough, Poseidon deposited another Greek man onto Taurian shores. He was especially pathetic, his small skiff in tatters and his mind in a similar state. Iphigenia almost felt pity for him as he was dragged from the gates up to the temple, babbling about world-eating whirlpools and many-mouthed beasts snapping men up like twigs. Still, she did not hesitate in preparing for the work of her station. Iphigenia was calm as she sprinkled the anointing oils, splashed the water of purification, and uttered a few words of dedication to the small statuette of Artemis that stood outside. She was the perfect image of a poised priestess, despite the waves of deep-seated trepidation that roiled within her as she looked down not on an empty altar, but a living, breathing human. She'd killed before, she'd sacrificed before, but this man was unwell, defenseless in his insanity.

Then the dagger was in her hands, and her focus was on the face of the man whose life she'd be snuffing out very shortly. He wasn't afraid; fear was the farthest thing from his expression as he licked his lips without taking his eyes off her.

"A bride," the man rasped, leering despite his bonds. "A Trojan bride to add to my spoils."

A sick dog, Iphigenia thought, trying and failing to tamp down the disgust bubbling up in her chest. He was sun-addled, and dehydrated too. The man had no idea where he was or what was about to happen to him. As his eyes raked down her body, she found that she did not care. Euthanization was the only cure for sick dogs.

When the knife bore through skin and sinew into the man's heart, she felt neither terror nor guilt, but a now familiar intoxicating plea-sure. It spread thick and hot through her veins just as quickly as the blood in the Greek's cooled. The man's death had thrown her into an ambrosial delight, she realized, so similar to that brought on by that divine drink of the gods.

"To Artemis of the beasts, Artemis of the wilderness, Artemis friend and soother of young girls, I consecrate this man," she prayed, trembling violently even as she poured the final libation over the altar.

The minutes after that passed in a blur. One second, she was scrubbing the blood from her forearms at the well so forcefully that her own blood threatened to join the man's, and the next, she was kicking at Medea's trapdoor, screaming to be let in.

Medea's arms held her tight as she wept, overwhelmed with anger and shame at the excitement she felt from taking that man's life. Medea was uncharacteristically quiet, only rubbing her back in circles and humming rather than providing her usual sardonic attitude. Iphigenia wanted nothing more. Empty platitudes and meaningless affirmations would be nothing to her, not in the face of something so vile locked inside.

* * *

Each time she performed her role, she went to Medea directly afterward. Iphigenia knew why, but she dared not voice it. There was no need, not at least until the fifth time. She'd been in Tauris months now, and this latest sacrifice had been the worst of them all, a trio of young men all pleading for their lives as she cut them down one by one. As she collapsed into Medea's arms, utterly spent, she wondered aloud when it would not be some grunt or lost infantryman, but her father who lay before her on the altar. Wouldn't it be an affront to the gods to feel pulsing pleasure at the death of her father, and by her own hand at that?

"They all might as well be," Medea remarked, stroking Iphigenia's now loose hair. It had grown long and wild over the winter, and as spring approached, she had taken to wearing it out more often, a far cry from the twin braids she'd worn all through her youth. "Your blood was the price for his war, and they willingly demanded the shedding of it. His crime is their crime. What you do is not vengeance, but justice."

Iphigenia's eyes burned with hot tears. This woman was her only constant in this strange land, her understanding of her going beyond mere language. Medea's words broke something in Iphigenia, and she surged upward, pressing her mouth against Medea's softly.

Medea returned the kiss, but it was all too brief; as she pulled away, a soft smile graced her lips. It did not reach her eyes. "You know I can't, Iphigenia," and the way she said her name — like it was the only name ever to exist in all creation — made her heart clench. "Not like you deserve."

"Not love," Iphigenia whispered, leaning her head against Medea's chest. She thought back to the words shared between her and a goddess in a cave without light, the same goddess who had eventually just abandoned her here. She couldn't do that again, but Medea...she was different. "Just a bit of comfort."

"Comfort, I can do," Medea replied, and she pressed a kiss to Iphigenia's temple before standing and gesturing towards the bed in the darkest corner of the chamber. "For you, always."

* * *

The first thing Iphigenia noticed when she sunk into the sumptuous sheets of her mentor was just how *different* Medea was. Where Artemis had been closed off, cautious to touch and even more hesitant to be touched, Medea was adamant that they cut straight to the chase. She was all long limbs and languid, lingering movements as the two women met in their embrace. Medea exuded confidence, and Iphigenia struggled to match it, not wanting to be outclassed. There had always been an inherent, undeniable eroticism to her lessons in witchcraft, and now it had been made manifest. Medea weaved magic with her mouth and spoke soft spells on her skin. Iphigenia relished in it, thrived under her hand — this was someone who understood her, who knew what she needed and didn't hesitate to provide.

It was right after one of these trysts that Iphigenia found herself burning with a question that had been threatening to fall out of her mouth all evening if it hadn't been otherwise occupied.

"Why are you helping me?" she asked.

Medea looked up from the chest of drawers across the room. She had just finished pouring wine from an amphora into two cups. She gave a short laugh as she walked back to the bed.

"Why wouldn't I?" Medea said, and Iphigenia gratefully took the cup she had offered. "Does it look like there's anything else to do around this shit-hole?"

"You and I both know there's more to it than that," Iphigenia pressed, then drained her drink. She set the cup on the floor and began to finger-comb her messy hair.

There was a pause as Medea took a sip from her drink before snuffing out the bedside candle. They were bathed in darkness, the solitary torch by the stairs their only source of light.

"How far would you go for your justice?" Medea asked, her tone neutral in a way that had Iphigenia on edge.

"You know the lengths I've gone."

"Yes, but not the whole breadth. So, how far?"

"I don't know."

"You've killed."

"Yes."

"Would you kill an army?"

"I've tried. You know this."

"A people? Would you wipe an entire race off the earth?"

"Gladly." The Achaeans were no good. They were a people united only by the desire to control and destroy — whether it be other nations or their own women and children. Iphigenia wanted nothing more than to see an end to the entire civilization.

"What about your own blood?"

Iphigenia looked at Medea darkly. "I want nothing more than my father's blood spilled on the ground before me."

"Your children? Would you take their lives, guilty of only being born, just so the cycle may cease with you?"

"What are you asking me?" Iphigenia cried, standing. She was truly rattled now, as Medea looked up at her with that same disturbingly neutral expression. She said nothing — then, Iphigenia realized.

"You're not asking me anything," she deadpanned. "You're telling me you...?"

"Go on," Medea coaxed, leaning back against the pillows and closing her eyes. "You're almost there."

Memories of Medea's body, lined with a mosaic of stretch marks, ran uninhibited in Iphigenia's mind.

"Who did you kill?" She whispered, despite wanting more than anything not to hear the answer.

"My brother, who was but a child," Medea began, and Iphigenia couldn't help but recoil, her thoughts immediately drawn to little Orestes in his swaddle. "He trusted me, his older sister, and I killed him. I hacked his little body into pieces just to taunt our father. He wasn't the only one; much later, I took the lives of two more little boys, even younger than sweet Absyrtus."

"And who were they?" Iphigenia, in her heart, already knew, but some morbid need to hear it spoken compelled her to ask anyway.

"My sons."

There was a crash as Iphigenia knocked over the bedside table in her scramble to get as far away from Medea as possible. Her mentor was a child killer. She had lain with this woman, guilty of the same crime as her father. "How could you?" She seethed. "You know what happened to me, and yet you dared...?"

"Who are you to judge me, Iphigenia of Mycenae? You, who would trade the glory of your civilization for one girl's selfish wish?"

"Selfish? I do what I do for my friend, for the girls of Troy—"

"Don't be so noble! Every girl becomes a slave to a man, Iphigenia, whether her master be literal, her father, or her husband. We are born knowing this."

"Not me," Iphigenia growled. "Never me."

"Then you agree — you only do this for your own desires. You took a god into you, you slaughtered dozens, all because you wanted to avoid an altar. You glut yourself on Greek blood because you're starved for vengeance. We're the same."

"Sacrificial or marriage, it was an altar all the same! I had no choice!"

"Then you understand why I had to do what I did. I loved my children." And for the first time, Medea's voice broke, heavy with grief. Iphigenia had never been more certain that she was telling the truth. "They were formed from my blood, my marrow, from the very bones of my teeth, and I gave it all willingly because I loved them. That is why I had to be the one to kill them. They were the last thing tying me to *him*, the man that had compelled me to kill my own brother, and he would have used them just as violently as he'd used me. Their destruction at my hand was the tenderest mercy I could offer them."

Iphigenia watched as Medea extended a hand toward her. She surprised even herself when she did not recoil but took it.

"I can't ever undo what I did," Medea whispered, "but if I can help you end this wretched cycle, then my life won't have been in vain."

* * *

Sacrifice became effortless after that. Iphigenia spent her days waiting on the cliffs of the Taurian seashore. It was fine; here, at least, she could be alone with her thoughts. On the rare occasion that she spotted a passing vessel, she clamored to her feet to wave her arms and shout, as if she were stranded on an island of cannibals. More times than not, the boats made haste for the shore, and she led the men who disembarked up over the dunes and towards Tauris. Her words, spoken in perfect Greek, were charming; that soft tone of voice her nursemaids begged her to use for her future husband finally got to see the light of day. The men in all their reckless abandon babbled about their exploits in Troy in an attempt to impress her, and she laughed, knowing they'd done naught but seal their doom. She knew them, even if they so clearly did not know her. They were all there at Aulis that day; they may not have been on that high hill, but they sailed on the breath of her blood all the same.

It didn't bother Iphigenia that they didn't recognize her. She was rather pleased. It only made her job all the easier. By the time they reached the gates of Tauris, the men were properly sedated, thinking they were merely liquored up instead of drugged. She praised Medea's crafty hands often, but her skill in poisonous brews may have been their greatest work. The boys of Tauris, now lanky young men, no longer needed to wrestle their captives into submission to drag them to the temple. Thanks to Iphigenia, they could now simply lead them by the hand, as if they were long-lost brothers. With the barrier of combat against seasoned war heroes gone, Tauris' youth had been able to grow into men and sire sons of their own.

Taurian towers had also sprouted from the ruins that once were, and the men passed them in awe as Iphigenia led the would-be besiegers to the temple, her temple, and snuffed out their lives as easily as they'd taken her own. Their names, purported to be renowned all across the Aegean and beyond, did not matter. The names of their victims— Andromache, whose baby was smashed upon the rocks at the bottom of Troy's mighty walls; Setaia, nailed upon a great wooden stake and abandoned until her death for daring to try and escape; Polyxena, youngest of Troy's royal daughters, killed on the grave of Achilles to provide a wife for him to lord over in the afterlife — those were the only names she cared to hear. It was for them that she did this now, the passion of revenge mellowing into the simple pleasure of justice. Her blade became an extension of her, no longer a simple tool, but a limb.

The men came not alone. Along with heavy stores of gold and grain, of dried meats and polished armor, there were countless women, stolen straight from Troy and her neighboring villages. These women, Iphigenia took under her wing. She washed the grime from their bodies, fed them, prayed with them, wept with them, and then brought them out of her temple, which had been expanded to accommodate them, into the Taurian fold. Many were already pregnant by their-now dead captors, such that within a few short years, the population of Tauris bounced back from near annihilation to that of a bustling city, its walls fortified and then expanded. If she hadn't watched the changes with her own eyes, Iphigenia would never have believed that it was once a desolate wasteland.

Throughout it all, Thoas grew as wide as his smiles, and he heaped praise upon praise on Iphigenia. The dinners grew so lavish that they became feasts, and the feasts became festivals, open to all the citizens of Tauris. Thoas' love for her multiplied with every Greek body tossed upon the pyre. If it weren't for his intense piety (and overwhelming appetite for strapping young men), Iphigenia would've believed that Thoas would have begged for her hand in marriage. That was one thing she'd avoided this far. The Taurian boys, half her age, avoided her like the plague. Medea was wholly uninterested in anything more than the purely physical, and Artemis had not made herself known to Iphigenia in years. It was as if she'd never roamed those vast forests and low valleys with the goddess at all.

It was no matter. To Iphigenia, Taurus had been the best thing that had ever happened to her. Here, she was not only respected, but *free*. All her earlier despairs had disappeared, replaced by total confidence. Thoas asked for her council, Medea educated her in things beyond human understanding, her trainees hung off her every word, the elder ladies fawned over her — it was everything she'd ever wanted and been denied. The Taurians were wrapped around her smallest finger, and it didn't look like that'd be changing any time soon.

One morning, shortly after her eighth anniversary in Tauris, Iphigenia was laying in Medea's bed when her mentor's body began to wrack with coughs.

"What's wrong? Take a hit from the wrong pipe?" Iphigenia asked, her tone playful. But when Medea did not respond, Iphigenia began to worry, thumping the woman's back until she caught her breath.

When Medea had recovered, she looked grimly up at Iphigenia. Blood stained the corner of her mouth, stark against her pale skin.

Iphigenia thumbed at it, her touch soft. She'd learned long ago that tenderness was the one way to Medea's true thoughts. "What's this?"

"Nothing," Medea had replied gruffly, pushing Iphigenia's hand away from her mouth and further down. "We have other more important things to worry about."

At the time, Iphigenia agreed. If Medea said she was fine, then she was. But eventually, the coughing fits became full body affairs, and more often than not, Iphigenia was holding Medea's long dark hair back as she spilled her insides into a chamber pot.

"Look at me," Medea said one morning as Iphigenia brushed her hair. The two of them were seated at a mirror, a rarity this far north. One of Medea's creature comforts, of course, one of the only things she'd treasured from her time in Korinth.

Iphigenia looked up, and the image that greeted her in the mirror was a grim one. She had hardly changed since the day she'd washed up on Tauris' shores, save for her hair, which had grown long, and her sides, which had grown themselves. She was well fed, and killing men hardly took the energy it did to track and take down full-grown deer.

Medea was who she had to worry about. The witch had lost weight where Iphigenia had gained it, her face gaunt and her hair graying at the temples. The bags under her eyes had grown apparent, and Iphigenia noticed just how Medea's hands shook as she reached for her face powders. Still, to Iphigenia, Medea looked just as wonderful as that evening she'd knocked at her door.

"I see you," she replied, running the brush through her mentor's silken hair. "You look as beautiful as ever."

"I'm dying," Medea responded, swiveling her head to look up at Iphigenia.

"Aren't we all?"

"I'm serious." And Iphigenia knew that she was. "As your power grows, mine wanes. There's no need for disciples of witchcraft when the goddess of them all walks the earth. You and I aren't so different, but here is where our similarities end."

"So they do," Iphigenia said, not meeting Medea's eyes. She knew she hadn't changed, not since the morning that cruel blade had been driven into her chest, but she had wanted to believe Medea was the same. Still, it had grown harder and harder to deny the truth as the years went on and Medea grew frailer, her movements slower, and her appetites diminished. That spark in her eyes was the same as it had been all those years ago, but all else had changed.

"The air is changing," Medea said, closing her eyes. "This world is on the verge of collapse. I can feel it, and even if I could be here for it, I don't want to be."

"But I need you."

Medea smiled. "You've far surpassed your teacher. Iphigenia may have needed me, but Hecate does not."

They sat in silence for a few moments before Medea began to speak softly again. "We have one last commonality. I foresaw it in a dream, just as my father did so many moons ago. A Greek man is coming to take you away."

Iphigenia recoiled in horror.

Medea grasped her wrist, stilling her. "Don't fear him. I refuse to witness it, but he shall not harm you."

"To take me *is* to harm me," Iphigenia lamented, her heart breaking. The loss of her mentor would be hard enough, but Tauris too? The city had become a true home to her at last, and now a *man* of all creatures was going to take it from her? The urge to retch was becoming harder and harder to resist.

"He's no Jason, but you will want to hate him as furiously as I did that man. Don't. Manipulation for even a taste of love can cause one to do terrible things. I know that better than anybody. Promise me you'll go quietly with him?"

And Iphigenia could only nod. Her world was falling all around her yet again, and as always, she was being told there was nothing she could do.

Anger bloomed in her chest. This time would be different. She hoped Medea would forgive her for what she had to do.

XXI

dance in measure round the fair altar

They laid Medea to rest on the darkest day of the year, the winds howling and the air bitterly cold. She'd hardly lived a month after that last prophecy she'd given. Iphigenia and Thoas were the only ones who attended the funeral pyre, as was to be expected. No one else in these lands had loved her, and it was not as if she had any children to mourn for her. Iphigenia couldn't meet eyes with the king; Medea was the one subject he'd never broached with her, and yet he'd come nonetheless. He was a true friend.

She poured frothy milk into a golden bowl, splashed dark wine in a high arc, and dribbled honey on top of it all. Then she sipped, passed the bowl to Thoas as well, then tilted it towards Medea's still, parted lips. The rest, she poured onto the earth, a dark libation for the god of the dead.

* * *

"Sentimental old woman," Iphigenia murmured, tracing a finger along a small vial mounted on the wall. She was in Medea's chambers, tidying up the last of the woman's mortal possessions. The vial in question contained her first poison that she'd brewed strong enough to kill. She'd made it under Medea's careful eye, and when it was finished, her mentor had asked if she would be allowed to keep it. Iphigenia had thought Medea had meant to *use* it, not treasure it like some delighted parent. The thought of someone being so proud of her, and that person being gone, made her heart ache in a way it hadn't in years.

Iphigenia was wondering just what else Medea had kept of hers when the sound of brass cut through the silence in the room. She ignored the sound at first, not understanding what she heard. When it repeated itself, she couldn't help but scramble up the ladder.

The sea watchmen were blowing their horns.

No one had dared journey into these waters in months. The old ships of the Greeks had begun to stink with the rot of abandonment, and she had assumed all those from Troy had either returned home or perished at this point. Who dared sail here, especially on this darkest of days?

She braced against the cold, wrapping her shawl tightly around her face as she emerged from the ground. A round face stared down at her from the wall above.

"Who is it, Opheltes?" she grimly called, and Opheltes, the boy who had once tried to kill her, now a grown man, responded.

"Two Greeks, quarreling something fierce. I can't tell if they want to kill or kiss each other!"

"Sounds par for the course." Iphigenia made her way to the closest gate. Opheltes walked parallel to her, up on the wall. "Are they at the temple yet?"

"Waiting only for you."

Iphigenia vowed to make this sacrifice quick. She was exhausted, and wanted to do nothing more than sleep for the next ten years. Medea was gone, and yet she was expected to continue on as if nothing had happened.

Then, she remembered Medea's words, and resolve alighted inside of her. A Greek was coming to take her away. It couldn't be a coincidence that two Greeks had washed up before Medea's ashes had even cooled. She picked up her pace, breaking into a sprint as soon as she passed through the gate.

The streets were blessedly empty, due to the dark and cold. It wasn't unlike that first night, but now her stride was a confident one as she dashed to the temple. The braziers out front were lit, and guards stood just inside its porticoes.

"Lead me to them," she murmured to one, who nodded and entered.

Inside, two men sat bound, one fiercely struggling against his bonds while the other focused entirely on the small statuette of her goddess. The staring one was dark haired and lanky, as if he had yet to finish growing, while the other, the one wriggling like a stuck pig, was stocky, muscles rippling with strength. A bored looking guard stood over them. When Iphigenia approached, the stocky one's attention turned fully to her.

"Please lady, whatever you do, kill me," he began, but before he could finish dragging the words out, the lanky one tore his eyes off of the statue and barked "No! Me!"

"They've been at this the whole time," the guard said, rolling his eyes. "I say kill both of them."

"Hush," Iphigenia said, pushing past the guard to peer down at the two men. Of course she planned on killing them, expeditiously in fact, but not without being sure — she had to know if Medea's words had been true.

"State your purpose here."

The dark haired one stared off to the side again, his jaw slack, but the stocky one was focused entirely on Iphigenia. His face was grim as he began to speak. "We're here to retrieve the goddess of this land."

Iphigenia felt her blood turn to ice in her veins as she took a step back. She had been aware of her changing nature for years now, had finally just started to embrace it, but to hear it put into words like this? Medea had been right on more than one count, it seemed.

She laughed nervously. "Goddess? There are no goddesses in Tauris; only widows and fishermen. You're rather far North of Mt. Olympus."

"Then who is that?" a voice asked, and it was as if its owner's throat had been scraped raw by the rough rocks at the bottom of the sea floor. Iphigenia looked at the dark haired visitor, who had a pale finger pointing shakily at her. He was an unnerving man; his eyes were as wild as his hair, and long scratches ran up and down the length of his arms. Madness had clearly alighted upon his mind, but that wasn't what had Iphigenia so nervous as he stabbed his finger towards her. No, it was the fact that the man looked devastatingly familiar despite her never having laid eyes on him, as if she'd known him all her life.

"Me?" Iphigenia said, placing a hand against her chest. Whatever these men were, they were straight to the point. No matter, it only made her job easier.

"Her!" The wild eyed man was straining against his bonds as he craned his neck to get a look behind Iphigenia. She turned, only to be greeted by the marble statuette of Artemis standing proudly beneath the flickering torchlight.

"That's a representation," Iphigenia replied. "Just an image, no more." No matter how many nights Iphigenia wished that it was something more, prayed for it to be, it never changed form, never drew breath, never spoke, never came to her. If she wouldn't appear for her, she wouldn't for these two vagabonds.

"It doesn't matter what it is," the stocky one said, taking over. "That statue is what we're here for. We'll just be taking it and—"

"Under what circumstances?" Iphigenia laughed. "Did you forget that you happen to be prisoners?"

"You look to be a hospitable host, Priestess," the stocky man argued. "Help us. You speak Greek, after all. You're really one of us."

"I am no such thing." Iphigenia felt the beginnings of a thundering headache, and for the love of the gods, would that mumbling idiot get his eyes off of her? Chill was starting to seep in, and she just wanted to be done with this dark day. These two wanted the statue, not her. They were not the one's Medea had spoken of, and somehow, that disappointed her. "Prepare the prisoners for sacrifice," she said out of the side of her mouth to the guard, who gave a firm nod.

She turned and made for the purification chambers to prepare, ignoring the gasp of affront from the stocky prisoner. It wouldn't do to keep her goddess waiting much longer.

* * *

The dark haired one, with the wild eyes, was to be sacrificed first. The other priestesses had done the difficult work of anointing the man and now he lay before Iphigenia on the altar, silent.

She looked down at him, grasping her blade firmly. While his friend's anguished cries rang out in the background, this man made no noise. He only looked up at her with a pair of unfocused brown eyes. What a shame. Iphigenia could recognize from his build that he would've made a great warrior one day, but madness had crippled his mind in such a way that he was as harmless as a newborn kitten. It was almost obscene that the guards had restrained him to the altar.

"Don't hurt him!" the other man yelled from his position on the floor. One of the guards had a knee in his back. "Pylades," the man on the altar murmured. "Everything's gonna be okay."

"That's right," Iphigenia cooed, stroking the man's hair. This was far easier than normal, even with Pylades' hollering. No one had come to her altar this calmly, not even the man driven mad by drinking seawater. The serenity of the man before her was oddly infectious, as she felt her own limbs growing more relaxed. She shook it off though. Iphigenia couldn't afford to let her guard down around these two, no matter how harmless they seemed. They were Greeks, and Greek men had never been kind to her. "Just go to sleep."

And the man gave a brief nod and closed his eyes, as if Iphigenia were his own mother laying him down for a nap. She raised the dagger high as she muttered the holy words, ingrained in her mind at this point. She'd make it quick and painless for this one. There was no pleasure in this killing, only the knowledge that it must be done. This was duty, and she was going to fulfill it.

The blade swung downwards through the air, and as it ended its journey in a splash of red, two things occurred. Firstly, the man on the altar jerked as the life began to spill out of him, and second, his companion wailed his name in the most heart wrenching cry Iphigenia had heard since that day in Aulis. But it was the name itself that had her stumbling backwards from the altar. The knife fell out of her hand, its blood stained metal clanging against the hard marble of the floor.

The build was right, and so was the age...even the hair, so thick and dark, was correct. He'd been so familiar...Iphigenia buried the sob rising up in her and rushed back to the man, praying that she wouldn't find what she was looking for. As the man convulsed beneath her, she pushed the mop of curly hair up and back out of his face. There, just above his eyebrow, sat a thin jagged scar running up and back to his hairline. So the name Pylades had cried, was one in the same with...?

Iphigenia pressed her hands to the wound, desperately trying to staunch it. "Get me a healer! A medic!" she cried out to the priestesses, who were staring, dumbfounded. "Now!"

Even as the girls began to scramble, Iphigenia knew it was too late. The man had grown still beneath her, and as his body began to cool, her cries joined those of Pylades.

* * *

She had wanted Pylades unchained, but the minute the first clamp had come off, he had lunged at her with all the fury of a wild lion. It had taken her strongest guards to wrangle the man back in again, and now he sat on his knees before her, his eyes full of tears.

Iphigenia was sure her face mirrored his, ruddy with anguish. Her baby brother, alive after all these years, and he had lost his life by her own hand. She wanted to scream; how much more were the gods going to take from her? But Iphigenia tamped down her emotions as best she could, and addressed Pylades.

"Why did you come?" She ignored the tremble in her voice as the man looked up at her, fire in his eyes.

"To atone for his sins," Pylades replied, jerking his head back at Orestes' corpse, still on the altar. "You weren't part of the program. He wasn't supposed to die!"

"His sins?" Iphigenia breathed. When she'd last seen him, Orestes had been a bubbly baby full of nothing but laughter. The idea that that same child could do something so heinous to drive him to the far reaches of civilization was beyond her.

"What did he do?"

"What's it to you, you murderous bitch?"

Iphigenia ignored the insult, even though she felt that she entirely deserved it. "He's my brother."

Pylades laughed then, but there was no mirth in it. "What are you, one of Agamemnon's bastards from the war? You're no true sister of his."

Iphigenia walked back to the altar, wishing with all her heart that Orestes' chest would be rising and falling just as her mother used to have her incessantly check in the middle of the night. She placed a hand on the hard plane of his front. No such movement occurred.

"Pylades, tell me, how old do you think I am?"

"I don't want to play your games. Just kill me." Pylades looks longingly towards Orestes' body.

"Answer the question."

"I don't know? 20 or so maybe? No older than us."

Ah. So that cleared up one of her suspicions. "Pylades, I used to watch you play." It was true; Iphigenia hadn't realized it at first, but her brothers' companion had once come to Mycenae, right as Orestes had been born. She hadn't paid him much mind at the time, enamored as she was with her new sibling. Now here he was, a grown man.

"Impossible."

"Your mother is my father's sister."

"You have no proof."

"My proof lies within the inner *megaron* at Mycenae. He has shown it to you, I presume?"

"When we were last there, yes," Pylades said, speaking out of the side of his mouth as if he were ashamed of something.

"And doesn't it depict Tantalus, Pelops, the battle between Thyestes and Atreus, all our relatives?"

"Orestes and mine, but not yours."

"They are mine all the same. Tell me, was the blood in the tapestry not woven from the very finest Tyrian purple thread?"

"It was. But this tells me nothing! You could be any nursemaid, turned rogue!"

Iphigenia sighed. "There should be a scar beneath Orestes' hair. Push it back and you'll know I'm telling you the truth — I am his older sister, Iphigenia."

Pylades stretched back from her. "No! She's been dead 20 years."

Iphigenia stepped closer. "I've been anything but."

"You have no proof, murderer," Pylades replied.

Iphigenia was just about to respond when there was a clang accompanied by a bright flash. She turned just as Pylades gasped; the guards and priestesses had already fled, and Iphigenia knew Pylades would have as well if he'd had the ability. Before them, the statuette hummed with power as it illuminated the room in silver radiance. Iphigenia cast an arm over her eyes, the brightness overwhelming after the dimness of the room.

"She is telling the truth," a voice said. Iphigenia sank to her knees. She hadn't heard that voice in almost ten years. "I myself rescued her, and the princess sacrificed on that altar all those years ago stands before you now as my immortal priestess."

Am I really yours? Iphigenia thought to herself.

"Now, on this darkest of days, she has continued the cycle she was once destined to break. Blood against blood, blade held to brother's neck."

Iphigenia dropped her arm, anger coursing through her. "Why are you here? Why did you have me do this?" She stared at the goddess, no longer statue, but flesh. Artemis, who had left her here with no guidance and no recourse.

"I told you; everything you did after that day was of your own free will."

"I would've never chosen this!"

"Who's to say? You don't even know of his crime."

"It doesn't matter...he was still my brother!" Hot tears coursed down Iphigenia's cheeks. "I never got to know him."

A warmth materialized at her shoulder and she shrugged it off. "You abandoned me," she muttered darkly. "You left me to do this horrible thing, and now you try to touch me?"

"It's not like that, I promise you," Artemis said softly. "There's still time..."

"Time?" Iphigenia laughed, bitterness staining her voice. "Twenty years wasted, just to end the same way it started, and yet there's still time?"

"Yes." Artemis' voice was firm. "Iset brought you to the path, and Medea handed you the lantern. All you have to do is light it and walk."

"But the cost —" Medea had warned her about dabbling in the realm of the dead. Even now, she could hear her mentor's voice, warning her that if she dared disturb her shade after she was gone, Medea would see to it that she drug Iphigenia to Tartarus herself.

"It's up to you to decide if it's worth it."

Iphigenia thought back to all those days spent in the sunshine, watching Orestes crawl over the blanket as she sat with her mother. She remembered the nights spent making silly faces to get her brother to laugh himself to sleep. And then, she thought of the promise she'd made to her mother all those years ago, that she'd protect Orestes until he was able to protect himself. She wiped her tears away and held her chin high.

"He's worth his weight in gold. I'll do it."

Artemis nodded at her, and then the statue was just a statue again, the light fading from the room.

"What the *fuck* is going on?" Pylades wondered aloud. Iphigenia had all but forgotten that he was there.

"I'm going to unchain you," Iphigenia said, her fingers making quick work of the young man's bonds. Pylades stood, cautiously rubbing his forearms.

"I should cut you down here."

"But you will do no such thing," Iphigenia replied, busying herself by snuffing out the torches and candles one by one. "Pylades, listen carefully. Do not leave Orestes' body. If this works, which I believe it will, it is imperative that you do not stray from this room. All will be lost if you leave him for even a moment."

"Explain."

"I cannot. You have to trust me."

"Trust a murderess?" Pylades scoffed. "Why should I?"

Iphigenia took a deep breath. "Because if you ever want to hold him again, you will."

The room was silent. Iphigenia snuffed out the last light, and they were plunged into darkness. "Go to him now."

She heard Pylades shuffle back towards the altar. Whispering filled the room, and while she couldn't hear what he was saying, Iphigenia was sure that Pylades was going to hold up his end of the bargain. Now, the true work could begin.

XXII

flitting among the shadowy dead

The dark, that ancient foe, had taken her into its maw, gnashed her between its rough hewn teeth, and gulped her down to the very bedrock of its bowels. There she churned, unable to determine up or down, right or wrong, life from death. Noxious gases dizzied her, snatching every belaboring breath from her throat before she could fully inhale.

Iphigenia longed to scream, to weep, to beg for the mercy on nonexistence as her body was assaulted on all ends by a force she had not the ability to understand. Iphigenia wanted all of those things, but Hecate, that burning deity within her, quaked with desire for the opposite. She would be a torch against that reeking chemical and alight the dark once and for all. A whispered prayer, and then the world exploded into fury and flame.

She was free. Iphigenia was overcome with gasps, sucking down greedy breath after breath. As tears streamed from her eyes, the first coherent thought that struck her was that she was undeserving to taste this air, no matter how acrid it was. Her second thought? That she would do it anyway.

No birds, no sky. Only dead, dry ground, and dead, dry corpses to keep her company on her umbral march.

"Hail, goddess," a thin voice, the first she'd heard in an eon (or was it three?), rasped out.

Iphigenia whipped around. A man stood, unwavering, his ghostly eyes clear. His bearded face was at once both familiar and alien.

"Atys," she whispered, the name coming as naturally to her as her own breath, and the man murmured his ascent, proud tears streaming down his face. For the first time in this desolate wasteland, Iphigenia smiled and raised her torch arm high.

"My living child, a goddess," the bearded man said as she grew closer. "The one with the power to avenge me has come."

"Avenge you?" Iphigenia asked. She'd come to avenge no one and nothing but her own transgression.

"End the bloodline of Agamemnon. Wipe it from the earth so that no Atreid ever walks within the light again."

Her face fell.

"Father, I promise you that I'm going to make things right, but I've not come here for vengeance—"

"You must!" Suddenly, the beaming image of a proud father distorted into a mask of rage, blood pouring from his snarling mouth and gaping chest wounds. The faint sound of a wailing infant rang in her ears, and Iphigenia wrenched herself away. Her father lunged at her, and without thinking, she swung the heavy axe. His ghost dissipated into nothing.

Nothing mattered more than retrieving Orestes. Not revenge, not ghosts, not truth and not lies. She soldiered on.

Beneath her feet, ashen gray became dotted with silken white. Asphodel bloomed in what she quickly realized was a path. Without hesitation, Iphigenia trod upon the flowers.

It was a gentle slope upward, and at its apex was a high, half moon dais nestled amidst a desolate field of ruins.

"Welcome to your trial," a familiar voice rang out. Medea sat at the high point, wearing a resigned grin.

"Fuck," Iphigenia swore.

"Good to see you too, kid. Don't worry, I'm far from the worst of your jurors."

From behind a pillar, two forms slunk out. Penthesilea glared at her, wearing a crushed throat and a weeping wound. Iphigenia only had eyes for the shade at her heels with the neutral expression and spear ruined chest. Iset. Iset, who she'd once loved. Iset, who she'd continuously dehumanized. Iset, who had died for her sake despite everything. Iphigenia ran up to the dais, sank to her knees in the soot, and bowed her head amongst the petals.

"Forgive me," she cried, attempting to wrap her arms around the shade's legs. It was an exercise in futility; they were as insubstantial as mist.

"Forgiveness is for the court to decide," deadpanned a voice she hadn't heard in two decades.

The world rippled, then morphed. She was seated in a high backed chair. More alarming than the thin chains binding her to her seat was the fact that she was also upside down before the now assembled court. The three of them were all seated according to the normal rules of gravity, looking rather disinterested. Iphigenia's head began to pound with the weight of her own blood.

"We are gathered here today to determine whether or not you, Iphigenia of Mycenae, Hecate of the In-Between, are to leave this place with the prize you seek." As Medea spoke, a pillar materialized behind the dais. It was painted in blotchy streaks of wine red, and a cloying metallic scent rolled off it in waves. "In my opinion, this is far too much stress for a bit of marble—"

"Orestes," Iphigenia corrected, for it was so obviously his representation that she could scream. "Give him to me."

"I thought I taught you patience," Medea said, scowling. "You must first plead your case, little witch, and plead it carefully. My fellow jurors aren't as sentimental as I, and they might opt to toss the two of you in Tartarus."

As if called by name, Penthesilea rose. Her hair, once a bright shade of red, had been reduced to a dull slate. She took a fistful of Iphigenia's own hair, as if jealous of its vibrancy, and tugged her head close.

"You killed me to eliminate the Greeks. You stole my army, my body, and allowed them both to be desecrated. Now you render that desecration meaningless by pleading for the life of one of those you sought to kill?"

Iphigenia had no answer for the hard eyes peering into hers.

"I'm sorry," was the best she could muster. Penthesilea turned from her in disgust.

Medea stepped forward now, tossing her heavy hair back. "You're lucky I even showed up to this. I was two steps from jumping into the Lethe and blessed forgetfulness. Why rescue this whelp? Let him die, and the Atreids die with him."

"I have to," Iphigenia murmured. "He's my responsibility."

Medea laughed, patting Iphigenia on the cheek in that overly familiar way that had once infuriated and infatuated her. "You don't know the first meaning of responsibility. Glad you're finally taking some initiative though."

As Medea returned to her seat, Iphigenia sought Iset's gaze. The ghost made no move to rise, only looking coldly from her high perch.

"Once, I thought you could save me. That wasn't a possibility. Why can't you at least avenge me? Did you ever really care about me?"

"I'm trying," Iphigenia pleaded desperately. "That's all I've ever wanted to do. I loved you."

"You've lied to me. You're going to save the last scion of that warmongering, slave owning race, and you're going to forget who granted you that power you so selfishly lord over everyone else in the first place."

"I've never forgotten you," Iphigenia whispered, unable to help the tears streaming into her hair. "Everything I've done, every life I've taken, every throat I've cut has been for you, Iset."

"Don't speak my true name. You don't deserve to."

"I want to. Let me deserve it — what must I do?"

"End this wretched cycle. Let the Greeks fade from the world. Their future rests on his shoulders."

"It rests on *mine*," Iphigenia corrected, "and has since that day at Aulis. Orestes is an innocent — he must live."

At this, all three women on the dais began to laugh, a hollow, alien sound in their grim locale.

"Orestes is far from innocent. His hands are stained as dark as mine," Medea said, wiping away an errant tear.

"Bring her out," Penthesilea murmured, a bored expression on her face.

"And here, our star witness," Medea announced with a little clap of her hands. Iset nodded, and from behind the pillar emerged the last person Iphigenia wanted to see.

Her mother, Clytemnestra, Queen of Mycenae, stood before her, the front of her gown soaked in dried blood, a grievous head wound exposing the pale bone of her skull to the air.

Words failed Iphigenia. She thrashed uselessly against her bonds, desperate to embrace the woman before her. Knives of guilt slashed at every nerve in her body — when had her mother perished?

"You shouldn't be here," she sobbed brokenly.

"But I am," her mother said, and it was at once the most beautiful and the most terrible sound Iphigenia had ever heard. Twenty long years, and it was still as if she'd been torn from her mother's pleading arms just yesterday.

"Do not weep for me, daughter. This is my natural fate; my punishment for my crimes. Now you must face your own."

"Queen Clytemnestra," Iset said, her voice thundering over Iphigenia's choked sobs. "Explain to the defendant why you stand before her today."

"I killed the man who took her from me. He'd taken one child already and had gone unpunished. I would not be aggrieved a second time without vengeance. I replay the moment I ended his wretched little life every time the god of clarity sees fit to bless me."

The axe embedded in the back of Agamemnon's shade, the very same one now on Iphigenia's hip, seemed to thrum with a self satisfied joy.

"Why are you here?" Penthesilea said, her voice soft.

"I took my husband's cousin for a lover. In my grief, in my longing for retribution, I neglected my two remaining children. They grew strange and bitter, and the spirits of madness took them for their own. They...are lost to me."

"Woman, please tell your child who took your life so I can get on with forgetting mine?" Medea said, shaking loose her dark robes. "I'm tired."

Clytemnestra's eyes, once as blue as the sea, were black holes as she whispered one word. "Orestes."

Iphigenia's world collapsed. The little infant Orestes, the baby who feared his own shadow, who'd still yet to even walk on his own at two years old, had grown up to commit matricide?

"Do you still desire him?" Medea asked, her voice cool.

"I...*why?*"

"You must choose," her mother murmured, ignoring the question. "We cannot be as Demeter and Persephone. Take him from this place, and you forfeit your natural death. You will never see me again. You will be as a god."

A radical thought struck Iphigenia. "And if I remain here with you?"

"Nothing will ever plague you again. You will be in my arms again, forever, and the House of Atreus will fall into little more than legend. Never again will the Greeks wage such terrible war."

"I want that," Iphigenia said quickly. "Let me."

And then her mother with a single word shattered her heart into dozens of brittle shards.

"No. The cost is too high, and I've favored you over the others for too long."

"Whatever it is, I'll pay it. I'll do anything," and Iphigenia knew her jury knew it to be true.

"The cost is Orestes," Iset said, her voice high and cold. "The fine for both his and your crimes is his condemnation to the deepest, darkest pit in Tartarus to suffer for the rest of time."

The cost was the one she'd descended into the bowels of hell to retrieve, the very one and the same with the one who had killed her mother.

"What shall you choose? What do you truly wish for, my gem, my Iphigenia?" Her mother spoke her name with such tenderness that Iphigenia broke into a fresh bout of sobs.

"I—he...Orestes is as much a victim as you or I," she said, fighting for every word. "He shouldn't be made to suffer for my own happiness. I will take him home to rebuild his house."

Her mother's smile was the softest Iphigenia had ever seen it. "Go forward in strength."

"I will, mother. I love you."

When Iphigenia next blinked, her mother's shade was gone.

"So now, you understand just who you bargain for. Do you wish to proceed?" Medea's voice was cool, but there was the hint of a smile still on her former mentor's spectral face.

"I do," she said firmly.

"And what is your argument for why we should allow you to leave with the man called Orestes, whom, I might remind you, *you* sent down here in the first place?"

Iphigenia steeled herself, gripping the arms of her chair tight. The tapestry in Mycenae's *megaron* loomed bright in her mind.

"Mother. Helen. Agamemnon and Menelaus. Atreus and Thyestes. Atys, my true father. Pelops and Broteas. Tantalus. They all share one commonality."

"What, being a member of the worst family since Kronos spat up Zeus?"

"That's exactly it," Iphigenia said quickly. "The gods, that is. They meddled with them, with all humans, and twisted us into these imperfect creatures riddled with evil and infirmity. Killing all the Greeks was never going to be the answer. We need to end the involvement of the gods."

"You know better than that," Medea said softly, almost disappointed. "Even without the gods, humans will always seek to harm each other."

"Then why this war? Why have the gods waged war against each other, using humans as pawns? What do they seek to gain?"

"It's not what they seek to gain," Iset said, standing again. "But what they want to lose. The Olympians seek a clean slate. The Trojan War is a war of annihilation, one you have gleefully participated in."

"I know this now," Iphigenia said softly. "And I oppose it. I will bring Orestes home, have him rebuild the house, and as divine intermediary between all realms, seal the gods from mortals forevermore. Humanity will make their own decisions."

All three women pondered her, curiosity alight in their eyes.

"You would cease the golden age of the gods, just as you come into your power?" Penthesilea asked.

"The golden age is dead," Iphigenia retorted.

"Is this what you truly want? Man will struggle without aid from the gods." Medea's voice was even as she posited her question.

Iphigenia thought of her mother's anguish at Aulis, of Artemis weeping in the belly of a cave for a long dead mortal, of Troilus' ripped open on the steps of Apollo's temple, of Achilles' clouded eyes looking down on her as Zeus loomed above.

"I want this."

She turned to Iset, who avoided her eyes. "Final remarks?"

Penthesilea leaned back in her chair. "You sacrificed peace for cruelty. You took my life, the lives of my women, my warriors."

"I did."

Iset's voice was next, high and cold. "I made you, and yet you treated me as a slave rather than an equal."

"And you've been my superior every step of the way. I'd give anything to remedy that, save for this."

Medea rolled her eyes as she spoke. "Your theatrics were a throbbing ulcer, both then and now."

"Okay."

This seemed to amuse Medea, who laughed as she stood. "I defer, if only because I've wasted enough time here. Good luck, my student."

"I defer," Penthesilea barked, standing as well. "I still don't like you, but warriors should battle on their own merits, without augments from the divine."

"I defer," Iset said softly, looking Iphigenia in the eye at last. "Do you know what this means?"

"I want to hear you say it. Teach me one final lesson."

"Divinity thrums beneath your skin like a snake ready to strike. Your days with humanity are slipping away like the sands of Kemet. The descendant of Orestes, of Electra? They shall forget you within a generation. Only the poets will remember, and even amongst them, a small portion."

"I am frail, fallible, undeserving and ill equipped for this gift you bestowed upon me," Iphigenia murmured. "I am not worthy of remembrance."

"But you are of my forgiveness. Go forth, Iphigenia."

"Goodbye, Iset."

As the words left her lips, the path to the pillar became clear. The bonds of her chair broke, and she hit the ground running in a sprint to the column. The words of purification, themselves as ancient as this place, flowed from her mouth as easily as blinking.

The judges were gone, the dais the only evidence of their ever having been. Here in this place, the thin shade of her brother was her only companion. There was color in his cheeks, she noted as she reached out a hesitant hand to touch him there. His skin was solid.

He slept. She traced her fingers from his face down to his hand, just as corporal. It was as soft as it had been when it was a balled up baby fist. These were hands that had never held a weapon in warfare. Orestes was pure now, as far from his father's son as one could be. Iphigenia took him into her arms.

Orestes stirred, groggy. He looked up at her first in confusion, then terror, raising his arms in front of his face.

"No more!" he yelled, trying to wrench himself out of her grasp.

"Orestes, I am your sister. I'm here to take you home."

At the sound of her voice, Orestes' shoulders softened. His eyes, still unfocused, peered up at her in suspicion. "You're not Electra."

"I'm not Electra," Iphigenia confirmed. "But I am going to bring you home to her."

"But how? We're both dead." Her brother, despite his height, still held onto a childish naivety.

"We're anything but. Now tell me, do you remember anything of your other sister, the one who died?"

Orestes face crumpled in confusion. "It's so hard to remember anything here."

"Then I'll remember for the both of us. Orestes, when you were a baby, hardly walking, you escaped from the palace. Everyone was scattered far and wide, searching for you, worrying that you'd been abducted by our father's enemies, but I alone thought to search not the roads or neighboring towns for you, but the woods. It took hours, but I found you at the overlook of the city, just babbling away at the birds of the sky and the bugs of the earth. Do you know what I did next?"

"What?"

"I carried you on my back all the way down the mountain, home to where you belonged. Orestes, do you trust me?"

She watched as her brother looked at her with trepidation heavy in his eyes. She was suddenly struck by just how young he still was. His beard had yet to come in yet. Barely out of childhood, and yet he'd suffered so much...how could he trust anyone?

Yet, to Iphigenia's surprise, Orestes nodded. "I believe you."

"Then I shall carry you one last time. Cling tight to me, just as you did all those years ago."

Iphigenia turned, and Orestes clamored onto her back, locking his arms around her neck. She hiked his legs up and started the long climb downwards. Orestes weighed as much as any grown man, but with each step Iphigenia took, she felt stronger and stronger until it was as if Orestes were a simple bag of grain being taken to market.

She was sprinting again, and her heart was so light that she had never wanted to break down into raucous laughs more in her life. Here she was, racing through her own field of Asphodel in triumph rather than sorrow. The river bank was coming back into view, and she knew the journey was nearing its end.

Her pace faltered when she saw not a shade, but a real man, dense with life, standing tall amongst them. It was not Hermes; the shock of recognition almost caused her to drop Orestes when it hit her. He looked far older than he had that day in Aulis, as if more than twenty years alone had aged him.

"Odysseus!" she yelled, thundering towards the man. Orestes' grip around her neck grew tighter as she nearly broke into a sprint.

The man in question looked up in shock from the shade he was conversing with; the ghost dissipated into little more than smoke as the little color in Odysseus' face drained.

"No," he murmured, taking a step back. "I expected you to be here, but *alive?*"

"I could say the same to you," Iphigenia spat, fingers itching for her axe. Agamemnon was long dead, but Odysseus still drew breath, still saw the light of day, still *lived* — never having paid for his role in that dark day. "You tore my family asunder."

Odysseus scoffed. "Your family had no need of my assistance in that area, that much is certain." He waved up at Orestes, who had gone suddenly still. "I see the curse still lingers."

"And I see you've yet to have enough of yours." Iphigenia hawked up a gob of spit at Odysseus' feet. "The weight of all the heavens themselves could not outweigh your hubris, and it shall be your downfall."

Iphigenia pushed past Odysseus, ignoring the man's hollow stare.

"Wait!" Odysseus called, and Iphigenia stilled. The voice that had lured her and her mother to Aulis held the same cunning note now as it did then, no matter how aged it had become. Odysseus was dangerous, incredibly so — which is why she stopped. She would be remiss not to glean all she could from his boasting.

"Speak, Son of Laertes," she coldly said, facing the inky water.

There was a clearing of the throat, and it sounded as if Odysseus had choked upon the thick ash underfoot. "How did you survive? How are you here?"

"I would ask the same of you, but your scheming knows no bounds. Gods know you'd slit the throats of your own men if it meant you could get ahead."

Odysseus, undeterred, took a step forward. "You've yet to answer my question."

"And I never will. I owe you nothing," Iphigenia said, stalking past the man. The atmosphere of the underworld was crushing, and she'd wasted enough time as it was.

Odysseus blocked her path, his narrow nostrils flaring. His eyes went wide, then narrowed. "Your skin reeks of *Circe*," Odysseus seethed, and Iphigenia had never seen the man more disheveled. His cheeks were ruddy, and he looked as if he were about to tear out her throat. "She sends me here, and low and behold you appear, stinking like the witch herself. All a ruse—"

Iphigenia just stared as he ranted, bemused. So, this is what Medea's famous and estranged aunt had been up to. If she didn't know Medea was halfway to oblivion by now, she'd have called out for her to witness this tantrum of Odysseus'.

"You shouldn't be so distrusting, King of Ithaca. It may lead you to something far worse—"

"Shut up!" the man yelled, his face ruddy. "You know nothing of what I have endured!"

"And I don't care to. Whatever it was, you deserved it." Iphigenia spat at Odysseus' feet. "Leave us alone."

"I'll kill you, and make sure the deed is finished this time." Odysseus lunged, and Orestes yelped, but Iphigenia held firm. When the warrior was within feet of them, Iphigenia whispered a word, the ground cracked and a wide ravine grew, separating them.

"I curse you, Odysseus King of Ithaca, for your second attempt on my life. You accuse me of witchcraft and conspiracy, and therefore your own conspiracy with witchcraft shall be your ultimate downfall."

Iphigenia spat once again and turned her back on Odysseus for the final time. It was time to go home.

Iphigenia had no need to cross the river when the key to the future was in her hand. She only needed to turn the lock.

XXIII

clipped with sharpened metal

The light of day was blinding. Iphigenia shielded her eyes as she stepped out of the temple. King Thoas stood at the bottom of the steps, surrounded by his attendants. Dozens of pairs of eager eyes turned to her.

"Well?" he asked, his chin wobbling. "Is it done?"

"Not quite, my King." Iphigenia's heart raced. She'd have to be very careful. "The goddess has rejected the sacrifice."

"Rejected!" A low murmur sprouted up amongst those who had gathered around Thoas. Never in all of her years of killing her country-men had Iphigenia faltered, and each sacrifice had been executed with the utmost precision. A rejected sacrifice was unheard of.

"That witch has cursed us," Thoas snapped. "She couldn't just die like a sensible person, no, she had to doom us with her."

"It has nothing to do with Medea. The goddess has rejected the blood of those men for their crimes and their crimes alone."

"What crimes? Murder? They're all murderers."

"Mother-slayers. One has extinguished the life of the one who gave him birth, and the other assisted in the act. They are marked men, unfit to be fed to dogs, let alone sacrificed to the Lady of the Forests."

"Gods above."

"They must be purified in the sea before they can be lain on the altar."

"I will send a contingent of guards at once. They cannot be allowed to linger on our land any more, lest they poison us all."

"It's not necessary. I can handle them; the mother-murderer is mad, and the other mad with love for him."

"I must insist; those mad with love have been known to strike at a moment's notice. Opheltes, accompany the High Priestess."

Iphigenia cringed as Opheltes stepped forward, excited energy roiling through his long limbs. He was just a boy, hardly old enough to hold a spear. He'd been there that first night, when she'd emerged raging from the sea. Opheltes had been afraid of her then; now, he took her hand into his, squeezing gently.

"I swear I'll protect you from those scoundrels, Priestess, on my life!"

* * *

As Iphigenia threw bag after bag of food provisions onto the boat, she couldn't help but let her eyes drift back to Opheltes. The boy lay face down on the beach, waves lapping at his still body. She hadn't wanted to do it. The horrified expressions on Orestes and Pylades' faces were confirmation of her own revulsion, even as her hands forced the boy's face into the seawater. He'd trusted her, and she'd bewitched him into dazed adoration so that when she lay him in the surf as one would a child they were teaching to swim, he did not fight as Poseidon snatched the breath from his lungs.

Entirely unbidden, a memory of Medea came to her. The older woman had been draped across a low *kline*, smoke curling around her ears as she told Iphigenia the dark tale of her flight from Colchis. She'd chopped her own brother into pieces as she fled, tossing them to be lost forever in the dark waves. She'd reduced the boy into little more than a distraction, a tool to help her carry Jason to Greece rather than a human being with an entire life ahead of him.

"I've got to bury him," Iphigenia said, setting down a bag of grain. The storehouses by the sea had been remarkably full for this time of year; the Taurians wouldn't even notice they'd taken anything for months.

"What? We don't have time," Pylades protested. "They'll come looking at any moment."

"I have to." Iphigenia had already begun to dig, using her bare hands.

A rough hand jolted her shoulder. "I said we have to go, now. There's no time for honor; it's not like these savages had any anyway."

"Get off of me." Iphigenia shoved away Pylades hand. "These "savages" were my *family*. I'll honor them how I please; either you can help, or you can fuck off."

Orestes kneeled next to her. A small trowel was in his hand — he must have retrieved it from the storehouse. "I'll help," he said softly. "I don't know what you did, but the voices are quiet now. Pylades," and he looked up at the stocky man standing with his arms crossed, "if I don't do this, they might come back."

"Fine."

Together, they dragged Opheltes' body from the sea and onto the soil of the nearby dune. While the boys dug, Iphigenia placed a coin in Opheltes' mouth, anointed his body with the last of her sacred oil, and sang a low funeral prayer. Hopefully Hermes would spirit the boy to Hades quickly. It was shoddy work, and incredibly shallow, but as the three of them heaved rocks onto the low mound that was to be Opheltes' grave, Iphigenia knew that she'd done right by him in death, even if she couldn't have allowed him to live. He would have alerted the rest of the Taurians; no matter how much he'd cared for her, Opheltes' first loyalty would always be to his nation. Taking him with them wouldn't have been an option either—he'd have fought them the whole way. No, dying in the land of his people at the hands of a friend, rather than in a violent struggle with strangers, was the only grace she could grant Opheltes.

The walk to the skiff was silent, and as the boys pushed off, Iphigenia knew they would not be followed. The Taurians would find the grave quickly, and they would have to mourn him for a solid week before they even thought about sending out their fledgling navy. Opheltes had been the hope of a future for an entire people, and she'd taken his life as easily as any one else's. She took Orestes' hand as Pylades lifted the sail. It made sense. Something always had to be given in exchange, right?

As they glided across the inky black water, she watched the flames of Tauris grow smaller until they disappeared entirely beneath the horizon. She knew she should be happy; she was reunited with her only brother, and after almost twenty long years, she was finally returning to the lands of her youth. Still, she couldn't shake the feeling of sorrow that crept up each time she caught her own reflection in the waves. Tauris had been more than a small fishing village in need of a priestess; the people had housed her, welcomed her, loved her even. Despite the dark duty she'd been forced to perform, her years there had been some of the most stable of her life. She'd betrayed them irreparably now; there could be no return.

By day, the hot sun beat upon her neck as she, Orestes, and Pylades sailed southwards. When the wind failed to blow, they took turns rowing. It was hard work, and calluses quickly developed on her palms, but Iphigenia almost relished in it. Anything to take her mind off what she'd endured, and of what might be waiting for her once she stepped foot on Greek shores again.

At night, the trio drifted, their vessel floating beneath stars innumerable. Iphigenia often caught Pylades pointing constellations out to Orestes as the two men sat huddled together at the aft of the small ship. Iphigenia was content to leave them to it, as she was still unsure of how to treat her brother as the man he now was rather than the infant she remembered him as, but one night, as she was drifting off into sleep at last, she overheard something she had to interject on.

"And that one there, those are two great warriors — they perished long ago, but vowed to never be apart."

"It wasn't that long ago," Iphigenia said, causing both men to look up from where their heads had been together. She stood, cautiously walking towards them in the dim lighting. She didn't want to fall overboard; it was one thing to swim in the sea during the day, but at night, a dip would be a one way ticket to the bottom of Poseidon's domain, newfound godhood or not.

"And how would you know?" Pylades replied coolly. "What, are you some sort of historian now too?"

Iphigenia ignored the taunt, sitting opposite the two men. "I know because those," she pointed skywards, tracking her finger to the stars in question, "are my and Orestes' uncles."

"Uncles?" Orestes asked, swiveling his head from her to Pylades. "I wasn't aware we had any uncles left, besides Menelaus—"

"Mother's brothers," Iphigenia corrected, "not Agamemnon's. Menelaus is no uncle of mine, blood or otherwise." For the first time in years, she thought of her Aunt Helen, so beautiful, so desired, that Menelaus couldn't conceive of her making her own choices, choices that did not involve him. He'd ended the world, just to regain possession of her. Iphigenia vowed that she would seek out her aunt, just as soon as she'd reunited with Electra, and that she would ask Helen what she wanted. If it involved killing Menelaus, then so be it. "Either way, you were right about them being great warriors, Pylades." Long afternoons spent racing across the training grounds with her uncles came to mind, and she was so sorry that Orestes never got to experience the genuine joy Castor and Pollux had brought to Mycenae with each visit. "They fought every battle with courage and honor. If they hadn't been murdered the night of Helen's departure, they might have convinced her to stay, and this awful war might not have happened at all."

"Departure?" Pylades scoffed. "The Spartan Queen was kidnapped—"

"Be quiet, Pyl'," Orestes interrupted, leaning forwards. His brown eyes were alight with interest, and for a moment, Iphigenia could've sworn that Pylades looked almost offended by his outburst. It quickly passed though as Pylades crossed his bare arms and pursed his lips.

"Yes, departure," Iphigenia continued. "Auntie Helen...had ways about her. Ways that make more sense to me with each passing day, in fact. She was kidnapped only once, as a child, and it was months before Castor and Pollux could rescue her. After she was taken as a child, she had vowed to never be stolen away again. Whatever occurred between her and Paris that night was of her own volition, I swear on it. He would've never left Sparta alive otherwise."

Iphigenia felt a flutter of happiness at Orestes' rapt expression. If he had been able to, she was sure he'd be taking notes. Even Pylades, sullen as he was, had perked up with interest. She had finally found a way to connect with the pair.

The rest of the voyage went in much the same way, with Iphigenia telling the stories of a generation that had almost completely wiped itself out, and the men listening as if she were imbibing them with some potent elixir. She supposed she was; after all, like Medea had once said, knowledge of the past was the key to the future. Both men were far too young to have participated in the Trojan War, and they were even further removed from the ultimate causes for it. Iphigenia would freely admit that despite her own role in setting the tragedies of the past two decades into action, she herself had only a hazy understanding of the events leading up to the conflict. She'd been scarcely more than a child when Helen had flown off to Sparta with Paris; all she knew at the time was that her favorite uncles were dead and her dearest aunt was missing, all lost on the same dark day.

She told as much to Orestes and Pylades as she could, until one day, when the sea had narrowed to a river and opened back up again, Orestes asked a question she didn't have the heart to answer.

"What did you do during the war? You were sacrificed, but somehow came to live in those barbarous lands? There must be more to your story, dear sister. It's the one I want to hear most of all."

"There is nothing more to hear," Iphigenia said, voice terse. "Agamemnon traded me for wind, and thus I came to live among the Taurians while the Greeks thought me to be long dead. That is all."

"You're lying," Pylades tossed over his shoulder as he adjusted the ship's lone sail. "It's plain to see; all you had to say was that you didn't want to talk about it."

"I don't recall asking for your input, Prince of Phocis."

"Please don't fight," Orestes said, placing his hands over his ears. "I promise not to ask again, just please, no more."

Iphigenia softened. Here Orestes was, his sanity barely regained, and she was arguing pettily with the only man who'd stood by his side though it all. She sighed and stood, ambling across the planks to where Pylades worked. She held out her hand.

"Orestes is right. Truce? At least until we reach land?"

Pylades seemed to consider her hand for a long moment, before taking it in his and giving it a hearty shake. "Truce. If it's for him..." Pylades said no more, and Iphigenia didn't need him to.

She saw her own youthful face reflected in his when he gazed on Orestes, called back to the way she'd once stared at the hunter goddess herself so many years ago. If he felt anything like she had, which she was sure he did, then Pylades had all her sympathies. Any lingering animosity she had dissipated.

From then on out, the rest of the journey passed in relative peace. They continued south, passing through another narrow straight before spilling out into the Aegean itself. Iphigenia felt a change come over her as they entered the familiar turquoise waters.

The trio were silent as they passed the blackened plain and collapsed towers of the land that was once Troy; whether it was from an abundance of caution or simple superstition, none of them spoke, lest it dredge up fresh tragedy out of that accursed place. From their boat, they could see the great mounds where heroes and nameless foot soldiers alike had been hastily buried when there was no longer time nor timber for pyres.

When they passed without incident, they all breathed a collective sigh of relief. No great monsters of the sea had emerged, the wind had kept their singular sail full when they had not the strength to row, and many islands had cropped up for them to stop for provisions. It was as if the gods themselves had blessed this journey.

In a way, they have, Iphigenia thought wryly to herself as Orestes cried out at the sight of land. One *did* do half the rowing, after all. The muscle definition in her arms would make even Heracles look twice.

Mountains could be seen in the distance, a telltale sign that this was no one off island in an archipelago, but authentic terra firma. They'd changed course westward after sailing down the coast of Troy, and Iphigenia knew that the warmer the water grew, the closer she was to the land she'd been born in and had effectively died in.

The thought made her sick with apprehension. She had conquered beasts as ancient as the sea they traveled on, walked through hell itself, come to terms with the crimes of the man she'd called father and had embraced the shade of her mother. A simple journey shouldn't have her retching like a newly pregnant bride, yet here she was, heaving over the stern of the ship as if she were emptying her body of its organs. To the men, she brushed it off as seasickness.

Then, there was a thunk on her back and her brother's face above her, a warm smile on his thin face. She wiped at her mouth as she straightened up.

"Smiles suit you, Orestes," she said, taking note of how he beamed.

"I'm sure they suit you too. I'd much rather see one of those on your face than that grimace you make when you're heaving."

"Very funny."

Orestes shook his head, his shaggy hair flopping around as his face sobered up. "I'm not trying to be. You're nervous."

"I'm more than nervous."

"Are you worried about Electra?"

"I'm worried about everything." Iphigenia couldn't help but wonder if this is what Medea had felt sailing to Iolcus with Jason all those years ago, on a path nearly identical to theirs.

Orestes leaned against the railing of the ship. "I'm worried too. Electra says when I return I am to be made king, but the people of the land…" Orestes shook his head as a mist welled up in his eyes, and at once Iphigenia knew of what he was referring to.

"I will crown you," she said hastily. "I'll have to prove to them that it really is me, and once they see that I of all people have forgiven you—" the word forgiven tasted like burnt oil on her tongue, but she soldiered on nonetheless, "—they will accept you as their king."

"And you will advise me?" Orestes' voice was eager with hope. Iphigenia frowned.

"I will not."

"But sister, you of all people—"

"Should not be ruling over anything," Iphigenia finished. "Orestes, I may have been raised there, but they're not my people. I know nothing of them. You and Electra are *his* children; I'm just the sister."

"You're more than that," Orestes said, his face crestfallen. "I can't do this without you."

"You have Pylades to help you, Orestes. And more than that, you have yourself."

"I don't understand." A whine was creeping into the young man's voice, one that Iphigenia quickly hushed.

"You have to make your own decisions. What good to his people is a puppet king? Good or bad, your decisions should start and end with you."

As Orestes looked down at her, awestruck, Iphigenia felt the realization that those were the words she had wanted someone to tell her, all those years ago. She then smiled.

"Now let's get you home."

* * *

It was the night before they were due to land on the shores of Mycenae and they had docked their ship at a small isle somewhere in the sea between Athens and Corinth. The air here was sweeter and warmer than Iphigenia had experienced since her time among the huntresses; where Tauris had often been bitterly cold and rainy, the islands proved to be the opposite.

Apollo was driving his sun-pulling chariot into the sea when Orestes announced that he was going to venture off in search of game. Iphigenia looked up from her position tending the fire. Her brother was all smiles as he stood on the beach, rough hewn spear in hand.

"Game?" she heard Pylades ask incredulously from his position behind the tree. From the sound of it, his bathroom break had been well needed. "This island is the size of a milk tooth and you want to hunt game?"

"Look, there's fresh water, and where there's water, there's game."

Iphigenia cracked a small smile. "Are you sure you hadn't been sent to Chiron's mountain rather than Phocis?"

Orestes looked at her blankly. "Chiron?"

Iphigenia's mouth popped open. "You don't know of Chiron? Pylades, did your father teach him *anything*?" Even the huntresses, those wild girls, had found time to teach her of the heroes and those who'd trained them.

Pylades rejoined them at the campfire, adjusting his shirt. "Only what was important. Fairy tales weren't very high on that list."

Iphigenia wanted to argue that Chiron was far from a fairy tale, but Orestes was already venturing toward the woods, swinging his spear almost happily as he walked on the tips of his toes. So that was who that fussy baby Orestes had once been really grown up to be. She couldn't imagine how he'd been compelled to have done such a heinous act as cut down his own mother, and to be frank, she didn't want to. Instead, she opted to watch Pylades as he set to sharpening his dagger with a whetstone.

"Do they not speak of the gods in Phocis?"

Pylades didn't look up from his blade. "Look, I'm sure the gods are very interesting and all, but we were just trying to survive. Passing around tales of some long dead centaur wouldn't put food on the table."

Iphigenia remembered of what her jury had said in the underworld, that the gods would begin to recede from the material world. Judging by Pylades' reaction, it had already begun. She would have to work fast then. Iphigenia was deep in rumination on this topic when Pylades stood, coming around the fire to sit next to her.

"What are you doing?" she asked, narrowing her eyes at him. Pylades still wouldn't look at her.

"Just trying to get warm. It's chilly."

Iphigenia scooted a bit to her left, away from her brother's friend. Here they were, in front of a rather healthy campfire, and the air was still balmy with the humidity of high summer.

"I'm no fool, Pylades. Try anything and I'll—"

"Marry me, Iphigenia."

There was a pause, and only the singing of the cicadas could be heard. Then, Iphigenia burst into laughter. She stopped when she saw that Pylades had his dark eyes trained on her in all seriousness.

"You're not joking?"

"I'm not. When this is all over, and Orestes sits on the throne, I want you to be my bride."

Gears were churning in Iphigenia's head. "Pylades, you can't stand me—"

"Look. I don't trust you. Whatever you did to save Orestes terrifies me. You terrify me. I don't even know what the hell you *are*, but..." Pylades' voice was soft, and he turned his gaze back to the sparse trees behind them. "You're as close to him as I'm going to get. Orestes will be expected to marry and provide heirs, just as I am. He and I only share a bond — the two of you share blood. This is the best way."

"Why not Electra?" Iphigenia asks, keeping her voice even as best she could. "She and Orestes are full siblings of the house of Atreus — that's just one reason she's more suited to you." She didn't mention the real reason she didn't think she was suited to marriage, with Pylades or any other man.

"Electra is..." Something seemed to have been caught in Pylades' throat, and he coughed for a moment before continuing. "She's not exactly stable. When we reach Mycenae, watch out for her. Not to mention," and here Pylades' voice took on a sad tone, "I'd never seen a pair of eyes as beautiful as Orestes'. Not until we came to Tauris. Yours are the same shade as his."

Pylades reached out a hand, and before he could touch her face, Iphigenia gently took it into hers and lowered it.

"Pylades, you don't have to do this," she said softly. "The old age is over. You and Orestes are going to be building a new world, and you can do it together." She remembered a friend's long ago dream, of a day where two lovers could just be themselves, free to be together without suffering the weight of heavy expectations written in the stars eons before their birth. She would be doing Achilles a dishonor by not helping others reach that dream.

Pylades eyes softened for a moment, wide, but then he scoffed, and the spell was broken. He pulled his hand back from hers. "Wishful thinking," he said, shaking his head. "Just because a bunch of heroes are dead doesn't mean the people will accept that. I need you to marry me, Iphigenia."

"I will not," she said simply, folding her hands on her lap. "My time amongst mortals is waning."

Pylades stood, kicking a log in sudden anger. Embers flared up as it fell deeper into the fire. "I should've never expected you to understand," he seethed, shoving his hands deep into his pockets. "All you talk about is gods and myths. You've never had to live this life!"

Iphigenia joined him in standing, her hands balled into fists at her side. "Just what are you implying, Pylades?"

"You've never tasted true responsibility. You're so far gone from humanity that you don't know what it's like anymore. You can't just snap and change the world."

"All I've ever been is responsible. I even let myself be killed, for the sake of the gods, Pylades!" Iphigenia was beginning to become exasperated.

"Horseshit," Pylades swore, his eyes flashing dangerously. "They may say you chose to go willingly, but I know the truth. They dragged you kicking and screaming to that altar. You had no choice in it."

"And so you throw it in my face?"

"Because it proves my point. You've never had the burden of making decisions. Everything has just happened to you—you haven't had to reckon with whether or not what you were doing was wrong. That's the burden of a royal," and Pylades turned from her, his arms wrapped tight around himself. He kicked a rock to the side.

"You don't know what you speak of! You don't know what I've had to do, who I've had to kill!"

"But I know you didn't walk away from any of it. You just did it, and damn the consequences for anybody else. That's not an option for me. I won't hurt him." Pylades began walking away.

"I chose Orestes," Iphigenia said softly, long after Pylades disappeared into the woods after Orestes. "I chose him despite everything. You should too."

XXIV

all held goblets and made libation

"Ho! Throw down the line!"

The sounds of the men preparing the boat to dock rang throughout the salt spray of the air, but Iphigenia couldn't focus on Pyaldes and Orestes as they wrestled with the sails. No, her vision was reserved for what lay at the shore of the bay they'd sailed into that morning. There, the waves transitioned into rolling golden hills, and craggy tipped mountains rose in the distance. If she squinted, she could just make out stone structures dotted amongst the hills; one loomed particularly large at the point where hills morphed into mountains.

Her stomach churned, dangerously close to betraying her once again, but Iphigenia swallowed the urge. She'd return home with her head held high.

There was a presence at her shoulder.

"We're home." Orestes stood next to her, shirtless. Despite the light provisions they'd taken on their journey south, he'd managed to put some weight on his slight frame, and days of constant sun had glazed his skin with an intense bronze. Iphigenia was glad for it. The gray pallor of the underworld he'd been coated in so recently might have never existed. The sun drenched lushness surrounding the bay made it so easy to believe.

"How do you feel?" she asked him tentatively. He looked at her in astonishment.

"How do *I* feel? You've been gone twenty years. I should be asking you that question."

"I think it's a fair assessment for both of us, considering the circumstances."

Orestes shrugged, turning his attention to the valley before them. The ship came to a stop, and there was a splash; Pylades throwing down the anchor.

"I don't know," Iphigenia heard him say. His brow was knitted. "It was never a happy place for me. I was always alone. I thought things would get better when father returned. Electra always told me they would, but then when he came—"

Orestes drew a finger across his neck. "That was that and mother had me shipped off to Phocis. I was only ten years old," he said, furrowing his brow. "I was so angry, and that's when the voices and nightmares came, but," he shrugged and gave a little smile. "I had Pylades at least. He was the first friend I'd ever had."

"We're not so different, then, you and I," Iphigenia said softly. She gazed overboard at Pylades, who stood in waist deep water, beckoning them to join him. A memory surfaced of her head in the lap of a goddess. Had circumstances had been different, if she hadn't been so caught up in her desire for revenge, could she have been as close to Artemis as Orestes was to Pylades? Would that have made her happy?

There was no time to ruminate. Orestes, his pack strapped to his back, had one leg over the edge of the boat. Iphigenia followed suit, gathering up her meager belongings: her torch, her keys, and an axe that shouldn't exist on the mortal plane yet somehow did.

Warm turquoise met her ankles as she sank down into the water. Pallid skies and chill winds had robbed her of the memory of just how pleasant the sea could be. She shuddered despite the temperature; the hot summer days she'd spent here as a child with her mother and sister felt like they'd happened in some far of age, as distant from her as the exploits of Theseus or the labors of Heracles.

The wade to the shore was short. A few cabins sat there along a stone wall, their windows boarded. Lonely fishing skiffs, their wood soft from rot, bobbed in the water alongside a massive dock. No merchants peddled their wares in the streets, and no artisans worked from their seaside shops. From her position on the boat, Iphigenia hadn't seen anyone; it was easy to blame it on distance them, but now that she was on solid ground, she could see that the port of Mycenae, once renowned throughout the Mediterranean for its wealth, was truly abandoned.

"What happened here?" She asked her companions as they shook the water from their bodies.

"The war happened," Pylades said, his voice gruff as he sized up the road ahead of them. "With most of the kings and men either dead, missing, or too old to do anything, raiders have had their pick of the whole Aegean. I don't know who they are, only that they come from the sea and they speak a language no one's ever heard of. Electra petitioned for aid, but Egypt wants nothing to do with us and all of the other cities are going through the same thing."

"The merchants are scared," Orestes added, patting one of the boarded up windows. "There was already little to trade, considering the famine. They've all retreated behind the walls of the city, last I heard. It's like a siege, without an army."

"Why didn't you tell me before we arrived?" Iphigenia asked, frowning. She knew raiders had ravaged Tauris, but they had been Greek. She knew how to handle Greeks. These sea people were a different story.

"We didn't think you'd care," Pylades said before Orestes could interject.

Iphigenia bristled. "Pylades, I've had enough of arguing with you. I just want to see that what's left of my family is okay."

"I'm not arguing," Pylades said, and Iphigenia could see from his calm tone and splayed hands that he was telling the truth. "I'm being genuine when I say this: the people of these lands, their kings, called for the war. Every bad thing that has happened since has been a result of that choice, what happened to you and Orestes included. I figured a few raiders would be the least of your concerns."

Iphigenia slowly nodded. "You have a point, I guess. But the people didn't do anything; my father and his soldiers alone were responsible for Orestes and me."

Pylades frowned. "And who do you think relied on those soldiers? Prayed for their return home?"

Before Iphigenia could begin the old argument anew, a cough sliced through the tension, and both she and Pylades' heads snapped around to see Orestes holding the reins of two mares.

"While you two were wasting air, I borrowed a couple of mounts for us."

"Orestes! Where did you find those?"

The young man aimed his thumb behind a long and low building. "Those stables are full of them. It's a miracle these guys weren't taken by any raiders." He gave one of the horses, the chestnut one with the sleek mane, a firm pat on the flank. The horse whinnied, and Orestes smiled.

"She's the first animal that hasn't tried to kill me in years. Pylades, will you ride with me?"

"And what of your sister?"

"His sister was riding horses while you both were still being kept warm in a pair of balls, thank you very much," Iphigenia deadpanned.

There was no further argument. Pylades grunted, taking Orestes' outstretched hand.

Iphigenia approached the other horse. Its coat was shiny and bright, a paler brown than the one the two men were sharing. She internally swore, mad that she'd eaten their last apple that very morning. If she had known there would be horses involved, she would have saved it a piece. She mounted it and they were off, trotting along the dirt road at a steady pace.

The journey through the valley felt longer than it was. All along-side the road stood empty houses and abandoned farmlands. The fresh green of spring, coming down from the mountains, met its end abruptly where blackened fields stood. The memory of her first steps in Tauris came to Iphigenia's mind, and she feared Mycenae itself would look very much the same.

Maybe the city should fall, something inside her thought. The voice was cruel, and all too familiar, even if she hadn't heard it speaking *to* her rather than *through* her in years. Iphigenia hadn't heard it since that dark moment in the underworld. *It's done nothing but bring you pain.*

"Get out of my head," Iphigenia murmured. When Orestes and Pylades looked back at her in confusion, she waved them off. She'd have to be more careful. While the Taurians may have encouraged her "communing with the gods," as they called it, she was sure that any remaining Myceneans—her travel companions included—wouldn't take very kindly to her babbling to voices no one else could hear.

They rounded a corner, and the cyclopean stone walls of Mycenae came into full view. Iphigenia breathed a sigh of relief when she saw that they were still standing. The hilltop citadel towered above them, and it was as if she'd never left. Even the banners flying her father's colors still hung from the walls. The mountain she'd spent many an afternoon exploring loomed over it all, and Iphigenia's heart thundered in her chest — it was beautiful, but she knew it was an empty beauty. The walls may teem with thousands of bodies packed tight to hide from the roving bands plaguing the land, but without her mother, it might as well already be a ruin.

She was about to lead Orestes and Pylades forward when there was the unmistakable whistle of an arrow's flight and the sharp thwack of it landing just in front of her mount.

"Halt!" A man's voice called out, and the trio pulled the reins of their horses tight. Iphigenia looked up, and along the top of the nearest wall to them stood a line of archers, all with their bow sights trained on them.

Ah. This song and dance again. "Do not shoot!" she called, her voice high and clear. "We seek an audience with the Queen."

One of the archers snorted. "You vagabonds look fresh off some stinking boat— those sea bastards probably sent you to kill her. No one's getting in."

"We're not vagabonds!" Orestes yelled, sliding off the back of the horse. He stalked forward, only stopping when the archers leveled their bows at him. "Look." He pushed back his long hair from his face with one hand, and with the other pulled a gleaming amulet from beneath his shirt.

"We come bearing the seal of the King of Phocis; all among us are royal."

"Wait!" one of the scrawnier archers yelled. "I recognize him! That's Orestes."

A dark murmur rang out amongst the men on the wall. They lowered their weapons, but the almost jovial attitude had fled, and in its place was one far more sinister.

"You were told to never darken these stones again, mother-murderer," the first archer seethed. "We knew you were shameless, but to continue to plague us—"

Iphigenia stepped forward, raising a hand to pause the man's speech. This cycle would end here.

"What is done is done. Orestes has paid his dues, and it is time for him to return home."

The archer scoffed. "There is no atonement for the killing of a mother. If it weren't for him sharing the blood of the one he slayed, we would have had his head ourselves."

Iphigenia smiled, and from within her robes she brought out the gleaming ivory that would be their linchpin. "Orestes, instructed by the god Apollo, has brought home to Mycenae a goddess, straight from Taurian shores."

There was a pregnant pause, and then laughter exploded amongst the men. "Woman, are you as out of your mind as he? That's nothing but a statue; the disgraced prince has brought no goddess here."

The speaker levied his bow at her. "We may be forbidden to harm him, but you, stranger, are a different story."

He loosed the arrow, and Iphigenia, too stunned to move, waited for that telltale pain to pierce her. When it didn't she opened her eyes that she hadn't even realized she'd squeezed shut.

Instead of sticking out of her chest, the dark feathered arrow quivered in the air, as if it had struck some impenetrable barrier. The men were all looking at her in alarm, and even Orestes and Pylades had shock written plain as day across their faces.

Iphigenia was warm, near burning even, and as she raised her arms to the arrow, she saw them encased in a shimmering gold haze. She touched the arrow, and it crumbled to dust beneath her fingertips. Cold power flickered there like flames, and she could trace its aureate journey through the blood vessels of her arms. Confusion gripped her briefly before realization had her smiling from ear to ear.

"I'm no stranger. I am Princess Iphigenia, she who was sacrificed upon the altar in Aulis, and reborn in the image of the gods by moon-drenched Artemis. Orestes has brought a true goddess to the doors of Mycenae, and she demands to be let in."

The walk up to the palace had been difficult. Outside its walls were the familiar narrow roads and stalls Iphigenia had known her whole life, but gone were the happy merchants hawking their wares to tired mothers; now, scarcely even a chicken stalked the streets. Instead, they were packed even tighter with makeshift tents and lean-tos, from inside which pale faces gawked at their entourage. It was a stark reminder of the state Iphigenia discovered Tauris in; she turned to Orestes, horrified, but the boy did not seem surprised at all.

"Orestes, why do you not weep at what has happened here?"

"Has anything new happened? It looks no different than when I was sent away."

Iphigenia watched as her brother absentmindedly picked a rock out of the dust and skipped it along the street. Clytemnestra had been Queen then...Iphigenia couldn't imagine her meticulous, overcalculating mother failing to maintain the glory of the kingdom.

"How long has it been like this?" she asked, pulling her veil tight around her face. It was unlikely, but she didn't want any lay people recognizing their long-dead princess just yet. It had been difficult enough keeping the soldiers from throwing her a parade then and there. No, she wanted no one knowing until she found Electra.

Orestes hummed, fingers stroking his chin. The first fuzziness of a beard was starting to begin there, Iphigenia noticed with a start.

"When I was a kid, it wasn't this bad," he began as they started up the sloping ramp that led to the palace's main entrance. "Then mother sent me away, and when Pylades and I arrived, we found it like this. It's not just Mycenae though; we sought shelter damn near everywhere, but all the towns were locked up as tight as this one."

"It's a wonder raiders didn't catch us and hold us for ransom." Pylades said, tearing his vision from a few emaciated looking women. "All we ever did was sleep under the open sky."

"It was better than any inn could ever be," Orestes muttered, and before anyone could respond, the gates to the palace proper swung open.

What had once been a neat and tidy courtyard had devolved into a shantytown, filled with the cries of numerous children. Their mothers tried to calm them to no avail, and one of the guards looked at them with anguish.

"Sorry for the noise. There's very little food; many of the women have had their milk dry up."

"You shouldn't be apologizing to us," Orestes replied. "Why haven't you taken care of them?"

They were silent as they walked through the courtyard, but all eyes were on them. Some of the women made the sign against evil while others averted their children's eyes. Iphigenia longed to give them some sort of relief, but the mens' strides were far too long. There'd be time for it after the *megaron*, she mused. More than enough, if everything went according to plan.

Burning sunshine became muggy dimness as they entered the castle proper. It was no time before the three of them reached an ornate door, made of solid bronze. It gleamed bright against the afternoon sun, and Iphigenia almost had to raise a hand against her brow to make out the massive lion standing out in relief upon it between the images of Perseus and Agamemnon. The image of the beast was captured mid snarl, no doubt one of Agamemnon's intimidation tactics, but Iphigenia couldn't help but feel that the lion of Mycenae was one trapped in a gilded cage, not a triumphant king of beasts. The thought struck Iphigenia that she was now standing in the same spot where, twenty years ago, everything had changed.

Then, the door swung open, the bright frescoes of the megaron were before them, and at the other end of the long hall, seated just beyond the center hearth, was a wild-haired woman drenched in scarlet robes. Her face was hidden beneath her unruly blonde tendrils, but Iphigenia would know her frame anywhere.

"Hail, Queen Electra!" one of the guards yelled, and while the men sank to their knees, Iphigenia stood firm. Electra's blue eyes, just as unfocused as Orestes had once been, met hers, and Iphigenia felt the words spill from her lips unbidden, as if Apollo himself had taken control of her speech.

"Mother-murderer, usurper, Queen; I know what you did. I've returned to make it right, once and for all."

Electra jumped down from her throne, thundering towards the group despite her petite size. Iphigenia could see the sharpness of her sister's bones through the thin skin of her face and wrists. Her eyes were wild and bloodshot, startlingly similar to those of the men Iphigenia had sacrificed.

"How many times must I tell you to begone! Foul shade sent by her, your ceaseless torment ends here!"

As Electra lunged, Iphigenia did the one thing she knew would calm the mad queen. She flung her arms wide, and Electra fell into them as if they were still children, before everything had changed. There was a pause as Iphigenia held her sister close; the men were staring, mouths agape.

And then, instead of pressing the knife in her hands into Iphigenia's middle, Electra began to sob.

"You can't be real," Electra cried, her fingers clutching at Iphigenia's chiton.

"I'm realer than I ever was," Iphigenia replied, pressing a kiss to her sister's head. There were strands of gray there now, but the scent was the same — of the garland of lavender woven throughout her hair, no doubt picked from the very same field they'd once upon a time wandered together.

"Orestes is too young."

"He's no younger than father—, excuse me, *Agamemnon* was when he took the throne."

"That was different. And why have you stopped calling him father?"

Iphigenia pinched the bridge of her nose. She and her sister were in a small audience chamber off to the side of the *megaron*, one which had been miraculously preserved, sharing an amphora of well-watered wine. The men had been led off to another room of the palace to get settled, after Electra had given them her blessing. For several hours, Iphigenia had been trying to explain what happened to her, what had happened to them all, but Electra had only asked after Orestes and how he was, and thus Iphigenia had directed the conversation to the quintessential matter at hand: Orestes taking the throne.

Iphigenia squinted, trying to get a better look at her sister in the dim light. She was taller now, and still just as devastatingly pretty as she'd been all those years before. Still, she was rail-thin, and dark bags marred the soft skin beneath her eyes. Iphigenia took one of those gray strands intermingling with the blonde into her hand. Electra was far too young yet for these. Clytemnestra had not yet gone gray when Iphigenia had parted from her, and here Electra was, scarcely above thirty, looking as if the past twenty years had been forty.

She watched Electra's thin hands tremble as she poured wine into her cup, and Iphigenia knew that this couldn't go on much longer.

"Tell me, Electra, how is the council taking things?" Iphigenia had never paid much attention to politics, but she did remember the seriousness with which her parents had referred to the council of elders.

Electra looked at her with confusion. "Council? I had them all dismissed long ago."

"Dismissed?"

"Bunch of no good lazy bastards. They're rotting at the bottom of the sea where they belong."

"Electra!" Things were worse than Iphigenia had thought. No council, bandits practically banging on the doors, Electra's mental health in shambles—. "Who is supposed to help you run the kingdom?"

"Don't need any help," Electra murmured into her wine cup. "Especially not from those leering maggots."

Iphigenia gently took the cup from her sister, replacing it with her own hand. "Electra. You need help. Let us help you. We love you."

"Love me?" Electra's eyes were unfocused as she scrunched her nose at Iphigenia. "You've always hated me. Mother said as much, said it even as I held her down and Orestes bashed her head in."

Iphigenia sucked in a sharp breath at Electra's words, uttered so nonchalantly. Guilt consumed her briefly, guilt for the role she'd played in their childhood animosity and guilt for what her mother had done to her siblings in her grief for her. "You're still my sister, no matter what you've done."

Iphigenia had not lied when she had said she had come to make everything right. No matter how much her heart screamed to take up her magic, to end her brother and sister for the crime of killing her mother—her only ties to a life stolen from her—Iphigenia still could not help but love them, and it was because of that love that she sought to make them whole again.

Electra stood suddenly, knocking the table off balance and causing the contents of the *amphora* to splash onto her front. "I didn't want to kill her," Electra cried, taking the clay container into her hands and hurling it against the wall. Iphigenia didn't flinch as it shattered into a dozen dagger-sharp pieces. "I was *so* lonely, Iphigenia."

Electra's hands shook as she began to pace the room, looking like one of the blood-stained shades Iphigenia had so recently confronted. "All I had was Orestes after you...left. Mother, she didn't care about us. Every day and every night, she could only weep. Years, Iphigenia, years. I raised Orestes alone. This went on until that *creature* slipped up from the nastiest sewer of the palace." Electra's tone morphed from anguish to outright malice. "Mother, in a fit, freed him, and it was as if the sun shone out of his ass. She let him do as he pleased," Electra laughed then, even as tears quickened at the corners of her eyes, "let his eyes wander at dinner and his body wander my halls at night."

"Who?" Iphigenia's voice was tight.

"Father's cousin, the one he and uncle defeated. Aegisthus."

Iphigenia remembered the night, years ago now, that she and Iset had gone down into the crypt. The memory of a thin man's hand reaching through cell bars hit her like a rock to the face. She'd been so close to freeing him herself...

"I tried to tell her, begged her to believe me, but she ignored me like you'd been her only daughter. It went on for so *long*, Iphigenia."

Some taut tendon deep within Iphigenia's heart broke at the crack in her sister's voice.

"I was afraid he'd go after Orestes next. Every day, I prayed for the gods to send father back to Orestes and I, and every night I prayed for them to guide his hand to Aegisthus' throat. Then, finally, the war was over, and the heralds announced that father's ship had docked in the harbor. That day...I alone prepared the whole house. Mother seemed disinterested, and that weasel had made himself scarce. It was no matter to me. I thought the gods had finally answered me, and Orestes, but a child, helped me to prepare as best he could.

"We waited in the family *megaron* for what felt like hours, but when father didn't come, I sought to find him myself. I told Orestes to stay put in case father appeared for his meal, and I set off to his chambers."

Electra laughed bitterly. "He wasn't answering his door, and so I pushed in. His bed, freshly made that morning by Orestes and I, was in total shambles, as if someone had—" Electra made a lewd hand gesture. "I heard a laugh from the bathing chamber, and I thought perhaps he and mother...so I entered. And do you know what I saw?"

Electra's eyes had taken on a faraway look. "Father, naked and headless in the bath, and mother, standing over him with a bloody axe, hacking him to pieces. She saw me, and next thing I knew, I had been carted off to the dungeons by that man...she said it had been for my safety. I didn't speak for a year after what he did to me. When I emerged, and I can't tell you if it was days or just hours later, Orestes was long gone, and I was alone again. The gods had heard my pleas, and decided they had bigger things to deal with. I'd have to answer my own prayers.

"That's why, Iphigenia." Tears slid down Electra's gaunt cheeks. "That's why I had to kill mother. Why couldn't she have loved me like she loved you?"

At that moment, Iphigenia felt like she was seeing her sister for the first time. Everything Electra had done as a child, every tantrum and every slight, made sense at last. She wasn't crazy, as the guards had said, nor was she the unstable mess Pylades had claimed her to be. No, Electra was strong, still holding on despite the horrific lot she'd been dealt. Iphigenia knew that she couldn't have been half as resilient.

"I'll make this right," Iphigenia promised, taking her sister by the hand. Her fingers were so thin and fragile that Iphigenia feared they may break. "I can't undo what mother did to you, nor you to her, but I can take care of you."

"How?"

"I'm going away again," she said quickly, "but I'm going to send for you. This place...Mycenae doesn't have a future. My own actions have seen to that."

"I know," and Electra began fiddling with her skirts. "The people say you cursed father and the whole kingdom the day you left us."

"I did. Do you hate me for it?" *It's okay if you do,* Iphigenia thought but did not add. All through their childhoods, Iphigenia had ignored Electra in favor of worrying about her own fears. She'd never given a thought to what Electra—always striving for parental affection and approval—might feel. Iphigenia may have been terrified of being married, but Electra's fear of being alone had already come to fruition long before that dark day in Aulis.

Electra looked up at her with bloodshot eyes. "I want to...but you came back. You brought Orestes home and whole. You're here."

"I'm here," Iphigenia whispered, clutching her sister close and wishing to the gods that she could stay.

XXV

by the cool stream the breeze murmurs

"Be careful," Iphigenia called, hands on her hips. "It's very heavy." She stood on a grassy knoll; below her, Orestes and Pylades marched in tandem. Across the valley, white marble columns surrounded by scaffolding rose out of the morning's dewy fog.

"We *know*," Pylades grunted, glaring up at her. "Can't you micromanage elsewhere?" There was a dull thunk as Orestes dropped the marble statue the pair were transporting on his foot. He howled, and Iphigenia had to hide her snicker with her hand as her brother apologized over and over again.

The dawn air was a warm caress, and the sun had tinted the mountains a glorious shade of flush pink. Iphigenia inhaled, the rich scent of the purple thyme that grew along this hillside permeating her every sense. It was a gorgeous morning to build a future, and where else but here? Brauron, for that is what she had named this place, was to be an enclosed settlement comprised entirely of women, so hidden and protected that no one would find it for generations. Iphigenia had secured the boundaries herself with a combination of spellwork, fortified walls, and a natural affinity for choosing prime real estate, untouched by famine or warfare. The fields were fertile, the stream was clean, and the land had been miraculously passed over by other Greeks and the raiders from the sea. It was as if it had been set aside by the gods.

In a way, it has, Iphigenia thought with a roguish smile.

Already a steady trickle of girls had begun to trickle into the grassy plain that would one day be the main square. The sound of their laughter floated up to Iphigenia as they shoved each other and staged mock battles with their rakes and shovels. Leading them with a smile was Electra, carried here by Iphigenia herself as soon as the first solid house had its hearth lit. Here, amongst these women, her sister would never be alone again.

Iphigenia pondered the populace below her from her perch. There were all sorts of girls. Orphaned daughters, fleeing from raiders, had been some of the earliest to arrive. Girls who had heard the rumors and were eager to study witchcraft at the feet of a goddess arrived next. There were even girls like Achilles and Beroe, whose families didn't want to acknowledge that they *were* girls. And, closest to Iphigenia's own heart, were the teenage girls who were just as desperate as she had once been to avoid marriages they wanted no parts of. All of them, she took in, and all of them she protected. The consequences of letting them suffer alone were too great.

Mycenae was no more, that much she knew. Even Sparta to the south, that rich city that was the home of her uncle Menelaus, had fallen. Helen had disappeared soon after returning, and this time, none knew where she'd gone, nor could they muster the energy to care. Menelaus' remaining allies, accusing their king of conspiracy, had turned on him immediately. Infighting brought Sparta to its knees. Her cousin Hermione, with half the beauty of her mother and twice the cunning of her father, had told her as much when even she had straggled into the settlement, half a dozen Trojan concubines in tow. Even she thrived now; she and Electra had become fast friends, cousins reunited after so many years, bonding over the ruins of their shared house. Iphigenia watched as the two of them eagerly greeted each other by a half constructed fountain.

"Iphigenia?"

Iphigenia looked up, startled. She'd been so deep in thought that she hadn't heard her own brother's approach. Pylades was still at the bottom of the hill, nursing his foot next to the great piece of marble the two of them had been carrying. The statue, a stunning recreation of Iset, stood proudly next to a pond so brimming with leaping frogs that the water was never still. Orestes' hand hovered over her shoulder, his brow knit in uncertainty. Iphigenia smiled, clasping his with her own and pressing it there.

"I'm real. You don't have to worry." She knew of Orestes' night terrors, of his visions. He may have been freed from the pursuit of the furies, but the trauma still lingered, and might always.

"I know that now. But Iphigenia, are you happy? Is this enough?" Anxiety colored Orestes' words, and Iphigenia knew he was thinking of what he'd heard in the Underworld, of the role he'd been foretold to play in the future. The assortment of kingdoms that had once banded together and called themselves *Danaans*, Greeks, no matter how mangled they were now, would ultimately rebuild and survive due to him.

"You'll always be enough," she replied, squeezing his hand. His eyes, so like her own, still held the wide innocence she'd remembered from her youth. "Orestes, feel no guilt."

"That's not what I asked. Is this enough to keep you? You won't go away from us again?"

Iphigenia considered her next words with care. Here, her family surrounded her. They were safe. No wars nor curses could harm any of them in this sacred place. And she had a renewed purpose; in helping all these girls, she could finally begin to atone for her many sins. She had *almost* everything she could desire.

"Nothing would bring me more joy than to stay amongst you all forever," she murmured, bringing a hand to her chest. Beneath her *chiton*, she felt raised scar tissue that had never quite healed correctly. She gazed westward as the old wound began to ache. "I will be with you through the end of the summer, but after that, I must love you all from afar."

She expected Orestes to argue, to protest, to weep as Electra had wept when she'd told her, but he merely nodded, looking more like a leader than he'd ever had. "I remember what they said in the underworld even as I forget. But you will be with us always?" Iphigenia knew Orestes referred to something even beyond her physical presence. She pressed the tiny statuette of Artemis that they'd taken from Tauris, the one she'd kept on her person ever since, into his hands.

"As long as there is light in the world, I will be with you."

"Then that is enough for me."

* * *

Iphigenia felt the familiar tingle of trepidation as she picked her way through bramble and underbrush. Her horse, long abandoned at the top of the ridge, would have gotten stuck, his panicked whinnies making too much noise. There was more to it than that, though. Her quest would end here. She would complete it on her own terms, and to do that, she'd need to walk on her own two feet.

As she descended, she gazed in wonder all around her. The glade looked frozen in time, as if it had been captured in the threads of a tapestry. There was the stream, its water running strong and clear. The altar in the center was just as broken, just as bright. Even the whining song of the cicadas was an immaculate reconstruction of her memory. It was as if the thorny bushes she'd fought through had been a portal to the past; Iphigenia felt that all she need do was blink and her father and his priest would be standing before her with an alabaster horse and an argument.

She plunged into the stream, not caring that her clothes were growing heavy with water. On the contrary, it was a welcome balm against the late summer heat; the soft fabric had been plastered to her skin for half the ride anyway.

The temperature may have been pleasant, but the stream was rough, the weight of its water threatening to knock Iphigenia down at any moment. Iphigenia struggled against the stream's torrential power as she fought her way upstream. It would have been easy to walk alongside the water, to let her sandals slap against the earth as she skipped to the terminus.

But when had Iphigenia ever done the easy thing?

And so she toiled against the water, losing her footing several times. Rocks ripped open jagged gashes, and she knew her flesh would be a collage of bruises as dark as the sea come morning. The terrain grew steeper and steeper until Iphigenia was forced to continue on her hands and knees, choking on water with every inch forward. The forest around her grew darker by the minute, murky with mystery. Anything could be in there, watching her. Still, her determination was ironclad. As she heaved herself over a waterfall, she tumbled into a pool. Iphigenia couldn't help but flail — goddess or not, she could not swim. Then her feet found purchase against the bottom of the pool, and here was a wall: she could stand. Her head crested the surface, and what she saw snatched her breath away all over again. There, in chest deep water so clear Iphigenia could see minnows flitting about, stood Artemis, bathing, her back turned to her. Her dark hair was plastered to her head. The goddess turned at the sound of her splashing. She was smiling, her sopping curls forming an elegant frame for her radiant expression. As the goddess sloshed closer, Iphigenia longed to reach out, to take those delicate strands into her hand, to caress that face that she both adored and despised. She didn't know what if she wanted to pull her into a bruising kiss or force her head into the water until the goddess begged for forgiveness. She settled on meeting the same gray eyes that had entranced her all those years ago.

"Join me?"

She could fight the current no longer. As if driven by a power beyond even the divine, Iphigenia plunged into the pool proper, just as twilight descended upon the valley.

"Artemis," she breathed, not daring to move.

"Iphigenia...or should I say Hecate?" She was as beautiful now as she had been the first time Iphigenia had laid eyes on her.

Her breath came in quaking little trembles that had nothing to do with her arduous trek through the stream. She wasn't sure if she wanted to laugh, cry, or hurtle curse upon curse on the goddess that had completely transformed her life. Drowning her was still on the table.

She settled on an even monotone. "I don't know. Call me whatever."

"And why would I do that?"

Iphigenia wanted to roll her eyes. Ten years, and yet this coyness still lingered. Iphigenia had a litany of things she wanted to tell Artemis, but if she kept this attitude up, the first thing she'd be telling her would be *off*.

"I've made peace with nearly everyone in my life, but I find it incredibly... challenging, to say the least, to confront you."

"Go ahead," Artemis said, and judging by the way she was wringing her hands, if Iphigenia didn't know any better, she'd say the goddess looked almost nervous. "Say whatever is in your heart."

"I fear divine retribution if I do. My anger goes beyond me, beyond memory." Iphigenia tilted her head upwards, closing her eyes. Flashes of lives that weren't hers, of dead children and charred flesh, churned through her mind unbidden.

"Do it anyway. I swear on the river Styx that I shall not harm you. Not that I could." Iphigenia heard the telltale splash of water and snapped her eyes open. She raised a hand, bidding Artemis to not take another step.

"Stop with your mind games! Don't you think I've been through enough?"

"I'm being serious, Iphigenia. We are equals now. Tell me that you hate me, that you want my head on a pike, that you wish to reach into my guts and disembowel me with your own two hands — it is all permitted."

Iphigenia looked at the goddess standing before her. Her beauty was still resplendent, but there was something dark in those gray eyes of hers, the same darkness Iphigenia had seen when she'd killed the bear and on the night of her trial, when Artemis had cried another's name — Kallisto. She looked on the verge of weeping, but Iphigenia ignored it.

She settled on a single question.

"Why did you abandon me?"

Artemis resumed her approach, moving slowly as if Iphigenia was a deer she'd been tracking for days and was ready at last to take. Iphigenia raised her hands.

"Stop and answer me," she said, voice shaky. She wanted her coming no closer until she knew.

"I don't have a good excuse for you," Artemis said, not meeting Iphigenia's glare. "I was scared—"

"And I wasn't? You dropped me on a godsforsaken beach with nothing more than a stick, and had me slitting the throats of strangers for a living!" Iphigenia's throat ached at the memories of having to re-enact her own deepest trauma. If it hadn't been for Medea's steady hand and teachings, she was sure she would've gone the way of Electra by now, or perhaps something even worse, driven mad by bloodlust.

Artemis, to her credit, had stopped at last, keeping her distance several feet away from Iphigenia. "It had to be done," she said, her voice wavering.

Iphigenia wanted to laugh. Was this the first time she was being confronted with the consequences of her own actions?

"The war threw everything off. Half the world had been destroyed, and the other half were going to go home conquering heroes with no regard for the gods that had supported their enemies. The war had left Troy and had descended upon Olympus. We were tearing each other apart, Iphigenia. To restore balance, to calm the rift among the gods, it had to be done, and it had to be done by you."

"I don't care about balance and I don't care about the gods and their quarrels, Artemis. I just wanted to live."

"And live you shall. Before, with me, you were caught in between. You weren't dead, but you weren't alive either. Your thirst for revenge kept you from living."

"I never felt more alive than when I was racing up and down mountains with you." Iphigenia could almost taste the cold air that had coursed through her lungs in those days, her laughter snatched away by the wind as soon as it had left her body. The huntresses had given her a home, a space to be herself. She had been, for the first time in her life, free. How had she not seen that then?

"The gods would have killed you for what you did at Troy. The Amazons would have hunted you to the ends of the earth, would have waged war with my huntresses. My father certainly wanted you for himself. For Iphigenia the girl to become Hecate the liminal, for you to become a true goddess, I had to send you away. It was one of the hardest things I've ever done."

"Did you ever ask me what I wanted, Artemis? Did you ever consider that I never wanted *any* of this?" Words that had been caught in her throat for years spilled out of her like wine from a broken cask.

"I didn't want you to die. I couldn't lose you, and I couldn't let my father harm you, so I did the one thing that I knew would save you. I sent you far beyond the reach of the gods."

"You said the ambrosia—"

"Had activated something ancient inside you. You were protected, but not immortal. Your friend, Achilles? You two were similar in that aspect, and I'm sure you've heard by now how her story ended." Artemis' voice began to break. "So, I sent you away to do the labor that I knew would finish the work of the ambrosia. You took it a step further, and became a hero in your own right."

"You mean the Underworld."

"I do. Few have descended and returned, much less with the soul of another."

"And yet I did."

"Yes."

Iphigenia leaned against the rim of the pool, frowning deeply. Artemis mirrored her action on the other side.

"So all of this, just to ensure you'd never lose me?"

Artemis nodded her head like a child eager for dates soaked in honey, and Iphigenia had a sudden urge to climb out of the water, head down the mountain, and ride her horse until the Earth blended into the sea. She stood her ground, however; there was one final question.

"What if I told you that I never want to see you again for what you've done to me? That the space between us is to great to ever reconcile?"

Artemis' face fell, and for a moment, Iphigenia could see silvery tears pooling at the corners of the goddess' eyes. Then, she turned from her, and in a strangled voice said, "If that's what you wish, I cannot and will not stop you. It's time you made your own decisions, and have them respected."

Iphigenia smiled then, knowing that the goddess could not see. "I guess for your sake it's good that I don't wish that at all. I don't hate you."

For a moment, both women were still. The only sound cutting through the early autumn chill was that of the cicadas, and the shallow breaths of the women. Artemis faced her again, tears cutting a silver path down her cheeks.

"You are sure?"

"Positive. I haven't forgiven you, but I understand why. Come to Brauron. See what I've made. Then we'll talk, openly and honestly."

There was the slosh of water once again, and then bow calloused hands, cool from the water, caressed her jaw with an aching tenderness. They were softer than they'd ever been all those years ago, and as Iphigenia felt the gentle press of a parted mouth against hers, she finally understood. Her sacrifice, the war, all of it? It hadn't been an end, but a beginning.

Acknowledgements

Thank you for reading *Now The Wind Scatters*! I've got a long list of people to thank for the incredible process that was writing and publishing the book of my heart. First and foremost, I want to thank Ashley for *everything;* for listening me rant about myths day and night, for bringing me hot tea and the absolute girliest coffee drinks imaginable, and for loving me through it all. I love you.

I want to thank Mic for late night conversations under the influence of Dionysus. Those wine soaked moments of enlightenment brought forth some of the wildest passages of this novel, and for that I cannot thank you enough!

All my love to Chloe for beta reading my stress relief fanfic and becoming a dear friend in the process.

Thank you to Abbey and Grace, the dynamic duo of legend, for hosting writing nights at the brewery, even if we ended up drinking more than we wrote.

Thank you to Mrs. Joyner for introducing me to classical studies in middle school, and same to Dr. Bradley for letting me nap during his Latin courses — that is how the roots of this novel were first dreamed up!

All of my twitter moots; you're awesome! You were all invaluable guides in this process!

Thank you to the Split Banana crew for allowing me the space and encouragement to complete this work — I'll always treasure your undying enthusiasm!

Believe it or not but I also want to thank Tony for pestering me to let him read my book so often that I decided to go ahead and publish so that he could do so without me having to actively know.

Big thanks to my brother Jalik for being my very first story telling partner. Without the influence of Hero Team, I'm positive that my writing would be nowhere near as unhinged.

Thank you to my assorted betas, critique partners, editors, etc; you are all the best and without you, this book would be a mess.

Thank you to Edwin Marion Cox, from whose translations of Sappho come the chapter titles of this book.

I can't go without thanking the OGs (and yes that means exactly what you think it does) — Euripides, Hesiod, Stesiochorus, Sappho, I literally could not have done it without you.

Finally, from the bottom of my heart, I thank *you* — without readers, a book is just a love letter lost on the wind. The moment you opened this novel, you gave it life, and by giving it life, you allowed its love to flourish.

About the Author

J. Donai is a former vice-mayor, anime figurine collector, and gamer. She holds a Bachelor's Degree in Political Science which she has since used to do exactly two things (that will remain undisclosed). She performs her own car repairs; publishing her own book is a natural extension of that. She lives nestled against Virginia's Blue Ridge Mountains with approximately 57.5 stuffed animals.

Ingram Content Group UK Ltd.
Milton Keynes UK
UKHW040111080323
418219UK00007B/36